SUPERNOVA

FALLEN LEGACIES BOOK 4

SUPERNOVA

JULIE HALL

USA Today Bestselling Author

Supernova (Fallen Legacies Book 4)

Published by Julie Hall

ISBN (paperback): 978-1-954510-08-1

ISBN (hardcover): 978-1-954510-12-8

ISBN (special edition hardcover): 978-1-954510-13-5

Julie Hall

www.JulieHallAuthor.com

Line Editing by Lee Burton.

Proofreading by Janelle Leonard.

Cover design by Mirela Barbu.

Interior artwork by Arz, Sara Mirza, Salome Totladze, and Lucas Hall

AWARDS

Winner, Speculative Fiction / *Stealing Embers*
2021 ACFW Carol Awards

Finalist, Paranormal & Supernatural / *Forging Darkness*
2022 Realm Awards

Audiobook Finalist / *Stealing Embers*
2022 Realm Awards

Finalist, Paranormal & Supernatural / *Stealing Embers*
2021 Realm Awards

Finalist, Young Adult / *Stealing Embers*
2021 Realm Awards

Finalist, Readers' Choice / *Stealing Embers*
2021 Realm Awards

Gold Medal Winner / *Stealing Embers*

2021 Illumination Awards

Parable Award Finalist / *Huntress*
2021 Realm Awards

Young Adult Finalist / ***Stealing Embers***
2020 The Wishing Shelf Book Awards

Finalist, Speculative Fiction / *Huntress*
2018 ACFW Carol Awards

Young Adult Book of the Year / *Huntress*
2018 Christian Indie Awards

Gold Medal Winner / *Huntress*
2018 Illumination Awards

First Place Winner, Religion / *Huntress*
2018 IndieReader Discovery Awards

Christian Fiction Finalist / *Huntress*
2018 Next Generation Indie Book Awards

Alliance Award (Reader's Choice) / *Warfare*
2018 Realm Makers Awards

Parable Award Finalist / *Logan*
2018 Realm Makers Awards

Gold Medal Winner / *Huntress*
2017 The Wishing Shelf Book Awards

Best Debut Author / *Julie Hall*
2017 Ozarks Indie Book Festival

Best Inspirational Novel / *Huntress*
2017 Ozarks Indie Book Festival

Second Place Winner / *Huntress*
2017 ReadFree.ly Indie Book of the Year

First Place Winner / *Huntress*
2012 Women of Faith Writing Contest

USA TODAY Bestselling Author
August 17, 2017 & June 21, 2018

PRAISE FOR THE SERIES

Filled with action, danger, romantic tension, and intrigue, Stealing Embers is absolutely addictive.

Casey L. Bond
award-winning author of *When Wishes Bleed*

With a dark, thrilling plot and beautiful, compelling characters, Stealing Embers is a fantastic take on angel lore that will keep you flipping pages long after bedtime.

Cameo Renae
USA Today bestselling author of the *Hidden Wings* series.

Packed to the brim with action, snark, angel lore, and characters you immediately fall in love with, Stealing

Embers will enthrall fans of Cassandra Clare and Sarah J. Maas, or anyone who loves beautifully written urban fantasy with a sizzling-hot dose of romantic tension. Prepare to become addicted!

Audrey Grey
USA Today bestselling author of the *Kingdom of Runes* series

This delightful read was everything I wanted in a book and more. Author Julie Hall kept me turning pages far into the night, and I wanted the next book in the series the moment this one was over. Stealing Embers just may be one of the best books I've ever read. Well done!

Michele Israel Harper
award-winning editor and author of the *Beast Hunter* series

Crazy-talented Julie Hall has leapt onto my auto-buy-author list! Stealing Embers is an enthralling story, that easily ensnared me with its compelling characters and quintessential Nephilim concept! I need the next book—NOW!

Ronie Kendig
award-winning author of the *Droseran Saga*

SUPERNOVA

1

onsters are real, and now everyone knows. I was raised on stories of the boogeyman—of soul-stealing monsters that craved my blood almost as much as they coveted my flesh—so this new world isn't so different for me. The same monsters who threatened my existence yesterday are still here today.

Same enemy. Same mission. Same fight.

It's humanity that's struggling to play catch up. A few months ago, humans went to bed on a Tuesday and woke up on a Wednesday to a completely different reality. A supernatural one.

Rumors and speculation circulated the globe, everything from aliens to the end of the world. The truth is that two realms have always existed, but since humans were ignorant about the spirit world and its inhabitants, when monsters from the other realm leaked through the veil, the apocalypse seemed like a fair guess. And it almost came to that. Our enemies nearly succeeded in destroying the barrier between the worlds, which would have resulted in literal Hell on Earth.

The barren and beaten down city of London stretching out before me is proof of that. Most of the buildings that stood in this once great city are now only piles of concrete and stone, and the sharp tang of ash and death hang in the air. The destruction reminds me of the photos in my *Human Histories* textbook of the Blitz.

London has a history of coming back from the brink, but not this time. As ground zero for the battle that almost consumed the Earth, a new dimension was created around its epicenter. The twenty-mile radius around the heart of the city has been dubbed the "Merge Zone," and at the location where the realms collided the rules that used to bind our enemies no longer exist. Fallen roam free, Forsaken walk in the daylight, and humans stupid enough to willingly enter the zone, or those unlucky enough to not be able to escape, are seen as one thing and one thing only—prey.

I squint against the mid-day light. It shines down from the bruised sky as bright as it would in either realm. The mash-up of the two dimensions caused a smattering of funky side effects. The sky isn't even one of the weirder ones. It makes sense that the blending of the mortal world's blue and the spirit realm's pink sky would result in purple, but the merge's effect on some animals is downright creepy. Fortunately, there wasn't much wildlife in the Merge Zone. I've been told the London Zoo, or what's left of it, is an absolute hot mess. Dogs have been spotted running around with scales, deer have fangs, and don't even get me started on bunnies.

Shiver.

I saw one racing across the open space we crossed, and

I'll have nightmares about it for years. No creature should have that many teeth.

Human and angelic DNA hasn't been affected, but who knows if it'll be just a matter of time. As a Nephilim, I have a mash-up of both sets of DNA, therefore I should be doubly protected against bizarre Merge Zone mutations, but I still sneak a peek at my hand to check for growing scales and run my tongue over my teeth to make sure they are still blunt.

Scales and fangs would be a hard look to pull off. I mean, I could do it—one of my special skills is being able to make anything look fabulous—but I'm pretty happy with the genetic cards I was already dealt.

My mind only half on my task, I accidently kick a chunk of concrete and it skids across the pavement, the sound echoing off the skeletal remains of the buildings around us. Up ahead, my dad—our team lead—freezes and then half-turns and levels me with a hard look. Other members of our group slant their gazes in my direction as well, and I wince and offer an apologetic grimace.

Coming level with my dad, my mom places a hand on his shoulder, tilting her head in a silent urging to keep going. He puts a finger to his lip in an unnecessary reminder for me to keep quiet and then starts off again. The rest of us follow.

My parents are my heroes. As Nephilim from the power-line of angels, we're born with a natural affinity for battle strategy and warfare. My parents are regarded as two of the fiercest and most respected power Nephs alive, but it's not only that, they also never talk down or placate me, they support me and my decisions, and always treat me with respect. I hate disappointing them. Bringing me into the Merge Zone with their unit today is a big deal.

Shaking off every thought that isn't mission specific, I refocus on the task: finding and extracting the human family we believe is still hiding in this borough. The Fallen and Forsaken are reported to be the most active in the epicenter, but the neighborhood we're in is relatively close to the edge of the Zone, so there's some hope of finding survivors and bringing them to safety without drawing unnecessary attention.

A crumpled beer can skids across the ground and bumps into the foot of the angel-born to my right. As a unit, we stop, our attention focused on the shaded alley it came from. There's a shuffling noise and then silence.

My dad glances at two members of our unit, Hendrix and Starla, and then tips his head, indicating they should check it out.

With a nod, they take off, padding soundlessly into the alley. The rest of our squad fans out around the opening, keeping an eye out for hostiles on the ground or in the air.

Only the Fallen—former angels who were booted from grace—can fly, and even though our intel says that most of them have congregated in the city center, we're not taking any chances.

It's far more likely that we'll encounter a Forsaken—a former Fallen who has possessed the body of an unfortunate Nephilim or human—rather than a Fallen. Outside the Merge Zone, the Forsakens' activities are restricted by the sunlight, which burns their skin on contact. But within this new, strange realm, they aren't bound by the same rules and can roam freely during daylight hours, which is why they've flocked to this area in droves. Even the conservative estimates of how many Forsaken now inhabit the Zone are chilling.

Luckily, old habits die hard and the Forsaken are still the most active at night, which is why we entered the area an hour after first light.

In less than five minutes, Hendrix and Starla return.

"Whatever it was, fled," Hendrix reports in hushed tones.

"If it was a Forsaken," my mom says, "it's probably going for backup. We need to check the location and get out."

My father casts a quick glance down the now-empty alley. His frown deepens, but he gives a quick nod. "I want us headed out of the Zone in under an hour, with or without the human survivors."

He doesn't wait for agreements or questions. As the mission lead, that was an order, not a suggestion, and he expects it to be followed.

There's a new tension in the air as we move through the city streets and alleyways. The fine hairs on the nape of my neck prickle. Keeping my eyes sharp, I strain my hearing, twitching at every piece of trash blown into the air. Despite the frigid winter gusts, I start to sweat, making my battle leathers uncomfortable.

I shouldn't be this jumpy. I've gone up against Fallen and Forsaken before and won. The anticipation of a potential ambush is worse than actually facing off against one of them. I'm not known for my patience. If there's to be a battle, I just want to get to it already.

We reach the target location, a brown-brick townhouse with a whitewashed ground floor, and start to search the premises in a leapfrog pattern the moment we're through the front door. When we reach the kitchen, it's my turn to enter the room first. I slide by my mother and through the arched doorway with both daggers held up and at the ready. My heart pounds like a bass drum, but no one would ever know. On the outside all I project is a trained and lethal predator. I'm good at appearances.

I do a thorough sweep of the room, checking every cabinet and hidey-hole possible before giving the "all clear" signal. We move through the rest of the house without finding a single soul. Our search ends in the small parlor off the front of the home.

Vespa, the third in command of our unit, asks, "We're sure this is the right location?" She sweeps her ponytail over her shoulder as her green-eyed gaze scans the room.

"The address and the GPS position match. Maybe the family moved on. Since we have cover for the moment, I'm going to call this into headquarters and let them know we're heading back." My father pulls a brick-like walkie-talkie from his belt. Cell phone signals can't reach outside the Merge Zone, but radio frequencies do.

Depressing the button on the side, he rattles off his call sign and asks to speak to his liaison. There's a crackle of response but I wander out of the parlor and into the hallway before the conversation begins.

Framed photos line the walls. I didn't bother inspecting the images when we swept the area, but now that I have a few minutes I do just that. A family of four used to live here. A mother, father, and two boys. The photos show the children's growth from infancy to early adolescence. There isn't a single photo where the older of the siblings looks more than twelve or thirteen.

A soft thump comes from below me and I pause. Tilting my head, I listen but I don't hear anything else.

My mom comes around the corner. "There you are."

"The basement got swept, right?" I ask.

"It's a cellar. Barely more than a small storage area, but Drake and Vespa checked it out."

I spot the door that leads to the cellar nestled under the stairs. "Mind if I give it another look?" I ask.

"Just don't be too long. We're leaving in five." My mom trails back into the parlor after I nod.

Angel-born are naturally tall, and this door must have been made for a hobbit rather than a human. I have to duck to fit through the opening. It's really more of an access panel than a door. I'm not even sure why I'm bothering to go down here if it was already checked, but something just feels off.

I pull my blades from their sheaths at my hips. The dilapidated wooden stairs creak under my feet with every step. When I reach the bottom, the ground is packed dirt and there's a musty smell in the air.

Scanning the small space, I don't pick up anything suspicious, but a block of unease still sits high in my gut.

A full minute goes by and the only sounds besides my own breathing are the angel-born walking around the house above me. I start to lower my guard when something clatters to the floor behind me.

My heart rate spikes as I whip around, dropping into a defensive stance and ready to take on an enemy. A large gray rat with tiny horns running down the ridge of its spine scurries across the dirt floor and then disappears into a crack in the wall.

I huff out a half-laugh, glad there wasn't anyone around to witness my freak-out over a rodent, when a very human cry comes from somewhere behind the wall where the rat disappeared.

"What the . . . ?"

Taking measured steps forward, I inspect the wall. There's a rough outline in the brick pattern that I didn't see before. Sheathing one of my blades, I run my free hand over the bricks, confirming with touch what I spotted with my eyes.

Could this be a door? Maybe the family is hiding because they're afraid? I wouldn't blame them—we did just storm their home.

"Hello?" I call out. "It's okay. We're here to help. We've come to take you out of the Merge Zone."

I strain my hearing, and sure enough, there's rustling and muffled sobs coming from the other side of the wall. Stepping back, I look for a way in.

It's a clever hiding spot. I can see how the first team overlooked it. If the rat hadn't disappeared into the wall, I would have missed it myself.

Noticing a notch in one of the bricks, I slide my fingers over it, and finding a concealed handhold I tug. It takes a little effort, but the door finally starts to grind open.

I'm mentally preparing myself to calm a frightened human family when something slams into me, tackling me onto the packed dirt floor.

The air whooshes out of my lungs and a sharp set of fangs snaps in my face.

Forsaken.

Because I'm not a novice, I still have hold of my dagger, and swing my arm forward, jabbing the nine-inch blade into the monster's side.

It's not a death blow but it does the job. The creature shrieks, and I smile.

That'll bring a few of my cohorts running.

While the Forsaken is preoccupied with the blade still sticking out of its ribs, I shove him off me. He pulls the weapon free as I pop to my feet, black ichor dripping from the blade.

The creature snarls, lifting his chapped and bloodless upper lip to reveal an elongated set of fangs still tinted red with blood. His dark brown hair hangs in greasy clumps that brush his shoulders, and the stench of rust and rot rolls off him, making me scrunch my nose.

It's hard to believe he was once human or Nephilim. There's something about stuffing a Fallen angel's essence into another body that makes them all nasty on the outside. I don't understand the mechanics of how or why but it's not pretty. Chalky skin, bloodshot eyes, and every single one of them in desperate need of a blowout.

"You'll pay for that with blood and bone, putrid halfling," the Forsaken spits at me.

"Putrid? You're the one who looks like they haven't showered in several decades." My heart is pumping wildly. The rush of blood through my veins pounds in my ears, but I don't let it show. "But do we really need to resort to name calling?"

The Forsaken snarls and then leaps at me, but I'm ready for that and have already pulled my second dagger, cleanly slicing into the creature's arm as I duck out of the way. Black blood seeps from another wound, which only infuriates my enemy more. I'm counting on his anger to make him sloppy, and he doesn't disappoint. He rushes me with claws extended and drool dripping from his mouth. If he's anticipating dining on a liter or two of my angel-born blood, he's going to be sorely disappointed.

I drop low and spin with one leg extended, taking out

his legs. His momentum propels him forward and he flies over my head and into a rack of pickled vegetables. Glass shatters, the rack tips, and the air fills with the acidic scent of vinegar—an improvement over the death-like stench coming from the Forsaken.

By the time the Forsaken regains his footing, my father, mother, and two other angel-born have pounded down the cellar steps and form a barrier between us. Whether he realizes it or not, the Forsaken doesn't stand a chance.

I don't bother watching them finish him off, already knowing they'll either sever his head or put a blade through his heart. Just like the vampire lore these creatures spawned, that's the only way to take out a Forsaken, the only injuries they won't heal from. But knowing the others will kill the creature isn't the only reason I don't watch.

The death cry of the Forsaken rattles behind me, but it's like it's coming from very far away. I have a direct line of sight to the interior of the hidden room, and I can't take my eyes off the carnage.

I take slow steps toward a boy huddled in a corner of the closet-like space, the bodies of his family are haphazardly tossed to the floor around him. I pay extra attention to where I place each foot so that I don't step on one of their limbs.

That monster. His death wasn't slow enough, but I hope it was extra painful.

When I reach the boy—the younger of the two children from the photos, probably around ten—I crouch, getting on his eye level. His lower lip trembles and he presses himself more fully into the corner. His eyes are wild and practically roll in his head as his gaze bounces back and forth. I'm not sure he even sees me.

"Hi, I'm Nova," I say softly. "Can you tell me your name?"

His gaze finally settles on me, but he starts shaking his head—violently. My instinct is to grab him to keep him from hurting himself, but I'm worried that will only make it worse. Since I don't exactly know what to do to calm him down, I just say the first thing that comes to mind.

"Did you know it's Valentine's Day? I have a box of chocolates. They're all filled with different types of jellies and caramels. I've been looking forward to having one all day."

That was so random it shouldn't have worked, but the boy stops shaking his head and then stares at me. His chest still moves up and down rapidly as he pants, but it's a start.

"Would you like to share them with me later?" I ask.

I hold my breath, half-expecting the child to start screaming or bashing his head into the wall. It takes a handful of seconds, but he slowly nods.

"How about we get out of here?" When he nods again, I ask, "Would it be all right if I picked you up?" I know he probably doesn't want to be touched, but he shouldn't have to walk around the bodies of his parents and brother.

It's an eternity before I get another nod.

Slowly pulling him into my arms, I urge him to wrap his arms and legs around me. When I stand, he buries his face in my neck.

Good. He doesn't need to see any more than he already has.

I pick my way back through the tiny room, trying not to look too closely at the bodies beneath me. The boy hardly weighs anything; he's not much more than skin and bones. He shivers, and even though his clothes are threadbare and splattered with blood, I don't think it's because he's cold.

My parents are waiting for me outside the hidden room. My mom places a blanket over the boy's shoulders, and I maneuver to wrap it around his body the best I can, a difficult task now that he doesn't seem to want to let me go.

"You can head upstairs. We'll do a check and then head out," my father says.

He means they'll verify the family is deceased, but he's being careful with his words. They've seen the slaughter, and their faces say they don't hold out much hope of finding another survivor. I don't disagree.

"Let's get you out of here," I whisper to the boy in my arms, who only presses his face harder against my neck. I'm starting to worry that he can't speak at all. Trauma can do horrific things to people.

He keens like a crying puppy and my heart starts to bleed. I rub a hand over his back, doing my best to soothe him.

"It's all going to be okay," I assure him as we emerge from the cellar, but in this new topsy-turvy world we all live, I wonder if it really will.

2

I paint on another layer of pale pink nail polish. I usually stick to reds, but the name of the polish, "So Many Clowns So Little Time," struck me as funny, so I'm going with it.

"Nova, did you hear me? I asked when you're coming back to Seraph Academy," Greyson says.

I take a moment to blow on my nails before re-focusing on the weekly group chat with my friends. Greyson is in the top left corner of my computer screen, Ash is in the box next to him, and Emberly takes up the bottom portion of my monitor. I'm in a tiny square on the bottom right.

I've heard everything they've said in the last thirty minutes, but I don't like to broadcast my attentiveness.

"Meh," I answer. "Eventually."

"You realize you really *are* going to have to go back someday, right?" Emberly says.

She looks so serious that I can't help but laugh. "You're one to talk. How's your schooling going?"

"Believe me, if I could, I would be back at the academy in a heartbeat," she says with a furrowed brow, and then bites down on her bottom lip.

Ah-oh, Council troubles.

Emberly is roughly the same age as I am, yet she holds a seat on our Council of Elders as the oldest Nephilim of the seraph-line. It's a role she didn't ask for and doesn't want, and it's forced her to remain at our leadership headquarters in Egypt these last few months. We have regular calls, and I can see the stress of the job wearing on her a little more every week. She has a horrible poker face.

A masculine hand reaches over from off screen and tugs Emberly's lip free. She scrunches her nose, giving the person a mini scowl, but she's not fooling anyone. Her blush is as bright as the red-tipped ends of her hair.

"Hey, Steel," I say, and he drops his head into the frame so we can all see him.

After jerking his chin in the typical "cool guy" greeting, he plops down on the couch next to his blonde girlfriend, slash fiancée slash soul-bonded mate. Emberly moves her computer back so they both fit in the display. With his arm slung around her and Emberly tucked into his side, they're the picture of domestic bliss.

Only a small twinge of awkwardness shoots through me before I shake it off. It's only a little weird that Steel and I used to date. If I didn't love both of them so much, I'd find their affection nauseating, but as it is, it's easy to admit that it's sweet. Emberly brings out a side of Steel I never saw. They're good for each other and I'm happy for them, mostly. Besides, even if I wasn't, I'm not about to argue with fate. The pair are literal soulmates.

Sterling shoves his face in front of Greyson's to talk to Steel. "Yo, bro. How's Dad?"

Greyson puts a hand on the side of his twin's face and shoves him out of the way. Sterling falls out of the frame and after a commotion he pops up behind his brother.

"Uncalled for," Sterling complains, but pulls a roller chair over and flops into it so he can sit and share the screen.

The dark-skinned beauty that takes up the remaining square in our group chat rolls her crystalline blue eyes. Her black corkscrew curls bounce as she shakes her head. Ash returned to school in Colorado with Sterling and Greyson after the battle in London but is calling in from her own dorm room. With Steel and Emberly in Egypt, and me in the UK, Ash is the sole remaining buffer between the middle Durand twins. She probably has her hands full, but if anyone can handle that pair, it's her.

Steel starts to update his brothers on how their parents are doing and I go back to painting my nails, happy they're all distracted from the topic of my return to Seraph Academy. I haven't told them that I've asked to be excused from my last two years of novice training. Angel-born usually attend one of nine training academies around the globe until they are twenty, but I've had more real-world experience in the last two months than some seasoned Nephilim warriors get in their lifetimes. I don't see what else I can learn from the professors and trainers back at Seraph.

I've outgrown the academy. My parents support my decision, and now I'm just waiting to get clearance from the powers-that-be to become an official member of my parents' special ops unit.

I've been reluctant to share the update with my friends,

who all think I'll eventually return to Seraph to complete my angel-born training and education. I've told myself there's no reason to let my friends know until it's official, but truthfully, I'm not exactly sure what's holding me back. Speaking my mind isn't something I struggle with. Maybe it's just that I don't want to see the look of disappointment on their faces when I admit I'm abandoning them. But that shouldn't matter. This is my life. Becoming a warrior for the cause is what it means to be an angel-born.

Maybe I'm going soft? That thought makes me frown.

"You doing okay there, Nova?" Greyson asks. "If you scowl any harder your face is going to get stuck that way."

I direct a glare at the camera at the top of my computer screen, showing Greyson what a scowl truly looks like. Next to him, Sterling shudders and holds up his fingers in the sign of a cross. I grin, glad to know I still have my edge.

Ash looks at her watch, her cheeks puffing out as she sighs. "We've got to go. Afternoon session is about to begin."

Everyone says their goodbyes and we sign out of the chat. When I close my computer, the room feels extra still. The night sky outside the single window in my bedroom is dark and starless.

I crawl off my bed. Since it's impossible to extend my arms wide without punching both walls of this minuscule room, I stretch toward the ceiling.

My parents' flat outside of London is tiny. It used to be a safehouse, but after they lost both of their downtown residences because of the Merge, they moved us into what was essentially their backup house. My bedroom is no more than a glorified closet. My twin bed touches three of the walls and the remaining floor space is taken up by stacks of clothes and shoes. There's only a narrow strip of hardwood floor exposed as a walkway to the door. In the past I would have balked at the lack of proper storage for my wardrobe, but I don't really mind anymore. My priorities have shifted. Finding the perfect pair of boots to match a new leather jacket is nice, but no longer "life-goals" for me.

Life has a way of punching you in the gut and showing you what really matters. My wake-up call came in the form of the loss of hundreds of thousands of human lives, the deaths of thousands of Nephilim, and the blending of dimensions in one of the world's most prominent cities. I also suffered loss during the near apocalypse, but that's something I actively avoid dwelling on.

Pushing through my bedroom door, I squint against the harsh overhead lighting in the hallway. There's a flickering bulb that's particularly annoying but I stop myself from jumping up and smashing it. Replacing it will be so much less messy, but I'm irritated.

My parents sit at the small table right off the kitchen. I'm surprised to see them. It was so quiet I'd assumed I was home alone.

"Did your patrol end early tonight?" I ask as I slip past them on my way to the fridge.

My father blows out a breath, and I glance over my shoulder at them before foraging for food. He rubs a hand back and forth over his head, a move he typically does when he's frustrated. I inherited my hair color and thickness from him, but right now his dark auburn hair is buzzed close to his scalp, military style, but if it were longer it would probably be a disheveled mess right now.

"Lochlan's unit took over for us a few hours early," my mother answers for him, but I can tell she's distracted as well.

Grabbing a chilled bottle of sparkling water, I shut the door and then lean back against the fridge, studying them as they hunch over a piece of paper and speak in hushed tones.

My parents may look like a young attractive couple in their late twenties, but thanks to our slow aging process you'd never know they are actually over three hundred years old. Humans would probably be skeeved if their parents only looked a handful of years older than them, but I'm not. That's just how it's always been.

My mom tucks a clump of shiny dark brown hair behind her ear and shoots me a look that has my spine straightening.

"Something's happened. Is it the boy we rescued earlier this week? Could they not locate a living relative?" I ask.

I try to compartmentalize the different parts of my life, locking any horrors away behind a steel door in my mind where they can never be accessed. It's just what needs to be done to keep myself sane, but the encounter with the boy who lost his family shook me. I've had a hard time not seeing his big brown eyes filled with tears and shaded with heartbreak when I close my eyes at night. The soullessness of the Forsaken is never clearer than when I witness the aftermath of such a tragedy.

"No, no. The boy is fine." My dad heaves a sigh. "Relatively speaking, of course. He started speaking again yesterday, and they found an aunt that lives in Newcastle. She has a husband and kids and he's being transported to live with them today."

"Killian, we need to tell her," my mother says as she taps the paper on the table in front of them.

"Yeah," he agrees with a nod, and then leans back, folding

his arms. "Nova, why don't you take a seat?" He gestures to a chair in front of them.

Narrowing my eyes, I set the bottle down and then cross my arms, mimicking my father's pose but remain standing. "Something tells me I'm not going to want to be sitting down in a minute."

"Your request for early graduation from Seraph Academy has been denied," my dad says. "They want you back in classes by the end of the week."

My stomach bottoms out. I was not expecting that. A few seconds of silence tick by before I erupt.

"What? What possible reason could they have for making me go back? They can use every able-bodied angel-born warrior available right now. The world's a mess."

My dad points to the paper he was studying with my mom. It must be the official rejection. How old school to send an actual piece of paper when the world is digital? Just goes to show how ancient Nephilim thinking can be.

"They said they'll reevaluate after you've gone through metamorphosis," he says.

Anger immediately lashes through me, its barbed tail slicing my insides as it demands release.

"What? Why does it matter if I have a set of wings or not?"

Metamorphosis is the stage when an angel-born comes into their full powers. For Nephilim of the power-line, that almost always includes wings and increased strength, but I'd already proven I was strong enough to fight Fallen and Forsaken without any extra abilities.

My mom stands and walks over to me. "You know if it were up to us, we'd keep you here and make you an official member of our team, but it's not. There's an angel-born hierarchy we have to obey."

I grit my teeth. My parents are good at toeing the Nephilim company line. They're incredibly powerful, passionate about their mission, but don't like to step outside the lines. In that way we differ. I was raised to believe in and obey the chain of command, but when the barrier between the mortal and spirit realm crashed, the world wasn't saved by the angel-born who followed the rules, but rather the ones who broke them. My faith in the higher-ups always knowing best was more than shaken, it was shattered.

Rising from his seat, my dad joins my mom and me. "You've been through a lot more than the average angel-born your age. You'll have your whole life to fight in this war. Taking a few more years to prepare won't be a bad thing. There'll be enemies to fight when you graduate."

"The need is here, now," I argue. "And I don't want—"

I cut myself off. Going back to the academy to be trained to fight an enemy I've already come up against definitely feels like a step back, but I'm not naive enough to think that's the only reason I'm reluctant to return. If I go back to Seraph I'll have space to process all that went down when the barrier between worlds fell. It'll only be a matter of time before the fortified safe where I sealed those horrors will crack, forcing me to relive the blood-soaked memories. I'd rather face off against a horde of Forsaken and Fallen than do that.

Forget self-reflection. Killing monsters is totally cathartic.

"It's going to be okay," my mom says, and then she and my dad lay a hand on my shoulder and each other's, and then wait for me to return the gesture.

With a sigh, I lift my arms and mirror their stance. We tip our heads, touching our foreheads together in the center of the triangle we just created—the traditional power-line gesture used for greeting, bidding farewell, or offering comfort. I know my parents are using it for the latter, but in this moment, it feels an awful lot like goodbye.

3

Turbulence causes the plane to bounce in the sky. My stomach dips and rolls with every jarring drop and violent rebound. It's eleven hours into what should have only been a ten-hour flight and I'm seriously regretting not having waited until the next day to catch a military plane back to the States. This aircraft must be operating on half an engine to take this long to get over the Atlantic Ocean. I'm not snobby enough to insist on traveling in one of the Council's private jets, but flying in this stripped-down hunk of junk was a mistake. Prisoner transports leave a lot to be desired.

The door leading to the cockpit swings open and the co-pilot yells back to me, "You doing okay back there?"

Rather than shout back, I plaster a smile on my face that I'm pretty sure is more grimace than grin and give a thumbs-up.

With a nod, he pulls the door closed just as we lose altitude. I lift an inch into the air and then slam back down, landing on my tailbone. Pain shoots up my spine.

Never again.

It's another thirty minutes before the turbulence stops. I wobble to my feet, needing to move around. I take three steps until I hit the other side of the plane, then turn around and repeat the movements. Rolling my shoulders, I crack my neck to work out the aches and pains from the last several hours.

After my fifth turn, I'm crazy bored. The interior of the plane resembles an empty tin can with steel benches. There aren't windows, so I can't distract myself with the view. The only thing of interest is the door in the back. Or more specifically, what lies beyond it, but that area is off-limits.

With a sigh, I pull out my phone and type a text to my friends. Of course, there's no reception, and it doesn't go through. I should have at least downloaded a game app or some movies before I jumped on this flight.

My gaze shifts to the closed door.

"What's that?" I say, knowing there's no way my voice will carry to the pilot and co-pilot. "There's a noise back there I should check out?" I tap a finger against my lips as if considering their nonexistent request. "I agree, I should see what's going on in there."

Maybe just a peek?

Running a hand over my ponytail, I pull it forward, draping it over my shoulder. These drab overhead lights do nothing to bring out my auburn highlights—not to mention what it's doing for my skin—but it hardly matters if I'm not at my best physical appearance.

I cast a glance over my shoulder to make sure the guys up front aren't watching, then stride toward the door at the back of the plane. I was warned several times not to open this door, go near this door, or even think about this door, but in my opinion rules are strong suggestions rather than hard guidelines.

Reaching the door, I flip the lock. If I'm not supposed to take a look-see at the cargo, this area should be secured better. As it is, anyone could get in here.

That's practically an invitation.

I open the door just wide enough to slide through and then shut it quickly behind me. It's pitch black. The crummy lighting in the main hold was bad, but no light is worse. I can't hear anything but the rumble of the engines.

It's creepy, especially since I know I'm not alone.

My angel-born eyesight, which works a bit like night vision, kicks in after a few blinks and I start to make out some of the details around me: shipping crates of various sizes holding who knows—or who cares—what, two jump seats to my right and left, and in the very back I can just make out the outline of metal bars. Beyond them, it's an abyss.

I slink forward, a bubble of anticipation growing in my chest. Just one quick look to satiate my curiosity.

It's not until I'm almost pressed up against the bars that I can make out the figure inside the cell. He's seated with his legs spread on a narrow bench, his wrists shackled to a rod that runs behind his neck and over his shoulders, forcing his arms to stretch in either direction. Taut chains connect to the ends of the rod and bolt to the sheet metal behind him. The contraption forces him to hunch awkwardly, but I know comfort isn't the Council's first concern when it comes to this particular monster.

With his head hanging forward, white-blond strands fall over his forehead and brush his cheekbones. Through the thin curtain of hair, he assesses me in a way that makes me feel like I'm the one behind bars instead of him.

"Enjoying the view?" he growls.

His voice isn't loud, but I still start. He was so still and silent, my mind tricked me into believing he was a statue rather than a living, breathing person. Frustrated with my reaction, I try to cover it with sass.

"Not particularly." I cock my head, exaggerating my inspection. "I'm trying to figure out what all the fuss was about. You'd think the leader of a Fallen and Forsaken army would be . . . bigger."

We haven't been formally acquainted, but this isn't the first time Thorne and I have crossed paths. The most recent encounter was right after Tinkle's death. My heart squeezes whenever I brush upon that memory. At the time, I was more than half-crazed with grief and fury and would have clawed Thorne's eyes out with my bare hands if my friends hadn't stopped me.

Good thing I hadn't, since it turned out we needed him to fry Seraphim out of Emberly and then use his power to break the magical barrier around the orbs to stop the apocalypse he helped start. But I suppose he could have done both those things without his eyeballs, so I'm back to being bummed I didn't get the chance.

"I'd probably enjoy it better if you were shirtless though," I add with a smirk as I pack down those memories. I'm still not up for deep diving into my emotional damage.

"If you'd like to relieve me of these shackles, I'd be happy to oblige." The resonance of his rumbled words is just the right timbre to cause a zing of awareness to fizzle over my skin. The slight British accent doesn't hurt either.

I'm annoyed but not surprised by my body's reaction. Thorne is my type, after all—emotionally unavailable tough guys who break hearts on the regular. Only the slightest twinge of guilt registers from categorizing Steel that way, but up until Emberly burst into his life, that description fit him to a T.

I look down at my nails, feigning boredom. "Couldn't if I wanted. Wouldn't if I could."

"Pity," he practically purrs. "I have a feeling you and I could get into all sorts of trouble together."

He jerks his head, flinging the hair off his face. I have to remind myself not to react. With his shirt on or off, he's one good-looking, evil angel-born.

"Trouble's not really my thing," I say.

"Liar."

I bite my cheek to keep from smiling. I do like a little trouble, but not the kind he's insinuating.

I open my mouth to shoot off a pithy remark but shut it again with a snap when I realize what I'm doing. Sure, seduction is one of my go-to deflection methods, but there's something very wrong with entertaining any type of flirtation with this particular beast.

My almost-smile melts into a scowl. I got my look; it's time to go. Nothing good can come from conversing with the devil.

I turn to leave, then the ground drops out on me. I'm airborne for three whole seconds before I plunge to the metal floor. My legs crumple under me like an accordion, and I land painfully on my back, stunned.

Flopping over on my stomach, I push to my feet and grumble under my breath. This stupid, defective, World War I era plane should have been decommissioned several decades ago. I suppress a groan. There's no way that spectacular lack of grace went unnoticed.

I'm expecting a snide remark or even a low chuckle from Thorne, but he remains quiet, so I can't help but peek at him before I go. His eyes are squeezed shut as he clenches his teeth. His facial muscles tense when he tries to roll his shoulders; the bar he's attached to now rests at an awkward angle.

That last drop must have popped his shoulder out of joint. But what can I do about that? Is there even anything I want to do? After all the death and destruction he caused, the pain from a dislocated shoulder is the least of what he deserves.

Old Nova would have laughed at his pain, but now leaving him like that seems wrong.

I scrunch my nose. More evidence I'm going soft. I don't like it one bit.

I spin away from the cage and force myself not to care about Thorne's injury. When something tweaks in my heart, I tell it to shut up, and it shrivels up and dies.

Weaving between the plane's cargo, I head back to the passenger section of the fuselage, but on the way there's a loud blast and the plane dips to the side.

My body goes weightless. I scramble for a handhold, grabbing a rope securing one of the shipping crates as I float above it, but as soon as my fingers wrap around the cord, the plane starts to roll. Like a shoe stuck in a clothes dryer, my body bangs against the shipping crates and curved metal ceiling.

I don't need to look out a window to know that we're going down. It's clear this isn't regular turbulence and that was a very real explosion.

Tasting fear at the back of my throat, I refuse to give into it.

It takes me a second before I get my bearings, locating the exit several feet away. I know that's where I need to go to get out of the tail, but I'm reluctant to abandon the rope chafing my hands to get there.

Gritting my teeth, I do my best to propel myself forward, keeping my gaze lasered on the door. It's not an epic fail, but it isn't a perfect shot either. I smash into the ceiling and crates, falling against the door as the plane keeps tumbling. Grabbing a safety bar anchored into the wall, I wrench the door open just as we stop spinning and go into a true nosedive. I almost fall through the opening but slam my feet against the doorframe to keep from toppling forward.

There's a hole in the side of the fuselage the size of a person.

A vortex of wind whips my ponytail forward and drags at my clothes. If I leave this part of the plane, I'll be sucked into the sky.

Up ahead, the cockpit door is gone, as is part of the wall. The pilot and co-pilot are wrestling with the controls, their safety straps keeping them secured to their seats. Through some miracle, the plane starts to level even as it shakes wildly.

I'm not about to breathe easy but flying horizontally is preferable to falling vertically.

The co-pilot turns his head and gestures wildly with one arm. I have no idea what he's trying to tell me, and I don't get a chance to interpret it because something detonates and obliterates the cockpit completely. The explosion propels me into the tail of the plane, where I collide with the metal bars of Thorne's cage with a bone-jarring thud.

What's left of the aircraft starts to nosedive once again, and I grab the bars just as gravity pulls my feet out from underneath me.

This is bad. This is *so* bad.

I don't have a parachute, and I don't have wings.

I'm going to die.

A repeated clanging rings out over all the other ruckus. Thorne's chains have broken. There's still a metal rod running behind his shoulders, forcing his arms out on either side of him, but he's not letting that stop him. Bracing himself against the opposite wall, he pounds away at the cell door with his feet. Some of the bars are bent, and the lock looks like it's about to give way at any moment.

After four more hits, it does just that.

The door swings wildly as what's left of the plane starts a death spiral. I have to adjust my grip on the bars to keep my hold, but Thorne, not able to grab on to anything, gets tossed around his cell.

"Get in here and get this thing off of me," he roars over the sputters from the dying engines and rushing wind.

I only pause for a half-second, then straining my muscles, I pull myself to the cell door and through the opening as quickly as possible. There's a ticking clock in the back of my mind. I don't know how high up we were before the explosions occurred, but every second that goes by we race closer toward the earth.

Thorne does his best to keep his back toward me as we're jostled around the small space. Finally getting a grip on the rod, I pull. It slides free from one of Thorne's cuffs, and then I'm slammed into the wall.

With one arm free, Thorne yanks the rod through the circle on the other cuff and tosses it out of the cell, where it clangs against the plane's metal interior. Thorne then forces his dislocated shoulder back into place, and I grimace.

"We have to get out of here," he yells.

I don't disagree, but where are we supposed to go? It seems to me that our choices are to die in the plane or die out of the plane. Is one really better than the other?

The door between the tail and what's left of the aircraft swings open and shut. Thorne shoves himself out of the cell and then makes his way toward the middle of the fuselage, a feat only a supernatural being could perform in a falling plane. I'm more focused on following Thorne as he jumps from one piece of cargo to the next than seeing what lies beyond.

Reaching the door, Thorne grabs hold of a crossbeam to stop himself. I grasp the same hold to keep myself from falling into the void, but almost lose my grip when I catch a glimpse of what's out there.

It's worse than I thought. The front end of the plane is gone, and we're hurtling toward sparkling sea below. We can't have more than half a minute before impact.

"The parachutes are gone," I yell over the wind.

Thorne scowls as his white-blond hair whips around his head. "We clear the plane, and I'll fly us down."

Great idea, except Thorne doesn't have a set of working wings. Steel ripped one of them off when they fought several months ago.

"How are you going to do that when you only have one wing?" I point out.

"One wing is better than nothing right now," he says as he grabs me.

Shoving my face into his chest, he ducks through the opening and jumps. His back slams into what's left of the plane's wing, and we ricochet into the air. The hit loosens his grip on me, and I start to slip, but I loop my arms around his neck and lock my legs around his waist, determined to stay connected even if he lets go.

I can barely tell which way is up or down as we plummet toward the water. The water below blurs with the sky above as we summersault through the air.

Thorne releases his wings, but all that appears is one full wing and the useless stump of the other. Our bodies tilt and jolt as his single wing catches the air, but one wing isn't enough to truly slow our momentum, and we spiral like a spinning top. Centrifugal force drags at us, trying to pry my body from Thorne's, but I tighten my hold and squeeze my eyes shut. I'm not prone to motion sickness, but this is too much.

The plane crashes into the water below us. Close. *Too close.*

With a roar, Thorne maneuvers his wing to minutely slow down our descent and rotation, but it's barely enough to cushion our impact.

We slam into the water, and it's like we've been chucked into a cement wall. My ribs crack; pain bursts along the right side of my body. Bubbles surge from my mouth as we plunge deep into the ocean's depths.

Thorne and I are a tangle of limbs as we disengage from one another and struggle toward the surface. I'm out of air, and only one half of my body will cooperate. My booted feet act more like weights than fins as I kick toward the ripples of light above me. My fingertips are almost there when a disc-like hunk of plane debris crashes into the waves above me.

The chunk of sheet metal slices into my shoulder and down my bicep. Red blooms around me as the salt water leaches the blood from the wound. It stings like crazy, but my lungs hurt worse from lack of oxygen.

Out of nowhere, there's a surge of power, and I'm forced into the spirit realm, phasing against my will.

I gasp, sucking in a mouthful of ocean water. Brightness surrounds me from every side, and I can no longer tell which way is up and which way is down.

My muscles jerk with involuntary spasms, and as my body begins to fail me, my resolve doubles.

I will not survive a plane crash only to drown in the ocean.

Committing to a direction, I fight, kicking and flailing to make progress toward what I hope is the surface. The water in the spirit realm is blindingly bright, so my eyesight is completely useless. I think I'm about to break the surface, but then something wraps around my ankle and hauls me deeper. I twist and squirm to escape, but my struggles are pathetically weak.

Fear and anger churn in my gut, giving me one final spurt of energy. My foot slips from the sea creature's grip, but the next moment it has me by the back of my jacket.

I hang limply in its grasp, my body no longer obeying my commands. At this point, I just hope I pass out before something tries to eat me. I don't want to be nom-nommed on while I'm conscious. What an awful way to go.

My eyelids start to slide shut as I'm hauled from the ocean and tossed on a flat surface. A fuzzy image of Thorne comes into view as he hovers over me.

Huh, not a sea creature after all, I think as I fight to keep my eyes open.

"Why were you swimming down? Are you *trying* to drown yourself?" His voice is sharp, but the look in his eyes is filled with unrestrained panic.

I may not be underwater anymore, but that doesn't mean I'm not dying. My attempts to suck in air around the water clogging my lungs are pathetic. I don't even have the energy to gasp, only open and close my mouth like a gaping fish. My vision dims.

Thorne utters something in Enochian—each syllable harsh and guttural—and then bends over. He pinches my nose and seals his lips to mine, blowing air into my lungs. It's not until the third breath that my body starts to take over. I cough and hack until salt water, and what's left of my undigested lunch, crawls up my throat and fills my mouth.

Rolling to my side, I spew the chunky mixture back into the sea. When I have control of myself again, I sit up. Thorne's scanning the water around us. I turn my gaze outward as well, but the brightness from the spirit world water is so overpowering that I can't see much except the pink spirit realm sky above us.

Looking down, I realize that we're floating on a square shipping crate. Our makeshift life raft is mostly intact, and bobs and sways when I displace my weight. There must be something airtight inside or it wouldn't float, especially not with both our weight on top of it. Pieces of the wreckage sink below the surface around us.

"Why were we forced to phase into the spirit realm?" I'm talking more to myself than Thorne, but he swings his gaze back to me, a snarl of disgust lifts his upper lip.

"Isn't it obvious?" he says. "I wasn't the only high value item being shipped on that plane."

4

Thorne jumps into the air, trying to use his one wing to lift him, but without the counterweight on the other side he barely ascends before he tips and plummets toward the waves. His head breaks the surface, and he flings wet hair off his forehead, spraying drops of water my way. It only takes a few powerful strokes before he's back at our makeshift life raft.

"Did you really think you'd be able to fly on one wing?" I ask as he pulls himself out of the water and onto the shipping crate. His clothes—a simple gray t-shirt and dark jeans —are plastered to his body and aren't doing a thing to hide his muscled physique.

He dematerialized his wings in the water, which makes sense because they probably just weigh him down—or at least the one remaining wing. There's hardly anything left on the other but an awkwardly angled footlong stump that he can move. It doesn't do a thing to aid with flight.

With a hand at his brow, he stops scanning our surroundings long enough to glance down at me. The look on his face isn't exactly hostile, but I wouldn't call it warm either. "I wasn't trying to fly, I wanted to see if there is anything around us. All this water is blinding."

He isn't wrong. My eyes sting from the reflection of the sun off the spirit world's crystalline water. It's like being stuck in a glass prism, and a headache starts to form.

I try to phase back into the mortal world for at least the tenth time, but once again I'm unable to do so. Besides his cryptic comment about there being another item of value on the plane, Thorne and I haven't really broached the subject of why neither one of us is able to phase, but I have an idea of what he believes is going on.

The only thing I know of that would force us to remain in the spirit world is one of the spirit orbs. There are only two of them in existence. One of them forces humans, angels, and angel-born into the spirit realm, and the other keeps them out of it. But even knowing that there's an orb that can disable our ability to phase out of the spirit world, I have a hard time believing that's what's causing this. The orbs are supposed to be under lock and key in Egypt, not on a random prisoner transport plane.

"So, is there anything out there?" I ask, pushing our phasing issue out of my mind.

We have more immediate concerns. Finding land or a boat—or anything beyond endless sea—will mean the difference between life and death.

Shoving to my feet, the crate bobs wildly beneath us and I reach out and grab Thorne's bicep to stabilize myself. He yanks away from my touch, and I pitch forward into the chilly water. I surface next to the crate, sputtering and with half a head of hair covering my face.

"Really? I just started to dry out."

Thorne glances down at the spot on his arm I touched and then back at me, but he doesn't offer any apologies. I guess I'm not really surprised by that.

As I heft myself out of the water, I notice that the slice on my bicep has started bleeding again. The blood is leaking into the ocean, turning some of the sparkling water pink.

Fantastic. Now it's going to be a contest to see what kills me first: dehydration or sharks.

Thorne's gaze trails to my injury as well. Smashing his lips together, he goes back to searching the horizon.

I feel like a drowned rat as I flop back onto the crate. I'm sure I look like one too, but that hardly matters. What I should be worried about is that I'm stuck in the middle of the ocean with a veritable psychopathic serial killer. Even though he technically saved my life by jumping with me from the plane and pulling me out of the water, the hard truth is that Thorne could decide to kill me at any moment. He was born and bred to be a lethal killing machine, and as much as it hurts my pride to admit it, I'm no match for him. His powers as a seraph Neph and skill levels surpass my own. Not to mention the ends of each feather on his remaining wing are razor sharp, giving him a weapon when I have none.

My blood chills at the thought, but I refocus and search for something to bind my wound. It only takes a few seconds to realize there's nothing to use except what's on my body, so shrugging off my shredded and now useless jacket, I grasp the bottom of my tank top and start to tear.

Thorne jerks toward me when he hears the ripping of fabric. I ignore him and continue to rip. When I'm done, several inches of my midriff is exposed, but now I have a strip to wrap around my wound. I try to wind the cloth around my bicep with one arm, but my efforts are clumsy at best, and the binding slides down my arm when I finish. Frustration bubbles in my chest.

Thorne crouches down next to me and the crate beneath us bobbles up and down. I look up at him sharply, but he silently tugs the cloth off my arm and starts to re-bind the wound.

I'm momentarily struck mute, confused that he's helping me.

With Thorne's attention on his task, I take the moment of peaceful silence between us to study him.

Like all angel-born, Thorne is tall by human standards, and although he may not be related to Emberly they both have the same pale skin and platinum, almost silver hair that is shockingly similar but can easily be attributed to their seraph parentage. In contrast to his blond hair, his eyebrows and lashes are thick and black, making his midnight blue eyes even more dramatic. I trace the straight line of his nose with my gaze down to his lips, which are full and pouty and form the perfect cupid's bow.

Thorne is handsome by anyone's standards, so much so I'd almost call him beautiful. Give the man some pointy ears and he'd be the embodiment of a fae prince.

A deceiving package for the shriveled heart that beats in his chest.

A muscle twitches in his square jaw as he works on wrapping my arm, betraying his annoyance—at me or our situation, I don't know. I hardly care either way and continue my examination of him.

His smooth skin lies over his high cheekbones, and like a hairline crack in smooth marble the only flaw in his face is a faint scar that runs through his left brow and ducks into his hairline.

Interesting, I think as I cock my head.

He must have gotten that injury at a young age. By the time a Nephilim reaches adolescence we heal from all non-life ending wounds, preventing us from scarring. For instance, the slices on my shoulder and arm will be completely gone by week's end—that is, assuming I live that long. Angel-born can go without food and water for longer than a human, but a week without water is pushing it.

I clear my throat and Thorne glances up at me, but I'm not worried he'll be able to guess at the jumble of emotions swirling inside me. My face is a mask and shield I've spent my life perfecting, and I know something as small as an arched brow and a half-smile can go a long way toward concealing my true feelings.

When Thorne finishes, he ties a knot and then moves behind me and pulls the strap of my tank down my shoulder.

"Whoa there." I swat at his hands. "Buy me a drink first," I say as I yank the strap back into place and shoot him a glare. I'm far from shy with my body, but seriously?

Thorne runs a tongue over one pointed canine tooth and then grinds out, "You have a cut on your back that's bleeding. I'm just checking to see how bad it is."

I roll my shoulder, only now noticing the tenderness.

"Oh, well, in that case, carry on." I scooch as far forward as I can to give Thorne room behind me. Keeping a hand on my shirt to stop it from slipping, I let him slide the strap of my tank and the sports bra beneath it down so he can inspect the lesion. His touch is surprisingly gentle as he prods the edges of the wound.

After a few moments, he grunts. I glance over my shoulder when his touch disappears and watch him peel off his shirt and then wring it out. I get a face-full of ripped man-chest, which suddenly makes me uncharacteristically shy, and I turn forward.

Pressing the soft fabric of his gray shirt to my upper back, he applies pressure to my wound. We stay locked in awkward silence for several minutes.

"Why are you helping me?" I ask, genuinely curious.

Why he even bothered to jump from the plane with me or save me from drowning is truly a mystery. We may both perish out here in the waves, but it would have been easier for him to just let me die in the crash.

Thorne snorts a half-laugh, but because he's behind me now, I can't read his face. "I'm not doing this for you, I'm doing this for me. Have you ever seen any of the spirit world sea creatures? They make sharks look like puppies. You're hemorrhaging in the water, which is like ringing the dinner bell for every carnivorous fish within a fifty-mile radius."

I can't help the shiver that racks my body. Being eaten is definitely low on the list of ways I want to die. If I have a choice, I want to go out in battle like any good power angel-born would want. Being a meal for an apex predator would be slow and painful, not to mention humiliating.

"What's the big deal?" I ask with fake nonchalance. "You could just blast any shark out of the water with your angel-fire."

Once the words are out of my mouth, I gulp, realizing he could just blast me with angel-fire too.

"Not with these cuffs on," he says, and shakes a hand

near my face, showing one of the silver shackles encircling his wrist.

The cuff is about two-inches wide and etched with symbols I don't recognize. Up close, it looks like a thick piece of jewelry rather than a shackle.

Strange. I've never seen anything like it before.

"They dampen my powers and make it almost impossible to use angel-fire," he explains.

My eyebrows jump up, and I glance sharply at Thorne. He keeps his gaze down and clears his throat and I get the impression he wishes he hadn't revealed that information. Trying to give him some privacy, I look back at the water, my mind wandering.

I didn't know the Council possessed something to mute angel-born powers, but I can understand why they'd want to weaken Thorne. As a seraph Nephilim, his powers are as strong, if not stronger, than the most powerful of us. I'm a little surprised Emberly never mentioned the cuffs, although in fairness she's rarely talked about Thorne over the last few months. It's clear she's conflicted about him. He kidnapped her—twice—and handed her over to his mother, but he also ultimately helped stop the realms from merging. I wouldn't be surprised in the least to find out she's the only reason he's still alive. Thorne's lucky she has a soft heart.

"But like I said before," he says, bringing me back to the moment, "sharks aren't what I'm worried about."

I roll my eyes, sure he's just saying that to freak me out. "You're making that up. There aren't different species of sea creatures in the spirit world."

For all I know, sharks might not even be a concern. There are some living creatures that can exist in both realms, but I don't know which ones. It's not something we study in school. And why would we? It doesn't have anything to do with fighting Fallen or Forsaken.

"They really don't teach you anything, do they?" Thorne asks, disdain dripping from every syllable.

"What do you mean by that?" I ask, sitting up straighter.

"There are whole subspecies of spirit world creatures."

I scoff. "No way. We would know about them."

Thorne scoffs. "It's hard to believe that Nephilim are so ignorant, but then again, angel-born aren't known to spend more time in the spirit world than they have to. The question is whether your Elders just don't know or if they're willfully keeping you ignorant. My money is on a combination of both."

I open my mouth to argue with Thorne, when he pulls the shirt away from my back and stands, sending the crate beneath us bobbing wildly. I lean back to keep from pitching into the ocean, squinting up at him as he scans something off to the left.

Suddenly, he drops his shirt and starts stripping. His shoes come off first; he tosses them at me with a hurried, "Don't lose these." His pants come next, leaving him in only a pair of black boxer briefs that leave very little to the imagination.

"Is this strip show for my benefit alone?" I ask with a wag of my eyebrows as I try to play it off like I'm not affected in the least by his near nakedness. The blush in my cheeks tells a different story, but I'm hoping he doesn't notice or thinks it's just coloring from the sun.

He chucks his pants at me too, and that's when I get annoyed.

"What do I look like," I snap. "A closet?"

"I see land. An island," he says, and then dives into the

water with barely a splash. When he breaks the surface he has a rope in his hand that's connected to the crate. "Don't lose any of my clothes or I'll take yours as payment."

This is normally when I'd throw something pithy out such as, "Is that a threat or a promise," but the words get jumbled in my throat as an unbidden image of him stripping me of my clothes rises in my mind's eye.

It's at that moment I realize I'm out of my league with this guy. I just pray he doesn't realize it.

5

It's late in the day when Thorne and I drag the crate onto the sandy beach. I'm achy and spent, and blood leaks through the binding on my injured arm, more of an annoyance now than a serious concern since we're out of the ocean.

The shoreline we're standing on stretches for maybe a mile in each direction before disappearing from view. A thick jungle lurks about fifty feet from the surf, and a volcano juts up in the distance, its curved mouth blessedly lava-free.

Everything around us is wild and untouched. Emberly always refers to the spirit realm as the spectrum world. Looking at the purple and pink sand at our feet, and the magenta and teal jungle a little ways off, the name is fitting.

It's beautiful, but unease gnaws at me, dampening its appeal. There's not a single thing that would indicate the island is inhabited, which is a giant problem. I have to get to a phone and notify the angel-born of what happened and where we are, but if there's no phone on this island, I'm out of luck.

Even though Thorne played the part of my reluctant savior today, he's still the monster that led the attack against London in his bid to take over the world. A couple of good deeds can't erase the black stains on his soul, and I don't trust him farther than I can throw him.

I need backup—a lot of it.

"Here ya go," I say, and then drop Thorne's clothes in a heap onto the sand, smiling to myself when the surf brushes over the clump and he has to dive to keep them from being swept back into the ocean.

He shoots me a glare that I pretend not to see. With effort, he tugs his wet jeans back on, but doesn't bother with his shirt. He squeezes the water out of it and then turns to slog up the beach toward the jungle. I swallow a gasp when I get the first good look at his uncovered back. It's littered with scars that crisscross over his skin from his shoulders down to his lower back. Some even disappear below the waist of his jeans.

Despite my dislike for him, nausea roils in my gut. These scars are nothing like the thin white line that runs through his eyebrow. These are thick and raised, which means they weren't tended to after they were received and got infected. The only explanation I can think of is that he was whipped, repeatedly, and at a very young age, since his body still bears the evidence. No one should have to go through something like that, but maybe there's another explanation.

Reaching a driftwood log higher up on the beach, Thorne lays his shirt over it before returning to the shoreline. I do a decent job of keeping my face blank and my eyes on the large wooden crate he insisted we haul ashore, pretending that I didn't notice his scars, even though I'm sure he knows I did.

He doesn't say anything before he starts tugging the planks off the top of the crate. I force myself not to stare at his back, busying myself instead with helping pull boards. I'm curious to find out what's inside the crate.

"What do you think is in here?" I ask.

"If we're lucky, there will be some food or water. Or maybe a tarp to use for shelter, and something to use for navigation inside," he says as he peels one of the planks off. "Knowing the angel-born though, this thing is probably filled with something useless like editions of the *Book of Seraph* or a shipment of academy blazers."

The thrill of finding dry land and knowing I wasn't going to be a shark's next meal had momentarily brushed the harsh reality that we're still in serious trouble out of my mind. Thorne is right. Food, water, and temporary shelter are the priorities, but when I first considered the crate's contents all I'd hoped for was a change of clothes and weapons.

Weapons mostly. I always feel better with a dagger in my hand.

I scrunch my nose. "Food. Water. Right."

Thorne lets out a sharp chuckle.

"What?" I snap and stop helping with the crate.

Thorne pauses to look at me. "I'm just not surprised you weren't thinking about what we need to stay alive right now. Teaching survival skills isn't high on the angel-born list of priorities. You guys are too busy learning human history and sharpening your online shopping skills at your posh academies."

"Excuse me," I argue, "foraging for food and enduring

extreme conditions isn't part of the curriculum for good reason. They teach us how to survive attacks from rabid Forsaken—you know, the monsters that have a taste for human and angel-born blood."

"Then they've left you at a disadvantage."

I cross my arms over my chest, annoyed that he's saying I've not been properly trained. I'm proud of my skill level and what I've accomplished. I've taken down more Forsaken and Fallen in the last couple of months than most angel-born warriors dozens of years older than me have in their entire lives.

"It's not like we have to search for Fallen or Forsaken in the boonies. They go where the people are—you know, their food source. The only survival skill I need for that is how to navigate a subway system."

Thorne scoffs. "As if you're fully trained if you've not prepared for everything."

"Oh yeah, like your psycho mom did a good job preparing you for the real world. She didn't even instill a basic knowledge of right and wrong in you."

Thorne stops trying to open the crate and stares at me. "My mother was a lot of things, a monster by most standards, but in that way she did right by me. I can survive in a wide variety of situations and in any climate on Earth. You can't say the same."

An image of his scarred back jumps to mind. If he has any idea what I'm thinking, it doesn't show on his face, but I can't help but wonder if regular beatings were one of the ways his mother prepared him to *survive a wide variety of situations.* I don't want to feel anything for Thorne except anger and disgust, but my stomach sours with the thought.

Thorne's gaze moves to the top of my head. "My guess is

that one day without your hairbrush and you'll be crying for the end to come."

I lift my hand to my hair before I can stop myself. My once sleek high ponytail now hangs from the side of my head with just as much hair still in the tie as has escaped it. It's a tangled and crunchy mess.

Yanking the band out, I grimace as clumps of hair pull out with it. Thorne catches the motion and smirks as if that proves him right.

"I can survive without a hairbrush," I grit out.

"Sure you can," he says with a shake of his head, and goes back to trying to tug planks off the crate.

Arguing with him about whether or not I can make it a day without a hairbrush is just stupid, so I take the higher ground and keep my mouth shut.

Thorne finally yanks the final board away and I peek inside.

Huh?

Within the crate something black sticks out from a sea of packing peanuts.

Thorne leans over and digs through the peanuts, pulling a sleek rectangular trunk about the size of a carry-on suitcase out of the crate a moment later.

Tilting my head, I scan its smooth black surfaces. There aren't any latches on the sides, but there's a long crack that runs diagonal across the top. The trunk was obviously damaged in the crash. Not surprising. Someone didn't do their job packaging very well. Packing peanuts only fill about a third of the crate.

Setting the small trunk down Thorne starts dismantling the rest of the crate, searching through the foam pieces for anything else inside. When that task is done and it's clear there's nothing else in the crate, he crouches to examine the trunk's sides, looking for a way to open and clearly frustrated when he can't.

He stands, shaking his head. "I don't see a way to open it."

I could have told him that ten minutes ago. *Boys.*

"Well, whatever's in there, someone didn't want anyone else to have it."

"I don't doubt that." Thorne lifts one eyebrow, shooting me a *you're-an-idiot* look.

I narrow my eyes at him. Fellow angel-born have lost teeth for milder insults than that. But I'm aware of what he's alluding to though. The orbs.

"It doesn't make sense that the Council of Elders would put one of the orbs on our plane. They have both of them sealed in their vaults in Egypt."

I'm less arguing with Thorne and more talking out loud. If they were transporting the orb, the Elders would have put some sort of security on it—multiple planes to escort it to a new location, angel-born to protect it. To think it was just sitting in one of the crates in the storage area of our transport plane is ridiculous. It's too precious, and dangerous, to be so cavalier about.

"It also doesn't make sense that someone planted bombs in our plane causing us to crash in the middle of nowhere either, yet here we are." Thorne waves his hand to indicate the blinding sea and purple sand.

I purse my lips, knowing he has a point but refusing to acknowledge it, at least out loud. But when I think about it, it strikes me as odd that there weren't guards on the plane to accompany Thorne. In a lot of ways, Thorne is just as dangerous as the orbs, yet I wasn't even told he was on board until we were already in the air. It all feels suspicious now.

Thorne runs a tongue over his top teeth as he considers the trunk.

"There's really no other explanation for our inability to leave the spirit realm," he says, oblivious to my inner thoughts and suspicions. "I know a lot about the artifacts and secrets of both worlds, and there's nothing besides the Starfire Orb that would force and then keep us in the spirit world like this. If the orb isn't in here . . ." Thorne raps the top of the trunk with his knuckles. "Then it's somewhere out there in the wreckage."

Starfire Orb? Interesting. The orb has a name. I don't think any of the Elders know that.

I tuck the information away for later and study Thorne as he casts a look at the trunk. His face is emotionless except for the glint of interest in his eyes. That glint makes me more than a little nervous.

I tense, covertly scanning for something I can use as a weapon as I slide in front of the trunk, putting my body between what might possibly be a powerful spirit world object and Thorne.

The angel-born don't know much about the orbs except that when they are brought together and saturated in a truckload of angel-line blood, they cause the barrier between the spirit and mortal world to collapse. Thorne's plan had been to merge the worlds and subjugate humankind with his Forsaken and Fallen army.

Granted, he seemed to have abandoned that endeavor, going as far as to help us stop his mother from bringing down the barrier, but who's to say, given the option, he won't try it again? People change their minds all the time, and he killed to get his hands on the orbs once before. I'm sure spending the last three months in captivity hasn't been his idea of a good time. World domination might be looking like a pretty attractive option once again.

Tracking my movements, Thorne pops his jaw in irritation. "Relax, I don't want that cursed thing anymore. I have no interest in bringing down the veil. I much prefer the spirit world to the mortal one. If I merge the two, I'd bump into angel-born all the time, and I want nothing more to do with your species."

I narrow my eyes, searching his face for signs of untruths. "You say that as if you're not angel-born yourself."

"I'm not. At least not in any of the ways that count."

I find it hard to disagree with him. Although Thorne is angel-born by birth, his mom was a homicidal Fallen seraph angel with zero regard for human life who raised him among soulless Forsaken and Fallen. It makes sense that he doesn't identify as one of us.

"What about your allegiance to your mother?" I ask, not convinced he'd give up his ambitions for world domination that easily. It's true that I don't know Thorne well. Our interactions before today have been brief and only on the battlefield, but imagining him living a life of peaceful solitude just doesn't seem to fit him.

"My mother's plans died with her. The only allegiance I have right now is to myself."

I scoff. "Well, that I believe."

He takes a step closer, his chest almost bumping into mine. I stare up at him, refusing to back down. As the former leader of a Fallen and Forsaken army, Thorne's no doubt used to people following his orders and cowering in his presence.

I'll do neither of those things.

"You'll do well to remember that. I'll be very clear right now so there's no misunderstanding between us. I have no intentions to kill you. We have no idea where we are or how to get off this island. Killing you would be rash when you might be of some use to me later."

Some use to him later? I lock my jaw, clenching my teeth to the point of pain.

"But if you become an obstacle to my goals, I won't hesitate to remove you from my way by whatever means necessary."

You'll kill me if you feel like it. Message received.

"And what would those goals be?" I ask, wanting to see how far I can push him.

Just then an unfamiliar roar, like a cross between an angry lion and the growl of a bear, booms from somewhere in the jungle. I can't help but wonder if Thorne was telling the truth about there being animals in the spirit realm angel-born don't know about.

Thorne flicks his gaze in the direction of the tree line before looking back at me.

"Right now, my only goal is to survive the night."

With that, he turns on a heel and stomps away. My heart thumps in my chest and I'm not sure if it's from the roar of the beast hidden in the depths of the jungle, or the threats of the beast I just faced off against. Either way, I know they're both dangerous and deadly predators I need to be wary of if I'm going to survive long enough to get off this island.

6

I need a shower so bad it isn't even funny. My hair is knotted and crusty from the dried salt water. My hip aches and my arm's numb from sleeping on my side. Itchy sand is everywhere and it's chafing some seriously sensitive areas of my body.

Cracking my eyelids, I look directly into the slitted eyes of a purple lizard that's chilling on a lump of sand in front of my face. The creature is maybe the length of my hand, a strip of pink spikes running down its back toward a barbed tail. I'm not really a reptile fan, but I think it's actually kinda cute. That is, until it opens its mini-shark mouth, revealing multiple rows of serrated teeth, and runs at me with a high-pitched screech.

I pop up with a shriek, backpedaling away from the bloodthirsty little beast. It tries to climb up my leg, but I kick out and it goes flying into the jungle. I keep my eyes focused on the direction I chucked the little monster, expecting it to come flying at my face like a hell-bat or something at any moment.

After a couple of minutes pass and nothing happens, I'm able to wrangle my heart rate back to its resting pace. No doubt I'm going to have nightmares about that for years. I'm not ready to admit that Thorne was right about there being spirit world creatures—I might not have recognized that little bloodthirsty reptile, but I'm not an expert so maybe that was just a normal lizard—but I'm no longer so confident he was lying. Either way, I need to learn how to sleep with one eye open on this island.

Last night had been as uneventful as it was uncomfortable. Thorne and I didn't talk again after our little tête-à-tête. I watched him pick up palm fronds for a while. Admittedly, the view of him scouring the beach and tree line for who-knows-what kept my interest for a bit, but I grew bored as the pink spirit world sky faded to dark purple and the red starlight appeared. Eventually, I ventured a little way into the jungle and fell asleep on the sand next to a palm tree.

As I stretch, still keeping one eye on the direction I punted the lizard just in case, I hear faint grunts and shouts in the direction of the surf. Carefully picking my way through the heavy underbrush and dodging trees along the way, I head toward the ocean, stopping when I spot Thorne on the beach.

Pink rays of the spirit world sun glint off the metal tips of Thorne's feathers as he runs through what looks like a training sequence, twirling and slashing with imaginary weapons. His shirtless torso is covered in a thin layer of sweat, telling me he's been at this a while.

His single wing flares with every spin as he practices using the sharpened edges of his silver feathers to slice into his enemies. One motion flows into the next, like an intricate dance, but I can tell he's off balance. He wobbles a little after each turn, taking extra steps to regain his equilibrium. His nostrils flare and he bares his teeth in a snarl every time he teeters, the frustration clear on his face as he works through movements that he probably perfected years ago but now has to relearn.

Dropping the context of fighting with weapons, Thorne's arms flow through the air in a way that makes me think angel-fire would be blasting from them if he were facing off against a foe. The silver magic-dampening cuffs make it impossible for him to produce angel-fire, but watching him go through the motions reminds me just how dangerous he'd be with his powers unleashed.

I've seen angel-fire in action. It engulfs its target and burns through flesh in seconds. One ball of Thorne's angel-fire to my chest and I'd be gone.

I shudder at the thought.

Crossing my arms, I settle against the trunk of a palm, taking the opportunity to study his movements, trying to commit his fighting stance to memory and learn his weaknesses.

I haven't given much thought to his recapture, but despite my bravado the night before, even maimed and with his power muted Thorne's going to be a hard target to bring in. He was only captured by the angel-born in the first place after he passed out from expelling too much energy helping Emberly separate the orbs; he was taken into custody while he was still unconscious. I don't know how long it took him to wake, but Emberly was out for days.

I tilt my head, watching his muscles bunch.

There is a flimsy truce between us at the moment, but who knows how long it will last, but there's little doubt it's going to come down to a fight at some point. Thorne wants his freedom and he's been crystal clear that he'll do whatever he has to in order to keep it. As an angel-born honor bound to protect humanity, letting him go isn't an option for me.

I sigh.

Hopefully, when the time comes to bring him back in, we'll only be taking him down, not taking him out. It would be a pity to snuff out someone that pretty.

Thorne's a machine. He keeps on with his drills for at least another hour. Eventually, he dematerializes his wings —his good one and the stump that remains of the other— and continues training. His movements without his wings are much more fluid and confident. I remain in the shadows of the trees as I watch, not wanting him to know I'm studying him.

The sun is almost directly overhead when he finally stops and faces the ocean. Bending at the waist, he rests his hands on his knees as he gulps in air. Sweat slickens his bare back and arms, and drips from the ends of his hair. His jeans ride low on his hips, and I wonder for a moment if he's lost weight during his captivity.

Something about that thought makes my stomach sour, so I bat it away. It's not my business how he fared the last three months. I don't care if he was treated well while he was rotting in some angel-born jail cell. People died because of him. Missing a couple of meals doesn't even begin to atone for his load of sins.

Stepping from my hiding spot, I start a slow clap, making my presence known. The only indication that I surprise him at all is the slight tightening of his shoulders before he forces them to relax.

"Enjoying another show?" he asks without turning in my direction.

"Immensely," I admit, as I join him at the water's edge, taking care not to let the gentle surf lap over the toes of my boots.

I don't want him to know how long I studied his moves, but I'm hoping the thought of me watching from the shadows throws him a little. When I catch the hint of a smile on his lips, I know I missed the mark. He either doesn't care I watched him or likes that I did.

My good mood evaporates, and I frown.

I thought I had the upper hand, but Thorne's blasé attitude makes me suspicious. He has a reputation for being a strategic genius as well as a skilled killing machine. Did he know I was there all along? If so, is he somehow playing me? *What's his angle?*

"Sleep well?" he asks, and my suspicion meter spikes even more. Why is he being so civil? The last conversation we had he basically said that if I got in his way, he'd end me.

I study his profile, openly taking his measure. He definitely has an angle.

Thorne turns to me, boldly returning my stare.

"I slept fine," I finally say.

"Good. It's going to be a long day."

"Why do you say that?"

"Because we're going to check out the island. We need to familiarize ourselves with our surroundings and see if there's anything useful. We also need to identify the dangers."

It isn't a bad plan of action, but I'm not about to admit it out loud.

I lick my lips. They're dry from the beginnings of dehydration. The action catches Thorne's attention, and he drops his gaze to my mouth. I'm close enough to see his pupils flare before he looks away.

I smirk, but then the smile slips from my lips. "Hey, where's the trunk?"

The black box isn't anywhere even though the remains of the crate that housed it are off to the side.

Did Thorne haul the trunk into the jungle while I slept?

I hope it didn't get taken away by the tide. Whether or not there's an orb in the trunk remains to be seen, but whatever is locked away in there is obviously something of value.

"I buried it."

What?

"You buried it?" I ask, furrowing my brow. Why would he have done that?

"That's what I just said."

I spin, searching for a splotch of unturned sand.

"Where is it?" I demand.

Thorne chuckles as he brushes past me, walking up toward the tree line. He grabs his shirt from where it's lying across the trunk of a sideways-growing palm and shrugs it on. The material instantly sticks to his sweat-slicked skin.

"Where did you bury the trunk?" I repeat.

"I don't intend to tell you," he says, and then marches into the jungle as I follow in his wake.

He stops when he reaches a bed of palm leaves and a small pile of coconuts. I stare at the makeshift bed longingly. It looks halfway comfortable and sand-free. I wish I'd had the same thought yesterday. It's going to take me days to pick the sand out of all my crevices.

"You have to tell me where you buried it," I argue.

Thorne snatches one of the hairy-husked coconuts and

places it against a palm tree, cracking it with a thump of his fist. Milky liquid starts to leak from the fissure in the shell and the sweet and distinctive smell of the fruit tickles my nose.

"I most certainly do not," he says, and then starts to drink the coconut water. He lifts his head high, his Adam's apple bobbing with every swallow. Watching him drink makes my throat extra dry.

"Yes, you do. That trunk, and whatever's inside it, isn't yours."

"It's not yours either," he says. The moisture from the coconut water coats his lips, and I can't help but lick mine as well. I'm so thirsty that I don't even notice I've stopped arguing with Thorne until he hands me the coconut. "Drink up. You'll need to be hydrated."

I'm not stubborn enough to refuse. Lifting the coconut to my mouth, I tip my head back and greedily gulp down every remaining drop of liquid. The coconut water is warm and slightly sticky, but still feels amazing as it slides down my parched throat.

Thorne offers me another when I finish, and I drink that one dry as well. As soon as I lower it, he hands me a piece of cracked shell, the white flesh of the fruit exposed. I glance up at him as he's biting into his own chunk.

"Eat up," he says unnecessarily.

I try to bite into the edible part of the coconut, but it's more difficult than it looks. The fruit is dense and curved the wrong direction, making it hard to get a good bite. After spending a few minutes chewing at the edge with my teeth and hardly getting any of the fruit off the shell, I finally stop and look down at the gnawed-on piece in my hand, huffing in frustration.

There's a whoosh and I look over to see Thorne has materialized his wings. Curving his one wing around him, he takes hold of a feather and plucks it without so much as a wince, then he folds the wing against his back and dematerializes it.

Taking the piece of coconut from my hand, he uses the sharpened tip of the feather he plucked to cut the flesh away from the shell, and then hands the white part of the fruit back to me, tossing the discarded shell to the side.

He doesn't meet my eyes as he goes back to eating, but makes an impatient grunt in the back of his throat and jerks his chin toward the fruit when I'm still blinking at him a minute later, confused by his thoughtful behavior.

Lifting the coconut to my mouth, I take a bite with relative ease, chewing slowly. It's not my favorite food in the world, but I'm thankful to get something in my stomach. When I finish the piece, Thorne hands me another, and another until I've eaten an entire coconut. Only then does it occur to me I should probably say thank you, but I don't. The list of things I should thank Thorne for keeps getting longer, and that just makes me grumpy. He saved me from the plane crash, saved me from drowning, found us food and water.

I don't like that I'm starting to feel indebted to him.

We eat in silence, both of us lost in our own thoughts. After we've had our fill of food and drink, Thorne haphazardly drops his feather to the sand and turns away from the beach to peer into the jungle. With his back turned, I snatch the feather up and quickly unzip one of the pockets of my pants. Thank goodness I decided on function over form when I dressed for this trip back to Seraph Academy. The pants I'm wearing have lots of useful pockets, the tank top is lightweight and dries easily, and my boots might not be useful for swimming but they're great for hiking.

As an added benefit, I look great in all of it.

I shove the sharp-tipped feather into the deep pocket at my thigh and re-zip it.

Thanks for the weapon, I think at Thorne's back with a grin. He just armed me with the equivalent of a four-inch dagger, and that was a mistake. I can do a lot of damage with a dagger.

Some of the tension that had been steadily growing over being stuck alone on this island with Thorne leaks out of me. I always feel better when I have a weapon on hand.

"All right, let's go," Thorne says, and then starts into the jungle without waiting to see if I follow.

I pause before trudging after him, casting a glance at the beach Thorne is so eager to abandon. By now, my parents and the Council will know that we crashed and will be searching for us. Is it really a good idea to leave the beach? We're more visible against the barren sand than buried deep in the jungle, so maybe we should stay put and wait for the angel-born to pick us up.

Turning to look in the direction Thorne went, I realize that it doesn't take long for the jungle to turn dense. Thorne's figure is already hard to spot.

"Hey," I yell as I move briskly to catch up to him. "Maybe we should stay on the beach."

Thorne looks over his shoulder at me without slowing his strides. "Be my guest," he says, and then faces forward once again.

Argh. He's so annoying.

"We have food and water, so why risk going inland?"

The idea of living off coconut fruit and water isn't appealing, but it will keep us alive.

"I just think it would be easier for someone to spot us down there," I say when it's clear he's not going to address my last question. But then again, will they even be looking for us in the spirit world? They could fly right over us and never know we're here.

Argh. If we could at least phase back into the mortal world, our chances of rescue would definitely increase.

"That's exactly what I'm worried about," he says.

"You don't want to get rescued?" I ask, my hands balling into fists as frustration bubbles in my chest.

He turns his head to look at me, arching his brow, as we march deeper into the jungle. "Do I want to get found by the angel-born and recaptured only to give whoever sabotaged our plane another chance to kill me? Not particularly."

He mentioned his theory about someone blowing up the plane yesterday. It's plausible, but I'm not sure I've bought into it yet. There are simpler explanations.

"We don't actually know that's what happened."

He laughs and the sound has sharp edges. "How else do you think the cockpit got blown from the plane?"

"It could have been faulty wiring or something that caught on fire and then caused an explosion."

"Two of them?" he asks, looking skeptical.

I cross my arms over my chest, annoyed that he's poking holes in my arguments. "It could happen. Like a chain reaction."

He gives me a side glance that practically screams, *Can it though?*

"Okay, fine," I say, throwing up my arms. "So what's your plan, then? You want to play Tarzan and Jane for the rest of our lives and live on this random island in the North Atlantic, making clothes out of fig leaves and talking to monkeys?"

"We're not in the North Atlantic," he says, throwing me off.

"Yes we are. Our plane was headed from the UK to the US. That big body of water between those two countries is the Atlantic Ocean."

And he razzed me about my education yesterday when it's obvious he never learned simple geography.

"I'm aware where the Atlantic Ocean is," he says, "but that's definitely not where we are. Thank you for the geography lesson though."

I wait for him to elaborate on why he doesn't think that's where we are, but he doesn't say anything else. Curiosity eventually gets the best of me.

"If you don't think we're in the North Atlantic, then where do you think we are?"

His eyes narrow as he studies something in the distance and then says almost offhanded, "Somewhere in the South Atlantic or Indian Ocean."

I start to choke on nothing. "The South Atlantic? That makes no sense."

Maybe he doesn't know his north from south. Plenty of hot guys are super dumb. I hadn't pegged Thorne as stupid, but I've been wrong about guys before. It's easy to be distracted by a pretty face.

"I agree. I don't think we're in the South Atlantic either. My guess is the Indian Ocean."

"The Indian Ocean?" I'm starting to sound like a parrot. "No way. There is literally no reason for them to go from London to Denver the other way around the world. It would take twice as much time, at least." I shake my head. "This is a pointless conversation. Like you can tell where we are anyway."

"As a matter of fact, I can. The stars don't lie, and we're definitely in the Southern Hemisphere."

My jaw drops. The stars might appear red in the spirit world, but they are in the very same position as they are in the mortal world. When I look up at the sky at night all I see are stars, but if Thorne knows his constellations, then he most definitely could tell which hemisphere we are in.

"But . . . the plane's flight plan said it was going to Denver." From Denver I was scheduled to pick up another plane to take me to a small airport in the Rocky Mountains near Seraph Academy.

I do a mental calculation in my head. We were probably into hour twelve or thirteen of the flight when we crashed. There's no reason it would have taken that long to get to Denver from London. At the time I just assumed the plane was flying ridiculously slowly, or maybe encountered a strong headwind or something, but what if I was wrong? What if there was a different reason we were in the air for so long?

"Are you sure about that?"

"Yes," I snap. "It's not like I accidently got on the wrong plane."

"Hmm," is all he says in response.

We both fall silent. Thorne seems to be focusing on the jungle around us, but my mind is tangled in how we could have ended up in the wrong half of the world. I can't make sense of any of it.

If not Denver, then where was the airplane headed? Did the pilots go rogue? Does this mean people are searching for us in the completely wrong place? If they are, we may never be found.

I cast a glance at Thorne as we pick our way through dense underbrush and around vine-covered trees. His mouth is set, and his eyes are alert as he scans the jungle around us, attentive and ready to face any threat that may appear.

I shock myself with the realization that although I've repeatedly reminded myself to be leery of him, I can't seem to muster up a sufficient amount of caution. The hard truth is that there's a part of me that's drawn to him. Maybe it's our darkness matching, or maybe I'm just vain enough to be swayed by a sharp jaw and a cut pack of abs? Could it be that I feel a demented sort of gratitude toward him for saving my life twice in the last day?

Whatever the reason, it's bad and wrong and I need to get my head on straight.

Picking up the faint burbling of rushing water, I stop and cock my head. Thorne takes three steps and then halts as well, casting me a look over his shoulder.

"I hear a waterfall that way," I explain, pointing to the right and then taking off in that direction.

Waterfall means fresh water, and although I'm not thirsty anymore thanks to the three coconuts I drank, I would give almost anything right now to wash the blood, sand, and salt water from my skin, clothes, and hair.

I don't have to turn and check to see if Thorne is following. Even though I can't hear his silent steps, I feel his presence behind me, like a buzzing sensation that makes the fine hairs at the nape of my neck prickle.

The farther into the jungle I travel, the surer I am there's a waterfall ahead somewhere. Cool moisture coats my arms, and the air ripples as the roar of water striking stone gets louder. After a few more steps I see the telltale sign of crystal brightness through an opening in the trees and pick up my pace.

I catch my breath as I break through the trees. In front of me is a cascading waterfall at least a hundred feet tall. The water looks like liquid diamonds as it spills into a small plunge pool beneath that sparkles, casting prisms of light in all directions. The leafy jungle canopy over the area is so dense that only small peeks of the pink spirit world sky can be seen through their blue-veined leaves.

I've never seen anything like this jungle oasis. The area is utterly enchanting, like a magical fairyland come to life. Angel-born don't typically spend more time in the spirit world than they need to, and I'm no exception. We train in the mortal world and only phase into the spirit world to battle our enemies. But standing on the edge of this crystalline pool I almost can't understand why we don't enjoy this realm more often—with the right precautions against Fallen of course. At this moment in time, it feels like the spirit world is a little slice of heaven we've denied ourselves.

"You shouldn't go in there," Thorne says, coming up behind me.

"Whyever not?"

"You don't know what spirit world creatures might be living in there."

When I turn to look at him, he's not staring over the water with awed wonder in his gaze like I am, but instead wary caution.

I shrug. "Whatever. I can handle a few fish."

"It's not a few pond minnows I'm worried about,"

Thorne says as I pull off my boots, a note of warning in his voice.

I roll my eyes at his overabundance of caution, but then I remember the creepy lizard from this morning, and a trickle of unease flits through me.

Raising my hand, I try to run it through my salt and sand-crusted hair, but my fingers get tangled and that settles it. I'll take the chance that there's a few sharp-toothed critters in the water if I can get clean.

The small ledge we're standing on is only about a body-length above the water, and without warning I jump from it. Thorne's shout reaches my ears right before I dive into the chilly pool, sinking several feet but not reaching the bottom.

The icy bite of the water is amazing against my over-heated skin, and I remain motionless for a moment, floating in a rainbow of light before kicking toward the surface. When I break through and take a deep gulp of air, I'm already feeling like a new person.

Looking up, I see Thorne still perched on the ledge above, his brow furrowed as he watches the water around me.

"You should join me and get some of that stink off you," I taunt.

Thorne continues his silent assessment of the water rather than answer me. What he's looking for, I don't know. It's near impossible to see anything through the sparkling brightness, and I'm sure if there is anything living in this pool, I scared it away already.

With lazy strokes, I swim over to a sunlit rock on the edge of the waterline, staying mostly submerged as I yank my socks off, squeezing them out the best I can before slap-ping them on the rock to dry. I struggle out of my pants next and then my tank top, spreading both of them on the rock as well.

I'm not in the least bit worried that Thorne will catch any peeks of my lady parts through the brightness of the water, but even so, I keep my sports bra and underwear on, which covers more of me than my bikini usually does. I don't bother to unwrap the strip of fabric Thorne tied around my arm yesterday. Even with my advanced Nephilim healing, the wound was pretty deep and might not have closed completely, so I'd rather keep it covered for another day or two.

My boots appear on the rock next to my discarded clothes, and I glance up to see Thorne watching me.

"Change your mind about a swim?" I ask with a grin, and then tip my head back to dunk it in the water.

Working my hands through my hair to detangle it, I let out a contented sigh when I'm finally able to run my fingers through without snagging on a knot.

"I suppose if you haven't been devoured yet, it's safe enough," he says in such a way that I'm not sure if he's joking or serious.

He pulls off his boots and socks and then yanks his t-shirt over his head. I tell myself to look somewhere else as he bends and scrubs his shirt in the water and then wrings it out, placing it next to my clothes. But my gaze appears to be stuck. It's only when he starts to unbutton his pants that I turn and swim toward the middle of the sparkling pool.

I don't hear Thorne get into the plunge pool behind me, but I still know when he does because my body starts to hum. I wish I could say my awareness of him is due to my sharp senses, but really it's just something about him that causes a physical reaction in me. I frown, more than a bit disturbed that I'm so attuned to his presence.

Thorne swims by me without a word, his arms moving in unhurried strokes as he cuts through the water toward the base of the waterfall. He ducks under the water, and I expect him to resurface eventually, but he never does. I don't start to get nervous until it's been several minutes and he still hasn't reappeared.

Images of tentacled monsters with sharp teeth float through my mind, and I jerk when I think something brushes up against my foot.

Another minute ticks by and I force my anxiety to morph into annoyance.

"Whatever," I mumble under my breath. "If he wants to drown himself, why should I care? One less evil villain in the world to worry about." But even as I'm grumbling, I start to drift over to the place he disappeared.

The roar of the waterfall drowns out any other noises; the air looks wavy and distorted. My toes brush over something below that feels like smooth pebbles. I squint to see through the waterfall, but it's too bright to make anything out beyond the cascade in front of me.

Where did he go?

I turn in a slow circle, still trying in vain to see through the water around me. I poke around with my feet but only manage to stub my toe on a rock.

"Ow! I swear, Thorne, when I find you I'm going to—"

Something wraps around my ankle and tugs, catching me off guard and pulling me under the water, yanking me to the other side of the waterfall before letting go. I pop to the surface, choking and blindly swinging my fists but only hitting air.

A deep rumble of laughter echoes around me and sends a shiver down my spine. Swatting the wet hair off my eyes, I find myself face-to-face with Thorne in a small alcove on the underside of the waterfall.

Splashing him, I back away as I glare up at his stupid face. Drops of water sparkle like diamonds on the ends of his dark lashes and trickle down his forehead and cheeks as he chuckles, and I have to stop myself from holding my breath.

I've never seen Thorne look so unguarded. His lips aren't curved into a smirk or a sneer, or even that suggestive knowing half-smile he likes to give me. They're upturned into a true humor-filled grin that completely transforms him. I am not prepared for the effect it has on me, and bite down on my lower lip—hard—and tell myself to calm . . . the . . . heck . . . down.

When Thorne's gaze drops to my mouth and his chuckles taper off, not even the icy water can cool my over-heated skin.

Still staring at me, Thorne licks the drops from his full bottom lip, and I force myself to keep my gaze locked on his eyes. Nothing good will come from fixating on his mouth. I might not be known for being the most discerning of girls when it comes to guys—truth is, I've always been a sucker for a handsome face and muscles—but I draw a hard line at murderers.

"That was incredibly childish," I snap, only now noticing that he's gobbled up most of the space between us.

I drift a few feet away, stopping when I back up against a rock wall.

"Was it?" he asks, looking genuinely curious, the brightness from the water below and to the side making his every expression perfectly clear to me.

Pursing my lips, I shoot him a look, equally as annoyed at myself as I am at him.

He shrugs. "I was never around children and certainly was never allowed to behave like one myself, so how should I know?"

Something tweaks in my chest when he says things like that, a reminder that he wasn't born a monster but made into one. But that doesn't change the fact that he *is* a monster, regardless of how he became one.

"When you couldn't find me, did you worry about me?" he asks, tilting his head slightly as he regards me.

I think he meant for the question to come out mockingly, but there's a touch of vulnerability in it that I'm not sure he's aware of.

I laugh, but it's forced. "Of course not," I say. "Just curious if some water beast had done me a solid and finished you off, so I could stop planning your demise."

Something flashes in his eyes, and for a wild moment I think he might be hurt, but then the look is wiped away. In fact, all emotion disappears from his face, and I shiver at how completely void he suddenly appears.

"Sorry to disappoint you by still being alive, but don't worry, there is bound to be a beast or two on this island that would enjoy making a meal of Nephilim flesh, so you may get your wish after all."

I roll my eyes, but a snake of trepidation uncoils in my gut. I'm starting to believe there may actually be things to fear in this realm besides Fallen and Forsaken.

"Let's go," Thorne suddenly says. "We've wasted enough

time. I want to cover more of the island before we lose light."

"Bathing is never wasted time," I shoot back.

He makes a non-committal noise in the back of his throat and then swims through the waterfall. I take a few beats to re-center myself before following him, but by the time I reemerge on the other side of the waterfall Thorne is already out of the water and pulling on his boxer briefs.

A half-second earlier and I would have gotten a nice solid look at his behind.

I get a little rush when I realize I'd been in such close proximity to him when he was completely naked. I can't decide if I'm glad I didn't know that at the time or not.

I pull myself up and out of the pool and then walk over to the rock where my clothes are drying and stretch out next to them, closing my eyes as I let the sun's rays dry me off.

"What are you doing?" Thorne asks. He's clearly annoyed, and that makes me smile.

"I can't put my clothes on while wet like this." I indicate my body with a flick of my wrist, not bothering to open my eyes and look at him. "I need to dry off a bit first."

"It's not safe to just lie on a rock like that. There are so many more—"

"Yes, yes. Scary spirit world beasts are afoot who want to rip us to shreds and feast on our innards. You're like a broken record. If you want to leave, go for it. I'm sure I can catch up," I say, calling his bluff. I don't actually think he'll leave me.

I hear him pull on the rest of his clothes, his motions jerky and rough, and smile more broadly when he utters something under his breath in Enochian as he struggles at one point to pull the fabric over his wet skin.

A moment later, something brushes against my bicep and I startle, my eyes popping open immediately to find him untying the knot he made when he bound my wound. I half sit up as he starts to unravel the fabric.

"What are you doing?" I ask, but what I really mean is *why,* since it's obvious he's checking on my injury.

In response to my question, he only glances at my face briefly with a raised brow before refocusing on his task.

Once the wrapping is off, I look down at my arm and notice two surprising things. The first is that the tips of two of Thorne's fingers are missing. The joints on his middle and index finger on his right hand are all there, but those two fingers end in a stub with no nail. It's another injury to add to the list of ones he must have gotten at a young age— but the real question is if the missing pieces of his fingers are due to an accident or if they were purposefully cut off?

The second thing is that the deep laceration on my bicep is completely closed and already turned into a fading scar.

I brush my fingers over the area. The skin is hardly even raised.

That's strange. I heal fast, but not *that* fast.

Thorne moves behind me and brushes my still-damp hair over my shoulder, checking the injury on my upper back that we never covered. "This one has scarred over already as well. Do you usually heal this quickly?"

Nephilim who have gone through metamorphosis and have their full powers sometimes heal faster than they used to. I'm probably under a year away from being a fully matured Nephilim—at least physically speaking—so maybe my healing abilities are starting to develop.

I shrug, not letting myself fret over something like this when there's so much more to worry about right now.

"The faster I heal, the sooner I'll be rid of the ugly scars," I say glibly, but then instantly wish I could shove the words back in my mouth as an image of Thorne's scar-covered back pops into my mind.

Thorne doesn't react other than making a small noise of agreement as he drops the now useless strip of material on the rock next to me.

"You're dry enough. Get dressed so we can get out of here," he says, and then turns and strides several steps away, making it clear he's giving me privacy to get my clothes back on.

I pause before doing anything, not liking the unsettled knot growing in my chest. Something about our last interaction isn't sitting well with me, but I'm not sure what.

With a huff, I push off the rock. My underwear and sports bra are still a little damp, but my skin is dry. I take a quick minute to braid my hair into a thick plait and then pull on my pants.

"You can turn around now. I'm decent," I say as I tug my tank top over my head.

Thorne only turns his head to glance over his shoulder at me, but that split second of distraction is the exact moment when a dark form shoots from the dense jungle and slams into him, shoving him to the ground.

7

One second I'm staring at Thorne's stony face and then the next he's on the ground beneath some sort of mutated beast that looks like a cross between a giant lizard and a Doberman with both fur and scales.

I'm trained to jump into action at a moment's notice, but the shock is so complete it takes me several seconds to react, and by the time I do Thorne has already managed to kick the beast off him, launching the creature back into the shadowy jungle.

Jumping to his feet, he releases his wings, the metal-tipped feathers on his good wing glinting when they catch a ray of sunlight penetrating the dense canopy above our heads.

We stare out at the jungle but it's completely quiet, making the moment even more creepy. We know that the mutant creature is still out there somewhere, but even with our advanced Neph senses we can't see or hear it.

Keeping my eyes fixed on the trees, I grab a large, rough rock—the single feather I have still concealed in my pocket isn't going to be enough against an animal that size. A rock isn't the most sophisticated of weapons, but it's the best option I have.

Ten seconds tick by.

Twenty seconds.

A minute.

"So maybe you were right about there being creatures in the spirit world Nephilim don't know about," I say, sneaking a glance at Thorne.

His gaze flicks to mine, his features pinched in a look that seems to say, *Yeah, you think?* But he keeps his mouth shut and focuses back on the jungle.

"What was that?" I ask after another minute ticks by without so much as a rustle of underbrush.

"It's a shadow dragon," he says. "They can camouflage their—"

A curse flies from his mouth when a streak of black shoots out of the forest again, but this time it's headed for me.

I swing my arm, smashing the rock against its side and jerking out of the way to keep from getting tackled like Thorne did, but the beast rakes its claws over my thigh as it sails by.

I don't let the bite of its sharpened nails bring me to my knees. Staying on your feet during a fight can make the difference between victory and death, and I'm all for staying alive.

Pushing the discomfort out of my mind, I spin, ready to deliver another blow with the rock and then my foot, but I never get the chance. Before the creature can even turn to make another pass at me, Thorne is there, arching a wing and bringing it down on the beast. His sharpened feathers slice into the animal's mid-section, almost severing it in two.

Shock and relief war inside me as I stare down at the creature. Shock at the ease at which Thorne's feathers sliced through scales, flesh, and bone, and relief that the hideous thing is dead.

Black blood and entrails spill out of the beast, bits of it leaking down into the plunge pool we just swam in, staining the crystal white water. Bubbles start to appear in the water and then a barbed tentacle breaks the surface, slithering toward us, following the blood trail to the creature Thorne just killed. As soon as the tip of the tentacle finds the body of the slain beast, four more tentacles shoot from the water and wrap around the carcass, dragging it into the pool.

I reel backward, losing my footing on the loose rocks and landing on my butt.

I look at Thorne, pointing toward the water and trying not to hyperventilate. "We swam in there with that thing?"

Those tentacles had to be connected to something.

Something large.

Something carnivorous.

"Maybe now you'll listen to my advice," he says as he dematerializes his wings.

"But . . . why didn't it eat us?" I ask, still sitting on the ground. I don't need to see my reflection in a mirror to know I'm wide-eyed right now because I am shooketh.

Thorne glances at the pool and then back to me. Shrugging, he says, "Krakens are actually scavengers. Despite the barbs, they don't hunt and kill their prey."

Krakens.

I blink back at him, and then look at the half of the

animal the kraken didn't grab. Shoving to my feet, I take a tentative and slightly wobbly step forward.

Even standing above what's left of the carcass of the dead beast, I don't understand what I'm looking at. The fur is black, but there are patches of iridescent scales over the body as well. The back feet of the beast actually look closer to hands than paws, each digit having a four-inch curved talon.

"This is a shadow dragon?" I ask. I've never heard of that before.

Thorne nods. "They, on the other hand, very much enjoy hunting and killing prey. Sometimes they do it for fun. They can camouflage themselves to blend into their surroundings, but now I know we're definitely in the Indian Ocean. They don't inhabit other parts of the world."

Mind. Blown.

"How do you know all this?"

"My mother made sure my education was . . ." He tilts his head, looking for the right words, and finally settles on, ". . . well-rounded. I told you there was a lot about the spirit world you aren't being taught."

I'm really starting to believe him.

I take a step and my thigh stings, reminding me that I was cut.

"Of course it had to tear my only pair of pants," I complain as I stick my fingers through one of the rips to inspect my newest injury.

Thankfully, it's not bad. Not much worse than a bad paper cut and barely bleeding. I'm not worried about it at all.

"Is it deep?" Thorne asks.

I shake my head. "Hardly a scratch."

"Pull your pants down and let me see," he commands as he steps toward me, and I laugh.

"Isn't that my line?" I say, and the corner of Thorne's mouth twitches.

"Seriously," he says.

"Seriously, I'm not pulling down my pants. You're just going to have to take my word for it that I'm fine." I clear my throat. "Do we need to be worried about another attack?"

Thorne narrows his eyes and for a moment I'm sure he's going to argue with me. "Probably," he says instead, and then tips his head toward the jungle. "Let's get going. Keep close."

His command to stay close both rubs me the wrong way and causes a little ball of warmth to unfurl in my chest. I'm about to tell him that I'm capable of taking care of myself but decide it's not worth arguing over. He can bark however many commands he wants at me. It doesn't mean I'm going to obey them.

***

Over the next several hours we travel through the jungle and then start to climb up the side of the mountain. Thorne and I don't say much to each other except a few words here and there. Half my focus is dedicated to watching for another attack; the other half is trying to work out the enigma that is Thorne.

I spend time picking apart every interaction we've had, from the first time I saw him in front of a burning Buckingham Palace to every conversation so far on this stupid island. The only conclusion I can come to is that nothing about him makes sense.

I go to swat a branch out of my way, but Thorne grabs it and pulls it to the side before I can, waiting until I've passed before he lets go. He's been doing stuff like that all afternoon, clearing the path, stepping in front of me whenever there's a rustle in the trees or underbrush. I don't know if he even realizes he's doing it or not.

By the time the sky is dimming, we've climbed high enough that the trees are sparse. We can see straight to the sea and the bright colors of the spirit world sunset reflecting off the water. From our vantage point, we can survey at least half the island, but there are only three things out there: jungle, sand, and sea. Not a single sign of civilization or any other land mass in view. Granted, the sparkling of the water makes it hard to search the horizon, but as far as I can tell, we really are stranded on a desert island in the middle of nowhere.

If Thorne is right, which he's been more often than not the last day, and we're in the middle of the Indian Ocean, that's on the other side of the world from where my parents and friends would look for our downed plane.

For the thousandth time that day, I wonder why the pilots flew us in this direction. I can't make sense of it any more than I can make sense of Thorne.

I remember the pilot and co-pilot not looking particularly happy when I showed up with my parents and they were informed they were taking on an extra passenger, but why let me on the flight at all if they weren't headed for the US? If they had reached their intended destination, what were they planning on doing with me?

"We should stay around here for the night. It won't be safe to travel in the dark," Thorne says.

I glance over at him but he's not looking back at me. Nor is he looking at the spectacular sunset either. He's scanning the dense jungle we just hiked through with a slight frown.

The warm tones from the setting sun reflect on his face, giving his usual stark white skin a hint of life. All Nephilim have dark hair and golden-to-dark brown skin tones with light eyes, but with his light coloring and perfectly proportioned features, Thorne looks more like an angel than anyone else I know—even more so in the spirit world with the soft white aura haloing his body. The only thing ruining the illusion are the streaks of black that occasionally flicker in the brightness, a reminder of his true nature.

As if he can feel my stare, he turns his gaze to me, meeting my eyes and holding them boldly. I won't be the first to look away.

"You say that like it was safe during the day," I say, thinking about the shadow dragon and kraken.

I suppress the shudder that wants to work through me when I think about how the kraken's lengthy tentacles wrapped around the shadow dragon and pulled it into the water to devour it.

"Saf*er*," he clarifies, and then turns and starts searching for shelter.

I don't bother contradicting or arguing with him. If he says it's too dangerous to travel after dark, I believe him.

We pick our way around for less than a half hour before we find a spot Thorne deems suitable—a cave whose mouth is covered by leafy and flower-covered vines. If I were looking on my own, I would never have found it, proving once again that I'm fully out of my element and making it even harder not to admit that Thorne had a point when he complained that my Nephilim education was lacking.

I wait outside while he scouts the cave. It's only a few minutes before he reappears, declaring the space to be "safe." Waving me in, he holds the vines out of the way, but I pause before joining him in the darkness.

Do I really want to be alone with Thorne in a confined space?

"Disappointed it's not the Four Seasons?" he asks with a smirk.

"Heck yeah I am," I admit, happy to let him mistake my hesitancy for simple disdain in the choice of shelter, but besides that I'm not going to apologize for who I am. I like nice things—or at the very minimum running water and a blow dryer. A dip in a pond isn't going to cut it for me. I want a real shower, or better yet a long soak in a giant bubble bath followed by a hot stone massage.

A now-familiar roar rumbles somewhere in the jungle. I sneak a peek over my shoulder, not seeing anything, but that doesn't mean the creature making that ruckus isn't nearby.

I quickly weigh my options—to hunker down with Thorne or risk facing a hostile beast—not liking either but knowing I don't have a choice except to pick the monster I know and hide in the space he found for us.

With a huff, I duck and squeeze through the vines Thorne is holding back for me. My shoulder brushes against his chest as I pass and I hear him take in a quick breath of air, but when I glance at him he seems completely unaffected. He's not even looking at me; his watchful gaze is trained out at the jungle outside the cave.

I don't get a good look at the cave before Thorne drops the vines, cutting off the little bit of daylight that still remains, plunging the interior into darkness. If it weren't for his slight white aura, I would have lost sight of Thorne immediately. As it is, I press my back against the rough stone wall as I wait for my Nephilim night vision to kick in.

It only takes a few hurried moments to be able to make out the shape of the space around me, but by that time Thorne has already taken off, soundlessly traveling farther into the cave and disappearing around a bend.

Sheesh, the guy moves like a ghost.

That realization is chilling.

"Come on," he calls softly from somewhere around the corner. "There's a more comfortable place to hole up over here."

A semi-hysterical laugh tickles the back of my throat, but I swallow it down as I push away from the stone wall to follow Thorne farther into a dark cavern. My friends already think I'm a little bit insane, but if they could see me now they'd know it was true. I can hardly believe I'm putting my trust in Thorne, but day two stranded on a desert island and here I am.

I round the corner and my breath catches. The cave dead-ends not far in front of me, but the area is lit by the soft teal glow of a thousand pinpricks of light speckled across the cave ceiling, along with dangling luminous strands as thin as spun sugar with dewdrop balls on them hanging low enough that I have to stoop to avoid them.

"It's beautiful, but you don't want to rub up against that," Thorne says, indicating the dangling threads. "It's a sticky mucus the glowworm uses to attract their prey. Like a spider's web. It'll be a real pain to get out of your hair."

I tear my gaze away from the softly lit ceiling to look at Thorne, who's seated up against the cave wall with one long leg stretched in front of him and the other bent with his arm draped over it. The way he's staring at me makes my stomach flip, so I look away.

"I can't say I've ever seen anything like this before." The cave looks nothing short of otherworldly.

"They use beauty to lure and deceive their prey," Thorne says.

"Just like the Forsaken," I say, and then glance back at Thorne. "And a couple other varieties of utterly dangerous creatures."

A slow smile spreads over Thorne's face and his eyes shine with an almost feverish glint. "There's no denying it's an effective way to bait prey. I thought you'd appreciate it though."

I tilt my head. "Appreciate what?"

"The light." He waves his hand toward the speckled ceiling and the glowing strands hanging from it. "I didn't think you'd feel comfortable in the dark with me all night."

That gives me pause. Why would he care if I was comfortable or not? Was this some weird ploy to get me to let my guard down around him? And if so, to what end?

"I can see fine with my Nephilim sight."

"Even so," he says with a shrug.

I go to the opposite side of the tunnel and sit facing him. Crossing his arms, he shifts a little like he's settling in. Tilting his head back, he closes his eyes and silence falls over the space. It's not a comfortable silence; rather a heavy one, weighted with suspicion and distrust.

The longer I spend with Thorne, the more I have to keep reminding myself what he really is—a killer, a psychopath, a savage monster—out of fear I'm going to forget the truth. But despite myself, I'm curious about him. About what it was like for him to grow up among Fallen and Forsaken and with Seraphim as a mother. About whether his actions this past Christmas were that of a foot soldier obeying the orders of a dictator, or of a ruthless leader fixated on domination.

Thorne remains quiet, and although his eyes are closed I know he's not sleeping. The longer the silence hangs in the air between us, the more curious I get until I can't keep the questions contained anymore.

"Why did you do it?" I ask.

Thorne cracks an eye. "Do what?"

"Attack London. Kidnap Emberly. Attempt to take over the world with an army of Fallen and Forsaken. Take your pick."

I don't miss that something flares in his eyes when I mention Emberly. I shouldn't care, but I've wondered about his feelings. Does he care for her? Is he in love with her? Is he even capable of those types of feelings?

Maybe. At the end of the day he chose Emberly over his own mother. There had to be a reason for that besides whim.

I lean forward, waiting for his answer.

"Because I could," he says, but that answer doesn't ring true to me.

"Lame," I say. "If you don't want to tell me, whatever. I'll just assume you were overcompensating for something."

Pretending to check my nails, which are horribly chipped and in desperate need of a manicure, I lean back against the stone wall, doing my best to look uninterested when I'm anything but.

I catch him scowl out of the corner of my eye, and smirk.

Gotcha.

"You know nothing," he says.

I take my time lifting my gaze. "Is that so?"

"You live in a pampered world of make-believe, where your species is just and noble when it's anything but."

I cock my head, studying Thorne as I see him become visibly agitated. I've hit a nerve, but I don't know how or which one yet.

"Are you going to try to convince me that Fallen and Forsaken are the true heroes of this story?" I raise my eyebrows. "If so, you should save your breath."

"Hardly," Thorne scoffs, "but at least they own who they are. They don't prance around pretending to be holier-than-thou, on a selfless mission to protect humanity. They are who they are, and that's at least something I can respect."

I try not to take offense, especially since I know he's trying to get me riled up, but that's exactly what I've been taught my whole life. That angel-born do exist to protect humanity. He's poking at the foundation of who I believe I am, or at least will grow to be one day, and that's starting to irritate me.

"What did the angel-born ever do to piss you off so badly?" I ask, trying to contain the real anger in my voice. "Or is it just that you've been swallowing down your mother's Kool-Aid since you were in diapers and don't know how to think for yourself?"

Thorne snarls. Actually lifts his upper lip and releases a low growl. "Watch yourself," he warns. "I have my limits, and you're nearing them."

Am I supposed to be scared?

Yeah, probably.

Maybe something is broken in me because his reaction just spurs me to keep poking.

No one ever accused me of being perfectly sane.

"You're not sorry at all, are you?" I ask. My body temperature spikes a few degrees.

"And what exactly do you believe I should be sorry for?"

Is he serious?

"How about unleashing the Fallen on London?"

Thorne tips his chin up. "That was technically my mother's doing."

"And you take no responsibility for that?"

"If Emberly had kept the bracelet on like I instructed her, Seraphim never would have taken her over. Once the hole was ripped in the barrier, there's nothing I could have done to stop the domino effect that occurred after."

"Wow, you just absolve yourself of all guilt? What, do you just avoid looking down so you don't see all the blood of your innocent victims dripping from your hands? That's convenient."

He narrows his eyes, a muscle in his jaw jumping like he might be clenching his teeth.

"I don't consider angel-born to be innocent."

"Fine. Let's not even talk about the angel-born. But what about the humans? The ones who lost their homes, their livelihoods, their lives. You can't claim they weren't innocent. They didn't even know the spirit world or any of it existed." I lean forward, holding Thorne's gaze, daring him to look away as I present him with the ugly truth. "I went into the Merge Zone just last week and rescued a boy who had to watch a Forsaken brutally murder his parents and brother right in front of him. He did nothing to you or your precious Fallen and Forsaken army, yet he'll live with that loss, with the horror of what he witnessed for the rest of his life. What do you say about that?"

I'm practically yelling by the time I stop talking, my breaths coming out in pants.

A flicker of some emotion sweeps across Thorne's face. It may be regret, but it moves over him too quickly to interpret. He looks away, staring down at his hands.

"What's done is done and cannot be undone," is all he says.

That's all he has to say? *How does he live with himself?*

I'm shaking with barely restrained anger. If I needed a reminder of how awful, how truly despicable Thorne is, he just gave it to me. I should thank him for setting me straight. For a minute there I had mistaken him as someone with an actual beating heart, but the truth is that Thorne is an imposter. He may look like a man but he's really a monster, and my mission concerning monsters is clear.

I kill them.

8

It takes at least a full hour for Thorne to completely fall asleep. Then I wait another thirty minutes to make sure he's not faking it before I pull my weapon—his discarded feather with the pointed metal tip—from my pocket.

I test its sharpness on the end of my finger and a bead of blood wells up from where I pricked myself. Wiping the blood on my tactical pants, I slowly creep over to Thorne, taking care not to make any noise as I place a booted foot on either side of his hips as he sleeps with one arm cushioning his head and the other lying across his chest. I stare down at him for an indeterminable amount of time, convincing myself the world will be a safer place without him.

Hardening my resolve, I crouch and then strike.

Well, almost.

Balancing my weight on my knee, I press the razor-sharp edge of the feather into the column of Thorne's throat, just short of cutting into his flesh.

His eyes flare open, instantly alert, and I tell myself I only hesitated because I wanted to see the look in them right before I ended him. But now that I have I can't seem to force myself to shove the blade into his neck.

Thorne stares at me, not making any attempt to save himself. In fact, while holding my gaze, he tips his head back a little, giving me even better access, and that makes me angry, igniting the fire in me.

Pushing the blade forward, I cut shallowly into his skin. A small line of blood wells up and leaks down in two lines over his neck, dribbling onto the dusty cave floor.

"I'll do it," I warn him, hating myself for the small quiver in my voice.

Thorne remains silent, his face a stony mask.

"I will," I shout at him, hoping he doesn't notice the tremor in my hand.

"Go ahead," he says. When I don't say anything or make a move, he adds, "You'll be applauded for it. Monster slaying is what you do after all, isn't it?"

I grit my teeth and scream at myself to finish him already, but I can't seem to make my damn hand obey me. If anything, I've decreased the pressure on the blade at his throat.

"Make sure to cut through my carotid artery or you might not finish me off."

"Do you want to die?" The question slips out, and it's not a taunt.

With the way he's acting, it genuinely seems like he doesn't care if he lives or dies. Oddly enough, that question is what makes him flinch.

We fall into a weird sort of standoff. I keep the blade

pressed to the sensitive part of his neck, but not hard enough to break skin again.

We're both breathing heavily. The light from bioluminescence around us, combined with my Nephilim eyesight and the faint glow of our auras, gives me a perfect view of his face. I watch for a flicker of something: fear, rage, or even resolve, but I have no idea what he's thinking. He's as closed off to me as he's ever been as he regards me with those blue eyes that are so dark that they swallow the black pupil.

Frustration boils in my gut, and then bubbles upward, filling my chest and creeping up my throat.

Why can't I just do it? *Why can't I end him?*

But even as I order myself to sweep the sharpened edge of the feather across Thorne's throat, I find myself loosening my grip on my weapon.

Thorne suddenly surges forward, and I have to yank my hand back to keep him from killing himself. Faster than I can track, he twists the feather out of my hand, throwing it somewhere out of sight, and flips me so I'm on my back and he's hovering above me.

I buck and twist, using my years of training to unseat him, but he blocks and outmaneuvers my every move, proving not only his superior strength over me but also his skill, and that makes me furious.

I redouble my efforts, but Thorne just captures my wrists and pins them to the ground on either side of my head, leaning into me more fully and subduing me easily with his weight.

In that moment I don't know who I'm madder at, him or myself. I had him and I let the opportunity slip through my fingers. Worse yet, I left myself vulnerable and now I'm at his mercy.

I bare my teeth in a vicious snarl, seething for allowing him to get the upper hand.

As my anger grows, a strange heat starts to warm my hands and I glance over to see sparks shooting from the tips of my fingers. I jerk in surprise, and Thorne's gaze darts from my face to my hands. His eyes widen slightly as he stares at the little zaps of lightning that sizzle over my fingers before they disappear.

The look in Thorne's eyes is calculated. "A skill you've been keeping from me?"

I open my mouth to confess I don't know what that was, but then press my lips together to glare at him instead.

Even as his cold eyes hold mine in a vise-like grip, I think, *He's going to kill me. I know he is.* I won't give him the satisfaction of looking away first or admitting I have no idea what that just was. Let him wonder what those sparks were and how big of a threat they pose to him.

Thorne looks like he wants to throttle me, but I simply plaster a taunting smile on my face, getting at least some enjoyment out of his growing frustration.

Logically, I should be terrified, but it's not fear that's thrumming through my system, making my muscles practically vibrate.

It's fury.

I'm so angry I can hardly see straight.

I'm going down, I know I am.

Thorne, even with those power-dampening shackles circling his wrists, is stronger and more skilled than I am on my best day. It chafes to admit it, but between the two of us I've always been outmatched. Even so, I won't go down without a fight, and I'm anxious to get on with it already. At least if we're battling, I won't be left to analyze my own death.

"No more talking. Let's just get on with this already," I snap at him.

Thorne's eyes flare, and rather than bringing his hands up to choke the life out of me like I expect, he stops breathing and his gaze drops to my mouth.

When his pupils dilate and he runs his tongue over his full bottom lip, my stomach bottoms out. He leans forward, bringing even more of his body into contact with my own, and I realize how much of his weight he was holding off of me before.

In a blink, his face is close enough that his breath puffs against my lips, tickling them, making them more sensitive than they've ever been before. It takes effort not to run my tongue over them to soothe the sensation.

What is going on? Is this some sort of weird form of torture? Does it give him a sick measure of satisfaction to mess with my head before he ends me?

"Stop toying with me," I growl, baring my teeth in a nasty snarl. "If you're going to kill me, just do it."

Thorne yanks his head back in surprise. I'm so wrapped up in my own messy and nonsensical feelings that I can't decipher the jumble of emotions that bloom on his face.

Sucking in a breath through his nose, Thorne's nostrils flare as a singular emotion takes control of him, one that I recognize instantly: anger.

When he speaks, it's almost more growl than anything

else. "If I wanted to, I could have killed you a hundred times over already. What makes you think I'd do it now?"

Despite the seriousness of the situation, I can't hold back the bitter bark of laughter that punches through me. Does he really expect me to state the obvious? That I expect a death blow because only minutes ago I held a blade to his throat and threatened his life?

I don't expect forgiveness from Thorne—considering the way he was raised; I honestly don't think that's something he's capable of—I expect retribution.

Instead of giving Thorne the satisfaction of listening to me beg for my life, I clamp my mouth shut, giving him nothing but silence.

His gaze brushes over my face, his anger morphing into an unreadable emotion.

Finally, he bares his teeth in a feral snarl, then releases my wrists and pushes off me. Springing to his feet in one fluid motion, he stalks toward the cave's entrance, leaving me lying on the ground in shock, wondering how the heck I'm still breathing.

9

I lie on the ground for at least five solid minutes before it truly sinks in that Thorne didn't kill me, that he probably never intended to, and most likely won't try to anytime in the future. With that realization, something inside me irrevocably shifts.

What if Thorne isn't all the things he's been portrayed to be?

No, that's not right. I know he's all the things everyone believes him to be, but what if there's more to him than *just* those things?

It's like one moment I'm sure the world is flat and the next I realize that I've been living on a sphere all along. I'm shaken straight down to my core in a way I've never been before, and that makes me unsure of everything I thought I knew to be true about Thorne, and to an extent about myself.

I sit up, my gaze catching on a flash of silver to my left and then settling on the sharp-tipped feather I used to threaten Thorne. Standing, I walk over to the weapon and stow it back in my pants pocket. Perhaps I won't need it against Thorne anymore, but today proved that there are creatures on this island I need to be wary of.

Taking a deep breath, I stare up at the glowing strands and try to decide where to go from here. I could try to find Thorne. I don't know if he's still in the cave or if he's decided he'd rather take his chances with the wild beasts lurking around the island. But if I find him, what would I even say? I did just try to kill him—with his own feather, no less—and even though there's a part of me that's relieved that I didn't go through with it, I'm not about to apologize for it.

Maybe Thorne is more than a murderer, but he's still definitely a murderer. My mission as a Nephilim is to protect the world and its inhabitants from creatures such as Thorne, so logically speaking I was in the right—the world would be a safer place without him.

I look toward the cave entrance, not able to see anything past the bend in the tunnel or hear anything besides my own breathing, but that doesn't mean Thorne left the safety of our temporary shelter. He can be as silent as the grave when he wants.

With a sigh, I sink back down to the ground, resting my arms on my bent knees with my eyes fixed on the blackness beyond the ring of faint light of the glowworm threads. My gaze never wavers as the hours tick by.

***

The jungle outside the cave comes alive slowly. I don't venture toward the entrance until I hear the squawking of tropical birds. I trail a hand along the cave walls as I make my way toward the entrance. The vines that conceal our shelter also block the morning light, but I can see well enough to know that Thorne isn't here.

Brushing aside the vines, I blink against the sun's brightness. Tears fill my eyes and I squint as I wait for my vision to adjust.

"We can go back to the beach now."

Startled by Thorne's voice, I trip over my own feet and pitch forward, only years of training keep me from face-planting against the rough rocks. My hand itches to snatch the feather out of my pocket as I turn to him. He's leaned up against the rock to the right of the cave's hidden entrance, looking outward.

"I thought you wanted to hike to the summit so we could check out the rest of the island?" My heart is beating fast, but I don't know if it's from the startle or something else altogether.

Thorne turns his head to look at me and his face is cold. There's no life in his eyes. "I already scaled the volcano and surveyed the island. There's nothing here except more of the same. We should go back to the beach, where it's relatively safer."

He hiked to the top and back at night? According to what he said last night that would be wildly dangerous.

I cast a glance upward, calculating the amount of ground he must have had to cover to reach the summit of the volcano and then return.

"Am I just supposed to believe you that the island's completely uninhabited?" I ask, eyeing him suspiciously.

I may be confused about a lot of things right now, but I do know that Thorne doesn't want to be recaptured by the angel-born. It would behoove him to keep me from reaching out to let them know where we are. If it's between recapture and living free on this island, Thorne may just choose the latter. Maybe he did find a way to reach out to the angel-born, but he just doesn't want me to know about it.

A flicker of something crosses Thorne's face, but the emotion flits over his features so quickly I can't discern what it is.

He pushes off the stones behind him. "Take your chances in the jungle, then, but just be aware there are beasts out there more vicious than the ones we've already encountered. A single one of my feathers isn't going to do you much good against them."

He walks away, back down toward the denser part of the jungle. There are three parallel slashes on the back of his forearm that look suspiciously like claw marks. The cuts don't look serious, but it's clear from the rust-colored marks on his arm that they were deep enough to make him bleed. With Thorne's accelerated healing, they've already mostly closed.

Hastily, I jog after him, uneasy with my knee-jerk reaction to stay close to Thorne. Despite what people may believe of me, I'm not rash in my decision making. The truth is that I'm calculating and methodical. I only like people to think I'm ruled by my emotions. There's a strategy in being underestimated.

We walk in silence. Thorne no longer moves branches and obstacles out of my way, and I don't blame him for not feeling particularly magnanimous considering what went down between us the night before. But he can't quite seem to help himself from moving slightly in front of me whenever there's a rustle in the underbrush, which is interesting if not also perplexing.

"Why didn't you just leave me?" I ask, my voice cracking the silence like a brittle branch.

Thorne looks over at me. A flop of silver-blond hair has fallen over his forehead, covering the scar that bisects his left brow. His other eyebrow is arched.

"Why, indeed?" The way he says it makes it seem like even he doesn't know the answer to that question.

"So, what's your plan? We live off coconuts for the rest of our lives?" I'm provoking him because I'm tired of being alone with my own thoughts.

"I'm sure it won't come to that," he says evasively. Then it grows quiet between us once again.

Okay, he's not feeling chatty. *Understandable, but still annoying.*

With every step, I become increasingly antsy. Thorne's supposed calmness brushes against me like sandpaper, grating on me until I can't hold my tongue any longer. "How did you know I wouldn't go through with it? That I wouldn't have killed you?"

He's a few paces in front of me and his shoulders tense before he forces the muscles to relax.

He glances over his shoulder at me. "I didn't."

I narrow my eyes, not believing for a moment that Thorne would have forfeited his life so easily.

"So, you're saying you would have let me slit your throat?"

With a shrug he faces forward. "I guess we'll never know."

I should be happy he seems to be putting this all behind him, but instead his apathy makes me angry.

"Okay, then, why didn't you kill me? You warned me that you wouldn't hesitate to take me out if I got in your way. Cutting into your carotid artery would absolutely put a dent in your plans for world domination."

"I've been very clear that I no longer have aspirations that lofty," he answers without stopping or turning, his voice still maddeningly level.

I snort a half-laugh. It is going to take a lot more than an unproven confession to convince me of that. "Sure, okay, let's pretend that's true. What are your *aspirations*, then?"

Thorne ignores me.

I hate being ignored.

"I still have a weapon. Don't you care?"

He laughs. "Of course not. I dropped that feather in front of you on purpose yesterday so you would stop being so skittish around me."

My toe catches on a root and I trip forward, righting myself quickly. It's on the tip of my tongue to call him out as a liar, but that wouldn't be the only thing he did to make me more comfortable around him. He said something similar about the light from the glowworms.

I'm overcome with the need to understand Thorne. To peel back his layers to see what really lives at the heart of him, but in order to do that I need more information. I need to get him talking.

"How do you know that I won't try again?" I taunt. I won't, but he doesn't know that. "You're going to leave a threat like that hanging over your head?"

As Thorne stomps along in front of me, I finally detect a note of irritation in him. It gives me a twisted sense of satisfaction to see that he's finally showing some sort of emotion. That shell of Zen serenity he put on before was boring.

"I already explained that if I wanted you dead I would have done it by now. I've had every chance to end you, including the very first time we fought." He casts a quick glance over his shoulder at me, making sure to catch my eye. "I could have killed you before you threw your first punch, but I didn't."

I grind my teeth as he refocuses on cutting a path through the dense jungle, annoyed that he's acting like it would be so easy to kill me—but also knowing he's telling the truth. The first time we fought, he mostly just blocked my attacks and then flew off. Like an idiot, rather than letting him leave I jumped and hung on to him, foolishly thinking I could still fell him. He could have dislodged me when we were high in the sky and I would have fallen to my death, but instead he only shook me off him when we were nearly back on the ground, and then flew off without me.

My ego wouldn't let me believe then what I can see clearly now. Thorne did in fact have several opportunities to kill me, but he didn't take any of them. He never even wounded me, and that makes zero sense stacked up against everything else I know to be true about him.

"And don't forget I've also saved your life . . . several times," he adds.

Right. There is that too.

My questions always boil down to: *Why?*

Why hold back from wounding me when we fought? Why not kill me after I attempted to do the same to him? Why bother saving my life when it would have been easier to just do nothing?

Not understanding his motives plague me like a festering wound.

"And why do you think you've felt compelled to save my life?"

Thorne remains silent.

"You don't know me. For all intents and purposes, I'm your enemy. Why go out of your way to save your enemy?"

Why? Why? Why?

I can't seem to let up, to move forward until I understand what makes him tick. One way or another, I'm going to break him. He doesn't know how relentless I can be.

Thorne cracks his neck and his muscles tense.

If I were smart, I'd stop pestering him. Aggression rolls off him in waves, but I can't stop myself. I have this morbid curiosity to see what happens when he blows.

"If it would be so easy to end me, why haven't you already? If you really are this big bad Neph warrior who commanded legions of Fallen and Forsaken, why lift a finger to help me, let alone make sure I'm armed so I feel safer around you? Why would you do that, Thorne? Why?"

Turning, he rounds on me. "I don't know!" he roars.

I stumble back at Thorne's sudden change in trajectory. He strides toward me, a wild look in his eyes that makes him appear unhinged. Adrenaline buzzes through my system and I hold up a hand to ward him off, seeing sparks and zings of what looks to be electricity dancing on the tips of my fingers—and I don't honestly know what freaks me out more, Thorne or the new power that's seemingly growing in me.

Thorne hardly gives the sparks a cursory glance as he steps into my personal space, his chest only inches from bumping up against mine, but I refuse to back down. My feet are planted, as if rooted into the very ground beneath me, and it will take more than Thorne's posturing to move me.

Thorne's voice drops to just above a whisper, which is somehow even more frightening than when he yells in anger. "I don't know why I didn't cut you down the first time you attacked me. I don't know why I've saved your life time and time again. I only know that cutting into you would be more painful than slicing my own flesh. I only know that I'd risk my own safety, my own life, my own freedom, to make sure you were unharmed. And I only know that even the *thought* of watching the light dim from your eyes overwhelms me with a depth of emotion I never considered myself capable of feeling."

Somewhere in the middle of Thorne's rant, I stop breathing. It's only when he stops talking that I release the air from my lungs. Whatever I may have guessed had kept Thorne from killing me last night, that wasn't it, and for the moment I'm shocked into silence.

Thorne moves even closer, and even though he leaves a thin sliver of space between us, I can still feel the heat from his body buffering up against me. He lifts his hand and runs a finger down my cheek, and I don't do a single thing to stop him.

"You consume me—mind, body, and soul . . ." The words rip out of his mouth like he's fighting them, then he bares his teeth in a snarl. "And I hate it."

With that, he spins and stomps off.

10

*J*keep my mouth shut as I follow Thorne through the jungle, leaving a distance of at least five paces between us as I digest his outburst.

"You consume me—mind, body, and soul . . . and I hate it."

I'm not a stranger to guys being obsessed with me. I'm not one of those girls who downplays their beauty to seem humble. I know I'm attractive. I've used my looks to my advantage in the past and won't apologize for it or feel bad. After all, broken hearts are healed easily enough. My appearance is just another weapon in my arsenal, and if someone is going to be stupid enough to be swayed by a pretty face and some curves, then that's their problem.

But whatever is going on with Thorne is different. For one thing, I can't seem to disassociate myself like I usually do. His confession pierced me, cutting through flesh and bone to sink into my heart. I felt what he said. That's not something I'm used to. I've always been able to shake off unwanted infatuations with a bat of my eyes and a flip of my hair, but this time I'm itchy in my own skin, as if different parts of me are at war but neither side will relent.

I don't know my own mind, and that's deeply concerning to me. If nothing else, I've always been someone who knows what they want and then goes out and gets it, but right now the only thing I'll admit to myself is that I want to stay alive. Anything beyond that is murky water that I'm not willing to dive into just yet.

The day is even hotter than the one before. The jungle canopy may be shielding us from the sun, but it also locks in the humidity, making it so it's like we're hiking in a steam room. I'm covered with a fine layer of wetness, and I'm not sure if it's the air sticking to me or my own sweat. Probably a combination of both.

Seemingly frustrated with the humidity as well, Thorne yanks his shirt over his head and tucks part of the material into the waistband of his pants, giving me another view of his scarred back. It's always a bit of a shock to see the raised, ropelike marks, and this time is no different, but the urge to run my fingers over these scars and tell Thorne I don't think less of him because of them *is*.

I clench my hands into fists as a fresh wave of fury for his sadistic mother rushes through me. I don't think for a minute a Fallen as cunning as Seraphim wouldn't know exactly how and when her son was marked, so the question is really just whether his scars were caused by her hand or her command.

I hated Seraphim before. How could I not? She took over my friend's body and tried to rule the world, killing and enslaving as she went. But my hatred for her burns red-hot right now.

My mind trips into dangerous territory, wondering if

Thorne ever really had a chance to be anything other than what his mother had molded him to become: a monster.

An unfamiliar sensation churns inside of me and a zap of power shoots down my arm, loosening my fists. Mini bolts of silver electricity dance over my hands. Raising them to get a better look, a stream of energy shoots from my extended hand and slams into the trunk of a nearby tree, singeing it.

What's going on?

This shouldn't be happening. Nephilim develop new powers in spurts, and only once a year, on their birthdays. Mine was two months ago and I didn't get so much as an increase in speed or agility. I was disappointed but resolved to the fact that I wouldn't gain my full strength as a power-line angel for another year or two. Since I've been taking down Fallen and Forsaken for the last couple of months without extra abilities, I was mostly okay with that.

The power coursing through my chest, arms, and legs feels strange and unnatural, a full-body buzz that is just short of uncomfortable. It's officially starting to freak me out.

"You don't know what that ability is, do you?" Thorne accuses.

I don't respond, but I'm sure my face conveys the truth. I played it cool in the cave when all I did was create a few sparks at the end of my fingers, but now that the bolts of electricity are covering my arms, the more panicked I get, the more it grows.

Thorne swears under his breath and then starts toward me. I hold up a hand to warn him off and a bolt of electricity zings through the air as if I shot a gun aimed at his chest. He hits the ground, narrowly avoiding getting hit.

"I don't think you should come any closer," I warn.

He stays down but looks up at me, his face a hard mask of determination. There's a roar in the jungle, but I'm too distracted to tell exactly where it's coming from.

The roar booms again, this time louder, and Thorne's gaze flicks to the side.

"You need to rein that power in," he says. "Not all spirit world creatures are frightened of angelic energy. Some view it as a challenge."

Oh shoot. Oh shoot. Oh shoot.

"Okay, full disclosure, I don't really know what this ability is or how to control it."

"You don't say."

"Not helping," I say as heat crawls up my neck.

"All right, I'm going to stand up. Keep your hands directed at the ground," he orders, and then slowly gets to his feet. "You need to look inward."

What the heck does that mean? Like . . . meditate?

"The power is coming from you, but you also control it. Calm yourself down enough to grab hold of the energy and bend it to your will."

I give a nervous laugh. "Just like that?"

"Yeah. Easy-peasy," he says, his voice a smooth murmur.

He continues moving toward me until he's close enough for me to reach out and touch him, but that also means he's too close to dodge another accidental misfire.

"Breathe in and out slowly." He takes a couple of unhurried breaths himself to demonstrate.

I guess it *is* a little like meditating.

I do as he says, and when some of the electricity starts to fade, I'm instantly relieved.

That is, until another roar echoes throughout the jungle

—this one louder than the last—and the electricity comes surging back full-force, strong enough that some sparks hit Thorne. He flinches when they make contact with his bare chest, but he doesn't complain.

A flock of birds screech off to my right, and I look over just in time to see them take flight, shooting through the air in a streak of colors before disappearing into the canopy above. Something explodes out of the underbrush—a dark form a lot larger than a shadow dragon, barreling toward us.

"New plan," Thorne says as he releases his wings and then twists toward the beast. "When it strikes, point your hands at it and unleash all you've got."

I don't have the time to freak out, and simply react by instinct, directing my hands toward some sort of giant black and gold striped cat as it jumps at us.

A bolt of sizzling electricity shoots from my outstretched hands and hits the beast in the chest while it's still mid-air. It lets out a piercing scream, and I twist out of the way as it thumps to the ground. Its limbs twitch and contort, reminding me of a dying spider, as the lingering effects of whatever power I hit it with work its way through its body.

Releasing a pitiful moan, the animal looks up at me from the ground, its hazel eyes the size of large marbles. The creature is huge. With the body of a jungle cat, it's easily larger than any lion or tiger I've ever seen. Stripes so gold they look metallic run through its black fur coat. Two long saber-tooth tiger-like fangs protrude from its mouth down below its chin.

It's beautiful, but also terrifying.

Next to me, Thorne raises his wing, preparing to bring it

down on the black-haired beast, cleaving it like he did with the shadow dragon.

"No," I say, rushing to put myself in front of the large cat, who is still mewing at our feet.

Thorne eyes me with a look of confusion. "What are you doing?"

I'm not even sure myself, but I'm overcome with the desire to protect this animal, even if it had been about to rip me to shreds with its curved claws and fangs only a moment before. I try not to think too deeply about why I want to save the beast, but an unbidden image of Tinkle shoots through my mind. I know the creature isn't a Celestial like Tinkle was, but I still feel compelled to protect it rather than end its life.

"I don't think we need to kill it," I finally say.

Thorne tilts his head. "Of course we need to kill it."

"No, look." I lift up my arms. "No more electricity. I'm all good. I'm sure it will just leave us alone now."

I don't even believe what I'm saying, but the words still fly out of my mouth.

Thorne's gaze shifts downward. When I look back, the creature is trying to get to its feet. I have to physically stop myself from bending over and helping it up.

Maybe that electricity fried some of my brain cells?

"Nova, get out of the way," Thorne says, and tries to sidestep me, but I shift to stay in front of him.

When the cat finally manages to lumber to its feet, it heads toward the jungle, but whatever I did to it makes it difficult for the animal to walk. It stumbles every other step and is still twitching, which I feel irrationally awful about.

"It's leaving. Just let it be."

The black and gold striped creature pauses to look back

at me before ducking into the foliage. Its large hazel eyes expressive for an animal.

Thorne frowns, also keeping his gaze locked on the creature as it staggers away. He doesn't say anything until it's disappeared from view. "You can't make it your pet like you did with that Celestial."

White-hot rage overtakes me in an instant and I round on Thorne, my new powers simmer and crackle beneath the surface. I'm only just holding myself back from throwing a punch.

"You don't get to talk about him," I snarl.

Tinkle was a pure soul who gave his life to protect me. He deserves more than to be referred to as a pet and called "that Celestial." It may not have been Thorne who loosed the arrow that pierced Tinkle's heart, but the blame can certainly be laid at his feet. We were battling his troops on that rooftop in London during a war that he helped initiate.

Thorne's eyes flash with anger, but the emotion dims quickly, replaced with something that looks a lot like sympathy.

Heat rises to my cheeks as he continues to stare at me, my breathing ragged and my fists clenched. I probably look unhinged—that's certainly how I feel—but I don't care. Thinking of Tinkle's death makes me equal parts ragey and grief-stricken.

"Apologies. I know you were close," Thorne says quietly, and dips his head in deference.

His words and gesture are so uncharacteristic for him that the fight inside me is doused as quickly as it was ignited, leaving me suddenly overwhelmed with exhaustion.

"What happened to that Celest—" Thorne stops and then corrects himself. "Rather, what happened to your friend caused you a great deal of pain. I'm sorry I didn't make it to the roof faster. I may have prevented his death if I had."

"I, ah . . ." I'm at a loss for words.

Thorne killed the Forsaken that had tried to take my life that day. The sincerity of his tone and the look on his face makes me think he's telling the truth. That if he had the power to go back in time and save Tinkle, he would, and for no other apparent reason than he knows how much Tinkle meant to me.

I'm unsure how to process that revelation, and with my rage subdued, grief wells in me, threatening to pull me under. The only way I know how to cope is to shove thoughts of Tinkle and that horrific day out of my mind all together. Stuffing isn't the healthy way to deal with emotional baggage, but whatever, we all have our own damage.

"How long have you had those powers?" Thorne asks, changing the subject. "And don't bother lying to me about it again. I know you're untrained."

I shove a few strands of hair that have escaped my braid out of my face, avoiding Thorne's gaze as I admit the truth. "Just last night."

"In the cave?"

"Yeah."

He's silent, and when I sneak a peek at him, the corners of his mouth are turned down in a frown.

"When's your birthday?" he finally asks.

"It was two months ago." I could lie, but I don't see a reason to.

He gives me a once-over, starting at my head and scanning down my body and back up again. Thorne's gaze is contemplative and lacking in heat, but I still bite my tongue at the rush of self-consciousness that comes with his scrutiny, instantly frustrated because I've never had issues with people looking at me before. In fact, it's something I usually enjoy.

"Would you like me to spin so you can get a three-sixty view?" I ask tartly, placing a hand on my jutted hip.

I have no idea what he expects to see. I look the same as I did yesterday, or even a few minutes ago.

"It's the Starfire Orb," he says, and I scrunch my brow.

"What is?"

"Your powers are emerging faster than they should because of your exposure to the Starfire Orb. Prolonged exposure to spirit world objects will force you through metamorphosis prematurely. Usually, it takes longer than a few days, but since you're relatively close to coming into your full powers anyway, it's happening faster."

That wasn't what I expected him to say, but something has to be causing these changes. Raising my arms, I look down at my palms as if I don't recognize my own hands, and then back up at him. "How do you know that's what's happening?"

Thorne runs a hand through his hair. "Because it's how Seraphim forced me to come into my powers before I was of age. But since I was younger, it took months for me to show the powers that are emerging in you in just a few short days."

I lick my lips. "How old were you when you went through metamorphosis?"

"Seven."

"Seven?" I gasp. "Why would she do that?"

"To make me stronger," he says matter-of-factly.

Horror steals my voice, and it's a moment before I can find it again.

"You were so young," I whisper. "Aging slows after metamorphosis. How old are you?"

I look Thorne up and down. If he's been aging slowly since he was seven, he could easily be over a hundred years old, but guessing my train of thought, he shakes his head.

"I'm only twenty. The Starfire Orb only forces your Nephilim healing to kick in and your powers to rapidly mature. It doesn't slow down or hasten your physical body's growth. I age like any other Nephilim."

Forces your Nephilim healing to kick in.

I feel my eyes widen. "Your scars," I whisper, bringing a hand up to cover my mouth.

If he went through metamorphosis when he was seven, that means he received all his scars before that. No matter how deep the cut, if the injury doesn't kill us after we've fully come into our powers, it will eventually heal.

Whatever Thorne sees on my face makes him harden his features. "You want to know about my scars?" he asks as he takes a step forward and then points to the thin white scar that bisects his left eyebrow.

"When I was four, a Fallen decided he didn't like the idea of a half-breed runt calling the shots one day, so he tried to shred my face. I managed to run from him and hide in the castle, but when my mother caught him she tied him to a pole in the middle of the courtyard and peeled his flesh off while he was still alive. As you know, the Fallen can regenerate body parts and organs, so she waited until he regrew his skin, and then I started training with weapons, using the Fallen that had attacked me as practice."

He moves a bit closer.

"I lost these when I was five," he says as he holds up his right hand, showing me the fingers where the tips are missing. "I wasn't picking up sword fighting with my less dominant hand fast enough. The Fallen and Forsaken would disarm me and then beat me bloody. My mother was embarrassed by my progress, so each time I lost a sparring session, she took a bit of finger, telling me that if I failed to learn to defend myself with both hands, eventually I'd only have one hand left. As you can see, I only ever lost twice after that."

He points to the thin line of a scar on his neck, one I hadn't noticed before. "When I was six, a starved Forsaken broke out of the dungeon and attacked me while I slept. Luckily, I kept a dagger under my pillow and severed his head from his body before my mother's Fallen guards found me."

Thorne grabs on to the waist of his jeans, a feverish look in his eyes. "I have more you haven't seen. Would you like to see them, or is your curiosity quenched?"

I put a shaky hand up to stop him from showing and telling me more. I don't think I could take it.

"Thorne, I'm so sorry."

"I'm not," he says, his voice barely above a whisper, but cold enough to cause a shiver to run through me. "I'm stronger because of it."

I'm instantly saddened that he thinks that.

I shake my head. "No, you're not. You're broken because of it."

"Did you know when a bone is fractured it heals stronger at the breaking point than it was before? I had to be shattered to emerge unbreakable."

"You may have been shattered, but I don't think you've

ever truly healed."

"Are you looking to heal me, Nova?" His tone is mocking, but what he doesn't know is that if it were in my power to do so, I think I would try. But I don't think anyone else can pick up Thorne's broken pieces and put him back together. He's the only one who can work through his damage.

Thorne moves even closer while I'm lost in my thoughts, and before I know it I'm blinking up at him, our chests practically touching. He wets his lips, and I can't stop myself from dropping my gaze from his eyes to his mouth, which is a mistake.

"Just a taste," he whispers so quietly that I think he's talking to himself.

I'm lost in enough of a haze that I don't fully process what he said until he's already ducking his head, and close enough that his breath feathers over my mouth. I can smell the sweet smell of coconut water on his breath.

A spark of electricity crackles on my lower lip, shocking some sense into me.

"No!" I shout as I shove Thorne away and stumble back.

I wipe my mouth even though our lips never touched, but they are sensitive and swollen as if we had.

My heart beats wildly in my chest as we both struggle to rein ourselves in.

There's chemistry between us. I don't bother lying to myself about that anymore. I was attracted to Thorne the first time I laid eyes on him, but just because you find the devil alluring doesn't mean you should give in to him.

"Don't *ever* try that again." My voice is low and shaky.

Thorne's features immediately shutter. He takes another step away as he straightens his shoulders.

"Got it," he says, his eyes cold and distant.

Part of me goes numb as he brushes by me. I know I hurt, or at the very least offended him, and I tell myself that doesn't matter, but something still pinches painfully in my chest.

Gritting my teeth, I strengthen my resolve by telling myself I can't feel anything for Thorne—I won't. Thorne will remain a prisoner for his whole life, or maybe even be tried and executed for his crimes. Eventually, the angel-born will find us, and when that happens, I'll do my duty and help them recapture him. There's no other scenario.

I turn, intending to follow Thorne back to the beach when a bolt of white-hot pain shoots up my spine, bringing me to my knees. Panting, my hands curl, my nails digging into the red dirt beneath me as I breathe through the aftershocks.

What was *that*?

Looking up, I scan the jungle. Thorne has disappeared. Maybe that's for the best. I don't need him bearing witness to any of my weaknesses.

When the pain fades, I shove back to my feet, but only get two steps before my muscles seize in agony and I fall to the ground once again. Streaks of lightning fill my periphery. The electricity that was a warm surge over my skin before now has become a blazing inferno that threatens to burn me from the inside out. The pain quickly becomes so acute that I'm not sure I wouldn't willingly succumb to death to escape it.

A scream rips from my throat as my world becomes a haze of white streaks. Electricity zaps off of me, hitting the trees around me as it grows in intensity, and wraps around my limbs and torso and then skates up my neck.

Twin slashes carve through the skin and muscle on either side of my spine. I'm not in control of my body anymore as my back bows and every muscle contracts. My jaw snaps shut, and I shriek through gritted teeth until my throat feels shredded.

I think I might hear my name being shouted. I'm too far gone in a dark abyss of agony to process anything besides the electric currents ripping through my body.

Molecule by molecule, I'm taken apart, until there's nothing left of me but exposed and raw nerves. I'm not aware of anything outside of the pain bubble I'm floating in. The torture goes on and on, an unrestrained juggernaut that gains strength and momentum every second.

I fear it may never end.

Until it does.

Like someone pulling a plug, the source of my suffering cuts off, leaving me slick with sweat and panting.

For a moment I think I'm blinded, until I realize that I just have my eyes squeezed shut. Blinking them open, I see Thorne's face hovering above mine. Concern puckers his brow and lips as he cradles me in his arms. There are three shallow scratches high on his cheek that I'm fairly certain I gave him.

"The worst is over," he says as he smooths a hand over my forehead, pushing away the wet strands of hair.

After the agony of what I just went through, his touch is amazing.

I open my mouth to ask him what just happened, but all that comes out is a low moan. My entire body is sore and over-sensitized. I try to sit up, but a weight at my back drags me back after I've only lifted a few inches.

Thorne's gaze slides off my face. When I turn my head to

see what he's looking at, blue feathers so dark they look black fill my vision.

Or are they so black they have a hint of blue?

"I have wings?" I croak.

"Beautiful," Thorne says, and then brushes a finger over the edge of one of the soft plumes.

Feeling the caress, I shiver.

Thorne was right. The Starfire Orb had triggered meta-morphosis almost a year too early, and now I have powers *and* wings.

A giddy sort of excitement flushes the memory of the pain from the last few minutes from my mind.

Power angel-born always have wings, so I've been excited about getting mine my whole life. Who wouldn't want wings? But as a power Neph I was never guaranteed extra abilities. The majority of our angel-line gets enhanced senses and strength when they mature, but not powers. I may not know how to control the electric currents yet, but once I do it's going to be an amazing asset.

Thorne helps me sit up, and then slowly push to my feet. The wings hanging from my back aren't terribly heavy, but the added weight still throws me a little off balance. I weave a little before getting my footing. My body aches, but the wonder of having the ability to fly helps me ignore the lingering discomfort.

The ends of my wings drag along the ground behind me as I take slow steps in a circle, getting used to the feel of them. I test out expanding and contracting them and I catch my breath when I've fully extended both of them. They must reach at least six feet in each direction. I arch them up and over my head and block out the sun completely.

Thorne watches me, his face impassive and impossible

to read, but something about his stance makes me think he's ready to bounce into action at any time.

He eyes the dark feathers. "You'll have to learn how to fight with the extra weight."

I know that already. It's part of the reason why angel-born don't officially graduate until they're twenty. They need time to train with their abilities before they are considered fully mature. But I'm confident I'll be a fast learner and won't need two years to get caught back up.

Giving my wings an experimental flap, I lift a couple feet off the ground, before floating down again. An idea flits through my mind and a wide smile grows on my face.

"Nova, don't," Thorne warns, but I'm not about to listen to him.

Gathering my strength, I arch my wings up and then flap them in a powerful downstroke. Immediately, I lift off the ground again, but this time I repeat the motion several times and ascend into the air.

"Nova!" Thorne shouts up at me from down below, but I'm hardly paying attention to him as I rise.

I let out a joyous laugh. Flying is amazing.

Just as I think I'm getting the hang of it, one of my wings clips the trunk of a tree and I bank hard to the left. I don't have enough time to right myself before I slam into another tree. My body twists mid-air, and I start to plummet.

The world is a jumble of leaves and bark as I fall, and I don't have the skill or time to right myself before I slam into the ground, my shoulder taking much of the brunt of the impact with a sickening crunch.

With a groan, I roll onto my back and look up to see Thorne standing above me.

"What I was trying to warn you against was practicing

flying in a dense jungle," he says, not bothering to keep the note of annoyance out of his voice. "Even the most skilled flyer wouldn't try to navigate an area like this."

Right. That's smart. I let my excitement override my common sense.

"I think I broke my arm," I say, wincing when I try to move my shoulder.

Thorne helps me up, and then gently probes my shoulder and bicep. I grunt a little when he reaches some tender parts. He slowly maneuvers my arm, testing its mobility.

"It's not broken, or even out of place, just a bad bruise. Your body is even more resilient than it was before and will heal faster. You'll probably feel fine by the end of the day."

I'm liking this more and more. Powers. Wings. A stronger, faster-healing body. So far, I'm not seeing a downside to triggering metamorphosis early.

There's a crack of a branch somewhere in the jungle and Thorne snaps his head in that direction. I freeze, forcing my senses outward, but I don't hear anything out of the normal. Thorne looks wary though.

"Let's go," he says. "We're running out of daylight, and I want to reach the beach by nightfall."

We start walking again, but I quickly learn that hiking with wings is a giant pain. The ends pick up bits of jungle debris as I knock into bushes and trees and get tangled in vines and low-hanging branches. The extra weight of the wings is also tiring me out.

"Argh!" I swat at a vine that's twisted in my wings, ripping a couple of my feathers out as I try to free myself.

Thorne doesn't stop to help, or even look back at me, but he does slow his steps so that I can keep up.

There's a weird tension in the air between us now that I'm doing everything I can to ignore.

As we walk, exhaustion weighs down my limbs. Fatigue had been tickling my consciousness since I blasted that giant black and gold cat with my powers, but if before it was gently knocking on the door, it's now busted through, ripping the door off the hinges and taking up residency in my body.

I weave another step forward and the world around me goes a little fuzzy. Stopping, I shake my head to clear the cobwebs, but that just makes me lose my balance again.

"I feel weird," I slur.

Thorne glances back at me, a frown on his handsome face.

The idea of walking seems completely out of the question. The only thing that I'm capable of right now is sleeping. I place my hand against the rough trunk of the nearest tree to keep upright and scan the ground, thinking that the clump of decaying leaves to my left suddenly looks like the perfect bed.

"You know, I think I'll just take a quick power nap," I say, not entirely sure if I'm coherent as I slide down the trunk and plop on the ground.

"None of that," Thorne says as he hauls me to my feet. "You can sleep later. Now we have to keep moving."

As soon as he releases me, my legs fold beneath me and I'm back on the ground. I tip over, resting my hands under my cheek and close my eyes. Thorne mutters a curse right before he sweeps his arms under my back and knees and lifts me.

Before I can muster the strength to complain, I'm already asleep.

11

The first thing I notice when I wake is that I feel good. Like, better than good. I'm energized and powerful in a way I never have been before. I'm not sure how I know, but I'm positive I could pick up a stone and crush it, run for hours without stopping, or hold my breath underwater for twice as long as I used to.

I was once a force to be reckoned with, but I'm no longer just a shining star, I'm a supernova, a stellar explosion that will take out anything in my path, and I like it.

I start to smile until I realize the lumpy pillow under my head is warm and someone is gently running their fingers through my hair.

I stop breathing and open my eyes, and the hand in my hair freezes. It's dark, but the faint glow of Thorne's aura illuminates his legs stretched out before me.

Sitting up fast enough to make my head spin, I take in the soft sparkle of the sea that shines through the trees ahead, and the rhythmic cadence of the surf gently breaking on the shore.

We're close to the beach.

The red spirit world stars and moon above are blotted out by the canopy of palm leaves hanging over our heads in the small shelter Thorne must have built.

I glance at Thorne. He's sitting quietly next to me, the look on his face unreadable. I'm pretty sure I was sleeping with my head resting on his thigh.

"Were you just petting me?" I ask, drenched in disbelief. I'm not sure how I feel about that yet.

"No," is his one-word answer, but we both know he's lying.

I pat my head. My hair is hanging loose down my back and over my shoulders.

He totally took my braid out and was combing his fingers through the strands. I should probably be creeped out by the thought of him touching me while I was unconscious, but instead heat rises to my cheeks, because before I was fully lucid, his ministrations felt . . . soothing.

"Where are we? What happened?" I fire questions as I shuffle away from him. The last thing I remember was getting my wings and . . .

Gasping, I contort myself trying to see over my shoulder. My wings are gone.

Did I dream coming into my powers?

"Your wings disappeared about an hour ago," Thorne says as he rises to his feet. Stepping out of the shelter, he brushes off his clothes, refusing to meet my gaze. "Your body needed time to adjust. It wasn't prepared to speed through metamorphosis like that."

Not a dream then. *Good.*

I take in the structure of the shelter. Thorne created a frame in the shape of a clamshell by connecting thick tree limbs together with vines, and then draping palm leaves over the outside. He spread palm branches underneath us, making it so we don't have to sit or sleep in the sand. Smart.

He's been busy while I was out.

I crawl to the entrance and then stand, reaching high above me and closing my eyes to enjoy the stretch. "Well, ready or not, I feel great now."

Thorne snorts. "You should," he says. I glance over at him with a question in my gaze. "Three days of rest will make anyone feel like a new person."

My jaw drops. "Three days? I was asleep for three days?"

"Technically, three and a half. It's almost dawn," Thorne says.

My stomach growls as if proving the validity of Thorne's statement. I place a hand on my belly, and it grumbles as hunger pangs shoot through me.

Thorne glances at my stomach and then at my face. He jerks his chin toward something next to me and says, "Come find me when you're done eating and we can get started on your training." Then he walks off toward the beach.

Beside me are a few pieces of white coconut, strips of what I think might be dried fish, a handful of pinkish berries, and an intact but cracked coconut.

He collected food for me while I slept?

It's not exactly a Michelin star meal, but considering the circumstances it definitely feels that way.

I pick up a berry and pop it into my mouth as I think about how I was completely vulnerable for over three days. Thorne could have easily left me in the jungle—where I would have become a meal for some spirit world predator— but instead he carried me all the way back here, protected me, and even thought to provide food for when I finally woke. It was sweet and thoughtful and caring, and another completely confusing contradiction.

Since when do psychopaths play nursemaid?

The sun is just cresting the horizon after I finish off the food and coconut water and go in search of Thorne. I find him waiting for me on the beach like he said he would, staring out at the ocean with his shirt off, his one wing and the stub of the other visible.

My eyes are instantly drawn to the scars on his back—the ones he hadn't told me how he got yet—but I quickly avert my gaze, feeling like a voyeur. Those scars tell a brutal story I haven't earned the right to know about yet.

I study his profile as I come up next to him. Thorne doesn't look at me as he says, "First and foremost, you'll need to learn how to materialize your wings and manipulate your power."

When I don't say anything, he turns his head toward me, and I immediately note the dark smudges under his eyes and the weariness etched into his features.

"Have you slept?" I ask.

He tilts his head. "We don't need much sleep."

"Angel-born might not need much sleep, but we do need some."

Is it possible Thorne remained awake the entire time I was unconscious? Four days—the three I was out and also the night I spent in the glowworm cave—is a long time to go without sleep, even for a Nephilim.

Before Thorne can respond, a low growl rumbles from the jungle behind us. I turn wide-eyed to Thorne, who just shakes his head and sighs.

"Your mercy seems to have created an admirer. The bastet has been prowling around for the last couple of days."

"The bastet?"

"The large cat-like creature you fried with your powers."

Oh. That.

"Has he attacked?" I ask, alarmed. I'm not sorry I saved the creature, but if it keeps coming at us, we might be forced to kill it.

"No." Thorne looks over his shoulder, scanning the jungle for the beast, but it's nowhere in sight. "I was concerned it would attack at first, or that it was lying in wait, but I think there's something else going on." He looks thoughtful, and then shakes his head. "I guess only time will tell."

Thorne turns toward me, and I mimic his pose. Even though his face is neutral as his gaze runs from my head to my toes and back up again, there's a spark in his eye that makes my stomach flip, but I do my best to ignore the butterflies.

"Release your wings," he says, and I bristle at the command.

I've been trained my entire life to follow orders—the power angel-born are like a human military in that way; we're supposed to obey our commanders' orders without question—but that doesn't mean I've ever liked that part of the job. I like it even less when it's Thorne, my veritable enemy, telling me what to do, which is why even though I know it's childish I cross my arms over my chest and say, "No."

"Okay, so if you can't materialize your wings, try to bring forth your power."

I lift my chin. "I didn't say I couldn't."

I totally can't. I honestly have no idea how to get them to appear.

Thorne gives me a look that says he sees right through me. "Are you planning on fighting me every step of the way?"

Part of me wants to say yes, but for no other reason than to be contrary, and that would be stupid. I really do need to learn how to control these new abilities. The faster the better.

"You really want to train me?" I ask, trying to let my guard down.

Thorne gestures to the empty beach. "What else are we supposed to do here? Seems like a decent way to pass the time."

A smile tugs at my lips. "So this is you just passing time?"

He runs his tongue over his top row of teeth before answering. "You could say that."

Hmm, my gut says there's something more to it than that, but is it worth my breath to call him out on it? The important thing is for me to be as prepared as possible, so if Thorne wants to keep his reasons for training me to himself, fine, I'll let him.

I bounce on the balls of my feet and crack my neck, stretching one arm over my chest and then the other, looking like I'm warming up to throw down. "Okay, Yoda, teach me the ways of the Jedi."

Thorne cocks his head. "What's a Yoda?"

Nephilim aren't exactly known for being up to date on human pop culture, but the fact that Thorne's never even heard of *Star Wars* is just sad.

"Never mind." I stop bouncing around like a cracked-out bunny. "Where do we start?"

A wicked smile flashes over Thorne's face and then he drops and spins, his leg sweeping out and knocking mine out from under me. By instinct, my wings burst free, and the next thing I know I'm lying on the sand with my hair flipped over my face and my wings extended awkwardly on either side of me as I'm covered in sand.

Shoving my hair back, I glare up at Thorne. "What was that for?"

He offers me a hand up.

"First lesson is on how to keep your wings from emerging until you want them to."

By the end of our fourth hour of training, I have a splitting headache and am one hundred percent convinced that George Lucas is secretly an angel-born. Thorne may not have ever seen or even heard of *Star Wars*, but the training he's been running me through is eerily similar to what Obi-Wan and Yoda forced on Luke.

"Don't let your emotions control you."

"Reach inside and feel your inner power."

"Center yourself and trust your instincts."

I grudgingly admit that Thorne is a patient and fair teacher. He doesn't lose his temper with me, seeming to have a wellspring of patience when I fail time and time again. And up until now, I've not complained, but as the sun's gilded rays beat down on us from on high in the mid-day sky, I hold up my hand, calling for a break.

The majority of our training has centered around mental exercises, but I'm more of an action-oriented girl, so all this training feels particularly difficult. Sadly, all that delicious energy coursing through my body when I woke this morning has been spent.

"I need at least five minutes," I say.

Thorne opens his mouth and I think he's going to bark at me to keep going, but then he just presses his lips together and nods. I don't wait for him to change his mind before trudging up the beach toward our shelter. There's a coconut with my name on it somewhere up there.

Once the shelter comes into view, I sprint, grabbing a coconut from our stash and smashing it against a trunk to crack its shell, and then immediately start to guzzle the sweet water. Good thing there seems to be an unending supply of the fruit on this island since I'm going through them like they're going out of style.

Thorne joins me and picks up his own coconut as I'm chugging from mine. It's only when I've sucked down all the sticky water that I wipe away the drop that spilled down my chin and then pry open the shell and bite into the flesh.

I mull over the fact that we haven't been found yet while I chew. With the three and a half days I was out, that means tomorrow we'll have been missing for a full week. My parents and friends would have started searching for me the moment they realized I was missing, so the fact that we haven't been rescued makes me think they're either looking in the wrong ocean, or the wrong realm. It's scary to think a rescue plane or boat might have flown or sailed right by us already without anyone realizing we are even here.

As many times as I've been over it, I still have no idea why the pilots flew us over the wrong ocean or what caused the explosions on the plane, but I think Thorne has some theories, and I'm curious to know what they are.

I quietly regard him as I munch on the leftover food. A

lot has happened between us in the last few days, and I wouldn't exactly call the silence between us comfortable, but it's no longer hostile.

"Why do you think we're here?" I blurt out.

Subtlety isn't really my thing.

Thorne glances over at me with an arched eyebrow, but he knows exactly what I'm asking. "I think someone wanted me dead. Someone high up with influence. Perhaps one of the Elders."

"But if the Council had wanted you dead, they could have just executed you. They didn't need to blow up an airplane to do that." I also can't see Emberly going for a plan like that.

"I didn't say the Council, I said *one* of the Elders. Your Council of Elders is a governing body that requires a majority vote. Maybe a vote didn't swing the way one of them wanted so they took matters into their own hands? Or perhaps one of them is tired of having to ask permission and wants to become a dictator. Power can easily corrupt."

I'd always been taught to see the Council as a wise and benevolent group of Nephilim. Sure, I don't think they're perfect—we're all part human after all—but for one of them to go against the others and stage something like this would be a huge upset. It's hard to believe, but on the other hand, I don't want to be so naive as to think Nephilim are incorruptible.

Thorne might be on to something. I think back to the strain on Emberly's face the last several weeks. She never spoke much about Council business, she wasn't allowed to, but the job was obviously stressing her out. Maybe there was dissension within the group she couldn't talk about?

"Okay, let's assume one of the Elders wanted you dead

but got outvoted by the majority. They stick you on a plane to be transferred to who-knows-where, but rig a bomb so the plane goes down, presumably killing you in the process, but then how does the Starfire Orb play into that plan? It's too much of a coincidence that you'd be on the same plane together. What would anyone, even an Elder, want with an object that forces people into the spirit world? I don't think there's someone out there crazy enough to want to try to merge the realms again."

"You have no idea the power in that orb. Under the right set of circumstances, a Nephilim could rule the world with it."

Chills skate down my spine and I'm not sure if it's because Thorne knows what those right set of circumstances are, or that someone else might.

"Why put you and the orb on the plane together?"

Thorne shrugs. "Two birds with one stone? Kill me and get the Starfire Orb out of hiding so they can collect it for themselves."

"Then why hasn't the person who planted the bomb come to collect the orb yet?"

Looking away from me, Thorne fixes his gaze ahead of him. "Why indeed?"

12

Thorne lets me rest for another ten minutes before standing and announcing we need to start training again. I mean, I want to learn to control materializing my wings and my new powers, but I don't get the rush. The one thing we have in abundance right now is time. Even so, I stand to follow him to the beach, but freeze when a branch snaps behind me, my instincts telling me that we're no longer alone.

Up ahead, Thorne stops and cocks his head, and then slowly turns and creeps back toward me as I turn to scan the jungle.

"Don't move," he whispers in my ear, making the fine hairs on my neck stand on end.

I don't have a chance to fret over my body's involuntary response to Thorne's closeness. There's a rustling in the underbrush followed by a growl that I would describe as a cross between a low rumble and a feline snarl. When I peer into the bush to my left, two hazel eyes stare back at me.

The bastet.

"Get behind me." Thorne wraps his hand around my bicep and tries to step in front of me.

But I'm not having it. According to Thorne, the bastet has been hanging around for the last several days. My gut tells me that if it meant us harm, it would have attacked already.

Tugging out of Thorne's grasp, I take several quick steps, spooking the bastet, who slinks farther back into the underbrush. Hunching down, I extend my hand, trying to get the giant cat to sniff me like a dog to see I mean it no harm.

"Hey there, big guy," I say to the creature, softening my voice. "I'm not gonna hurt you."

"Nova . . ." Thorne's voice is full of warning and laced with caution. I can practically feel the waves of tension rolling off him.

"Chill out, dude. Animals love me."

There's a whoosh, and without looking I know Thorne's released his wings, but I do my best to ignore him, focusing on the pair of eyes staring back at me.

After what feels like an eternity, the bastet starts to creep forward. Eventually its head appears, poking through the fuchsia-colored leaves of the bush it was hiding behind. I stay perfectly still, trying to portray a calm presence even though my heart is pounding. Regardless of what I said to Thorne, I'm very aware this creature is strong, and can definitely do some damage if it decides to attack. I'll never admit it to him, but Thorne's presence behind me is reassuring.

"Here, kitty-kitty," I whisper as it creeps even closer.

Thorne makes a noise that's part strangle, part half-laugh.

The creature is even bigger than I remember. Its head is

easily twice the size of mine, and even though I just referred to it as a cat, it's not like one I've ever seen before. Its body is large like a lithe jungle tiger, but its stripes are metallic gold laid over a midnight-black coat, and its white saber teeth jut at least two inches past its chin.

I hold my breath as the creature gently butts its head against my hand. I scratch behind its ear. Its fur is thick and incredibly soft, and it closes its eyes and starts purring.

I dart a quick look over my shoulder at Thorne. He stares back and forth between me and the beast with a wide-eyed look of astonishment on his face and his mouth open. I have to stuff down the giggle that tickles my throat.

The bastet twists and shoves the side of its body against me, and I almost lose my balance. This time I do let out a light laugh.

"Hey there, big guy. Are you just looking for some cuddles?" I say as I run my hands over its back.

"It's a girl," Thorne says.

I glance over at him with an arched brow and a smirk. "You checked?"

Thorne rolls his eyes. "The males are smaller and have rosettes like a jaguar instead of stripes. The females are also more vicious."

"Vicious? No," I say as I look into the creature's large hazel eyes, feeling like she's trying to communicate with me. When I scratch under her chin, her eyes close and she starts purring again. "She's just a beautiful big baby and I think I'm going to keep her."

Thorne starts to choke. "You can't keep her. She's a wild animal. She's a wild *spirit world* animal."

"Don't listen to him," I tell the beast. "We're going to be great friends."

Just then a flock of birds take flight and the bastet jerks her head in their direction, perking up like a retriever and then scrambling off after the commotion.

I stand, brushing off my pants as I smile after her. I know she'll be back.

"Bastets are attracted to angelic powers," Thorne says with his gaze trained in the direction the beast headed. "They attack anything with our type of angelic powers. They have a particular taste for angelic flesh, Fallen or otherwise. But maybe this one is defective?" he muses.

"She's not defective. In case you haven't noticed, I'm just irresistible." I toss Thorne a flirty smile and pretend to fluff my hair.

Heat flashes in his eyes as he looks at me.

"Oh, I've noticed," he says, turning on a heel and heading back toward the beach.

I swallow, wetting my suddenly dry throat.

"Nova," I say out loud to myself. "Girl, you are in so much trouble."

With a last glance toward the jungle, I take off after Thorne, unsure whether the wiggly sensation in my stomach means I'm dreading getting back to training or looking forward to it.

Over the next couple of days, I'm pretty proud of myself at how quickly I adjust to having wings and controlling my powers. Thorne isn't one to shower praise, but even he admits I've come along rather quickly, and I get the vibe that he's relieved about it. He's much less wary, and each day spends less time scanning the jungle for threats. He still stands watch over me when Cleo—I named the bastet after Cleopatra because she's nothing if not a queen—comes to visit, but he doesn't grumble about it anymore.

I'm not super awesome at flying yet, but I'm not beating myself up about it either. I don't expect everything to come easily to me, and although I've taken several rough tumbles, I'm enjoying the process.

"What are you doing?"

I open my eyes, squinting up at Thorne hovering above me. He steps to the right, shading me from the worst of the sun's rays so I can see him clearly. His brow is scrunched as he stares down at me as I lay on top of my wings as if they are a beach towel. I rolled my tank top and tucked it into the bottom of my sports bra.

I have to suppress the grin that wants to break free at his obvious confusion.

"Soaking up some vitamin D," I say. I close my eyes again and wave my hand, indicating he should get out of my sun.

When he doesn't step out of the way, I crack an eye open to peek at him. He's standing exactly where he was, staring down on me with the same confused expression as before.

"Never seen a girl working on her tan before?" It's impossible to keep the smile off my face this time.

"Actually, no."

I guess that makes sense. Forsaken can't be exposed to the sun without bursting into flames and Fallen are all gray skinned, so I assume they don't tan. I'm not sure if he's taken note of it, but Thorne's marble-white skin has started to bronze up a bit, giving him a more life-like appearance than he had before. It suits him.

"Join me," I offer without much forethought.

Thorne tilts his head, but after only a few seconds plops

down on the sand next to me. He sits with his arms draped over his knees, continuing to watch me out of the corner of his eye.

"And you do this to appear more attractive?" he asks.

I laugh. "I could shave all my hair and be covered with mud and I'd still be plenty attractive," I say confidently. Thorne releases a noncommittal snort. "But despite the risk of pre-mature aging and skin cancer, I suppose that's what humans do. Honestly, I just like the feel of the sun on my skin. Especially combined with the ocean breeze. It feels good. Like a soft caress. It's relaxing."

"Relaxing . . . hmm," he says.

Rolling onto my side, I prop my head on a hand. "Yeah, relaxing. Have you ever tried it?"

His eyes scrunch, and I think he's actually struggling to remember a time when he just chilled out.

"Idleness wasn't exactly encouraged where I come from," he finally says.

After everything he's told me, I don't doubt that. But the fact that the guy doesn't even know how to take a few moments to himself to unwind is extra sad. No wonder he's wound so tight.

I pat the sand behind Thorne. "Come on, release your wings and lie back. Maybe you'll enjoy it."

He gives me a look. "My feathers aren't exactly downy."

Oh, right. The tips are all razor sharp. He'd probably accidently slice and dice himself if he tried to lie on them like I've been.

"One sec," I say and then pop up and jog into the jungle.

I grab a couple of palm leaves from the roof of our shelter and head back. Thorne watches as I situate them behind him.

"There. Now lay back," I order.

He doesn't move until I nudge his shoulder and then he reluctantly reclines.

"Now, close your eyes."

"So you can stab me when I'm not looking?"

I grin. "Tempting, but no. You have to close your eyes to get the full effect."

He rolls his eyes before shutting his lids.

"Now what?" he asks.

I lie back down next to him. Far enough away that we aren't in danger of touching, but even so I'm so aware of him we might as well be.

"Now . . . just be," I say, sucking in a lungful of salty air.

It isn't long before I notice Thorne's breaths evening out, and I sneak a peek at him, confirming that he's asleep.

Good, he needs the rest. I don't think he's actually slept since the night in the cave when I tried to slit his throat.

I consider it for a second. I guess if I'd woken up to someone straddling me with a blade at my jugular, I'd be reluctant to rest in their presence as well, but even so, over a week with no sleep is extreme.

I stare at Thorne as he rests, feeling like a bit of a creeper but not caring enough to stop. His head is tilted a little to the side; a rebellious chunk of hair hangs over his forehead. My hand twitches with the desire to brush it back. I order it to stay still. His lips are slightly parted as he blows shallow puffs of air as he sleeps.

My gaze skips over his face and I take note of every small imperfection. The faint scar that bisects one dark brow. The small bump on the bridge of his nose. There's a small bit of cartilage missing from the top of his ear that I haven't noticed before.

Maybe some people would think the small imperfections would mar Thorne's beauty, but I don't think so. If anything, I find the subtle reminders that he's only mortal after all add to his allure.

I know I shouldn't do it, but I reach forward and run a single finger over the arch of his brow and down to the top curve of his cheekbone. When I lift my hand and he hasn't woken, I get a little bolder and move my hand toward his mouth and lightly trace his bottom lip with the pad of my finger.

I'm so enthralled with what I'm doing I don't notice that Thorne's blue eyes are open and watching me until I reach the cupid's bow of his top lip. I freeze with my finger still lightly pressed against his mouth as our gazes connect.

With a gasp, I start to pull my hand back, but fast as a viper he snatches my fingers and brings them to his lips. With his eyes holding mine, he presses a soft kiss to my fingertips before releasing my hand.

"Thank you," he says, his voice deliciously thick with sleep.

"For what?" I whisper, swallowing to wet my throat and then darting a tongue out to do the same to my suddenly dry lips.

"Perhaps I'll tell you someday," he says with a soft smile.

"Thorne?"

"Hmm?"

Now might not be the time to bring this up, but something inside compels me to ask. "Who gave you the scars on your back?"

I'm not sure if he'll answer me. Something about those scars seems weightier than the others. Like they hide a story that I need to know. A piece of Thorne that he's kept to himself that I want unearthed.

Thorne pauses before answering. I think he may be holding his breath.

"My mother," he finally says.

That's not a surprise. Maybe I was wrong and the corded marks on his back just tell another story of Seraphim's cruelty.

But he's not done. "The Fallen. The Forsaken . . . and myself."

"Yourself?" My heart thumps against my ribs.

Thorne nods. "I was taught that failure mustn't go unpunished. That weakness has to be beat out of you."

I know what he's saying. He was taught to hurt himself. Some of those scars were from his own hand.

Thorne watches my face carefully from his spot on the sand.

There's something else I have to know. "Are you still hurting yourself?"

He shakes his head.

"I've stopped. For good. She doesn't own me anymore," he says, conviction sharpening his voice.

"Good." If I could bring Seraphim back to life only to kill her again—slowly—I would.

After repositioning himself on the makeshift bed of palm leaves, he closes his eyes again, not saying anything else.

In contrast to Thorne's relaxed posture, I'm tense and my heart beats fast enough that I can hear the blood rushing in my ears.

Something is happening to me—between us—that I don't want to admit.

I push to my feet and head into the jungle, practically tripping back toward our shelter. My mind is a messy jumble that I don't quite know how to unravel, but one thing is glaringly obvious—I need to get off this island. Every day I spend with Thorne, he becomes less of a monster and more of a man, and that terrifies me.

13

Walking back through the jungle with clean-ish clothes and freshly washed hair makes me feel like a new person. Cleo walks beside me, and I brush my fingers over her gold-streaked coat, not in the least bit concerned about any spirit world animals sneaking up on us while she's by my side.

I smile, thinking I could kiss Thorne for finding the small waterfall that we could use as a makeshift shower, and then shake my head with a self-deprecating laugh.

Who am I kidding?

Shower or not, I just want to kiss Thorne. The urge to press my mouth against his, to taste his lips and hear what sounds he makes when I run my fingers in his hair, grows stronger every day, and I'm tired of fighting it. I've never been great at self-restraint, and the longer we stay on this island the further away the outside world and every logical reason to keep Thorne at a distance feels. It's just been the two of us for two full weeks now, long enough to make me think we may never be found.

I stop by our shelter to find Thorne taking a nap in the shade, something that would have been unheard of a week ago. Going up to him, Cleo nudges his side. His eyelids crack as he lifts an arm and scratches behind her ear. She purrs, tipping her head in his direction, and I can't help the bud of warmth that starts to bloom in my chest.

"What have you been up to?" I ask.

Thorne gives me a lazy smile that makes me go a little gooey inside.

I've officially gone soft, but I can't seem to muster the energy to care. It's all I can do to keep from pouncing on him.

"I've been practicing that relaxing thing you taught me last week," he says as he stretches.

His shirt rides up, showing a sliver of his tanned and flat stomach, and I glance away quickly, only now noticing the large fish being cooked over a fire, and the pile of coconuts that weren't there when I left. I haven't had to forage or hunt for food once because Thorne's been almost obsessed with making sure I'm well fed.

"Oh yeah, looks like you've really been taking it easy," I say with a raised brow.

Thorne shrugs and then climbs to his feet. Stealing his spot, Cleo stretches lazily on the palm leaves and closes her eyes. She's getting spoiled.

"I'm not used to being idle, so that's why I have to practice it," Thorne explains, his voice still a little rough with sleep, which is really doing it for me right now. I have to ball my fists to keep from reaching for him and pulling his mouth down to mine.

I'm not sure if he knows he's doing it, but this side of Thorne—the warm side I don't think he's ever revealed to another soul—is wearing me down. I'm like a string that's pulled so taut one pluck will break me. Part of me almost wishes he would go back to being harsh and callous toward me, because this feels like torture.

Reaching forward, Thorne brushes my hair back and I hold my breath. His fingers caress the shell of my ear before he drops his hand, and I half expect to spontaneously combust right there on the spot. A ripple of power shoots down my arms, creating a few sparks.

There's a hint of laughter in Thorne's gaze that tells me he knows exactly what he's doing, but my body is wound too tight to be angry. I just want him to do it again.

Instead, he turns and walks away, heading toward the beach. "Come on. Afternoon training session," he calls over his shoulder.

I follow, shaking my head when we get to the edge of the tree line. "No way, I just showered. I'm not baking away in the sun again."

"Don't worry," Thorne says as he grabs my hand and tugs me forward. "No flight training. You can work on target practice."

He drops my hand far too quickly and leans over and grabs the shell of a rotten coconut, setting it up on a drift-wood log.

"Fine. But only because I like blowing things up."

He chuckles and it moves over me like a caress. "That's the spirit."

Pull it together, girl, I scold myself as Thorne and I trudge about a hundred feet away from the target, farther than I usually practice, but that's probably because I'm so good he knows he needs to up the challenge.

I crack my neck and make a big show of doing stretches

both of us are aware I don't need to do in order to manipulate my power.

"Limber enough?" Thorne asks with an arched eyebrow.

"Just a sec," I say, and then stretch out both my arms, twisting my damp hair up into a messy bun at the top of my head. "Okay, now I'm good," I announce with a cheeky smile.

Thorne rolls his eyes and crosses his arms over his chest. "Let's practice precision today. The goal is to hit the coconut without damaging the log it's sitting on."

I scrunch my nose. That's going to take a lot of concentration. Hitting the target from this distance won't be a problem, but hitting it in a way that won't char the driftwood, that's a totally different challenge. I'll need power *and* accuracy. I'm better at the power part.

I nod my understanding. Thorne steps behind me and out of sight as I build my power. It's hardly any time before it's crackling along my torso. I command it down my arms to my hands.

"Take aim," Thorne says. He's far closer than I realized, having slid up right behind me while I was concentrating on stoking and moving the electric power inside.

The electricity that zigzags over my hands flares and I clear my throat, hoping he didn't notice, and then lift my hands, directing them at the target in the distance.

"That's good," Thorne says, and his breath brushes against the back of my neck, causing the fine hairs to tingle. "You'll need enough power to shoot the electric currents the distance. Only a small stream or you'll blow up the coconut and the log."

Giving a small nod, I take a steadying breath, squinting at the coconut.

You've got this, I say to myself.

Just as I go to release a concentrated amount of power, Thorne's lips brush against the base of my throat, right where my neck meets my shoulder, and I short circuit. Rather than a powerful but concise amount of electricity being shot toward the target, a blast of energy like I've never produced before explodes from my hands, shooting across the beach, blasting the driftwood log to pieces. I stare as the bits of wood splatter over the sand and shoot through the air toward the jungle and sea.

Thorne's laugh booms and I turn on him. "You did that on purpose," I accuse.

"I absolutely did," he admits.

"That was dirty and unsportsmanlike." And absolutely something I would have done.

He reins in his chuckles enough to respond. "Life rarely hands you a fair fight."

I don't disagree with him. The people who are winning at life are the ones who bite and claw to the top, not the ones standing on a moral high ground. I'm not saying it's right, but that's how it is. Anyone who expects life to be fair is an idiot.

"I'm trying it again," I say. Thorne lifts his hand and gestures toward the mess I made on the beach as if to say, *Be my guest*.

Turning, I search until I spot a charred coconut.

Great, I didn't even manage to hit the target.

"I'll shoot a hole right through the middle," I say, not having the slightest idea if that's even possible. So far, I've only managed to either blow up objects or scorch them. Shooting through them as if I have laser precision isn't something I've really attempted before.

"Feeling ambitious are you?"

I smirk at him before refocusing on my target.

"Do your worst," I mutter as I re-build my power.

It takes a little longer to gather than before. After I expel a lot of energy I need some time to recharge, but I'm determined, and in under less than a minute white and silver bolts are once again dancing on the tips of my fingers.

This time, I'm fully aware when Thorne comes up behind me. He trails a finger over my shoulder and down my bicep. I clench my jaw to keep from reacting.

I lift my hands knowing Thorne is going to try something, so I'm ready when he brushes a finger over my cheek just as I'm about to release hell on that coconut. Instead of blasting my target, I suck my power back into myself and reach up and grab Thorne's hand. Bending as I yank, I pull him forward, and then with a jerk flip his body over my shoulder.

The idea was for him to thud against the sand with the wind knocked out of him, at which time I would gloat about my superior reflexes, but the man is like a cat and somehow manages to twist in the air and snag my leg, taking me down with him.

I land on top of him. As my brain scrambles to make sense of how we ended up like this, he uses ninja skills to reverse our positions, and then I'm trapped beneath him.

"You have *got* to be kidding me. That plan was flawless."

He grins down at me. "Nice try, but too slow."

"I'll show you too slow," I say as I swing up at him in frustration, but he snatches my hand before it connects with his face, laughing as he presses it back into the sand above my head.

"You didn't actually think that would work, did you?"

It's my turn to smile.

"Oh, it definitely worked." I pinch his side to show him I could have had a dagger impaled through his eighth and ninth ribs while he was distracted with my other hand.

His eyes flare in surprise but return to normal in a blink. "Impressive."

"I know."

This is the point when Thorne should lift off me, but he doesn't. I'm acutely aware of his weight pressing into me, and I can't say that I mind. A fire grows in his eyes that I'm sure is mirrored in my own, and all of a sudden whatever it is that's been holding me back dissolves like sugar.

"Kiss me," I whisper.

His gaze drops to my lips, and I know he wants to, but he doesn't move.

"You told me not to," he mutters, but then slides his tongue out to wet his lower lip and I have to squash the moan that wants to rise up my throat.

I want to taste this man. I want to taste him right now.

"Are you really going to argue with—?"

Thorne's mouth descends on mine before I can finish the sentence, and his lips are just as warm and soft as I imagined they'd be.

Heaven.

One of his hands grips my waist, his thumb brushing lightly over exposed skin as his mouth connects with mine again and again through kisses that are exploratory but in no way tentative or lacking in passion.

With a low moan, I sink into the web of sensations that he's expertly weaving, happy to surrender the lead as long as he never stops kissing me.

Encouraged by the soft noises coming from the back of

my throat, Thorne gets bolder, and gently sucks on my lower lip.

I. Am. Undone.

I'm no stranger to kissing, but never has it felt like this: soul consuming, mind bending, earth shattering to the point where I don't know if we're lying in the sand or floating in the clouds.

It's clear that however lacking Thorne's upbringing may have been, this isn't an area he's unfamiliar with, but that realization causes a spear of jealousy to pierce my chest and I'm suddenly desperate to have him be as lost for me as I am for him.

Deepening the kiss, I slide a hand to the back of his neck and grab a fist of his hair, bringing him closer to chase the ghosts of any other girls who came before me from his mind.

Something rumbles deep in Thorne's chest, and he matches my aggression, no longer testing the waters, but jumping right in, devouring me in a way that leaves me absolutely breathless.

Shifting some of his weight onto his elbow, he sinks a hand into my hair and the tiny tugs only urge me on.

Something clicks deep within me, like two puzzle pieces coming together, and a fierce urge to lay claim to this man —body and soul—rises up in me.

Under different circumstances I might be alarmed, but my mind spins, drugged on the taste of his lips. The world around us could catch fire and I doubt I'd care.

A horn blares from somewhere in the distance and Thorne pulls away. His muscles lock under my palm as he stretches his senses, instantly alert.

Unlike me . . .

I blink up at him, my thoughts hazy and wholly focused on his lower lip, which is now red and plump from my kisses. I lift my head and try to take his lip between my teeth in a gentle bite, but Thorne leans back, keeping his mouth out of reach.

How annoying.

Shoving off me, Thorne springs to his feet and takes several steps toward the surf with a hand at his brow to shade his eyes. The sun now sits low in the sky, its bloated belly brushing the tops of the crystalline waves.

I sit up and watch him scan the horizon as I slowly—and reluctantly—come back to myself. My body fights me. I have to give my head a firm shake to fully regain my senses. When I do, I push to my feet and try to brush the sand off me.

Gross, it's everywhere.

Making out on the beach sounds romantic until you're picking sand off your scalp and wondering how it got in your underwear.

The horn blasts again, and this time I'm as alert as Thorne. Jerking my gaze seaward, I spot something in the distance. A grayish-brown smudge not much bigger than a pinprick.

"Is that . . . ?"

. . . a ship?

It isn't that I wasn't hoping to be rescued eventually, just that I hadn't been expecting it to happen any moment, and I'm suddenly deeply conflicted and a little pissed about the timing. My plan before was to be on the angel-born side when they finally came for us, helping them subdue Thorne and return him to captivity. But with my lips still throbbing from his kisses and the taste of him lingering on my tongue, I'm not sure I can do it anymore.

I squint, and slowly the brown and gray blotch in the distance turns into the shape of a four-masted ship, a weird looking one with white sails billowing in the wind and a hull made of metal. It looks half-warship, half-pirate ship.

The ship rushes toward us, and I know I have only moments to make a decision about who has my allegiance: Thorne or the angel-born.

I don't know what Thorne's thinking. He silently glares at the approaching vessel. A muscle tics in his jaw, and although he doesn't look afraid, I'm still surprised that he's not running. I realize then his plan is to do the opposite. To stand his ground and fight, because I know he won't be taken willingly.

Panic flares when I think of him going up against a group of highly trained Nephilim using only one useful wing, his powers still bound by the silver cuffs circling his wrists. The thought of him getting injured or even killed fills me with terror like I've never experienced before.

I can't stop my wings from emerging, which startles Thorne.

"Nova, put those away," he orders as he rounds on me, trying to back me toward the jungle.

"Heck no. If I'm going to protect you from the angel-born, I'm going to need my wings."

Thorne's breath catches. He stops trying to shove me away from the shore. "You'd really do that for me?" he asks softly.

I clear my throat. "Listen, don't go getting all mushy on me," I say, and then shrug. "I just think you're not a half-bad kisser and it would be a pity to see your skills go to waste before getting to try them out again."

The corner of Thorne's mouth lifts in a smirk. "That would be a pity," he says. Then all the warmth leaches from his face. "But this is serious. You have to listen and do exactly as I say."

"Um, have you been around the last couple of weeks? You know that's not going to happen."

"Nova, I'm not kidding. You don't understand what's about to happen."

Over his shoulder, I catch sight of three figures launching off the ship, soaring high into the air and on a trajectory toward us.

Shoot, the angel-born are almost here.

I consider grabbing Thorne and trying to fly him somewhere into the jungle but dismiss the idea quickly. I'm not a strong enough flyer to carry Thorne anywhere, and what would that really accomplish anyway? We have to face the angel-born sooner or later. It might as well be now.

Thorne grumbles something about it being too late to hide me and then lays a hand on my cheek, startling me. The way he's looking at me says he wants to kiss me again, and although my body is on board with that, the timing couldn't be worse.

"Thorne, this isn't the time to be—"

"Whatever happens next, you need to know none of it was a lie."

"What are you talking about?"

"You'll see," he says, turning and placing himself in front of me just as a figure drops from the sky, landing in a crouch on the sand before Thorne.

I hold my breath as I take in his black wings, hardened

leather armor, red eyes, and gray skin as he stands to his full eight-foot height.

Understanding dawns. That isn't an angel-born rescue vessel, it's some sort of Fallen warship.

I hear two more telltale thuds of bodies landing—one behind us and one to the side—but I don't take my eyes off the monster in front of us.

The giant Fallen smiles, revealing his sharp fang-like canine teeth. "Prince Thorne, you saved a snack for us. How thoughtful."

14

With a flap of my wings, I spring into the air, vaulting over Thorne as I aim a right cross at the Fallen's face. I may be outnumbered, but I'm not going down without a fight.

The Fallen rears back before I can make a solid connection and so my punch grazes his cheek instead, but when I land I follow up with a jab to the nose and an uppercut that snaps his head up and sends him stumbling back a few steps. If it wasn't for our significant height difference, those blows would have laid him out, but there's only so much power I can get behind my punches when I have to aim so high.

The Fallen shakes his head, then releases a roar of outrage and rushes me. I try to spin out of the way, but my wings still make me a little clumsy and I end up stumbling a bit and the Fallen plows into my side, snatching me around the waist and lifting me high. I'm not able to twist out of his grasp before he chucks me. I tumble through the air in a ball of limbs and feathered wings, slamming into the trunk of a palm tree hard enough to crack it. When I fall to the sand, I'm instantly showered with coconuts.

Through hazy vision, I see the three Fallen stomping toward me.

I'm trying to push to my feet when I hear Thorne bellow, "I said enough!"

Two of the Fallen pause but the third keeps advancing. He wipes at a trickle of blood under his nose with the back of his hand, but doesn't make it two full steps before Thorne is tackling him to the ground and then wrenching one of his wings back. The snap of a bone cuts through the air and the Fallen bellows in pain, but Thorne isn't done. He delivers a booted kick to the Fallen's head, then wrenches the giant former angel over and onto his back and delivers a series of bare-knuckled blows to his face in rapid succession. Thorne doesn't stop until the Fallen goes unconscious, and even then he gets in a couple of extra jabs.

Whoa.

I must be a little twisted, because I absolutely thought that was hot.

Thorne shakes his hands as he stands and black blood splatters the sand. Wiping the sweat from his brow with the back of his forearm, he glares down at the Fallen in disgust as his chest heaves from exertion and rage.

After barking in Enochian at the two other Fallen, he comes over and offers me a hand up. It's only then I realize I was so enthralled by the beatdown he laid on that Fallen that I hadn't gotten to my feet yet. I take Thorne's hand, even though there's still some blood on it. It's not like I'm squeamish.

Stepping close to him, I ask in a low voice, "So what's the plan?"

"Are you hurt?" he asks, ignoring my question.

I do a quick body assessment, including my wings. "I'm fine. Just a little sore."

Keeping my gaze fixed on the two remaining Fallen, I rub a tender spot on my head, feeling a lump growing where a coconut beaned me. "Do you want to take the one with gray wings and I'll take the brown-winged one?"

Between the two of us, I know we can take them out, then we can deal with however many are still on the ship. It's a long shot, but if we can get control of it, we could sail to safety.

I'm mentally going through my plan of attack when Thorne turns to the Fallen. "Good work tracking the Starfire Orb, Balthazar. Go dig it up and let's be on our way. I'm not interested in spending another hour on this godforsaken island."

The one with the gray wings nods, then casts a glance toward the Fallen that Thorne throttled. "What about Dagon?"

"Haul him back and throw him in the brig. I'll deal with him properly later."

"And her?" the Fallen says, gesturing toward me.

Thorne looks over at me, his eyes deadened. "Put her in my cabin. I'll deal with her properly there too."

Gasping, I shoot Thorne a harsh look. Betrayal flashes hot and fast, searing my insides, casting a shroud of doubt over my mind.

Sure, I thought it was the angel-born coming to rescue us, not Fallen, but I still assumed it was Thorne and me against a common enemy. I'm starting to see I was so very wrong.

"Get a dinghy out here to take us to the *Soulless*," Thorne barks at the other Fallen.

"You don't want to fly yourself?"

Thorne turns a stare that's cold enough to freeze fire on the Fallen, and the brown-winged former angel hefts Dagon into his arms and then launches into the air.

The first Fallen, Balthazar, is already trudging down the beach. It looks like he's holding something, but I can't see what it is. He drops to his knees and starts digging with his bare hands.

I round on Thorne. "What's going on?"

Thorne only glances at me from the side of his eye. "Let me handle this."

"Umm, how about no."

"Nova," he growls in warning.

"*Put her in my cabin. I'll deal with her properly?*" I recite back to him, my blood pressure spiking. "Emberly may have allowed you to lock her up in a room like some damsel in distress, but that's not going to happen here. I may technically be a damsel, but I don't jive with the distress part. If you try to lock me away for my own good or otherwise, I'll rip your arm off and beat you with it, got it?"

Thorne finally turns to me. His mouth stays flat, but there's a look in his eyes that makes me think he's trying not to smile. "Got it."

"I'm not Emberly," I say again, feeling compelled to remind him.

His gaze travels from head to toe and back up again, before clashing with mine.

"I'm acutely aware of that fact," he says, and I'm not sure if I should be flattered or offended. "Nevertheless, this will go better if you follow my lead."

"Follow your lead, or pretend to be your prisoner?"

Thorne glances at the ocean. I track his gaze to see a flying Fallen towing a small wooden boat along the water toward us.

"Please. Just trust me," he says, his voice low enough that one of the Fallen couldn't pick it up.

He's asking a lot right now. He's asking me to walk myself into enemy territory without putting up a fight, and that goes against every molecule of who I am. He's asking me to put my full trust in him, and I'm not sure I'm ready to do that. But what other choice do I have?

I set my jaw and give him a curt nod, clearly broadcasting that even though I agree to go along with this, I don't like it.

Relief streaks over his features just as the Fallen hauling the boat reaches shore. Tipping his head in the direction of the dinghy, Thorne gestures for me to get in. I only hesitate a moment before slogging into the surf.

When I reach the boat, the Fallen—an oversized beast with thighs as large as my torso and a barrel chest that strains the confines of his leather breastplate—goes to grab my arm, but I jerk out of reach.

A low rumble comes from Thorne's chest. "Don't lay a hand on her," he growls. The warning in his voice is more than clear.

The Fallen shoots him a look of confusion and takes a step away from me. I can feel his gaze as I heft myself into the dinghy. I settle onto one of the plank seats and let my eyes trail over to the Fallen who is digging in the sand. Thorne gets into the boat, sitting in the seat opposite me just as Balthazar hauls the black trunk out of the hole.

Unbelievable. It was so close the whole time. I should

have pressured Thorne to tell me where he'd hidden it, but in all honesty the magical object had kind of fallen off my radar.

The boat jerks, and within seconds we're turning and being towed toward the wood and steel warship. I take a final glance over my shoulder at the island Thorne and I have called home the last couple of weeks and spot a black figure emerge from the jungle. My heart drops to my feet.

Cleo.

She eyes the Fallen as he hefts the cracked trunk into his arms and then sprints toward him. I'm out of my seat and jumping into the air in a flash. Thorne shouts my name, but I'm singularly focused on getting back to that beach before the Fallen kills Cleo.

How could I have forgotten about her?

I fly faster than I ever have and land on the shore just as Cleo leaps at the unsuspecting Fallen. If I knew she wouldn't get hurt, I'd let her take him down, but I'm not convinced she's strong enough to do that. When she rakes her claws over his back, cutting deep into flesh and feathers alike, the Fallen roars and spins, pulling his blade.

"No!" I scream and throw myself between Cleo and the Fallen.

The Fallen, not knowing what I am to Thorne but being wise enough to know he'd be mega pissed if he cut me in two, hesitates. Cleo does her growl-roaring thing, and he lifts his sword at the ready, silently telling me he'll cut through me if he has to. I flare my wings, hopefully cutting off his view of the dark shadow creature prowling behind me.

"That's enough," Thorne barks as he joins us. He's dripping wet, making me think he dove into the sea and swam back to shore. "Take the trunk and go back to the *Soulless*," he orders the Fallen. "See if anyone can get it open."

Balthazar snarls in my direction but picks up the trunk and jumps into the air. I get a little bit of satisfaction seeing that it's difficult for him to fly with an injured wing.

"We can't bring her with us," Thorne says.

Folding my wings, I turn to Cleo, crouching when she approaches and running my hand over her head to scratch behind her ear.

"Okay, then just leave me here with her. The angel-born will find me eventually."

Probably. Maybe.

A muscle in Thorne's jaw twitches. "I'm not leaving you here."

"Then you're taking her too."

Thorne sighs and then his tone softens. "She doesn't belong where we're going. You know that, Nova. She's better off here."

Closing my eyes, I rest my forehead against Cleo's. Thorne's right, I know he is. But Cleo already feels like a part of me, and I don't want to be parted from her.

My heart breaking, I open my eyes and stand, taking in her beautiful black and gold striped fur. I haven't uttered a word, and it's not as if Cleo could understand me if I did, but she mewls sadly like she knows what's coming anyway.

I start to walk with Thorne toward the boat the Fallen has towed back to the beach, and Cleo follows. I want so badly to bundle her up and take her with us that it's physically hard for me to put one foot in front of the other. My eyes start to prickle, a warning that tears are coming; that's huge for me. I'm an expert at bottling emotions, so I almost never cry, but right now I'm not sure there's anything I can do to stop it.

I climb into the dinghy with Thorne on my heels and refuse to look back at Cleo. Cats hate water, so I'm sure she'll remain on the beach well away from the surf.

We jerk forward as the Fallen starts to haul us to the *Soulless*, and a hot tear streaks down my cheek.

Thorne reaches forward and takes my hand. "I'm sorry," he whispers.

The knot in my throat keeps me from responding, and even though I know it will only hurt more, I can't stop myself from looking back toward the island.

I gasp. Cleo's head bobs in the water as she frantically paddles after us. She seems to be a decent swimmer, but there's no way she can catch up. As if knowing she's not going to make it, she lets out a loud mewl and tries to swim faster, her movements becoming jerky. Her head dunks under the water when a wave hits her.

I can't take it and jump to my feet. "Thorne, stop. Get him to stop! She's going to go out too far and drown!"

I'm a half-second away from diving into the ocean and swimming back to her when Thorne shouts something in Enochian and the Fallen stops tugging us toward the warship. Cleo finally catches up, and Thorne helps me haul her into the boat with us. I throw my arms around her, shoving my face into her wet fur. She's shaking but settles at my feet.

Thorne runs a hand through his hair and then shakes his head. "This is going to be a disaster," he mumbles, but then shouts another command I don't understand, and we start moving again.

Cleo won't allow any Fallen to get close to her, so they have to haul her up on the boat with two ropes looped under her chest and stomach. Not amused, she squirms and growls the entire time she's ascending. I watch from below with my heart in my throat, terrified she's going to wiggle her way out of the ropes and fall. As soon as she disappears over the railing, I hear her snarl and Fallen shouting.

I jump into the air, beating my wings to reach the deck. Thorne said he wouldn't allow any Fallen to hurt Cleo, but I don't know how much control Thorne really has on this group. He seems to be hiding that he's missing a wing from them, and his angel-fire powers are still suppressed by the cuffs around his wrists.

I spot Cleo in the middle of a ring of Fallen. Flying over to her, I land at her side, electricity crackling along my knuckles in warning as I bare my teeth at the closest Fallen. Cleo's hair stands on end as she growls at the group surrounding us.

The circle parts in front of us and Thorne strides forward, a hard look on his face reminding me of the first time we met. Cold. Distant. Unreadable. The perfect winter prince for a Fallen and Forsaken court. What scares me in the moment is that I don't really know which of his personas is the act. This cruel and untouchable ruler, or the thoughtful protector who gathered food and created a shelter for us that I was beginning to get to know.

Thorne barks something in Enochian and the Fallen start to slowly disperse. Many cast angry glares in my direction as they do, but they still seem to be obeying whatever command Thorne gave them. All except a single Fallen, who scowls at Thorne with open contempt.

"You're allowing a bastet on board the *Soulless* simply because the girl doesn't want to be parted from her *pet*," the Fallen says and then spits on the wooden planks beneath us. "Your mother never would have allowed it."

Angel-fire shoots from Thorne's hands so fast I didn't even see him move. The golden blaze engulfs the Fallen before he has a chance to dodge. His shrieks pierce the air as his wings are nothing but ash within seconds; then I watch in horror as his gray skin melts right off his face. I force myself not to look away as the angel-fire completely consumes the monster, leaving nothing left but a pile of cinders lying where the Fallen stood only moments before.

Swinging my gaze back to Thorne, I check his wrists, seeing that one is bare and there's a prominent two-inch tan line where the cuff once was. A Fallen comes forward with a contraption that looks like a pair of sharp pliers and says something to Thorne. Without taking his gaze off the charred remains of the Fallen he just blasted, Thorne holds out his arm. The Fallen with the pliers quickly snaps off the other cuff and then Thorne dismisses him with a jerk of his chin.

A satisfied smile lifts the corners of Thorne's mouth and my blood chills. Thorne could have only wounded the Fallen if he'd wanted to, but he's clearly sending a message to the Fallen aboard about what happens if they defy him. I'll be the first one to admit that the only good Fallen is a dead one, but that death was particularly gruesome. I can still hear the Fallen's shrieks as he succumbed to the angel-fire.

"Lilith." Thorne gestures to a group of Fallen and a

female with muddy wings steps forward and drops to one knee in front of him.

"Yes, my prince." She keeps her eyes downcast.

"Take Nova and the bastet to my cabin and arrange for them to be brought food and drink." Thorne's gaze slides to mine. "And make sure they are locked inside."

"Oh. Hell. No." I take an aggressive step toward Thorne, my power surging, electricity skating up my forearms. Cleo easily reads my mood and a low growl rumbles in her chest, causing some of the Fallen to shoot uneasy glances at her. "You promised," I whisper-yell.

Thorne's gaze is impassive. "I said what I needed to say to get you off that island and on this ship without a fight."

I go numb. *He played me.*

"Go with Lilith or I'll throw you over my shoulder and haul you there myself."

"I won't forgive you for this. For lying to me," I snarl.

Thorne tips his head back and laughs. "I desire a great many things from you, Nova." He allows his gaze to roam my body suggestively. "But forgiveness isn't one of them."

Several of the nearest Fallen laugh. There's a flash of something in Thorne's eyes, but it's only wishful thinking to believe it's regret.

With a nod toward Lilith, he turns on a heel and stalks away, shouting for someone to get him some decent clothes to change into.

I watch Thorne's retreat, seething. A cold hand wraps around my bicep, and before I can jerk out of its grasp, Cleo rakes her claws over Lilith's arm, drawing blood. Slapping her hand over her wound, the Fallen spits out something in Enochian that's probably a curse word and backpedals away from us.

"Good girl," I praise Cleo.

The Fallen's gray face darkens. I'm almost certain she's going to retaliate, but she stops herself, checking over her shoulder and seeing Thorne watching us closely. With a growl, she says, "This way," and jerks her chin in the direction of a door that I'm assuming leads to the lower decks.

I hold my head high as I follow Lilith, Cleo at my side the whole time as visions of disemboweling Thorne become the thread I hang on to as I march to my new prison cell.

15

I smile in satisfaction. Thorne's cabin looks like a hurricane ripped through it. Unable to rage at the man himself, I took out my frustrations on his quarters. I do feel a little better for it. Especially considering how neat it was before I tore into it. Everything had its place, and now stuff is strewn all over the space. Cleo even joined the fun and shredded the heavy velvet drapes that covered the windows, digging deep groves into the floorboards with her claws. Not liking to be confined any more than I do, she paces back and forth, her tail whipping in agitation.

"I know exactly how you feel, girl. Captivity isn't my thing either."

For Cleo's sake, I try to calm myself, knowing how intuitive she is and that she feeds off my moods.

Someone knocks on the door and I spin toward it, putting my hand out in front of Cleo to keep her in check. Surprisingly, she listens to me, but lowers her body into a hunting position.

"What?" I snap.

"I have food and a change of clothes for you," says a muffled female voice from the other side of the door.

I glance down at myself, lifting my upper lip in disgust as I take in my ripped and stained clothing. On the island, I tried not to focus on how long I'd been in the same underwear, but the truth is I'd kill to get into fresh clothing.

"Enter," I say, putting as much haughtiness into my voice as I can. I might be a prisoner, but that doesn't mean I have to act like one.

The door slowly opens and a petite girl at least a head shorter than me backs into the space with a silver tray in her hands. Blonde hair hangs in stringy clumps over her shoulders and when she turns after entering, I see her chalk-like skin, confirming that she's a Forsaken.

I blink twice, confused. I've never seen or heard of a Forsaken looking this weak and sickly before. Fallen prefer angel-born vessels not only because they don't need our consent to take us over as vessels, but also because we're traditionally tall and strong. On the occasion they do manage to trick a human into offering up their body as a host, they choose physically strong ones. This girl can't even walk without limping and it's only when she passes me that I notice her foot is twisted at an awkward angle.

Cleo lets out a warning growl as the feeble Forsaken shuffles over toward the round table that's lying on its side and pauses. Carefully setting the tray on the ground, she rights the table and then sets the tray on top. She has a bag slung over her shoulder that she places on the tabletop next to it after mumbling something about clothes. She points to one wall and says I can bathe, and then eyes Cleo cautiously as she scrambles out of the cabin.

So weird.

The minute the door clicks shut behind her, I'm on the food. I'm hungry, but really I just can't wait to taste something that isn't coconuts, salty fish, or berries. When I get a look at the food I stick my lip out in a pout. It's only a mash-up of canned meats and pickled veggies. Not exactly the luxurious meal I was hoping for, but it makes sense. We are on a boat in the middle of the ocean, and as far as I know, Fallen and Forsakens' diets consist mainly of human or angel-born blood.

That thought reminds me how the Fallen Thorne beat to a pulp back on the island looked at me with visible hunger in his eyes as he referred to me as a "snack."

After opening what looks like a can of cat food and sniffing to discover it smells like that as well, I set it on the ground for Cleo and go explore the spot the Forsaken gestured to when she mentioned bathing. There's a bookshelf against that wall that holds several ancient texts. I'm not the least bit interested in any of the reading material, but what does catch my eye is that the shelves look sunken into the wall and roughly the size and shape of a door.

"Sneaky," I murmur, moving closer to inspect it, and after only a few seconds of probing I'm able to get the bookshelf to swing open. Through the opening is a small bathroom complete with shower, sink, toilet, and gold clawfoot tub.

"Fancy," I say to Cleo with an eyebrow popped. The bastet ignores me completely as she licks the can of mystery meat clean and then plops her front paws up on the table to inspect what else is up there.

I snatch the bag of clothing before she gets pickle juice or something on them and go into the bathroom, casting a longing look at the gilded tub before deciding on a quick shower instead. Bubble baths will have to wait until I'm not in mortal peril.

The shower is nothing short of heaven and I'd be lying if I say I didn't do my best to use up all the hot water on this ship. I was unsuccessful, but not from lack of effort.

As I dress in the black battle leathers that the Forsaken had left for me, I do my best not to think about how they had them, since they were obviously angel-born issued. I'd probably never know how they got them, and nothing good could come from me finding out anyway. Not bothering to collect my old clothes from the floor. I open the bookshelf door and walk back into Thorne's cabin, feeling like a whole new girl as a billow of steam follows in my wake.

Thorne stands in the middle of the room, and I tell myself not to notice that he looks good, but that's impossible. Having ditched his thread-barren jeans and t-shirt for black leather pants and a fitted long-sleeved shirt he looks extra yummy. A single piece of armor covers his right shoulder, the straps holding it in place cross over his chest, and a sheathed sword hangs from a belt around his waist.

"Was this really necessary?" he asks, hands on his hips as he surveys the wreckage that was once a very clean and tidy cabin.

I was able to get some perspective as I cleaned up, and although I don't appreciate his methods, I think Thorne was doing the best he could to get me and Cleo out of eyeshot of his bloodthirsty crew. His cabin is probably the safest place for us on the *Soulless*, but I am still a little peeved, so I don't feel bad at all for the mess I left.

"I trashed the room to let off some steam in lieu of ripping off your arm and beating you with it like I warned you I would. So, I don't know, you tell me?"

"If those are my choices, I suppose I should be thanking you for your leniency, then."

I cross my arms over my chest and lift my chin as if to say, *Damn right you should be thanking me.*

"Cleo helped," I say, notching my chin toward the feline sleeping under the table. All the jars of pickled veggies are smashed, and the cans of processed meat are ripped open and licked clean as well.

Thorne picks up one of the wooden chairs I knocked over and sits down heavily, looking like he has the weight of the world pressing down on him. After unstrapping the armor from his shoulders and chest and dropping them to the ground, he scrubs a hand down his face and then looks up at me. "I'm sorry for all that before. I needed to get you hidden down here while still maintaining control of my crew. This situation is precarious. I didn't think they would find us this quickly."

"This quickly? You knew they were looking and would be able to find us?"

He nods slowly, his eyes focused as he watches my reaction carefully.

"How?"

"The Starfire Orb," he answers. "The crack in the trunk let its power leak out. I knew it was only a matter of time before my army, or what remains of it, would track it down."

"You're blowing my mind. You have a way to track the orb?"

"Yes. The backup plan if we failed in London was always to retrieve the orbs. They haven't been able to until now because your Elders figured out a way to conceal their power in a special case. When the plane crashed, the casing around the Starfire Orb was damaged, letting its power leak out. Of course, like we discussed, that's also what kept us stuck in the spirit world the last couple of weeks. But once the orb's power wasn't concealed anymore, they were able to start tracking it to where we were."

So Thorne knew the entire time that Fallen and Forsaken were on their way and he never said a word. "Why didn't you tell me they'd be coming?"

Thorne looks away. "I was going to. But . . ."

But he didn't trust me? Is that what he was going to say? And if so, can I even blame him? I did try to kill him in his sleep. He probably thought I'd pull something if I knew they were coming, and he'd be right.

I let out a sigh. *What a mess.* "Okay, what's the new plan, then? Where do we go from here?"

Thorne's head snaps toward me, fire crackling in his eyes. "That's it?"

"At first I thought you betrayed me, but when I calmed down I realized what you were trying to do, and I get that it was for the best. If I were in your shoes, I probably would have done the same, so whatever." I shrug. "Like I said, I took out my frustration on the room, so as long as you promise to keep me in the loop moving forward, we're good."

Thorne stands and stares at me from across the room. In three long-legged strides, he's in front of me, gently taking my face between his hands. "You truly are an amazing woman."

I crack a smile. "Of course I am."

Pfft. As if that was ever in question.

"Now tell me what we're going to do about that orb and how to get ourselves away from this horde of Fallen and

Forsaken. Figuring out how to keep you out of an angel-born jail wouldn't be a bad idea either."

"Later," he says, right before he presses his lips to mine.

I fall right into the kiss, reveling in the feel of his mouth as it moves against mine and his hand gripping my hip as he pulls me closer. His thumb teases a spot behind my ear and a delicious shiver runs down my spine.

Mmm.

He tastes just as good as I remember. Who needs food when they can feast on this man?

Using the hand he has woven in my hair, he tips my head sideways and then drags his mouth from mine, pressing an open-mouth kiss to my neck and then slowly working his way up. When he reaches my ear, he bites down gently on the lobe and tugs, and my eyes roll back in my head.

The sensations running through my body are nothing short of explosive. I'm sure I'd be embarrassed about how thoroughly he's owning me right now if I didn't love it so much.

I don't realize that Thorne's steered us across the cabin until the backs of my legs bump up against something. Reaching down, he scoops me up and sets me on the polished wood tabletop. He executes the whole maneuver without removing his mouth from my overly sensitized neck.

Skills.

As Thorne moves into the space between my legs, I have a fleeting thought that I'm probably sitting on pickle juice and bits of mystery meat, but I push it aside. I'll just take another shower. It'll be totally worth it.

My hands are pressed up against his chest, and when he

kisses a spot behind my ear a little burst of power causes sparks to fly from my fingers.

I gasp, leaning back a little because I know I must have shocked him. Thorne lifts his head but pulls me closer. Now that I'm seated up high, our eyes are almost level. The blue in his irises looks like a churning midnight ocean. His cheeks are adorably flushed, and his hair is a hot mess—emphasis on the hot.

How I managed to last two weeks alone with him on a desert island without tasting his lips until today is truly a mystery for the ages.

"Sorry," I whisper.

Thorne licks his lips and I bite down on my lower one to keep a moan from slipping out. I've not even had close to my fill of him yet.

A lazy smile spreads on his face. "I'm not. I kinda like that I can make you lose control."

A nervous laugh bubbles up in my throat.

He has no idea. I've kissed my fair share of guys and nothing, *nothing*, has ever felt like this before. When Thorne kisses me I become completely consumed. He's quickly becoming an addiction I won't soon give up.

Is it the same for him?

I want to know, but I'm too scared to know his answer to ask.

I'm spared from trying to speak by a quiet knock on the door. A shadow instantly falls over Thorne's face and he drops his hands, resting them on top of my leather-covered thighs and then barks, "Enter."

When the door slowly creaks open, he checks over his shoulder to see who it is. The same Forsaken who delivered the awful food and bundle of clothes enters the cabin, her shoulders hunched, her stringy blonde hair hanging over one eye. This time she's carrying a small trunk about the size and roughly the same shape as a shoebox.

Cleo stirs on the floor, letting out a feline yawn and sniffing the air. She licks her chops as she stares at the Forsaken, whose gaze flicks toward the bastet before returning to the deck at her feet.

"You ordered this brought to you," she says meekly.

Thorne points to the bed that Cleo made a mess of. "Set it down over there and leave."

She moves as quickly as she's able and sets the black box down, handing Thorne a small key before scurrying out of the room.

"What's up with that?" I ask Thorne after she shuts the door behind her. "I've never seen a Forsaken like that before."

Stepping away from me, Thorne rolls his shoulders, weariness evident on every inch of his face. "That's my mother's doing. One of her favorite forms of punishment. She'd force Fallen to take a weak human vessel and then defang them."

My stomach churns. "That's sadistic."

He inclines his head in agreement. "That was my mother."

I crinkle my nose and hop down from the table. Nothing like talking about someone's evil mom to ruin the mood.

I'm not sorry I never met Seraphim. Technically, maybe I had since she was hiding in Emberly's mind for a while, but she hadn't wrangled full control of her body until after we'd separated, so I don't think that counts. The little peek I'd gotten of her on the roof of the Savoy Hotel when she was in the process of draining an angel-born of blood was more than enough to know that she was pure evil.

"Do you ever miss her?" I ask, and Thorne tenses.

Maybe that question is too personal, but my philosophy is that once someone's tongue has been in your mouth, you don't have to hold back anymore.

Thorne catches my eye, not even blinking when he says, "Never. Not even for a second."

I'm hit with a wave of relief.

"But . . ."

I hold my breath, waiting to hear what he's going to say next.

He sighs and runs a hand through his hair. "I do miss what could have been. What *I* could have been if . . ."

"—your mother hadn't been a homicidal maniac obsessed with ruling the world?" I finish for him.

He snorts. "Yeah, that."

Going over to him, I capture his face between my hands, forcing him to look at me. "I think that's what you're figuring out right now. You have some big choices ahead of you. Your mother is gone. What happens from here on out is all up to you. I don't think it's too late for you to become the man you want to be rather than the man your mother tried to make you."

"Be careful. If you keep talking like that I may never let you go."

My stomach flips. That idea more attractive than I would have thought, but I cover my truth with a toothy smile and a wink. "You'll have to get in line. No one *ever* wants to let me go, but no one's been able to hold on to me yet."

Thorne arches an eyebrow. "Do I look like a man who waits in lines for things?"

I give him a once over, silently admitting he doesn't look like a man who waits for anything. With a face and body like his, it wouldn't surprise me if he snapped his fingers and Forsaken females tossed themselves at his feet.

Whatever. I'm worth the wait.

"Don't get ahead of yourself. You still have a horrid public image issue we have to straighten out before I'd even consider saying yes to a date."

Calling it a "public image issue" is a giant understatement, but it helps me not to freak out about him being the Nephilim public enemy number one and knowing they'll throw him in a jail cell for the rest of his life, or worse, if he gets recaptured. Flirting makes everything feel less serious.

"Enough nonsense. We need to get down to business," I say as I step away from Thorne. "Let's start with that." I point at the box on the bed, assuming that the Starfire Orb is inside it.

"Right, that." Going over to the black box, Thorne runs his hand over the top. "This box blocks the orb's power, so you could phase back into the mortal world now." I start to get a little excited until Thorne says, "But please don't or you'll be dumped into the ocean."

Right, the *Soulless* is a spirit world ship, which means it doesn't exist in the mortal world. I don't want to be stuck in the middle of the ocean again.

"I have some news I need to tell you though." He looks at me, watching my face for my reaction. "It was one of mine that planted those bombs on the plane—a Forsaken. They intercepted intel that I was still alive and being transported. Both bombs were on a timer. They put the explosives far from the cell in the back, assuming I'd be able to survive the crash."

That *is* news.

"So it wasn't someone from the Council or an angel-born higher up that downed the plane after all."

He shakes his head. "No, but my men thought the plane was being flown to the States as well. They were searching for me in the Atlantic Ocean, and of course couldn't find me or the wreckage. If they hadn't picked up on the Starfire Orb, we may truly never have been found."

"Which means we still don't know why those pilots flew in the wrong direction." I absently rub my bottom lip as I try to work all the puzzle pieces together.

"Right. But we do know it had to be part of an angel-born plot, not a Fallen or Forsaken. According to my men, they had no idea the orb was on the plane with me."

"Only an angel-born with power and influence would have been able to get those pilots to fly somewhere they weren't supposed to," I say, resigned.

"Exactly."

That's certainly some information to munch on.

I nod toward the box. "So what should we do with that?"

"I was telling the truth when I said I didn't want anything to do with the orbs. The only thing to do about it now is to figure out a way to return it to its origin. Once it's back, it will be near impossible for anyone to remove it again. It's protected by magic. Seraphim almost died retrieving them the first time." Thorne nods to himself. "Yeah, returning it is the only way to ensure this one stays out of the hands of any Fallen, Forsaken, *or* Nephilim who may have nefarious intentions for it."

That's exactly what we were trying to do back in

December, return the orbs to their origins, but Thorne had intercepted our team in Scotland and taken the one we had from us and then dutifully delivered it to his mother.

"Do you know the location of the origin of the Starfire Orb?" I lean forward, interested in hearing what else Thorne has to say. The origins of both orbs are so top secret that Camiel, Emberly's seraph angel father, would only reveal them to the leaders of each of our groups.

Thorne pauses. "I know the general location."

I grin. An idea forming in my head that I know Thorne is going to hate. "I guess it's lucky that I know who would know the exact location, then."

"Absolutely not," Thorne says as he starts pacing back and forth.

I grin at him from my reclined position on the bed. Cleo purrs next to me as I pet her. I'm amused by Thorne's reluctance to go along with my plan when we both know he's going to give in eventually. Meeting up with my friends only makes sense. We are going to need the backup since there's only so long before Thorne's crew realize he's not on the let's-take-over-the-world bandwagon anymore. And I have no doubt that Emberly will be able to get the Starfire Orb's origin location from Sable. We won't be able to get squat done without that location, so unless Thorne knows an angel who's willing to confide in us, my friends are the only option we really have.

"Shall we address what this is really about?" I ask with an arched brow.

"You mean that any angel-born we try to work with is more likely to try to capture or kill me than help us?"

It's cute he thinks I'm going to believe that's what he's all worked up about.

"No. I mean how you just don't want to have to work with Steel."

Thorne stops pacing and pins me with an icy stare. "I'm not working with that bastard."

I chuckle. "Admit it, you're just salty because you went up against him in a fair fight and lost."

Thorn snorts. "That was the furthest thing from a fair fight."

"How do you figure?"

"I was injured. One of your friends shot me in the chest the night before."

That would have been Greyson, and I don't blame him for shooting Thorne. Thorne broke his leg, sidelining Greyson from the battle, so they're basically even.

I shrug. "You shoot angel-fire and Steel doesn't, so I'd say if anything you being shot leveled the playing field."

He scowls and my grin only grows. I'm having a great time. Teasing him is fun.

But then something occurs to me, and the smile drops from my face.

Maybe I have it all wrong and Thorne's deep-rooted dislike of Steel goes deeper than one lost battle and a missing wing. Could this actually be about Emberly? Did I misjudge his relationship with her? The last thing I want is to catch feelings for another person who's really in love with someone else. Losing Steel to Emberly only pricked my pride, but if Thorne is in love with her . . .

"What's wrong? What's that face for?" he asks.

"Are you in love with Emberly?" I demand as I swing my legs off the bed. I want to be standing for this conversation.

"Where did that come from?" Thorne looks more confused than defensive, but that doesn't do much to cool me down.

I come at him, poking my finger into his chest for emphasis. "Because if you are and you dared to kiss me—" I'm suddenly so worked up I can't even finish verbalizing that threat.

He looks down at my finger with a knitted brow, but then it smooths out and a grin stretches his mouth. "You're jealous."

I throw back my head and laugh. Not because he's wrong. The thought of him being in love with Emberly makes me so jealous I can taste the bitterness in the back of my throat. If I look in the mirror right now, I won't be surprised to see I've turned a shade of green.

No, I'm laughing because this idiot doesn't realize that he's about two seconds away from experiencing my wrath in the form of an electric bolt to his handsome face.

I let a bit of my power out; a streak of blue electricity runs over my knuckles. Thorne doesn't miss the silent warning. He makes a lame attempt to tamp down his amusement but the corners of his mouth quiver with a suppressed smile.

"Nova. I'm not in love with Emberly." His tone is just shy of patronizing.

I lift my chin. "How do I know that? From what I heard about you, you seemed decently obsessed with her."

All merriment melts off of Thorne's face. "I'd rather not talk about that."

Looks like I hit a sore subject. *Good.* "We're having this conversation whether you feel like it or not."

"Can't you just take my word for it?"

"No."

Backing away from me, Thorne runs a hand through his hair, agitation evident in his jerky movements. "Are you forgetting that my mother used Emberly as a vessel? If I were in love with Emberly, it would be a little like I was in love with my own mother."

"Grosser things have happened."

His face screws up and pales, but then he sighs. "Okay, fine. I'll admit it. I was a bit . . . obsessed with Emberly."

I'll kill him. Right here. Right now.

My hands light up with power.

"But it's not what you are thinking," he quickly adds before I have a chance to fry him. "I am not in love and have never been in love with her. The truth is I saw Emberly as someone who was like me. Before even meeting her I'd built her up in my head as the only person who could ever relate to me, to what I'd been through. But even though we're both seraph Nephilim, Emberly isn't like me. I'd hoped she would be, but she's not. She'll never be able to understand my darkness."

In a split second I go from being furious with Thorne to feeling sympathy so strong my heart aches. I douse my powers, and the severity of my reaction to this whole situation leaves me a little shaky.

I don't get jealous . . . ever, because I don't get attached. Although I do care deeply for my friends and family, I've never been accused of being overly compassionate. I don't know when it happened, but I'm in it deep with Thorne, and that scares me.

This is bad. *This is really bad.*

Clearing my throat, I turn away from Thorne and walk over to the bed to stroke Cleo's fur. She's turning into my emotional support animal. "Yes, well, at least we have that out of the way and settled and such and can get on with business. What's the best way to contact one of my friends? Do you happen to have a cell phone somewhere on this ship?"

When Thorne doesn't say anything, I peek over my shoulder at him. He's silently studying me, his gaze seeming to see more than I want him to. I school my features. I've already revealed more than I intended to today, and the half-revelations I'm discovering about myself leave me uncharacteristically exposed.

After a long pause, Thorne sighs in resignation. "No mobile phone. I'm afraid it's not going to be as easy as that."

16

Making contact with my friends proves to be harder than I imagined it would be. I didn't really expect Thorne to be able to whip out a cell so I could call them, but we truly are in the middle of the Indian Ocean, so we have to wait until we make landfall to reach out to anyone. Thorne tells me it will take the better part of the next two days to get to Australia, which is where Thorne claims is the origin of the Starfire Orb. Cleo and I spend all night and the morning of the first day held up in Thorne's cabin until we're both stir crazy. I get so bored I even clean up some of the mess we made, just for something to do.

Even though technically we're sharing the same cabin, Thorne only comes in to check on me periodically, never staying more than a handful of minutes at best.

"We're making good time," he says on one such occasion. "We should reach the coast by mid-day tomorrow. Then we'll go ashore and find a phone."

"I've hit my limit. I need to get out of here and stretch my wings. Figuratively speaking."

Cleo growls and circles Thorne, her tail lashing back and forth.

"Cleo too."

Thorne looks like he's about to say no.

"I'm not asking for permission."

We have a silent stare-off but then Thorne nods and says, "All right. I get it. Can you at least stay close to me?"

I smile. "Of course."

"And please don't get prickly over anything I say or do up there."

"Who, me? I'd never."

Rather than commenting on that, Thorne just arches a brow and then gestures toward the door.

Five minutes later, the sunlight hits my face as Cleo and I walk on deck. The pink sky of the spirit world isn't as pretty as the blue tones in the mortal world, but after a day sequestered away, it's still a welcome sight.

Letting go of the door he held open for us, Thorne steps next to me. I warm a little that his manners are still intact, even in front of his crew members.

Thorne informed me that his crew consists of Forsaken and Fallen, but since it's mid-day, only Fallen are on the deck. We get a lot of looks as Thorne guides Cleo and me to the quarterdeck until he snaps something in Enochian and then they avert their gazes, returning to their tasks. I still get a couple of sneers behind Thorne's back, but I hardly care. I don't like *them* either.

Up a short flight of stairs is another flat deck. Sheets of metal cover the deck rather than planks of wood, and there a female Fallen grasps a large wheel that I'm assuming is what steers the ship. When we near the Fallen there's way more than just a wheel in front of her. A whole control board with knobs and pullies and even a few buttons are laid out on a dash on both sides of the pirate-ship-looking wheel. I have no idea what any of it does. It's just another weird mash-up of old and new on this vessel that makes it a fascinating mystery.

The Fallen eyes us as we draw closer. She hisses at Cleo, who responds by sinking into a crouch and letting out a low growl. I pat Cleo on the head, murmuring praises rather than dissuading her from taking a chunk of flesh from the Fallen.

"You're dismissed," Thorne says, waving the Fallen from her position.

Before relinquishing the wheel, she casts a glare in my direction and spits a few Enochian words at me.

She must have said something particularly rude, because Thorne is immediately in her face, snapping back at her in the same tongue. Like always, I don't understand anything they say as they argue back and forth. These conversations in Enochian are getting old fast.

I lay a hand on Thorne's arm and he looks down at me. "As macho as it is that you keep defending me, I couldn't care less what the Fallen think of me."

The female Fallen starts to laugh, but Thorne cuts her off with a single stern look.

"My crew *will* respect you," Thorne says, his gaze still locked on the female. "Or they will pay the price."

To my surprise, a flicker of fear crosses the Fallen's face.

Okay, I take it back. He can defend me all he wants. Seeing him exert his authority is crazy hot and I have to stop myself from lifting a hand to fan my face.

The female finally lowers her gaze, half bowing to Thorne before leaving. He takes hold of the wheel.

"That was intense," I say.

Thorne's grip on the wheel tightens and he presses his mouth into a thin line.

Something's wrong, but it's not as if I can just ask him outright with all the Fallen ears around us.

I duck under Thorne's arm so I'm standing directly in front of him and then reach up, looping my arms around his neck as I move in close. With my lips almost touching his ear I ask, "What's wrong?"

He tenses, but then flips a switch on a panel next to the wheel that locks it in place and wraps his arms around my waist. He lowers his head and buries his face in my hair, which hides his lips from view. "I have tenuous control of the crew right now. They're looking for weaknesses. If the crew thinks they can disrespect you without consequences, you'll no longer be safe."

I want to tell him I can take care of myself, but on a ship full of Fallen and Forsaken, that's not really true. I'm tough and a good fighter, but not that tough and not that good. Truth is, there isn't an angel-born alive who could handle this crew besides Thorne. He's truly the only thing keeping them from killing me, or worse. The Fallen have been sizing me up since I stepped foot on this ship, and now I'm beginning to wonder how many of them are plotting to make me their vessel.

Becoming a Forsaken is a fate worse than death.

A shiver works its way through my body. Feeling it, Thorne pulls me in even closer. "I won't let anything happen to you. I promise."

"I know," I say, because it's what he wants to hear, but if

he does lose control of this crew, he might not have anything to say about it.

———◆———

Cleo stands with her back feet on the deck and her front paws propped up on the railing I'm leaned up against. She has her eyes closed, the wind skimming over her face, lapping at the salty air like a dog hanging its head out a car window. It truly couldn't be cuter.

While she's enjoying the clear-skied day, I'm pretending to split my attention between the sea and the movement on the upper decks, but mostly I'm watching Thorne as he stands behind the wheel, keeping the *Soulless* sailing on track. Every time I order myself to look somewhere else, my eyes veer back to him. At the way the sea breeze ruffles through his white-blond hair. At the set of his shoulders as he grips the knobs on the wheel confidently. At the look on his face as the *Soulless* plows through the crystalline ocean waves.

There's just something about him in this element that seems right. It also ups his level of attractiveness by about a million, which is bad news for me.

A brawny Fallen with cinnamon brown hair and matching wings approaches Thorne. He carries a long, thin bundle wrapped in a white cloth. Curious, I push off the railing and head toward Thorne just as he gestures another Fallen over to take the wheel.

"It was constructed exactly to your specifications," the Fallen is saying as I join them. He hands the item over to Thorne.

"What is it?" I ask.

The Fallen refuses to look at me, but it's a step up from being sneered at.

"I'll show you," Thorne says. He doesn't smile, but there's a note of excitement in him.

He quickly unwraps the object, which turns out to be a long and flat but rather thick piece of metal about the length of my arm. I have no idea what it is.

He runs his fingers over the hunk of metal with a barely-there smile on his face, and then sets it at his feet when the Fallen hands some sort of harness to him. Unbuckling his shoulder pauldrons, he hands them over to the Fallen and then releases his wings. Slinging a strap over one shoulder and around his wing, he adjusts a few buckles around his chest. Once that's done, he picks up the metal object and then slides it over the stump of his missing wing, much like he would if he were sheathing a sword on his back, and it snaps into place with a clang.

"Um, ohhhh-kaaay." I'm still confused.

With a smirk, Thorne does a fast shrugging motion, and with a whoosh a full-sized replica of his severed wing appears, but rather than downy feathers the whole thing is made of thin shards of metal.

Whoa.

My mouth drops open.

"Ah. That feels better," Thorne says.

There's just enough left of his original wing that he's able to expand and contract the prosthetic limb. Thorne gives it a couple of gentle test flaps before nodding to himself.

"That will be all," Thorne says, dismissing the Fallen, who leaves after a bow of his head.

Thorne tucks his wings and I circle him, noting how

each metal feather comes to a sharp point and how similar in shape and size it is to his other wing.

"They made that on board?" I ask, my voice full of wonder.

He nods. "We have a forge below decks."

"How does it work?"

Thorne makes another shrugging motion and the wing collapses, folding into itself until it's just a long metal bar. With another shake, it releases again, becoming a full-size wing.

"They cast my right wing and made this one an exact replica. I can stow it when I don't need it and release it with an exaggerated shrug."

"Wow. I'm impressed. Can you fly with it?"

He holds out his hand. "Care to find out?"

"I don't need you to fly, remember?" I say with a tilt of my head. "I have my own set of wings."

"True, but I'm a much better flyer than you are," he says with a cocky grin.

I roll my eyes. I'm a little shaky but I'm still learning. "Maybe you should give that hunk of metal a test drive first."

"Scared?"

"Never."

"Good."

Reaching out, Thorne scoops me up into his arms and then shoots into the air. I have to swallow a scream at the unexpectedness of his action. I wrap an arm around his neck as he flaps his wings, and we fly higher than the tallest mast on this ship. Looking down, I spot Cleo pacing in anxious circles below.

"She'll be okay," Thorne assures me. "I've made it very clear what will happen if anyone touches her."

With another powerful downstroke of his wings, we ascend even higher, the wind pulling at us as we streak into the sky.

A laugh bubbles in my throat and spills over as Thorne banks and swoops through the air.

I love flying. There's a freedom in cutting through the air, no limits, no rules, no restrictions. Like my troubles are glued to the world below, unable to stretch this high and reach me.

I lean into him, brushing my lips against his ear, and goose bumps break out on his neck. "Looks like you're back in working order."

When I pull back, an unguarded smile tugs at his lips. "Do you remember the first time we flew together?" he asks.

We're high enough now that clouds hide us from the view of the Fallen on the *Soulless* down below.

"You mean when we jumped from the falling plane? I remember less flying and more falling."

"No, before that."

It takes me a minute to realize when he's talking about. The first time we met, I went after him with two daggers and enough bravado to fill a stadium. I threw everything I had at him that day and only managed to nick him with my blade. When he tried to fly away, I jumped and climbed him like a tree and tried to sucker-punch him mid-air. We ended up crashing in a park.

Looking back, I now realize how easily he could have killed me that day.

"You didn't fight back. You only blocked my attacks, not giving me so much as a bruise. Why?"

Thorne looks at me, his eyes bright. "Why do you think?" he says with a secretive smile. Before I have a chance to answer or even process his response, he says, "Your turn," and with a mischievous wink he tosses me.

The scream I swallowed before bursts from my lungs as I tumble through the air. It takes me a few seconds, but I manage to stop myself from spinning, and then spot Thorne diving along next to me with both wings tucked close to his body.

"Think it might be time to release your wings?" he shouts over the rushing air beating against me.

Right . . .

I manifest my wings and they immediately billow, catching the wind so I'm gliding rather than falling. I flap them to gain altitude, wobbling a little before I really get the hang of it.

Thorne swoops into the space next to me and I glare at him.

"You dropped me," I snap.

"As you so sweetly reminded me before, you don't need me to fly," Thorne says, completely unrepentant.

I'm more irritated at how he had to remind me to release my wings than him dropping me, but he doesn't need to know that.

"Let's see what that new wing of yours can really do. Try to keep up," I say, sounding more confident than I actually am.

I'm not an expert flyer yet, but even so I fold my wings and dive through a cloud, expecting Thorne to give chase.

As I punch through the vapor, I flare both wings, angling them slightly and banking hard to the left. I check over my shoulder and Thorne is there, following close behind. I'm not surprised he's able to keep up. He's already flying with his prosthetic wing like he's had it his whole life.

I'm not sure how long Thorne and I dip and dive through the clouds, hidden from the Fallens' gazes down below, but eventually I start flagging and notice a growing soreness in the muscles on either side of my spine. Thorne doesn't look the least bit tired gliding through the air next to me. If anything, he seems rejuvenated, but if we don't head back now I might have to ask him to carry me part of the way, and I have enough pride to not want to do that.

When I tell Thorne we should head back, he nods and tells me to follow him. We drop lower so we can see the sparkling ocean and the *Soulless* in the distance.

Spotting something out of the corner of my eye, I look to the left. The brightness of the ocean in the spirit world makes it difficult to spot much—it's even hard to see the *Soulless*—but there appears to be something else floating in the sea off in the distance.

"Hey, Thorne," I call to get his attention and he glances back at me. "What's that?" I ask as I point toward the object.

I can't see his face, but his shoulders tighten.

"We have to get back to the *Soulless, now,*" he says.

17

Thorne doesn't say anything else until we touch down on the deck.

Cleo shoves through two Fallen and then rushes forward, practically tackling me. With her front paws on my shoulders, she tries to lick up my face like a popsicle. I dodge and weave as I mutter assurances that I'm fine, coaxing her back on all fours.

Thorne shouts some commands in Enochian. Four Fallen shove off the deck and streak into the air. He turns toward me, strain written on his face even though I know he's trying to hide it. "I'd order you back to my cabin, but I don't think you'll listen to me, so I'll save my breath."

"Wise choice."

One of the Fallen returns, landing right next to us. He glances at me and then turns to Thorne, who gives him a curt nod to let him know he can speak freely in front of me.

"It's as you expected. A Nephilim vessel," the Fallen says, his voice deep and filled with gravel.

Could my parents be on that other ship? Or maybe Steel

or Emberly?

A bud of hope grows in my chest.

"Should we prepare the weapons?" the Fallen asks, casting a wary look my way.

Time seems to stop as I wait for Thorne to answer, realizing he's in an impossible position. Surely, he can see the hope on my face, but if he turns the *Soulless* over to the angel-born, he'll be recaptured and imprisoned again, or maybe even worse.

After a small eternity, Thorne nods and the Fallen takes off, shouting orders in Enochian that I don't understand.

"You can't do this, Thorne. You have to stand down and turn the Starfire Orb over to the angel-born."

"And turn myself in along with it?" he asks.

I shake my head. No, of course I don't want that. I was ready to fight with him against the angel-born and that hasn't changed, but I need to think. There has to be a solution that doesn't involve an all-out battle.

I check the sky, realizing that the sun is hanging low and it won't be long until night comes. When that happens, the Forsaken crew members will be able to fight as well.

Sensing the tension in the air, Cleo starts pacing. Low growls emanate from deep in her chest.

The deck of the *Soulless* becomes a flurry of motion as Fallen arm themselves and take up battle positions. They even start to roll several large machines into place that look like a cross between a cannon and a machine gun.

I start to panic. What if my parents are on that other ship and a shot from that cannon kills them?

"Thorne," I say, and grab his arm, letting the desperation slip into my gaze when he finally looks at me.

"What if I fly over there and give them the orb? Surely

that's what they really want. You could sail away without a fight." The words are hard to get out. What I'm suggesting will separate us and just the thought of that gives me anxiety that I don't understand, but if it means he'll be free and we can avoid bloodshed, it would be worth it.

A muscle pops in his jaw as he grinds his teeth.

"Just promise me you'll take care of Cleo," I say.

Thorne's brow drops low, and he shakes his head. "No, we're not separating. If there's an Elder on that ship, they're not going to be satisfied with only the orb, they're going to want me as well. Handing the orb over to them isn't going to stop this from happening." Relief filters through me and then I'm immediately swamped with guilt because that's what I wanted him to say.

What's wrong with me?

One of the Fallen shouts something in Enochian. Thorne's nostrils flare and he spits out what I'm guessing is an Enochian cuss before turning and marching toward the middle of the deck. My heart is a slow sinking ship until I hear him shout, "Aim for the water around the vessel and hold all fire until I say."

Several of the Fallen manning the heavy artillery snap their heads in Thorne's direction, their gazes sharp enough to cut. They keep their mouths shut, but I catch them exchanging pointed glances with each other before they go back to preparing the weapons. I'm not sure if Thorne caught those looks, but it makes me uneasy and I remind myself to watch my back.

A Fallen appears next to Thorne and tries to hand him two thigh holsters with sheathed daggers attached, but Thorne shakes his head and directs the Fallen to give them to me. The Fallen reluctantly hands me the weapons, his upper lip pulled back in a snarl as he does. I accept them since Thorne still has a sword belted to his side and two functioning wings to defend himself.

After quickly attaching a holster to each leg, I pull the foot-long daggers from their sheaths, palming one in each hand and instantly feeling better with my fingers wrapped around the weapons.

"No matter what happens, you need to stay close," Thorne says. "I can't guarantee how all of this is going to go down, but I can't protect you if we get separated." Thorne glances down at Cleo, who's prowling back and forth in front of us, scanning the Fallen on the deck. The fur running down her spine stands on end. "Try to keep her calm," he says, but she seems to be getting more keyed-up with every moment that passes.

"I'm not sure I have enough influence over Cleo to keep her caged if things escalate, but I'll do my best."

Thorne gives me a sharp nod, accepting my answer and then looking over my shoulder toward the horizon. Turning, I follow his gaze, easily spotting the other ship in the distance, as well as the tiny figures moving around the top deck.

The angel-born ship looks nothing like the mismatched *Soulless*. Steel from bow to stern, lacking in sails but loaded with artillery, it looks like a true military ship. I can't imagine angel-born having built the ship in the spirit world, but I have no idea how else they would have gotten that war machine here.

"What's the play here, Thorne?" I ask, once again torn over who I should regard as friend or foe.

He opens his mouth to answer me just as a boom rents the air. I spin back toward the Nephilim ship, seeing a streak of orange fire headed right toward us. Thorne tackles me to the ground, covering us with both his wings just as the *Soulless* is struck. The force of the impact makes the deck shudder. I peek out of a break in Thorne's wings to see pieces of debris flying through the air and Cleo bolting toward a group of Fallen.

"Cleo!" I shout and try to wiggle out from under Thorne. He pops up, dragging me to my feet with him but holding my arms tight when I try to take off after the bastet.

"Nova, stop. Cleo knows how to take care of herself. I need you to stay with me." When I look into his eyes I see a wildness there, a sliver of panic I've only spotted in him when I've been in danger in the past. "I *need* you to stay with me," he reiterates. "If you don't, I won't be able to think clearly."

"I'd risk my own safety, my own life, my own freedom to make sure you were unharmed." Thorne's confession on the island echoes in my head, and looking into his eyes, I realize he was telling the truth.

I cast a glance in the direction where Cleo ran but look back at Thorne and nod, letting him know I'll stay with him.

He releases a breath, relief evident on not only his face but in his body posture as well.

"Come on," he says as he grabs my hand and pulls me toward the quarter deck.

"The half-breed ship is within range. Permission to fire?" a Fallen calls to Thorne when we ascend the steps.

"Hold," Thorne says just as the Nephilim ship fires on us again. This time their shot goes a little high but still rips through the tip of one of the masts, shredding the topsail. Bits of flaming white fabric float down from above.

"What are they shooting at us?" I ask, watching Fallen fly up to try to extinguish the fire before it takes the whole mast down.

"Angel-fire cannons," Thorne answers with a grim look on his face.

I stare at him in surprise. *Angel-fire cannons?* I've never heard of such a thing, but now's not the time for twenty questions.

"We have to return fire," a Fallen shouts. Black blood drips down his face from a gash on his forehead, and one arm is mangled, but he doesn't seem to notice his injuries as he bellows at Thorne. "If we wait much longer, our destruction will be sealed."

"I said *hold*," Thorne growls back at the gray-winged monster.

"You'll get us all killed," he says, but Thorne just stares him down.

Another loud boom rents the air as a ball of angel-fire takes off the long metal bowsprit that extends from the ship's bow.

Thorne doesn't flinch, and I start to wonder if he might be trying to down the *Soulless,* or if he's just holding off on firing on the other ship because of me.

When I look over the water, I notice the Nephilim vessel has gained ground on us in the last few minutes and can't be more than a mile away. Several dozen angel-born dot the top deck, and even more man angel-fire cannons that are pointed right at us.

I'm starting to wonder if I shouldn't have asked Thorne to hold off on firing against the ship. They certainly aren't using the same restraint on us.

An amplified voice booms from across the waves. "We

have the superior ship and weaponry. We're looking for Thorne. If he's on your vessel and you hand him over now, we'll cease fire and allow you to sail away."

My gaze flicks to Thorne. He was right, they do want him back, but he doesn't react to their demands.

Scanning the Fallen closest to us I'd be lying if I said they didn't look tempted.

"Line up your shots to spray the water in front of their ship," Thorne orders, and it takes a beat for his Fallen to obey.

"Fire!" Thorne shouts, and a volley of shots land in the sea near the bow of the angel-born vessel, causing a wall of water to shoot up into the air, but it does nothing to stop the ship from plowing forward.

The ship is now close enough that I can make out the color of the wings of the angel-born aboard it as they launch into the air. Several Fallen to my left and right shoot skyward to meet them and suddenly an aerial battle has broken loose.

Thorne shouts something in Enochian. It sends Fallen scurrying over the deck. The next thing I know, the injured *Soulless* is lurching forward. I flick my gaze up, expecting to see the sails bloated with wind, but the ones still intact are hanging loosely, flapping in the breeze.

Rushing to the rail, I look toward the back of the ship for churning water from a motor, but instead I see at least two dozen oars moving in tandem, propelling the *Soulless* forward and slowing the distance gained by the angel-born ship with every stroke.

Someone drops from the sky, their feet thudding on the deck behind me, and I spin just in time to dodge a sword as it arcs toward my head.

Pulling both daggers from their sheaths, I arm myself, ready to deflect another strike, but the angel-born male standing there freezes.

"You're not a Fallen or Forsaken?" His voice is filled with confusion.

"No, I'm definitely not," I say, letting down my guard.

"Are you—?" A sword punches through the angel-born's chest and he stares down at the blade in horror and disbelief.

I'm as shocked as he is, so when the sword is ripped back out the way it came in, and the angel-born falls to his knees with a trickle of blood leaking out of the corner of his mouth, I just stand there and stare at him.

The angel-born looks up at me and I think he's about to say something, but then a blade cuts through his neck, taking his head off in one swipe. Squirts of blood shoot from the stump and his body tips over. A puddle of red quickly grows beneath him. I backpedal to keep the blood from touching my feet, but I can only go a couple of steps before the railing stops me.

The Fallen who struck down the angel-born grins at me, his red eyes practically glowing with bloodlust as he takes a step forward and raises his sword again.

I'm about to dart forward, aiming for his unprotected underarm and then to stab him in the back, when the Fallen is struck by a ball of angel-fire. He screams and bats at the flames, but before he can be consumed Thorne is there, flaring his wings and decapitating the Fallen.

"Are you okay?" Thorne asks as he tries to pat me down for injuries. I swat his hands away.

"I'm fine. But what are they doing?"

Brawls between angel-born and Fallen have broken out

all over the *Soulless*. I don't understand why the angel-born would have flown over here to fight. There's no way they can hope to win against so many Fallen.

"Being epically stupid," Thorne answers with a shake of his head.

I bite my tongue to keep from asking him to stop his Fallen from battling the angel-born. He's already on thin ice with his crew; issuing an order like that would be suicide for him.

There's no going back. Do or die, we're in it together now.

Someone bellows Thorne's name loud enough to be heard over the chaos. We both twist toward a black-winged Fallen who's striding toward us. His matching black hair is shaved on the sides, giving him a short mohawk; his face is splattered with red blood. He lifts his arm, pointing the tip of his long sword at Thorne. "You've made us vulnerable by failing to strike at our enemies."

"Who are you to question my authority?" Thorne asks as he stares down the Fallen.

The Fallen bares his teeth, his red-eyed gaze shifting to me. "The girl has made you weak."

Thorne steps forward, flaring his wings and blocking my view of the angry Fallen.

"Look at her again and I'll carve your eyeballs out of your skull," Thorne growls.

"You've changed," the Fallen accuses. "You're not fit to lead us anymore."

Thorne's body practically vibrates with rage as he arcs his wings up, a clear warning to the Fallen.

Something moves in my peripheral vision. Four Fallen

are closing in on us, their weapons drawn and already dripping with the red blood of downed angel-born.

"Thorne!" I scream just as the group rushes.

Thorne twists and shoves me to the side to protect me, but the Fallen he was arguing with wants in on the fight and tries to sink his blade into my midsection.

Dropping low, I kick out, hitting the Fallen's knee straight on, hearing the satisfying crack as it breaks. The Fallen drops to his other knee with a roar of rage and agony. I deliver a front kick to his chest, and he topples over. Just as I fall atop the Fallen and sink my dagger into his eye socket, an ear-piercing boom splits the air and a projectile streaks from the *Soulless* toward the angel-born vessel, punching a hole in the hull of the other ship.

Black smoke instantly starts to pour from the crater. The explosion is followed by a volley of smaller shots that pepper the deck of the angel-born vessel, starting a few fires. The other ship must be crippled, because the *Soulless* starts to pull away.

Shoving off the Fallen, I swing around looking for Thorne, spotting him just as he beheads the last Fallen. Thorne doesn't even wait for the Fallen's body to hit the ground before spinning and searching for me with a wild gleam in his eye that only dims when our gazes lock. He sprints the short distance to me, and when he starts to talk I can hardly make out his voice over the noise of Fallen shouting and the small battles raging on the deck around us. "Go to the cabin and—"

"No." I'm shaking my head before he can finish the sentence. "You know that—"

He grabs me by the shoulders, his fingers digging into my flesh just shy of painful. "Go to the cabin and get the

Starfire Orb." He shoves something into my free hand, and I look down to see the silver key. "You won't be able to get the case open without this. Once you have the orb, hide it somewhere on you and don't tell anyone you have it. Lock the trunk so it looks untouched and then come back."

Oh.

Thorne's gaze snaps over my shoulder. He then spins me, flaring his metal wing and taking the brunt of a hit—from an angel-born or Fallen, I don't know.

"Go!" Thorne yells right before he shifts, swinging his sword at whoever attacked him.

I take off, dodging two fights between Fallen and angel-born as I go, ducking rounds of angel-fire from the Nephilim vessel. I push through the door to the lower decks to come face-to-face with a pack of Forsaken that are just waiting for the sun to set to rush into the battle. They hiss, and one even snaps at me as I shove through the group, but no one makes a move to detain me. Looks like they haven't gotten the memo that Thorne might be losing control of his crew.

I exercise an extreme amount of self-control by not cutting a few down as I pass by them myself, but I don't want to antagonize the creatures any more than they already are. I'll never be able to get to Thorne's cabin and secure the Starfire Orb if I start a fight in the narrow corridors. I'm also wildly outnumbered.

After several twists and turns, I reach Thorne's cabin and bust through the door, slamming it behind me. The trunk containing the Starfire Orb is sitting on the desk, exactly where I last saw it.

"I saw her run that way," booms a voice from down the hall, and I have the sense to flip the lock.

They are coming for me. The locked door won't stop them, but it will slow them down.

Rushing to the trunk, I shove the key in the lock and twist. The lock disengages and when I flip the lid, I'm immediately blinded by the light emanating from the Starfire Orb. I blink away the tears forming in my eyes from the brightness as I reach for the round stone that's roughly the size of a large marble.

Someone rattles the cabin doorknob and then slams into it when they realize its locked. I hear more Enochian and know my time is almost up.

I'm glad the Starfire Orb isn't anywhere near as large as the other orb—that one is almost the size of a bowling ball —but it's still going to be difficult to hide.

Slamming the lid shut on the trunk, I lock it and then shove the key into a side pocket. Rushing to the bed, I tear a strip of fabric off the sheets and wrap it around the orb to hide its light. I glance down at my battle leathers, looking for a place to hide the orb, but there aren't any options in my tight-fitting clothes.

There's a loud crack. The doorframe is about to give.

Shit.

I shove the orb down my shirt and between my breasts. It leaves a small bulge in the middle of my chest, but it's hardly noticeable.

Good enough.

Dashing to the other side of the room, I start pulling books and scrolls off the shelves, trying to make it seem like I'm looking for something there to distract them from looking at the trunk.

There's a groan, and then splintering wood as a Fallen finally crashes through the door.

A black-haired Forsaken leans around the large Fallen and hisses, "Take her."

I throw a book at the Fallen stomping toward me, which harmlessly bounces off his massive chest. It's my nature to fight with everything I have in me when cornered like this, but I'm worried too much movement will dislodge the orb. It's not like my boob-pocket is a super secure hiding place.

The first Fallen lunges at me and I call up my power, not holding back. The zigzags of electrical magic crackle along my skin right as the Fallen reaches me, and when his hand wraps around my bicep he gets blown back across the cabin as if he's been electrocuted. I don't think he's dead, but his hair is standing on end and steam rises from his gray skin as he sits slumped against the far wall.

That felt good.

"I've been waiting to do that since the minute I stepped on this ship," I say with a smile. "Who's next?"

A Forsaken rushes me, and more appear in the door behind him. I take him out with another bolt of power and then another two right after, but eventually there are too many Fallen and Forsaken in the cabin for me to be able to fight them all at once. I go to deliver a front kick to the opponent in front of me, but something hard cracks over my head and I'm out before I even hit the ground.

I come to while being dragged between two brutish female Fallen. We're still in the ship's corridors, so I must not have been out for very long. They have me by the arms, and the orb starts to slip. Quickly standing, I try to yank out of their grasp, but my head is fuzzy and I'm as weak as a limp noodle, so they continue to haul me forward with ease.

Reaching for my power, I come up empty, which leaves me at a complete disadvantage.

We reach the deck and it's flooded with Forsaken.

Dusk has fallen.

I don't see any angel-born on the deck anymore, but a pain-filled scream pierces the air and then cuts off abruptly. To my left, there's a small swarm of Forsaken almost piled on top of each other, and a growing pool of blood soaking the planks beneath them. I turn away, not wanting to watch them make a meal out of a fellow angel-born, but I can't ignore the thick scent of fire and blood in the air.

Scanning the deck, I search for Thorne. I don't see him anywhere.

A ball of angel-fire hits the water right off the starboard side of the ship. The *Soulless* rocks violently. The Fallens' grips on me loosen, and I take advantage of the distraction to rip free and sprint toward the railing. Reaching inside my pocket, I grab the key to the trunk and drop it over the side. I try to watch it plunk into the ocean, but a clawed hand wraps around my neck from behind and yanks me back into a hard chest. A Forsaken's sharpened nails press into my tender skin, drawing blood.

"You're not getting away that easily."

Gag. His breath reeks.

"Loosen your grip, you fat Teletubby. You break it, you buy it, and I can tell you right now I'm out of your price range."

The Forsaken growls in my ear and squeezes tighter, making my blood run all the more freely, and then spins me away from the rail.

A rage-filled roar almost loud enough to shake the ground beneath me has the Forsaken behind me going stock still. I turn my head as much as I can while still in the Forsaken's grasp and spot Thorne off to my left. He's splattered with black Fallen and Forsaken blood, gripping the hair of a severed Fallen head in one hand and grasping his sword in the other.

A Forsaken rushes him from the side, fangs out and hands ready to slash at Thorne's face, but before I can open my mouth to shout a warning, Thorne flares his metal wing and slices right into the Forsaken's middle, causing his guts to waterfall out of his stomach.

I'm impressed. A bit grossed out, but also impressed.

Thorne's eyes are a blazing dark blue inferno as he strides toward me. Lifting his sword, he points it at the Forsaken restraining me. "Release her," he growls, but the Forsaken only grips my neck tighter. More of my blood streams down the front of me, soaking into my top. It probably looks worse than it actually is, but I am starting to feel a little dizzy.

Good thing I'm in all black. Getting blood stains out of fabric is a real pain.

Seeing my blood makes Thorne go berserk. His face contorts in rage as he sprints toward us. Angel-fire shoots down his arms, turning the Fallen's head in his hand into a ball of fire that he chucks to the side with hardly a thought.

The Forsaken tries to flee with me in his grip. I shuffle backward, craning my neck to keep his claws from cutting too deep. We're not moving nearly fast enough to escape Thorne, and within seconds he's only a handful of steps away.

I smile, thinking of how Thorne is going to rip apart this monster who made me bleed, but just before he reaches us a chain-link net drops from above, covering Thorne completely. Four Fallen drop from the sky, landing on the edges of the net, securing it to the deck as Thorne rages from within it. He tries to slash at the metal webbing with the ends of both his wings and his sword, but he can't cut through it. As one, the four Fallen inch forward, which pulls the mesh tighter and eventually forces Thorne to a knee.

Thorne pants as he pins the Forsaken behind me with a deadly glare.

"Touch her and die," Thorne growls.

In defiance of Thorne, the Forsaken licks up my neck from shoulder to ear, and I gag, only just keeping the vomit from crawling up my throat and shooting out my mouth.

"Delicious," the Forsaken taunts.

A noise comes from Thorne that's more animal than man, then he explodes with angel-fire. The explosion knocks me and my Forsaken captor, as well as the Fallen securing the net, off our feet at the same time Thorne shoots skyward, tossing the net off him as he ascends.

Landing on top of the Forsaken, I don't waste a moment. I jab my elbow back into his gut. Grabbing one of the daggers sheathed at my thigh, I twist and then bury it into the Forsaken's eye socket all the way through his skull and into the deck beneath his head.

"I wanted to do that," says a deep voice above.

I look over my shoulder and Thorne is there. He offers me a hand up, which I take, but rather than releasing me when I get to my feet, he tugs me forward and wraps an arm around my waist. Pressed up to his body like this, I can feel the tremors racking his frame as he eyes the wound at my neck.

"It's not as bad as it looks," I say.

I think he's about to say something, but he clenches his jaw, stopping whatever sentiments are trying to break free.

He gently settles a hand behind my head and pulls me forward, planting a kiss to my forehead.

The sweet gesture brings tears to my eyes, and I blink against the rush of emotions. This isn't the time to melt.

The unmistakable growls of Forsaken and grunts of the Fallen fill the air. When I look up, we are completely surrounded. Fallen are braced with their feet apart and swords at the ready. Forsaken are crouched, ready to pounce and rip us to shreds.

This isn't looking good for us.

I push against Thorne's chest. Reluctantly, he lets me go, but he keeps his hand in mine, making it clear he doesn't want me to go far. I don't mind humoring him as I pull my remaining dagger from its sheath with my free hand, flipping it casually as I eye the closest threats. I then gesture toward the dead Forsaken at my feet to remind them what I can do with a blade.

They don't look impressed, but they don't come any closer either.

"You have two choices," Thorne calls out, his voice loud enough for every Fallen and Forsaken on the deck to hear. "You stand down and let us leave. Or . . ." He scans the Fallen and Forsaken creeping closer to us. His mouth curves in a smile that makes me think he's hoping his former crew will take whatever option he's about to present them. "You fight back, and I kill each and every one of you."

I immediately assume Thorne is bluffing. There are dozens of Fallen and Forsaken on this ship, but from the way they shift back and forth and eye Thorne nervously, I start to think that maybe he could actually take them all on singlehandedly. After all, there has to be a reason beyond his mother's influence that the Fallen and Forsaken willingly followed him. It makes sense that his skills as a warrior were impressive enough to persuade the Fallen and Forsaken to respect him. Or if not respect, at least fear, which seems like what would motivate these creatures.

A Forsaken with a shaved head steps forward. I don't recognize him but can tell his vessel was angel-born. His arms and legs look like tree trunks and he's only a few inches shorter than the Fallen around him. Humans just aren't built like that.

"We have the orb. We no longer need this false leader," the Forsaken calls out. "Let the half-breeds have him and his *hashic*." He spits the last word out of his mouth like it's poisonous.

Thorne bristles next to me.

I don't know what *hashic* means, but I get the gist that he's talking about me and it's not flattering.

Thorne's hand tightens around mine. The air seems to vibrate with the energy it's taking to keep himself in check. It's clear he'd like nothing better than to separate that Forsaken's head from the rest of his body.

I, for one, think he should go for it.

"You'd let this traitor flee without spilling his blood?" a Fallen shouts. He rolls his shoulders, his black wings arching aggressively. "Why should we show mercy to this betrayer?"

The bald Forsaken frowns at the Fallen who spoke up. He may want to just be rid of us, but probably doesn't know what to say that won't paint him as weak.

As the Forsaken and Fallen grumble around us, I release my wings. They emerge with a whoosh. There's still a thin layer of fuzziness in my mind from the hit I took, but it's clearing quickly, and my powers respond when I reach for them this time. Pulling my hand from Thorne's grasp, I allow the electric energy to zip up and down my arms.

I'm ready to throw down with this bunch. If this is the way I go out, so be it—I'll definitely be taking some of these bastards out with me.

The anticipation makes me antsy, and I bounce on the balls of my feet. Thorne shoots me a look that says to stand down, but I'm not in the mood to take orders. I'm in the mood to kick ass.

Just as I'm about to fry a Fallen who clearly wants a go at Thorne and me, he pitches forward, landing on his stomach in front of me. He screams and black blood shoots from his neck like a geyser. I'm confused for a second, until Cleo appears out of thin air. Her front claws are dug into his shoulders and her mouth is covered in sticky black blood. It drips from her jaws as she looks up at me with something akin to a smile on her furry face.

"Cleo can go invisible?"

"Apparently," Thorne answers.

Chaos explodes on the deck as the group of Fallen and Forsaken converge on us. Cleo bends down, rips out what's left of the Fallen's throat, and then pounces on another. I don't know where she's been this whole time—maybe invisible and waiting for the right moment—but my heart jumps into my throat as her growls fill the air as she attacks the Fallen.

I snap out of it when a Forsaken leaps at me, and I barely dodge her strike. Before she gets a chance to come at me again, Thorne is there, flaring his wings and decapitating her in a single motion.

"I had it," I say. But he just grabs my hand and yells, "Let's go!" as he tries to yank me into the air.

"Cleo!" I shout, and he glances back at me. We can't leave without her.

Thorne nods and shoots a blast of angel-fire off to the left, which burns away several of the ropes holding the dinghy out of the water. The weight of the boat can't be supported by the remaining ropes, so they snap and the boat falls to the ocean.

"Go," he yells, "I'll get her."

I don't second-guess Thorne. I sheath my dagger and fly as fast as possible toward the boat now bobbing in the waves next to the *Soulless*.

Fallen jump into the air after me and Forsaken throw daggers and whatever else they can as I flee. I have managed to clear the deck when something hits one of my wings, sending me spiraling toward the sparkling spirit world ocean.

I splash into the water, a streak of pain temporarily paralyzing me, but I have enough sense to dematerialize my wings and the blinding pain becomes a phantom throb. I didn't get a look at my wings before I put them away, but I'm pretty sure the left one's broken.

Clawing my way to the surface, I take big gulps of air. The dinghy is only a few strokes away and I swim for it, pulling myself up and over the side. I scramble to my feet, ready to defend myself against any Fallen who have followed me, but there's no one there.

I jerk my gaze toward the *Soulless* just as an explosion rocks the ship and I'm blown back, landing hard on the bottom of the dinghy. I cough as I struggle to my feet, gasping when I see the hole in the side of the mighty ship and most of the deck lit with orange flames. A gust of wind brings with it the scent of burnt wood and flesh as it blows my hair around my face.

I scan the ship for any signs of Thorne or Cleo, then release my wings with the intent to fly back and search for them, but the moment they are free the pain in my left wing brings me to my knees. Looking over my shoulder, they seem fine, but there's no way I can fly. The pain is too distracting, so I pull them back into me hoping they heal quickly.

Right as I'm about to dive into the water, a figure shoots up through the smoke covering the deck of the *Soulless*. Thorne beats his wings as he flies toward me, Cleo hanging awkwardly in his grasp.

Dropping Cleo into the boat next to me, he swoops down to grab the rope to pull us farther away from the *Soulless*. Cleo lands smoothly on all four paws and presses her head into me, asking for a rub. When I touch her head, it's wet with enemy blood.

Yuck.

But I still say, "Good girl," as I scratch behind her ear.

Thorne tugs on the towline, his wings beating against the air, and we move off. I almost lose my footing with the sudden movement, but Cleo helps me stay on my feet. I keep my eyes fixed on the *Soulless* and watch as three Fallen launch into the air after us.

"Thorne," I yell, "we have company!"

Thorne checks over his shoulder and then flaps his wings faster, probably hoping to outrun the Fallen, but it becomes clear after only a few moments that isn't going to be possible. Thorne just can't fly as fast while also hauling the dinghy.

Snatching the dagger from the holster on my thigh, I

take aim at the Fallen closing in on Thorne, knowing I'll only get one shot, so I need to make it count.

I let the dagger loose. It flies end over end and pierces its target, the Fallen's temple. The Fallen tumbles from the sky, landing with a splash in the ocean, but there's still two more of them on our tail.

When they are only a body's length away from Thorne, I shout a warning and he drops the rope and swoops up. The Fallen jet skyward to chase him. A loud boom rents the air and one Fallen is struck in the chest with angel-fire from the angel-born ship. It envelops him, turning him into a giant ball of fire as he falls toward the ocean.

Now that Thorne isn't tugging us anymore, Cleo and I bob on the water. There aren't any lingering fires on the angel-born ship. There's still a large hole in the hull, but now that there isn't smoke billowing from it, it doesn't look as big as it cuts through the waves toward us.

I turn my gaze to the *Soulless* to see that it's turned and limping in the opposite direction, the oars moving back and forth in the waves the only thing keeping the ship moving. Frankly, I'm surprised it's still floating at all, but the remaining Fallen and Forsaken on board must have decided it was better for them to flee than bother going after us.

"Put down your weapons and we won't shoot again," a voice calls from the angel-born vessel.

I immediately put my hands in the air, showing them I'm unarmed, but when I look up, Thorne and the Fallen he's battling ignore the warning completely. I sink my teeth into my bottom lip, worried that any moment Thorne will turn into a fiery ball of flames just like the Fallen that tumbled from the sky.

Thorne and the Fallen come together again and again,

trading blows in the air while they attempt to stay aloft. It's a dangerous aerial dogfight that takes a couple of years off my life as I watch from below. Thorne kicks the Fallen's jaw, and before the creature can recover, Thorne twists, slashing his sword and cutting the Fallen's head off. The Fallen's body splashes into the ocean but his head drops in the boat with Cleo and me. Cleo immediately pounces, grabbing the downed Fallen's cheek and shaking the head back and forth like a chew toy.

Thorne lands in the boat with a thud, sending it rocking. There's a shallow cut high up on his cheek, and one of his sleeves is covered in a mix of red and black blood. Sweat has dampened his hair, and dark strands stick to his forehead and the nape of his neck. He scans me from head to toe.

"Are you injured?" he asks, and I shake my head. I'm not really, at least not seriously.

He lifts his free hand like he's going to reach for me but flicks a gaze over his shoulder at the approaching angel-born ship and makes a fist instead, dropping it to his side. "And you have the orb?"

A smile touches my lips, and despite his reluctance to touch me, I grab his hand, bringing it up and laying his fingers on my chest. He looks confused for a split second before he feels the round object under my shirt.

"I locked the trunk and tossed the key overboard. That should keep them from realizing they don't have the orb for a little while."

"Smart girl," he says with an appreciative gleam in his eyes.

"This is your last warning," a voice blares from the angel-born ship. "Drop your weapons."

I don't have any weapons to drop, but I stare up at

Thorne, waiting to see what he's going to do. He's motionless.

"What do you want to do?" I ask him, ready to dig deep for the energy to fight the angel-born aboard that ship if he wants me to.

After a heavy sigh, he releases his sword and it clangs on the bottom of the dinghy, startling Cleo, who has chewed the Fallen's head past recognition. With his back to the angel-born ship, Thorne lifts his hands in the air, signaling that he's weapon-free.

A handful of angel-born launch off the ship's deck and fly in our direction. Cleo nudges past Thorne to get to me and then twists to watch the angel-born soar through the sky.

"What's our play?" I ask, concern for him and Cleo rising up in me. We only have a few moments to come up with a plan.

Thorne pins me with a hard stare. "Keep the orb away from whoever is in charge. Get a hold of your friends and return it to its origin as we'd planned. Don't trust anyone on that ship."

I nod. Of course we still need to get this orb back to its origin, and being overly trusting isn't like me anyway. "Right. But what about you? We need to come up with a premeditated escape plan."

His gaze softens as it roams my face, taking in each of my features. A pit starts to grow in my gut. I don't like that look.

"Nothing about me. You hang on until you can get off that ship and get with your friends. After you return the orb, you get on with your life and you don't look back."

"Thorne . . . *no*. That's not what's going to happen. I'm not leaving you in some angel-born jail to rot, or worse."

With a sad smile, he trails a finger over my cheek and back toward my hairline. He traces the edges of my ear, making me shiver. "I did a lot of bad things. Atonement. Forgiveness. Redemption. Those aren't meant for me."

"Not everything that went down in London was your fault. Your mother—"

"My mother may have pointed me down a path, but I chose to follow it. People like me don't get a happily-ever-after. For a moment I thought . . ." He trails off and he shakes his head. "I'm ready to face the consequences of my misdeeds. I know I'm headed for Hell, and I won't take you down with me."

A large angel-born with snow-white wings lands in the dinghy behind Thorne. Thorne puts his hands back in the air.

"I won't put up a fight," he says.

Cleo growls at the newcomer, but I quiet her with a hand on her head as I helplessly watch the angel-born slap shackles on Thorne and then roughly force him to the bottom of the boat, a knee in his back as he cuffs his hands. Thorne complies without a fight, his cheek pressed up against the rough boards as the angel-born calls up to one of his friends to haul the small boat the short distance to the ship.

Four other angel-born, all dressed in battle leathers and loaded with blades, circle at various heights above us. One of them swoops down and fishes the rope that Thorne dropped out of the water.

"Are you Nova Kelly?" the angel-born asks, drawing my attention as we start to move.

I only nod. I can't find my voice around the rock lodged in my throat.

"Good. We've been looking for you. Your parents are on board and will be relieved we've found you."

"My parents are here?"

The angel-born nods. "Is that thing dangerous?" he asks, gesturing with his chin toward Cleo.

Cleo's tongue darts out and licks her lips as she stares at the angel-born, anticipating her next meal.

"She's domesticated."

Huge fat lie. Cleo is most assuredly dangerous and far from tame, but I'm not going to give them an excuse to lock her up or hurt her. It's starting to feel like I've lost Thorne. I refuse to let anyone take her from me as well.

The angel-born eyes Cleo like he doesn't quite believe me—*smart man*—but doesn't say anything else. The boat falls quiet as we skim the waves toward the ship.

18

The first words out of my mouth after my mother releases me from the biggest hug she's ever given me aren't "I missed you," or "I love you," or even, "Did you bring my favorite snack because I've been on a diet of coconuts and seaweed for two weeks?" No, the first words out of my mouth are, "Where are they taking him?" as I watch two angel-born haul Thorne across the deck and through a door.

My mom looks confused for a moment, and then glances over her shoulder just as Thorne and his angel-born guards disappear. "Don't worry. They'll put him somewhere secure. He won't be able to hurt you."

That is not why I asked, but I'm not ready to explain my convoluted feelings toward Thorne right now. Certainly not before I'm able to unravel them myself.

My father lays a hand on my shoulder and squeezes lightly, pulling my attention. "Are you unharmed?" he asks, and the look in his eyes says he's asking about more than just my physical well-being.

"Yes, I'm fine."

My mom searches my face. "Honey, you can tell us anything. If he did something to you that you don't want to talk about, it's okay."

"No, no. Mom, I really am all right. Thorne didn't do anything to hurt me. Honestly, I probably wouldn't have made it two days on the island if it wasn't for him."

My parents exchange a concerned glance, one that says they don't quite believe me. I open my mouth to defend Thorne when Cleo shoves between me and my mom, herding me away from my parents. She's been skittish since the moment we boarded the *Dauntless*, the angel-born warship. I was happy she hadn't attacked anyone yet, but the night was still young.

"Miss Kelly, I'm so glad to see you are safe and sound," says a vaguely familiar male voice, and when I look over a man with black hair and gray eyes is walking toward us. Malachi, the cherub Elder.

I don't know Malachi well, but I've met him a handful of times. He's the oldest of the Elders on the Council, or at least he used to be before Nikias, the angel-line Neph Elder, was initiated a couple months ago. He looks to be in his late forties or early fifties, which is rare among our kind. I'm not sure how old he is, but it's possible his age has four digits.

My last face-to-face interaction with Malachi wasn't stellar. It was his idea to bomb London, which is what led to the death of Emberly's father. I'm not sure she's forgiven him for that fateful decision yet.

I peek over Malachi's shoulder and spot Zara and Draven, the dominion and throne Elders. They stop talking and glance my way but stay rooted where they are. Zara's light gray stare drills into me, leaving me feeling exposed, like she can read all my secrets on my face. After a pause, they return to their conversation.

My mother clears her throat and I realize it's my turn to say something.

"I'm glad to be in one piece as well." I scan the deck of the *Dauntless*. Where the *Soulless* looked like a cross between a pirate ship and a spaceship, the *Dauntless* looks like a sleek military vessel.

"I didn't know the Council had any ships that could navigate the spirit world," I say, blatantly fishing for information.

Malachi's smile doesn't quite reach his eyes. "As I'm sure you can understand, we don't make everything public to every Nephilim."

I smile and nod, since I know that's what's expected of me, but inside my mind is weighed down with suspicion. How much has the Council concealed from the general angel-born population?

"I'm sure after the ordeal you've had, your priorities are food and rest, but I was hoping to have a word with you first." Malachi glances at my parents. "Killian, Ciera, would you mind if I talk with your daughter for a few minutes before you get her settled?"

This ought to be interesting.

My dad frowns but says, "Yes, of course," before turning to me. "We'll just be over there," he says, gesturing off to the side. "When you're done, we'll show you to a cabin and you can get some rest."

Malachi waits until my parents have moved out of hearing range. Cleo plops her butt down right next to me, eyeing the cherub Elder warily.

Malachi only gives the large bastet a fleeting glance

before turning his full attention to me. That's interesting. I'd think a spirit world creature would be of more interest to him.

"Nova, I'd first like to say I'm so sorry for the ordeal you have just gone through. A plane crash and then enduring two weeks on an enemy ship crawling with Fallen and Forsaken. It's truly hard to fathom what you've been through." His words drip with regret and empathy, but I'm still wary.

"Two days," I correct him.

"Excuse me?"

"I was only on the *Soulless* for two days. I spent the better part of the last two weeks on a desert island with Thorne."

Interest flashes in Malachi's eyes making me instantly regret offering that information.

"Is that so? Was this island near the crash site?"

I nod slowly, uneasy in his presence.

"What can you tell me about the island?"

"Umm, it had a beach and a jungle."

"Anything specific that might give us an idea of where it's located?"

"Not really. Only that there weren't any humans on the island, and we couldn't see any other land in sight. Who knew there were still undiscovered bits of land out there?" I say, going for nonchalance.

"Did you check for signs of human or angel-born life in the spirit *and* mortal world?" he asks eagerly.

Busted. The dude just tipped his hand. It's obvious Thorne and I had been in the spirit world, or the Fallen, who can't travel to the mortal world, never would have found us. There's also Cleo as evidence we were in the spirit world. He's fishing to find out if we were actually trapped there though, which means he knows the Starfire Orb was on the plane with us.

I'm not about to reveal I know about the orb, especially since it's currently sitting in my cleavage. Let him think it's on the bottom of the sea and go on a wild goose chase for it. That will give me time to figure out how to get it back to its origin,

"Yeah, no signs of humans or angel-born anywhere." Technically not a lie. "It was a true desert island. I'm still trying to figure out if I was really lucky, or really unlucky."

He takes a step closer and Cleo growls. Frowning down at her, he backs up again. "So, you have no idea where the island might be?"

"You found me, you have Thorne back, so who cares where the island was?"

"We'd like to find the wreckage of the plane, if possible. You know, for the families of the pilots who perished."

Um, yeah. I'm sure that's why you want to find the wreckage.

Internally, I'm eye-rolling. Malachi thinks the Starfire Orb is at the bottom of the ocean somewhere near that island and wants to retrieve it. Good, that's what I want him to think.

"Honestly, I have no idea where the island is. I wouldn't have even known we were in the wrong hemisphere if Thorne didn't know how to read the stars."

Interest flares in Malachi's eyes, and I'm suddenly worried for Thorne. The look on Malachi's face tells me he'll do anything to find that orb. I've no doubt he's not above roughing up a prisoner for information.

It's probably just my imagination, but the orb burns against my skin. My fingers itch to reach up and touch it beneath my shirt, but I ignore the impulse.

The only reason Malachi doesn't realize the orb is on the *Dauntless* with us is that we are all already in the spirit world. Here in the middle of the ocean, there's no reason for anyone to attempt to phase back into the mortal world. They'd just dump themselves into the water. But once we get to shore that could all change. I need to get off this boat before we reach shore if I'm going to keep Malachi from realizing the orb is on board.

"And so you're saying that the Fallen and Forsaken found you and Thorne after you'd been on this island for several days?"

"Yeah."

"How do you think they found you?" he asks, an interested gleam in his eye.

I'm not sure if he knows the Fallen and Forsaken can track the Starfire Orb when it isn't concealed, and it's not information I'm about to offer up.

"No idea," I lie easily. "How did you know to look for us in the Indian Ocean rather than the Atlantic?" I ask, turning my questions on him instead. "The plane I got on was supposed to be headed for the US. Any ideas why it flew in the wrong direction?"

"Not yet," he says. "But we're looking into it. Someone went to great lengths to hide the flight itinerary, and the pilots turned off their tracking system. It was actually your parents who figured out the general location. No one seems to know why the pilots were flying this way, but when your plane disappeared and we couldn't figure out what happened, your parents were able to track your position on your phone. The last time your phone picked up a signal was over Yemen, which tipped us off that something was up."

The plot thickens.

If it wasn't for my cell phone and my parents digging into it, the only people who would have known the plane flew this way were the pilots, and whoever they were working with or for. My intuition says that person is Malachi. That he put Thorne and the orb on that plane for a reason. That he was trying to take both the orb and Thorne somewhere—but where? and why?

"Where are the prisoners held on the ship?" I ask, changing the subject.

Malachi's eyebrows lift. "Why do you ask?"

"I'd like to see Thorne behind bars." *So that I can come up with a way to break him out.*

"I can assure you he's safely secured. There's no chance he could escape."

I cross my arms over my chest. "I'd feel better if I could see that for myself."

Malachi pauses, silently considering me. "I'm sorry, but that won't be possible. We don't allow our prisoners to have visitors."

Well, that's inconvenient.

"But don't worry. We're less than a day away from the coast of Australia. You and your parents will be offloaded from the *Dauntless* and I can promise you won't ever see Thorne again." His smile is just shy of condescending, and I half expect him to pat me on the head like I'm a small child.

I force my mouth to curve into at least a semblance of a smile. "Great. Just what I wanted to hear," I lie.

With a nod, Malachi turns and walks away.

Fantastic. I have less than twenty-four hours to figure out where they are keeping Thorne, break him out, and then get him, Cleo, and me, off this ship, all without being caught or anyone discovering what I'm hiding down my shirt.

⁓

"Mom, Dad, I swear I'm fine. I couldn't eat another bite if you paid me."

My parents are not the doting types. If anything, they're the throw-their-child-in-the-deep-end-to-teach-them-life-is-sink-or-swim types. It's not that they don't love me, I've always known they have, but their identity as power Nephs, warriors, and defenders has always come first, and they expect the same from me. So, it's extra strange to see my mom fluffing my pillow and my dad asking if he can get me a bottle of water before I go to bed. I suppose thinking their only child burned up in a fiery plane crash has shaken them a bit.

"Seriously, I'm okay. I think I just want to get to sleep," I say, only a little guilty that I'm really trying to get rid of them so I can sneak out and search for Thorne.

"What about Cleo?" my mom asks, and I glance down at the black and gold furred feline snoring on the floor.

"Cleo's fine, Mom."

She nods. "Okay, okay. We'll leave you alone."

"We'll be in Australia by mid-day tomorrow," my dad says and then checks his watch and realizes it's past midnight. "Or rather, later today. And then we thought we'd all take a few days together before you returned to the Academy."

"Like . . . a vacation?" I ask, and my dad nods.

That surprises me. When I was little, we used to take family trips with the Durands, which is why I've known

Steel and his siblings for so long. My mom and dad were close to Laurent and Eloise when they all attended Cherub Academy in France a couple hundred years ago. But we haven't taken a family trip together since I was thirteen.

"I'd like that," I say sincerely, even though if everything goes how I want it to, I won't be able to make that trip with them. I'll be returning the Starfire Orb to its origin instead.

I briefly consider telling my parents everything but decide against it. It's not that I don't trust my parents. I do. I trust them with my life, but something feels off about this whole thing. At this point I'd rather they have plausible deniability if it hits the fan.

After another round of hugs my parents leave. The smile slips off my face as soon as the door latches behind them. Reaching a hand down my top, I take the orb out and pull away some of the ripped sheet wrapped around it. The orb shines just as brightly as before and I quickly re-wrap it.

Looking around the small bare-bones cabin, there isn't much to see. There's a tiny twin-sized bed that I'm sitting on, and a desk built into the wall with a metal chair. Cleo sprawls out on the ground, taking up a lot of the floor space. I debate hiding the orb back down my shirt, but I don't want to carry it any longer. Just because I haven't been caught with it yet doesn't mean I won't. If someone finds me poking around looking for Thorne, there's a chance they might get suspicious. Last thing I want is someone patting me down and finding the round orb wedged between my boobs.

Lifting up the thin mattress, I shove the orb under it. There's literally not another place to hide it in this stripped-down cabin. I scratch Cleo's head and tell her I'll be back soon, but the bastet truly doesn't care. My mom brought her so much raw meat to eat that her stomach bulges a little as she lies paws-up on the ground.

I check left and right before stepping out into the narrow passageway. It's late, so I expect many of the angel-born aboard to be asleep, but not all of them. I keep my senses stretched as I slink forward.

As I duck through an entryway, I keep a lookout for the stairway. My assumption that they have Thorne tucked in somewhere in the bowels of the ship are based on my limited movie experience. It's a shaky theory, but it makes sense to me they'd hide him as far away from the other angel-born as possible.

Twenty minutes later I'm still searching for a way to descend into a level below the one I'm on. I've found two sets of stairs, but they only lead up.

A door catches my attention at the end of the corridor, and I make my way to it. There's nothing on the door that indicates where it leads and there's a keypad off to the side. When I yank on the handle it doesn't budge, which tells me that it's probably exactly where I need to go.

If only I had Aurora with me. She's a little lockpicking genius and could probably hack her way past the keypad in a couple minutes flat. But as it is, I'm stumped.

Voices come from behind and I only have a second to duck into a small closet next to the locked door before two angel-born round the corner. I keep the door cracked and pray they don't notice.

"Have they gotten anything out of him yet?" a male asks.

"No," replies a higher female voice. "Not a single word, let alone given up any information about the orb."

My heartbeat skips.

They're talking about Thorne and the orb.

I hold my breath, trying to catch every syllable that drops from their lips.

One of them heaves a sigh. "I hope they get something out of him or they're going to have us dredging the whole ocean for that orb. Have you been able to get out of Malachi what's in room thirteen yet?" the male angel-born asks.

I knew Malachi was part of this. Shady old dude.

"He's tight-lipped about it. As far as I can tell, only the Elders have access to that room."

"We could always—"

"Don't even think it, Shane. It'll be our heads if anyone finds out."

"The mystery is killing me," Shane says with a chuckle. "Just a little peek. I even know the code. Ninety-eight forty-three."

"I didn't hear that."

There's a beeping followed by the clank of a lock disengaging, and then the telltale whoosh of a heavy metal door being yanked open.

The pair keep chatting as they walk through, and even though I can't be sure they've passed the threshold, this is my chance. I shove out of the closet, snatching the door an inch before it clicks shut, and then freeze waiting to see if the angel-born notice the door didn't latch behind them.

Seconds tick by and their voices fade, and I can finally take a full breath. I carefully open the door wide enough for me to slip through, and then soundlessly let it close behind me.

Bingo.

On the other side of the door is a stairway that leads down. There's a round red button to the left of the door on this side. I hope it's there so you only have to push it to exit.

I'll be in trouble if I need a keycard or code to get out of here. I had an excuse rehearsed in case anyone caught me poking around one of the other decks, but this area is restricted, so there's not an excuse good enough to hold up if I get caught.

I creep down the steps and three deck levels before the stairwell opens to a passageway with white walls and blue-tinted overhead lights that flicker every so often. It gives off major horror-movie vibes.

Thorne, you owe me big time for this.

Numbered doors line the right and left sides of the corridor. I pull open the first one and peek inside, but it's just an empty room about the size of my cabin, with no windows. I go to the next room and the next and the next, zigzagging across the corridor following the numbers on the doors, and find more of the same. Every time I check a new room it's like I'm playing Russian Roulette. At any time I might open a door and come face to face with an angel-born.

I get to a door with a keypad lock and glance up to the number plaque fastened on it. Thirteen.

Have you been able to get out of Malachi what's in room thir-teen yet?

This is the room the angel-born were talking about. They can't have been talking about Thorne since they know about him already and whatever is behind this door is a mystery to them, but I'm super curious to know what else Malachi is hiding down here. I lift my hand to the keypad, remembering the code the male angel-born rattled off.

Ninety-eight forty-three.

I shake my head. It's not Thorne, so it's not a priority.

I force myself to move on to the next door but opening

and peeking into another ten rooms doesn't reveal much. Why in the world are there so many empty rooms down here? What's the point?

I'm up to room twenty-four and so used to seeing the same thing, an empty windowless room, I peek my head in and then move on to the next room before registering this one isn't like the others.

Gasping, I twist back to room twenty-four and slide into it. Against the far wall is a long desk with several computer monitors and keyboards, and then a row of screens above, which show activity all over the *Dauntless*.

"Shoot, they have the whole ship under surveillance," I whisper to myself.

Moving closer, I tap the spacebar on one of the keyboards and the monitor comes to life.

"I need him talking," a muffled voice says on the other side of the door.

Malachi.

Turning away from the screens and monitors, I scurry to the door, pressing my ear against it and crossing my fingers no one comes inside.

"He's resilient," says a deep female voice. I don't recognize this one, but I wonder if it's Zara.

"Not unexpected," says a new male voice. *Draven perhaps?* "His sadistic mother no doubt trained him to withstand torture."

Torture?

I clench my fists so tight that my nails pierce my skin and sticky warmth starts to coat my palms.

It was what I feared, but hearing they tried to torture information out of Thorne causes rage like I've never felt before to detonate in my chest.

Squeezing my eyes shut, I clamp my teeth together and breathe through my nose, knowing I'm hanging on by a very thin thread. The Elders pass by my room and move down the passageway in the direction of the stairs, all the while discussing how to get Thorne to talk. Each of their suggestions are more vile than the last, and when their voices finally fade, I'm relieved.

I count to ten before forcing my hands to unclench. Droplets of blood drip to the ground from the tips of my fingers, making tiny puddles of red by my feet.

Wiping my hands against my pants, I rub off as much of the blood as I can, and by the time I'm done the crescent-shaped wounds aren't bleeding anymore.

Score one for advanced healing abilities.

Slipping from the room, I move from room to room with renewed vigor. When I reach room number thirty-two I hear voices on the other side—the male and female angel-born who unknowingly let me into this secret corridor. I'm about to move on, skipping the room so I don't have a confrontation, when a familiar timbre stops me.

"You're wasting your time," Thorne says, and my breath catches.

Relief floods my system, making my fingers and toes tingle.

"Ah, he speaks," says the male angel-born, Shane, but Thorne doesn't respond. "You know, if you don't start talking, the Elders will move on to the girl," Shane finally says, frustration clear in his tone.

The girl . . . that must be me.

There's a pause and then Thorne says, "Why would I care?"

Ouch.

"Maybe you don't," Shane says, "but they're starting to speculate that she might not have been as unwilling of a captive as they first believed."

Silence falls over the room again.

"Angel-born aren't trained to withstand torture like you've obviously been. They're beginning to see her as an easier mark to break than you are," the female angel-born adds.

A loud clang startles me and then Thorne growls, "If you touch one hair on her head, I'll make you eat your own entrails before I take you apart piece by piece."

Graphic. But oddly romantic.

But also, exceedingly stupid. He just revealed that I'm important to him, which only makes me look guilty. I'll forgive him though. No one has ever threatened to make someone eat their own innards on my behalf. I'm a little touched—touched and a tad demented because his gruesome threats make my heartbeat skip and bring a smile to my face.

Shane laughs. "I guess that answers that question. Thanks for the confirmation. Alessandra, go let Malachi know we definitely need to question the girl."

Thorne goes ballistic and starts hurling insults at the two in English and Enochian and the clanging from before gets louder and repetitive.

"Is he going to be able to break out of there?" Alessandra asks, sounding concerned.

"Naw. We're safe. Those bars would hold back a charging bull. Go on ahead, I'll hold things down here. If he gets too feisty, I'll give him another zap."

Not if I can help it, you prick.

Concentrating, I stoke my power, the electric streaks

from the tips of my fingers down to my toes. I would have preferred to sneak in and get Thorne out of here without any witnesses, but that's not an option anymore. I can't have that chick telling anyone about Thorne's reaction to the mention of hurting me, at least not until I can get us off this ship and away from the Council members on board.

Forgoing subtlety, I kick the door open, taking aim at the first angel-born I lay eyes on. My bolt of power slams into her chest and she goes flying, smacking into the wall behind her and slumping to the ground, either out cold or dead, I'm not sure which.

Thorne shouts a warning and I duck just as a blade slides over my head. That pisses me off and I shoot another bolt of power at the remaining angel-born. He tries to dodge my attack, but there's just not enough room in the space for him to go far, so rather than hitting him in the chest, my stream of electricity strikes him in the shoulder. The force is strong enough to spin him around but not to take him down.

I don't give the guy time to recover. Just as he's turning to face me, I grab his head, shoving it down and bringing my leg up to knee him in the face. His nose shatters and blood gushes from it. I deliver a quick but powerful jab to the temple and he's out, falling to the ground next to his downed companion.

I pant as I stand over the bodies of both angel-born. There's a steady rise and fall to each of their chests, telling me that they're still alive.

That's good . . . I guess.

"Impressive," drawls Thorne.

When I spin to face him, he's leaning against the bars of a small cell with his mouth twisted into a half-cocked smirk.

There's a bruise high on one cheek, but no other visible injuries.

Something inside me unclenches.

"I told you to forget about me," he says with a head tilt, a spark of curiosity in his eyes.

"Good thing I didn't. You just put a target on my back."

"I had it covered."

I roll my eyes. "Sure ya did." I look pointedly at the bars he's trapped behind.

His face softens. "I never would have let anyone lay a finger on you."

"Oh yeah? And how would you have stopped them?"

Lifting his hand, Thorne beckons me closer with a finger. I drift toward him as if being pulled on a string. When I'm close enough, he reaches through the bars and takes hold of my hand, lifting it to his mouth and turning it over. He presses a soft kiss to my wrist, his eyes never leaving mine. It's just an innocent kiss, but it makes it feel like the temperature in the room went up fifty degrees.

What this man can do with his lips is unbelievable.

With my mind firmly in the gutter, he moves my hand to the bar in front of him, smoothing it over one spot in particular. It takes me a moment to catch on, but then I feel it.

The hairline fracture in the metal rod.

"A couple more hits and I would have been out," he says. "I just needed the proper motivation to bust out of my jail."

There's a moan behind me and both of us swivel toward the angel-born on the floor.

"The controls to the cell are back there," Thorne says, gesturing to a panel on the far wall.

I rush over to the controls and find the release to the

cell. The door swings open and Thorne strolls out, a ball of angel-fire hovering above his hand.

"Thorne, don't," I warn, and he blinks at me.

"Whyever not? When someone finds them, they're going to tell them exactly what happened."

"Malachi and the others aren't stupid." *Unfortunately.* "They're going to figure out what happened anyway. There's no need to kill them."

"I assure you it won't take long," he says.

"That's not what I was worried about. Let's just lock them in the cell. I plan to be off this ship before anyone finds them."

Thorne frowns but doesn't argue with me. I find two pairs of shackles on the wall as he drags the unconscious angel-born into his cell. We bind them to one of the bars to keep them from getting out, and then lock the cage with them in it.

Rushing to the control panel, Thorne pushes some buttons and a compartment opens in the wall to reveal his collapsed metal wing. Snatching it, he quickly secures the straps around his chest and over his shoulder.

Time to go.

I start toward the door, but he grabs my hand and tugs me against his chest. He swipes a thumb over my cheek and then slips his hand behind my neck, tilting my head back.

"Thank you for ignoring me when I told you not to come for me."

Thorne's close enough that his breath feathers against my mouth. My throat is suddenly dry, and I slip my tongue out to wet my bottom lip.

Thorne's gaze drops to my mouth, and he lets out a frustrated groan. "Not enough time," he mumbles.

"Maybe we have a little bit of time," I say, my words breathy as I tip my head back even farther, lining up our mouths.

"Not for what I plan to do to you," he says, then his arms disappear from me.

My body is pulsating as he skirts me and heads toward the door, stopping to glance back before pushing it open.

"Come on. We gotta get out of here before they find these two," he says, jerking his chin toward the unconscious angel-born.

Huffing a breath, I nod. No turning back now.

19

"This passageway is disturbing," Thorne whispers.

"Agreed. I keep imagining a wave of blood coming at us." I shiver. Not much frightens me, but a wave of blood definitely would.

We creep back down the passageway, the idea being to leave the same way I came. "Hold up," I say to Thorne when we reach the room with the screens and monitors. "I'm going to call for reinforcements," I explain when he gives a quizzical stare.

Thorne's brow slams down and he shakes his head. "I don't want any other angel-born involved."

I get where he's coming from. My friends aren't exactly Thorne's biggest fans, but I have a strong feeling we're going to need their help. "Trust me, okay?"

Thorne presses his lips together, looking more concerned than convinced, but nods.

We slip into the room and Thorne keeps the door cracked to act as a lookout as I rush to the computer.

"I have no idea how they got this equipment on a spirit world warship, but I'm glad it's here," I say, searching for a way to get a message to Emberly.

"There are spirit world stones that allow you to bring materials from the mortal world straight into the spirit world," Thorne answers even though my question was rhetorical.

Never heard of that before, but I add it to the list of things the Elders are hiding from the general angel-born population.

"Yes," I hiss when I figure out how to work the angel-borns' internet communications system. Sterling would be proud of me right now. With my heart in my throat, I type out a hurried note to Steel, while I silently thank Greyson for insisting we all learn how to send each other coded messages and cursing myself for not paying better attention when he tried to teach it to me. I honestly never thought I'd have a reason to use it, but now that I know how epically shady Malachi and some of the other Council Elders are, I'm not taking any chances that their personal correspondences aren't monitored.

After I finish what I hope is seen as a nonsensical email about animals and geometric shapes to anyone who reads it besides one of my friends, I hit send and send up a prayer that Steel gets this quickly. I wasn't able to tell him exactly where to meet up with us since I don't have those details hammered out yet, but I basically told him to get his butt to Australia, STAT. I'll have to reach out to him again once we get to land and find a place to hunker down, but with any luck my message will be enough to get him and Emberly on a plane.

"Done," I announce, then we're back out the door and rushing down the corridor.

We're close to the stairs that lead to the upper decks when Thorne stops.

"What?" I ask, looking back at him frozen in the middle of the passageway.

He tips his head to the side, his eyes slightly unfocused. "There's something here," he says. "Something . . . angelic."

"Umm, both of us are part angel."

Thorne shakes his head. "Technically, we're part Fallen, but this energy is pure." He looks at me. "Can't you feel it?"

"No, I really can't." But when I stop to think about it, it does feel a little like something is running over my skin, but I never would have noticed it if he hadn't pointed it out.

Thorne shrugs. "Never mind, we should get going."

"No, wait," I say, realizing we are standing in front of room thirteen. "There's something important in there. I heard the angel-born talking about it, and I know the code. Let's take a look."

Before Thorne can weigh in, I punch the code into the keypad and with a beep it pops open. He grabs my arm before I go into the room.

"Should we be doing this?" he asks.

"Probably not," I admit. "But I've got to know what's in here. Maybe it's something we can use to escape, or leverage against Malachi and the others later."

"Okay, but let's make it fast. We're pushing our luck as it is."

I nod. Thorne lets go of me, and we enter the room.

The room holds a bunch of machinery I don't recognize but reminds me of medical equipment. The corner of the space is draped with curtains from ceiling to floor like something you'd see in a human hospital. The machines and contraptions around us are interesting, but I'm instantly drawn to whatever is behind those curtains.

Thorne stays close as we walk over to the curtained-off area. Grabbing the off-white fabric, I pull it to the side, gasping when my gaze lands on the large angel strapped to the table in front of me.

Thorne mutters in Enochian.

The angel's eyes are closed, but his chest rises and falls steadily. His three sets of gold wings are folded under his oversized body, and no less than six thick straps secure him to a flat table.

"That's Camiel, Emberly's father," I say. "Emberly thinks he's dead. We all did."

Thorne steps around me, moving closer to Camiel to inspect a catheter that's inserted right below the crook of the angel's arm, and the suction cups attached to his temples.

"He doesn't look good," I say. "What's he doing here?"

The last time I saw Camiel, he was larger than life. The six-winged seraph Angel of War literally glowed with heavenly power and could cut through a Fallen with ease. In contrast, the being laid out before us is hollow-cheeked and dull-skinned. His once-shining golden locks hang in clumps, and his wings look to be missing at least half their feathers.

It has been three months since Camiel was spotted, and in that time his body has atrophied to such an extent it would be easy to mistake his identity. I only recognize him as he's the only angel I've ever met in real life, so he made an impression.

Thorne glances at me. "I think the question is less what's he doing here, and rather what are they doing to him?"

"Well, they aren't going to be able to do it to him anymore. We need to take him with us."

"You can't be serious," Thorne says, his eyes wide with disbelief and a touch of fear.

I point to Camiel. "That's Emberly's father. We can't just leave him here. It looks like they are experimenting on him or something."

Thorne shoves a hand through his white-blond hair and then rubs the back of his neck. "What that is, is an angel. He's going to smite me the first chance he gets."

"I won't let him."

Thorne lets out a snort of disbelief.

"Besides, Camiel is different," I go on. "I've met him. I just need to explain to him that you're sorry for what you did and I'm sure we'll be all good."

Thorne shoots me a look. "You're going to explain that I'm sorry and you expect the Angel of War is just going to accept that and move on?"

"Yeah," I say with a shrug. *No biggie.*

Thorne swipes a hand down his face and shakes his head. "You're going to be the death of me."

"Hey," I say, somewhat offended.

"Fine," he says. "Let's figure out how to wake him up. There's no way we'll be able to carry him out of here. He's huge."

After pulling the needle from Camiel's arm and removing the suction cups, we unstrap him. He remains unconscious the whole time. I try waking him with some light pats to the face and repeatedly saying his name, but that doesn't work.

Dude is out cold.

"What do we do if we can't wake him?" Thorne was right, we can't carry him.

"Stand back," Thorne says, and walks toward Camiel gripping a giant hypodermic needle full of who-knows-what. "You don't want to be within swinging range when this stuff kicks in."

"What is it?" I ask as I take a few steps back.

"Adrenaline. I think."

"You think?" I squeak just as he plunges the needle right into Camiel's chest. Thorne depresses the plunger, emptying the contents into Camiel's system.

And then . . . nothing happens.

Thorne looks at me and shrugs as if to say, "I'm out of ideas."

Camiel's eyes fly open, and he jackknifes, his upper body and legs coming off the table below him with a roar.

Thorne is in front of me in an instant.

How cute. The boy thinks he's going to protect me.

Patting his arm, I sidestep him, putting my body in front of his. If anyone is protecting anyone in this scenario, it's me protecting him.

I hear the whoosh of Thorne releasing his wings and then the clicking of his metal feathers rubbing against one another.

Camiel's brow is furrowed, heavy with confusion, until his golden gaze settles on us and his eyes start to glow.

Yikes. Time to defuse this situation before he shoots us with angel eye-laser beams, if that's even a thing.

"Whoa there. I'm Nova. We met in London. We fought together, remember?" Putting my hands up, I take a step forward. Thorne tries to pull me back, but I shake him off.

The hard look on Camiel's face says that he doesn't remember me. He surges to his feet, his movements aggressive and making me nervous for the first time.

"I'm friends with your daughter," I quickly spit out, hoping he doesn't remember I insinuated that he was a deadbeat dad the first time we met.

Camiel stops short. "Emberly?"

"Yeah, that's right. Emberly. I met your daughter at Seraph Academy in Colorado. We're like besties. She would be really upset if you killed me." Pretty sure she would be upset if her father fried me, but the besties part is a bit of a stretch.

Camiel takes a shaky breath and then stumbles, catching himself on the gurney he was strapped to before.

"I remember you now," he says, but then his gaze tracks over my shoulder and hardens. "And I remember him as well. He kidnapped my daughter and started the Fallen War."

"Er, right. I agree that Thorne was super bad, but what you don't know is that he helped free Emberly, who was possessed by his mother, and then used his powers to stop the spread of the Merge Zone. He's totally on 'team good guy' now." *Kinda.* "I promise we can explain everything later, but we gotta move. Do you know where you are?"

Camiel shakes his head. "I wasn't conscious the whole time."

"We're on an angel-born warship in the spirit world. I don't know what's been going on down here," I gesture to the table he was strapped to, "but it doesn't look consensual to me. I'm assuming you want to get off this ship?"

Camiel nods.

"Then follow our lead. You don't look like you're in any

shape to take out a boatful of angel-born, so we're going to have to sneak off the *Dauntless*."

Camiel growls. "If I was at full strength, I would find that cherub Elder and wipe him off the face of the Earth."

His eyes glow again, and it's on the tip of my tongue to ask what Malachi did to him, but we truly are out of time.

"When the time comes, I'll help you," Thorne says, startling me. "Nova, lead the way."

I nod, and we only get a few steps when Camiel freezes, closing his eyes and scrunching his face in concentration.

What is it now? Every second that passes, the urgency to flee grows stronger. My skin practically itches with the desire to get going, knowing we're operating on borrowed time.

"I sense an orb somewhere on this ship," Camiel finally says.

"Yeah. It is. I stored it back in my cabin. We'll swing by and get it and Cleo on the way out," I say.

"Do the Nephilim Elders know it's on board?"

I shake my head. "Not yet."

"Good. Grab that," Camiel orders, pointing at a small box the size of my fist on a shelf. "We can conceal the orb's energy in that. We've got to get it off the ship and away from your Elders."

Good to hear Camiel's on the same page as we are.

As Thorne palms the box, I take a minute to explain the layout of the hallway and the set of stairs we need to ascend to Camiel. The plan is to return to my cabin and get Cleo and the orb, and then steal one of the ship's lifeboats. Flying would be easier, but there's no way to get Cleo off the ship that way. She's too big and would be too awkward for one of us to carry, so the lifeboats are our only option.

Thorne dematerializes his wings and exits the room. We find the creepy horror movie corridor still empty. It is a true miracle that we make it back to the passageway in front of my cabin without getting caught. There were two close calls, and I experience a rush of sweet relief when I twist the handle to my cabin and shove the door open.

I rush through the door, Thorne and Camiel right behind me.

And come face-to-face with my parents.

Oh, angel-fire.

My father is holding the orb that I apparently failed to hide well enough, and my mom is crouched over Cleo, her hand frozen mid-pet. It takes them a half-second to assess the situation. My dad's gaze lasers in on Thorne and he pulls a sai from a sheath on his back. My mother rises to her feet, her eyes wide with shock as she looks back and forth between me, Thorne, and Camiel.

"What is going on here?" my father asks, and I'm just glad that he didn't immediately attack, although the room size might have something to do with that. As it is, the five of us plus Cleo barely fit.

Cleo pops to her feet and pads over to me, nudging my hand with her head.

"Camiel?" my mother asks, taking in the towering, weakened form of the Angel of War. "We thought you died."

"Because that's what your Elder wanted you to believe," he says, and my mom gasps.

I know my mom well enough to recognize that her reaction is genuine. She has no idea what Malachi and the others have been up to—not that I suspected either of my parents had anything to do with Camiel's imprisonment.

"Nova, get behind me," my father says, slipping the orb

into a pouch on his belt to free his hand so he can grab the second sai. His gaze never leaves Thorne.

"We truly don't have time for this," Thorne says and then sighs like he's bored, but I think it's just an act.

"Don't worry, it won't take long for me to plant my blade in your brain," my dad says, changing his grip on his weapon and then striking out at Thorne.

I move without thinking, throwing a hand out to stop my father from impaling Thorne, and the pointed tip of my father's sai sinks straight through my palm.

My father's face goes white, and I drop a cuss word that I normally would never utter in front of my mom.

"Nova, your hand," my mom says, trying to reach for me.

Thorne tries to jump my father, but I block him with my body, and Cleo lets out a low rumble.

"Everybody chill out!" I yell, holding up my hand with the sai still embedded in it. "And someone please shut the cabin door before an angel-born strolls by and sees us."

The door clicks shut. Thorne grabs my hand, yanks out the weapon, and I release another colorful swear. Grabbing a sheet, he rips off a strip of fabric and starts wrapping it around my hand, his face stormy as he works.

When I glance over at my parents, they're watching Thorne bandage my hand with wide eyes.

"I'm so sorry, baby," my father says, regret shining from his gaze.

"It's okay, Dad. But how about we all calm down and talk for a minute."

It takes a solid thirty minutes—thirty minutes we don't really have—for Camiel and me to bring the whole group up to speed. I tell my parents everything about what went down from the moment I stepped on that doomed plane to when I reunited with them on the *Dauntless*. Well, almost everything. They don't need to know about the kissing, but they *do* need to know how Thorne repeatedly saved my life, and after watching him tend to my hand I think they might actually believe me. I also tell them how we met Cleo and how exposure to the orb sped up my metamorphosis. I kinda wish I could show them my new wings, but there isn't enough room in the cabin.

After I rush through a recap of the last couple of weeks, Camiel explains how he hadn't died but had been badly injured stopping the bomb from exploding in downtown London, how Malachi, Zara, and Draven found him and used his weakened condition to imprison him. Goose bumps erupt all over my arms and legs when he talks about the experiments they conducted on him, proving just how corrupted Malachi and the others have become.

Apparently, unsatisfied with their own abilities, some of the Elders believe they can extract an angel's power and use it for themselves, so they subjected Camiel to a bevy of painful tests and experiments that slowed down his natural healing abilities. They also restricted his food and water intake to keep him purposefully weak, knowing that if he ever got to full strength he'd rip them apart.

It's not clear which Elders are part of the cover-up outside of Malachi, Zara, and Draven, but according to Camiel they were going to start experimenting with the orb to see if they could use it to extract his powers—solving the mystery of why the orb was being transferred.

We still don't know for sure what they'd planned to do with Thorne, but the running theory is that they were going to try to steal his power as well.

When Thorne asks if it's possible to use the orb to steal

an angel or angel-borns' powers, Camiel evades the question, and I remember back to London when Camiel said that angels weren't permitted to touch the orbs. I'm instantly suspicious that's the reason why, which becomes just another reason to keep the orb away from Malachi and the others. The Elders are powerful enough.

Once Camiel finishes, we move on to discussing how to get off the *Dauntless* without tipping off the angel-born on board. We are only a few hours off the Australian coast. It's good that we won't have too far to travel before reaching land, but the sun will be up in under an hour, and if we don't leave before then, it will be even harder to escape unnoticed.

"Leave Cleo with us," my mom says, surprising me. "The lifeboats have trackers on them. They'll find you before you reach shore. You can escape easier if you fly low over the water, and you can't take her with you that way."

I'm already shaking my head. "No, you need to come with us. We all leave together."

My parents exchange a look, and I'm sure there's some silent communication happening between them. After a long pause, my dad gives a curt nod and then the both of them turn to me.

"We need to stay here and create a diversion so that the angel-born on board don't notice you leaving," my mom says. "Cleo can help immensely with that task. With any luck, you'll be long gone before they realize you've fled."

"Mom. Dad," I say, ready to argue, but my father cuts me off.

"Your mother and I can take care of ourselves," he says. "We've been doing it for a long time."

"But Malachi is willing to torture people to get the information he wants. What's to stop him from doing that to you?"

"We don't intend on letting him think we know anything. We can create a distraction, and then thirty minutes later report you're missing to Malachi, taking the suspicion that we know where you went off of us."

"That's assuming no one discovers I'm gone before that and reports it," Thorne says.

My parents share another meaningful look and then my dad says, "I'll make sure no one gets to him before that."

This plan makes me anxious, but I have a lot of faith in my parents. If anyone can pull this off, it's them.

I glance down at Cleo. "I can't leave her here, though. She's not on her island anymore because of me. I can't just abandon her."

My mom lays a hand on my arm. "You won't be abandoning her. Your father and I will make sure no harm comes to Cleo. We'll protect her." My mother pets Cleo's head, obviously having quickly bonded with the large cat.

My heart aches at the thought of leaving Cleo behind, but my mother is right. Escaping with her will decrease our chances of success. We can fly faster than the *Dauntless* can sail, but in a lifeboat, the larger ship has as better chance of catching up to us when they discover we're missing.

Cleo is surprisingly calm in the midst of all the angelic beings crowded around her. She blinks back at me as I stare down at her, almost like she understands what we're saying and is just waiting for me to make up my mind.

"I don't even know if she'll stay with you," I confess. "The last time I tried to leave her behind she jumped in the water to follow me."

"Tell her the plan," Camiel says. He's seated on the bed to

the left of Cleo, having needed to get off his feet a solid twenty minutes ago. It's obvious that he's weak, and even more obvious that he hates that he is, but he wisely decided to save his energy while he could. "Bastets are highly intelligent. If she's bonded with you, like it seems she has, she'll be able to understand."

I shoot him a look, finding that hard to believe.

"She's a spirit world creature," he goes on to explain. "Angels and bastets used to have a very special relationship. We fought side-by-side against our enemies until the Fallen killed most of them off. Cleo here is probably one of the last of her kind in existence."

Wow. Okay. It's worth a try.

Crouching, I get eye level with Cleo. "Is that true? Can you understand me, girl?"

Cleo tilts her head, and I'm not sure if that's supposed to mean anything.

"Are you going to be okay if I leave you here with my parents until we can all meet up again?"

Cleo lets out a soft trill and then butts her head up against mine. Closing my eyes with my forehead pressed up against her soft furry brow, I take a deep breath, feeling in my soul that Cleo does understand and is trying to offer me comfort.

I stand, looking between Cleo and my parents. "Take good care of each other. You're all very important to me."

I have difficultly speaking around the knot in my throat.

My mother and father lift their arms, placing a hand on my shoulders and each other's, and I follow their lead. Cleo sits in the middle of our little triangle. When we separate, we're all business again. My family loves deeply, but we're also warriors through and through, and know when we need to push emotions aside to get a job done.

"Take this," my father says as he unstraps the small pouch he put the Starfire Orb into from his belt and hands it to me. He turns to Camiel to ask some more details about the Elders plans, wanting to find out as much as he can about which ones might still be uncorrupted.

"You okay carrying the orb?" Thorne asks as he hands me the small box that Camiel said would conceal its power.

Pulling the orb from the pouch, I place it inside the box and then back in the pouch, securing it to my belt.

"Pfft. I'm just glad I don't have to put it in my boob pocket anymore."

Thorne arches an eyebrow. "Your boob pocket?"

"Don't ask," I chuckle.

"How's your hand?" he asks.

I open and close my fist a couple of times. There's only a twinge of pain. "I'm good. It will probably heal over in a few hours."

He takes my hand between his own and gently flips it over, checking for blood leakage, but there is none. "I'm so sorry," he says, looking into my eyes.

"You don't have to apologize," I say.

"I do. If I hadn't antagonized your father, he wouldn't have struck out."

"Um, pretty sure my dad would have taken a shot at you no matter what."

He winces and rubs the back of his neck. "I don't really have any experience with fathers."

I start to laugh at that but catch my mom eyeing the two of us with a frown.

Clearing my throat, I look away from Thorne, one

hundred percent certain that if my father knew the full truth of how close Thorne and I had become on that island, he'd throw a punch at the seraph angel-born.

My parents give us instructions on how to get to a weathertight door that will allow us to leave from an opening below the upper deck, and on the other side of the ship from where they plan to create a diversion. Finding my mom's suspicious gaze on me more than once, I do my best to keep my attention focused on anything but Thorne.

My parents prepare to leave first. They are supposed to make sure the passageway is clear for us. If they don't come back in five minutes, that means the coast is clear and we should head straight for the exit on the deck above us.

My father kisses me on the forehead, and Cleo licks my hand. My mother lays a hand on my cheek and says, "Be careful."

"Aren't I always?"

Her gaze flicks over my shoulder. I don't need to turn around to know she just glanced at Thorne. "For your sake, I hope so," she says, and gives me as close to a disapproving look as I've ever seen from her. My stomach sours. I'm not used to seeing disappointment on my mother's face.

I open my mouth to reassure her that of course I'm being cautious, but when it comes to Thorne, I'm starting to think that maybe I haven't been careful at all.

20

Thorne, Camiel, and I make it to the exterior door without issue, and the minute we hear Cleo's roars followed by panicked shouts we take flight. I have to force myself to ignore Cleo as we speed away from the *Dauntless*, knowing that we planned for this. My parents will take care of her and in turn she'll protect them.

The sky is just starting to brighten as we fly low over the gentle waves. If I stretch my arms toward the ocean below, my fingertips will skim the water, but I'm doing my best to make sure none of my body parts touch it. We don't want to kick up any spray that might draw attention to us as we flee, but we also can't fly more than fifteen feet above sea level because then the angel-born could pick us up on radar.

It's difficult though to fly at a fixed altitude. Whenever I flap my wings I rise but then drop low again when I start gliding.

Next to me, Camiel appears to be struggling as well, but not from lack of skill like me; he's just exhausted. His face is even more drawn and pale than when we freed him, and he wobbles frequently. It's a good thing he has so many wings. He's missing so many golden feathers that if he didn't have those extra sets, I'm not sure he'd be able to keep himself airborne.

Only Thorne, who's flying on my other side, is steady. He keeps shooting me worried glances every time I teeter in the air. I want to snap at him to stop worrying about me, but I don't dare talk until we're farther away from the *Dauntless*. I have to settle for shooting him a couple of icy glares.

We've been flying for almost an hour when Camiel tips to the side, his right wings dragging through the water. He tries to flap to gain altitude, but he only lifts a couple of feet and then tilts in the other direction, weaving and wobbling in the air like a baby bird using its wings for the first time.

I glance at Thorne as Camiel continues to struggle.

Camiel flies so low his feet drag in the water. Flying higher would be less strenuous, we could coast for longer periods of time, but with the radar that's not an option. Camiel grits his teeth as he forces his wings to keep flapping, but it's only a matter of time before his body gives out on him.

I don't know what to do.

A gust of wind blows my hair over my eyes as Thorne swoops over me and levels off right over Camiel. He reaches between the angel's first and second set of wings and hooks him under his armpits, securing Camiel's back to his front and taking his full weight.

"What are you doing?" Camiel says angrily, trying to twist out of Thorne's grasp. The pair bob in the air.

"You're not going to make it," Thorne says through gritted teeth. "I'm not so happy about this arrangement either, but there's no other way to get you to shore. Once you crash into the waves, we're not getting you out of the ocean."

"I can fly on my own," Camiel argues, but we all know Thorne is right.

"You can take a swing at me for this when we reach land, but until then stop fighting and making this harder on both of us."

Camiel's face twists into a disgruntled expression, but he stops trying to get free. Strain shows on Thorne's face as he flies with the bulky eight-foot angel, but when he catches me staring he gives me a lopsided grin and a wink. I chuckle. The picture of Thorne hauling Camiel is going to stay with me for a long time, but when Camiel shoots me a side-eyed glare I cover the laugh by clearing my throat.

"Don't worry, big guy," I say. "This stays between the three of us."

If anyone had told me a month ago that I'd be fleeing angel-born Elders with Thorne and Camiel, I'd have told them they were delusional.

Shaking his head, Camiel sighs and rolls his eyes.

Camiel is the almighty Angel of War, so I can't imagine he's used to having to rely on others like this. It must burn even more that it's Thorne he's forced to accept help from.

Refocusing on the horizon, I squint against the brightness from the water below to try to spot land. We are flying faster than the *Dauntless* is capable of traveling, so we should reach the shore soon.

Another twenty minutes pass and the toll from carrying Camiel's extra weight starts to show on Thorne. Sweat plasters his hair to his forehead and he puffs out ragged breaths.

I open my mouth to ask if I can help somehow when Camiel speaks up, "Shoreline up ahead."

Although Thorne tries to hide it, I catch the look of relief that flashes over his face.

"Let go, Thorne," Camiel commands. "I can fly the rest of the way."

The pair disengage smoothly. Thorne flies over me to flank my other side, trailing his fingers over my feathers as he does, making me shiver. Flushing, I shoot him a look of reprimand that has zero heat in it.

After a few minutes we touchdown on a magenta beach. Small houses set back from the water dot the landscape.

"We need to find a place to lie low and rest. Then I can figure out a way to reach out to Steel again and let him know where we are." I scan the beach, not having really any idea where we are except that it's somewhere on Australia's west coast.

"We should phase into the mortal world," Thorne says. "The angel-born looking for us won't think to search there first."

Camiel tenses up. Angels are practically forbidden from entering the mortal world. In London he was even hesitant to enter the mortal realm to protect his own daughter, although he did in the end.

"Let's wait until we have a little more cover before phasing," I suggest. "We don't want any humans spotting us."

Thorne and Camiel both agree, and we trudge up the beach toward the houses. We luck out and the third house we find appears to be a vacated vacation rental. The furniture is covered with sheets, and there are no humans in sight. Thorne breaks the lock, and once we're safely inside the cottage we all phase out of the spirit and into the mortal world.

It's been over two weeks since I've been in the mortal world and the first few moments are a shock. I'd gotten used to the vibrant colors of the spirit world, so everything looks dull in comparison. It doesn't help that the house we've broken into is painted in shades of gray and lacking any pops of color, but even the blue sky through the windows looks muted.

"It's part of the reason I prefer the spirit world," Thorne says, reading my face correctly. "The mortal realm is so boring and bland. Why would anyone choose to live here if they could live in the other world?"

"Tell that to the Fallen and Forsaken," I say with an arched brow.

Thorne shrugs. "That has more to do with food source than anything else. And it chafes them to not have the freedom to pop back and forth between the realms."

Camiel walks over to a couch and sits heavily upon it without even bothering to remove the sheet covering it. His lids droop low over his eyes and his head lulls forward. His once-brilliant wings hang limply from his back and his shoulders are hunched. It's truly horrific to think what they might have done to the mighty angel to make him this weak.

Emberly is going to go biblically ballistic on Malachi and the others when she sees what they've done to her father.

I start toward Camiel but stop when a white film appears over his eyes, and he goes into a trance-like state. I've seen him do this once before, so I know he's reaching out to another angel. I'd somehow forgotten he could communicate telepathically.

I chew on my bottom lip as I wait for Camiel to come back to himself. Camiel's the commander of *all* the angel armies, and although a horde of angels would be great for our Malachi problems, it would probably be dangerous for Thorne. Not all angels are as accepting of angel-born as Camiel, and on top of that they must be aware of the role Thorne played in the invasion of London and subsequently the creation of the Merge Zone. If we tripped across an angel right now, they'd be likely to smite him first and ask questions later.

Thorne watches Camiel with a pinched brow, and I can't help but wonder if he's thinking the same things as I am.

Letting out a frustrated grunt, Camiel shakes his head as his eyes clear.

"Is the cavalry coming?" I ask, trying to keep my tone light and my body language loose. If angels are on their way, we're just going to have to adjust our plans.

"No," Camiel snarls. "My weakened state has prevented me from being able to communicate to my brethren since I regained consciousness after the explosion. I was hoping I'd be able to do so by now, but I'm still not strong enough."

I'm a bit conflicted about that, but Thorne looks visibly relieved.

"How about we all get some rest?" I suggest as I eye Camiel. "There's no way Steel and the others are in Australia yet, so we have the time to catch up on sleep." *Sleep.* When was the last time I did that? Two, three days ago? "I'll go out and buy a burner phone in a few hours and leave him a coded message with a place we can all meet up."

"I'll go with you," Thorne says immediately, but I shake my head.

"It's best if I run out and do it alone."

"No," he says, and crosses his arms over his chest.

Is that supposed to be intimidating?

"It's cute you think you have a say."

"I'm not letting you go out there alone."

Oh no he didn't.

Squaring off with him, I cross my arms, matching his pose. "You're right, you're not *letting* me do anything, because I'm not asking for permission."

Thorne's nose flares and his eyes narrow. It's time to nip this thing in the bud. He needs to know he doesn't get to tell me what to do.

"Maybe you shouldn't leave alone," Camiel says, and I shift my glare to him.

Oh, they want to gang up on me now, do they?

"Let's be honest, boys. Out of the three of us, who do you think will do the best blending into the mortal world?" When it looks like they might argue, I point a finger first at Camiel and say, "You have three wings and have probably spent a total of what, a couple of days out of your intensely long existence in the mortal world? And you," I continue, pointing at Thorne, "grew up among Fallen and Forsaken in the spirit world and haven't ventured into the mortal world much more than he has.

"Also, you might not know this, but your picture has been plastered all over the globe as public enemy number one for what happened in London, so if you're spotted here there's a decent chance someone might report seeing you to the local authorities. If that happens, it's only a matter of time before the angel-born catch wind of it and are crawling all over the place looking for us. I'm not arguing this point with either of you anymore. I'm the most familiar with the mortal world and the least likely to be recognized as a supernatural being. I'm going, *alone*, and that's final."

I glance at Camiel, expecting him to argue, but it looks like he's sleeping sitting up.

Good. He won't be a problem.

Thorne forks a hand through his hair and paces away from me, his movements stiff. Agitation rolls off him in invisible waves. Heaving a sigh he turns toward me, and when our gazes connect, there's a hint of familiar desperation in his eyes.

As we stare at each other a muscle jumps in his jaw and he presses his lips together, as if he's having difficulty holding in words that want to burst free. Giving me a curt nod, he marches right past me and down the hall, disappearing into one of the rooms.

I should feel triumphant that I won the argument and stood up for myself, making it clear to Thorne that he can't intimidate me, but there's a slimy sensation in my gut, like worms are wiggling around in my stomach, making me slightly nauseated. When a few minutes pass and the feeling doesn't go away, I head after Thorne, pausing in front of the room he's in.

I stare at the wood grain on the door, fighting with myself. Why should I care if he's upset? When have I ever cared when someone didn't like something I did? Especially a guy?

Never.

Steel was the closest I'd ever come to catching feelings for someone, and in our own way, we do love each other, but I know if he ever got upset over something I did or one of my decisions, I would laugh in his face and tell him to deal with it. But the longer I stand in front of the bedroom door thinking that Thorne might be somehow suffering on the other side because of me, the more troubled I become.

What is going on with me?

I've only known Thorne a short amount of time, and sure it was an intense couple of weeks, but I still don't understand why I can't laugh this off like I normally would.

"Are you going to stand there all day?" Thorne says, his voice not even muffled by the door between us.

Awkward.

"I can hear you breathing," he says when I don't make a move to open the door or leave.

I cringe, squeezing my eyes shut, embarrassed and steeped in indecision. The next few moments feel big. Important. Like stepping through this doorway isn't just passing through a physical barrier, but an unspoken one as well.

I rock on my feet and then take one step back. The door swings open and Thorne appears, staring at me with a raised brow. His hair is slightly disheveled, and I have to fist my hands to keep from reaching up and brushing back the strands that have fallen into his eyes.

He tilts his head as if to say, *Well? In or out?*

I take a slow breath through my nose and take another step back.

His eyes narrow slightly, and now I think they're saying, *Wrong choice.*

Before I have a chance to consider my next move, Thorne snatches my hand and tugs me over the threshold, shoving the door closed behind me and then pinning me up against it.

He stands with his body less than an inch away from mine, one hand positioned above my head and the other grasping my waist. I'm surrounded by him and maybe that should make me uncomfortable, but I know if I put my hand against his chest and push, he'll step away.

No, I don't feel uncomfortable. I don't feel intimidated. I feel *alive*.

"You were just going to walk away?" he asks quietly, but it sounds like an accusation rather than a question.

He's not wrong. I was. Would I run from a battle? Never. But if I'm honest with myself, running from complex emotions is kinda my M.O.

This thing, or whatever it is between us, is really starting to scare me. It's easier to brush it off as an intense attraction that will eventually burn itself out, but deep down I know it's more than that. I'm just not ready to see this for what it really is. It's too big. It's too intense.

When I remain silent, a muscle jumps under Thorne's eye. "I see."

He does? What does he see?

I want to know, but also don't.

"It's okay if—" he starts, but my body has a mind of its own and my hand snakes out and wraps around his neck, pulling him down to me so I can taste his lips.

Whatever Thorne was about to say dissolves like mist the moment our mouths meet.

This kiss is hungrier than any of the others. All the confusion swirling inside me and the pent-up fear I felt when he was taken by the Nephilim come out in this kiss, and rather than shying away from it Thorne matches me, drinking from my lips as deeply as I am from his.

I may not be willing to figure out what's happening inside my own heart, but I do know that the chemistry between us is off the charts.

My other hand dives into his hair and I clench the silky strands at the base, holding him in place even though he's not going anywhere.

Thorne makes a masculine rumble deep in his throat and tugs me forward so we're flush with each other. Nerves I didn't even know I had spark with the full body contact. I'm positive that if we were in the spirit world my skin would be crackling with electricity right now.

I'm in a racecar going a million miles an hour, headed toward a curve I can't possibly make. I'm losing control in the sweetest way possible.

I reach down, grabbing the bottom of Thorne's shirt, wanting the barrier between us gone, but when I inch the fabric up his ribs he stops me and pulls back, denying me the pleasure of his soft lips and the warm skin.

"Why were you going to walk away?" Thorne asks, his cheeks flush, lips reddened, hair more tousled than when he tugged me into the room.

My throat tightens, preventing me from speaking even if I had an answer that I was willing to share.

Our breaths and heartbeats slow as the seconds slide by. He untangles my fingers from where they are gripping the edge of his shirt, and bringing my hand to his lips, he kisses my knuckles before releasing me.

"I won't push you, but someday . . ." Thorne lets his unfinished sentence float in the air between us. His face is an open book, and what I read on his face is a mix of longing, desire, and adoration.

I don't know what to do. Why is it easier to fight by his side, battling friend or foe to protect him, than to just open up? Maybe parts of me are as broken as Thorne.

He takes a step back, and the air that rushes between us

feels infinitely colder than his body. I miss his warmth right away.

Reaching forward, he grabs the knob next to my hip and pulls the door open. I have to move to get out of the way.

"Take the room. You need the sleep," he says, gesturing to the bed. "I'll crash on the armchair out in the living room."

And with that he leaves, walking through the door and shutting it behind him. I don't move right away. Instead, I stare at the closed door and wonder where in the world I'm going to go from here.

21

I try to rest, I really do, but I'm too keyed up to fall asleep. After tossing and turning for a half hour, I sneak out of the room to find Thorne and Camiel asleep in the living room. I dozed a little when we were on the *Soulless* but Thorne didn't, so even if he probably didn't intend to fall asleep it still happened, proving he is, in fact, part human.

I hold my breath as I tiptoe past Thorne and Camiel—not that I need to be concerned about waking the warrior angel; he's sleeping like the dead. I don't think angels sleep often, but it's clear he needs it. Some of the color has returned to his ashen skin.

The door creaks as I'm closing it behind me and I wince, but after I wait a minute and Thorne doesn't come busting out the front door after me, I take off in search of a place I can steal a burner phone and some food.

I'm gone for less than an hour, but when I get back to the cottage the door flies open before I reach for the knob and Thorne yanks me inside. He doesn't say anything about me going off alone, but I can tell from the tension in his jaw that he wants to.

He only relaxes after scanning me from head to toe, and then toe to head, seeing that I'm completely unharmed. Releasing a breath, he steps back, rubbing a spot on his chest like his heart is aching.

"If you're going to leave again like that, please just let me know first," he says without meeting my gaze.

I thought it was best to leave while they were both asleep, but maybe that was a bad call. Ideally, I would have gone and returned before either of them woke, but it looks like I just took a couple of years off Thorne's life.

Good thing Nephilim are extremely long lived. He won't miss those couple of years. But still, giving him a heads-up isn't a lot to ask.

"Sure," I say. "I can do that."

Thorne meets my gaze, his lips forming the shadow of a smile. "Thanks."

Over Thorne's shoulder I catch Camiel still sleeping on the couch. Thorne must have thrown a blanket over him, which makes the corners of my mouth twitch.

"He's in restorative sleep," Thorne says. "Angels only do that when their bodies are on the verge of shutting down or they are severely injured. He'll probably be out for the next couple of hours, but he should feel a lot better when he wakes."

I nod. That's good to hear. If there's any time to get rest, it's now.

Thorne and I stare at each other, neither one of us saying anything or making a move.

I clear my throat. There's an awkwardness between us that wasn't there before. I try to shake it off as I strut past

Thorne to the small round four-seater table in the kitchen, but the uncomfortable feelings cling to me, making my skin tight and itchy.

Pretending like the awkwardness doesn't exist, I set the bag of food on the table with a flourish.

"I brought home a banquet." Truthfully, it's only a couple of sandwiches, chips, and sodas, but it's still a step up from the canned meats his Forsaken crew tried to feed me on the *Soulless*. "Dig in."

Thorne pulls a chair out and waits for me to select a sandwich before taking one for himself.

I pop a chip in my mouth, closing my eyes and moaning. Have artificial barbeque flavors ever tasted so good?

When I open my eyes Thorne is staring at me with an amused look on his face.

"I'll never eat coconut again," I say, and he chuckles.

I smile. It feels like we've broken the ice. "So. . ." I start, "we're in a small town called Lancelin. It's about eighty miles north of Perth." Perth is the capital of Western Australia, but that's about where my knowledge of the city starts and ends. "From what I gathered, Lancelin is somewhat popular during their summer months, but it's practically dead now. Which is good for us and probably why this cottage is vacant, but it made stealing this food and a burner phone a bit of a challenge. I was the only one in the store, so the clerk in the little grocery store wouldn't take his eyes off me."

Thorne cocks his head, giving me a knowing look as he chews on a bite of his roast beef sandwich. "I doubt he wouldn't stop looking at you solely because you were the only one there."

"We all have our special skills," I say with a shrug as I pop another chip in my mouth. I was able to swipe all this food because I charmed the clerk into going in the storage room to check for a particular brand of chocolate for me. He was rather accommodating after I hinted at meeting up with him after his shift. I do feel a little bad about not paying for the food and phone, but it's not like I have any cash on me, and this definitely qualifies as desperate times. "The important thing was that I was able to get a coded message off to Steel."

After brushing crumbs off my fingers, I pull the small flip phone out of my pocket and lay it on the table. "I'm hoping he calls back soon."

Thorne looks down at the phone, a crease between his eyebrows. I don't know if he's worried because Steel might call or if it's because he might not. He's been vocal about not wanting to work with Steel, but he also knows our chances of getting the orb returned to its origin before the Elders find us is better if we have help. As mighty an advocate that Camiel would usually be, in his current state he's more of a hindrance than a help.

Just then the phone rings, making me jolt. Only Steel has this number, but that was way faster than I imagined it would be.

I pick up the phone and flip it open, but don't say anything.

"Nova!" barks Steel on the other line and Thorne scowls.

"Is this a secure line?" I ask.

"Of course it is. I got your message on my cell and am calling you from a burner. It's not like I'm an amateur."

I smile at the irritation in his voice.

"Are you okay?" he asks, his voice softening.

"Yeah, I'm good."

"We were worried about you," he says, and I know he's being sincere. Steel and I may have a slightly twisted history, but we've been friends since childhood.

"Aww, nothing really to be worried about," I say, playing it off. I don't need Steel getting mushy on me right now. "I just took a couple weeks beach vacation. Can't wait until you see my tan."

I can almost hear his eyes roll on the other end of the line.

"Where are you now?" I ask, getting down to business.

"Over Indonesia on our way to Darwin."

"Can you reroute to Perth?"

Steel pulls the phone away from his mouth to shout to someone with him. It only takes a few seconds before he's back on the line. "Yeah, we can do that," he says.

"Good. Go to Perth. We're in a small beach town north of there called Lancelin." I rattle off the exact address we got from a piece of junk mail I snagged from the mailbox.

"Okay, I think we can be there in six hours. Maybe a little sooner. But who exactly is 'we'?" he asks.

Thorne narrows his eyes, his Neph hearing making it easy for him to pick up my conversation with Steel.

"Who's with you?" I ask to delay answering.

"Emberly," Steel says. "Ash, Greyson, and Sterling are on their way as well, but they are flying from the opposite direction."

"Aww, the band's getting back together. How adorable. Are you sure no one knows where you all are? Even other angel-born?"

"Of course." Steel pauses. "Nova, what kind of trouble have you gotten yourself into?"

I suck my lips into my mouth as my gaze drifts over Camiel and then lands on Thorne. "The sticky kind."

Steel blows out a loud breath. "Are you going to tell me who you're with?"

Thorne tilts his head, waiting to see what I'm going to do.

I chew on my lip as I weigh telling Steel the truth. He's going to flip about Thorne, and Emberly is going to flip about Camiel, but it's probably best they are prepared. Maybe if they have the next six hours to think on it they'll be a little more chill when they arrive.

"So, I'm here with your favorite uni-winged angel-born and—"

"What?" Steel roars into the phone before I can even finish the sentence. Thorne shoots me a glare for the "uni-winged" comment. "What are you doing with Thorne? He's been missing from his prison cell for the last two and a half weeks and—" Steel cuts himself off. "He's been with you this whole time?"

"Yep. We're basically best buds now."

"Put him on the phone," Steel demands.

"Noooo," I say. "I think it will be best for your reunion to happen in person. That way I can actually watch your head explode."

Thorne chuckles at that.

"Nova," Steel warns, "I mean it. I want to—"

"I'm here with Camiel too," I say, cutting off his rant.

The line goes so silent that if it weren't for the buzzing of the plane in the background I would think we've been disconnected.

"He's alive?" Steel finally asks.

"Yeah, he is. He's not in awesome shape but he's here.

The Elders found him after the battle in London and have been experimenting on him for the last three months."

Steel lets out cuss. "It sounds like you have a lot to catch us up on."

"I really do. I'll leave it up to you to decide whether or not to tell Emberly about him."

"Tell me about who?" Emberly's muffled voice comes across the line. "Is that Nova?" she asks, her voice rising in excitement. "Nova! I was just napping," she yells from somewhere behind Steel, which is totally unnecessary. "I'm so glad you're all right."

Hearing Emberly makes me smile. I probably should hate the girl—she's a little too sugary sweet for me—but she's also such a badass warrior that I can't make myself dislike her. I happen to glance over at Thorne. He's gone ramrod straight and wiped any and all emotion off his face.

"Tell your girl I say 'Hey,' and I'll see you guys later today. I gotta go," I tell Steel and then snap the phone shut.

I watch Thorne as he crumples up his empty sandwich wrapper and then shoves it into the grocery store plastic bag.

"So, they'll be here tonight?" he asks, deceptively calm.

"Yep." I lean back in my seat, watching him. Gauging his current mood.

"You nervous about seeing Emberly or something?" I ask, cutting right to the point.

He shakes his head.

I think he's lying.

"Steel, then?"

A wicked smile curves his lips. He lifts a hand and a small ball of angel-fire forms in his palm. "I'm actually really looking forward to seeing him."

I should probably scold Thorne and tell him to play nice with Steel, but, honestly, I'll enjoy watching that throwdown. It's a pity I didn't snag a bag of microwave popcorn when I was out. If something does go down between them, it's guaranteed to be quite a show.

But Thorne's reaction to Emberly tells me there's something going on there. Was I stupid for believing him when he said that his feelings for her weren't romantic? I guess I'll know soon enough. In about six hours to be exact.

Leaving the rest of my uneaten food scattered across the table, I push to my feet.

"What are you up to?" Thorne asks as I brush past him.

"I'm going to try to get some shuteye. It might be the last opportunity I have for a while." I strut down the hall toward the bedroom, pausing when I reach the door. "I was a little too keyed up before to fall asleep," I say with a sultry smile and a wink before shoving through the doorway, chuckling at the heated look on his face. "Let's see who's too worked up to sleep this time," I whisper to myself as I fall on the bed and cuddle a pillow under my head, a wide smile on my face.

It feels like minutes later when someone is gently shaking me awake, but hours must have passed. Orange evening light kisses Thorne's cheeks when I blink open my eyes. He steps back, giving me space. My limbs feel weighted and my head hazy as I struggle to a seated position.

"What time is it?" I ask, my voice rough with sleep.

I run a hand through my hair and wonder if I have time to grab a shower before Steel and the others get here and things start to get dicey.

"About an hour before sunset," he says, confirming I was

right about it being late in the day. "I expect your angel-born friends to show up anytime. I thought you'd want to be awake when they arrived."

"Yeah, definitely." After rubbing my eyes, I give my head a shake, trying to brush off the remnants of sleep. I usually wake very alert, but not this time. I must have been sleeping deeply because I'm downright groggy.

"How's your hand?" Thorne asks, nodding toward the hand my dad accidently skewered.

When I pull off the wrappings, the injury is sealed. I open and close my fist a couple of times, not even feeling a twinge of pain. Nephilim healing is the best.

Thorne takes my hand, gently running his thumb over the place where the sai punctured my palm. There's hardly a mark to be seen.

"I'm sorry," he says.

We've already been over this. "There's no need to apologize."

He frowns and lets go of my hand with a sigh. I know he doesn't agree with me.

It happened. I'm fine. Time to move on.

"How's Camiel?" I ask.

"He's grumpy because he still can't reach out to any of the other angels, but he's been up for the last hour."

"Did you wake me as a buffer?"

Thorne chuckles. "That, and so you can be the one to let him know his daughter will be here soon."

Shoot. He should have a heads-up about that.

"You didn't tell him?"

Thorne shakes his head. "The guy doesn't want to look at me, let alone talk to me."

I don't doubt that's true, and although Thorne doesn't

look hurt by that, a little part of my heart twists for him. Has there ever been a single person who's treated him with respect and decency? His own mother certainly didn't, and even though the Fallen and Forsaken respected him to an extent, there's no doubt they were always looking for a weakness in him to exploit.

After what happened in London, he's going to be hard pressed to find an angel-born willing to give him the benefit of the doubt either. I never would have if I wasn't forced to spend two weeks with him alone.

Looking into Thorne's future is pretty depressing. If he manages to stay out of Neph jail, where else will he be able to belong?

Swinging my legs over the side of the bed, I get to my feet. Thorne has to put out an arm to steady me when I wobble, and I smile up at him gratefully. "Sorry, I was just really dead to the world."

"No worries," he says. The tips of his fingers feather down my arm when he releases me.

I don't know if he was trying to be smooth or not, but even that gentle brush starts the blood pumping through my veins. He steps away though like he has no idea what effect simply his nearness and a soft touch has on me.

Nova, girl, you're in trouble.

"Someone's coming," Camiel calls from down the hall, breaking whatever mini-spell I was just under.

"Oh, yeah, about that—" I start to say as Thorne and I leave the room and head into the living room, but the front door crashes open and Emberly, fully angel-fied with her gold armor and gilded wings, bursts into the room.

"Where's my father?" she demands, but before we can answer she spots him and sprints across the short space between them, throwing her arms around Camiel. "I thought you were dead," she sobs with her head pressed into his chest.

Camiel looks shocked at Emberly's reaction. It takes him a couple of seconds to react. When it finally sinks in that his daughter is crying in his arms, he wraps them more fully around her and hunches over to press his cheek into the top of her head.

"It would take more than a human bomb to kill me," he says.

Watching the two of them reunite starts to feel a little voyeuristic, so I tilt my head at Thorne, indicating we should give them a moment. I step out onto the front porch with Thorne trailing behind.

I'm two steps over the threshold when I hear the meaty smack of flesh striking flesh and spin to see Thorne stumbling back as he recovers from a blow to the face from Steel. Straightening, Thorne wipes blood from his lip with the back of his hand and then stomps toward Steel, who looks like he's winding up for another punch.

I react without thought, advancing on Steel before Thorne can reach him, delivering a front kick to his solar plexus that has him flying through the air and landing on his back in the sandy yard.

Thorne steps up next to me as I glare down at Steel. Rather than readying angel-fire like I thought he'd be, he stares at me with a funny look on his face, like he's confused about what just went down.

Truthfully, I'm a little confused by my reaction as well—it's not like Thorne can't take a punch or hold his own—but no one needs to know that.

"What the heck, Nova?" Steel says as he shoves to his feet

with his fists clenched and his hate-filled gaze directed at Thorne.

I pop a hip and flip my hair back. "I'd apologize but I'm not sorry."

"Of course you're not," Steel grumbles, and then tugs me into a bear hug.

Thorne tenses, making a grunt of displeasure in the back of his throat, but doesn't try to yank me from Steel's arms.

When Steel lets me go, he bares his teeth at Thorne. "You deserved that and more."

Thorne only lifts his chin and stares down Steel.

"Yuck." I pinch my nose and fan the air between the two of them. "The sudden rush of testosterone sure does stink."

Steel rolls his eyes, breaking his silent stare-off with Thorne first.

Emberly pops her head out the doorway. She's back in regular clothes, and although her eyes are red-rimmed and her face is splotchy, there's a giant smile on her face.

"Everything okay out here?" she asks.

"You just missed the pissing contest," I say, and she scrunches her nose in disgust. "Not literally," I add.

"Oh, good. Come on back in the house. We have some planning to do." She throws Thorne a wary glance and then steps back so we can enter the cottage.

"Emberly," Thorne says by way of a greeting, and nods as he passes her.

I study their body language closely, but Thorne has himself on lockdown and Emberly just looks suspicious of him, which considering their history is to be expected.

"Hey, girl," I say as I follow Thorne into the cottage.

Emberly takes a step in my direction and then stops

herself. "Glad to see you safe and sound," she says, and gives me a giant smile.

"Pfft. As if a little thing like a plane crash could take me down."

Her chuckle turns into a squeal when Steel enters behind me and wraps her in his arms. Dipping his head, he whispers something in her ear.

The connection between them is obvious to anyone with eyes—even if you didn't have eyes you could probably still sense it. I can't seem to look away, even though watching them makes me ache, and not because I want to be with Steel, but because they have something so precious that I'm starting to want too.

We settle into the small living room. Emberly sits on the couch next to Camiel, and Steel takes the recliner on the other side of her. I pull over a chair from the kitchen and plop down, but Thorne chooses to remain standing a little ways away from the rest of us, his shoulder propped up against the wall as he leans against it.

"Grey, Ash, and Sterling should be here soon," Steel says, his gaze fixed on the cell phone in his hand as he punches in a message.

"Good," Camiel says. "We need to get moving."

"Yeah, by now Malachi and the other Elders have to know we're missing and are probably scouring the entire Western Australia coastline for us."

Emberly leans forward. "Your coded message said something about some of the Elders, but the details weren't exactly clear."

Steel snorts a laugh. "Yeah, I don't think you remembered Greyson's code correctly. Your message said they were 'fuzzy bunnies that needed to be vaccinated.' That's probably not what you meant to say, was it?"

"Whatever, I was only ever half-listening when Greyson explained the code anyway. The important thing was that you guys got it and now you're here. Malachi isn't who you think he is."

Steel and Emberly exchange a look, some sort of silent communication going on between the two. I think Steel's look is saying something along the lines of, *I told you so*, and Emberly's is saying, *Yeah, you were right.*

With a sigh, Emberly looks back at me and then Camiel. "Tell us everything."

Twenty minutes later, Emberly's eyes are filled with tears. I quickly sped through the story of Thorne and I being on the same plane, the crash, finding the Starfire Orb, getting picked up by the Fallen and Forsaken, and then everything that happened on the *Dauntless*. Camiel picked up the story after I told them about how I broke Thorne out. He explained how he ended up as Malachi's prisoner after he intercepted the bomb, glossing over the details about the experiments they put him through.

Camiel ends by saying, "Your Council needs to be stopped."

"Agreed," Steel says. He moved from the chair to sit on the arm of the couch so he could hold Emberly's hand when she started getting emotional.

"But how do we know which Elders are corrupt?" Emberly asks. "I'm an Elder and I didn't know about any of this. In fact, before you went missing I'd been trying for weeks to find out where they were keeping Thorne and came up empty."

Out of the corner of my eye, I catch Thorne cock his head.

Emberly tried to locate Thorne? *Interesting.*

"And I had no idea anyone had removed the orb from our vault at the compound in Egypt. There has definitely been some shadiness going on with the Elders. Steel and I have been talking about it for a while, but I can't be the only Elder who didn't know any of this was happening. At the very least, I'm sure Nikias didn't know either. He would have told me and fought tooth and nail to free you."

"I don't think Sorcha or Lyra would have gone along with this either," Steel adds about the virtue and power Elders. "I'm not sure one way or the other about Riven or Arien though."

"How can we know for sure?" I ask.

"My point exactly," Emberly says. "Let's assume we are able to depose Malachi, Zara, and Draven from the Council, the ones we are positive are corrupt . . . will we ever really know that we've cut the cancer from the Nephilim governing body?"

"Perhaps your whole system needs an overhaul," Thorne says. Up until now he's remained completely silent. "Some humans have an interesting system of electing a leader."

"That's rich coming from you," Steel says with a sneer. "You rule your horde of fiends through a dictatorship."

Not anymore.

"Let's take this one step at a time," I say, stopping a verbal sparring match between Steel and Thorne before it starts. "We first need to get the Starfire Orb safely back to its origin so the Elders can't misuse its powers."

"Nova's right," Camiel says. "If the Elders get their hands

on the orb again, they can use it to steal an angel's powers for their own."

Interesting. Camiel wouldn't admit that before. Perhaps having his daughter around puts him in a sharing mood.

"Your powers can be stolen?" Emberly says, alarm written over her face.

He nods. "That doesn't leave this room," he says, and then shoots a stern look at Thorne. I wonder if for a moment he forgot Thorne was here. His gaze slides back to his daughter. "And so can yours."

Steel shifts on the arm of the couch. "No one is taking Emberly's powers."

"What about the other orb?" I ask. "The Elders still have access to that one."

"That orb has different properties. We don't have to worry about them using it to take our powers, but I still think that one should be hidden away as well."

"What if we return it and Malachi figures out where we put it?" Emberly asks.

"You don't need to worry about that," Camiel says. "Once it's returned to its origin, the orb will lock in place. There is a very specific set of circumstances that need to happen to remove it again."

Thorne nods. "He's right. My mother nearly died getting it the first time. As far as I know, she never shared with anyone how she did it. I highly doubt Malachi will know how to retrieve the orb once it's back in its resting place."

That's good to know. I'd hate to go to all this trouble only to have Malachi track the orb and snatch it again.

"All right, then where are we headed?" I ask as I push to my feet.

I've had enough of this talk, it's time for action. The orb

still hangs from a pouch attached to my belt, and I'm anxious to get rid of the thing. Figuring out how to deal and what to do about the Council of Elders is a future Nova problem. Actually, I'm not really into politics, so that's a future Emberly problem.

Camiel starts to say something and then freezes, cocking his head and getting a faraway look.

"Everybody down," he yells, dragging Emberly from the couch and covering her with his body.

The next thing I know, Thorne slams into me, taking me down and releasing his wings just as the room explodes.

22

Smoke fills my lungs, and I hack as Thorne tugs me to my feet.

"Steel!" Emberly screams.

"I'm here," he answers, but I can't see anyone besides Thorne through the smoke and fire.

"Out the back," Camiel commands.

I take shallow breaths as Thorne pulls me toward the rear door, the one that leads to the beach. We are almost there when I hear unfamiliar voices above the noise from the flames and falling beams, followed by a series of pops.

"They're shooting at us," I say to Thorne, my throat raw from smoke inhalation.

Tucking me against his side, he flares his metal wing and wraps it around me and then shoves open the door. He doesn't waste any time shooting a blast of angel-fire as he pulls me outside.

We sprint out onto the beach but there is zero cover. Thorne points to the left at a sand dune and we run for it, falling after we crest the top, sliding down the other side on our butts. When we hit the bottom, I twist to look for threats. The dune does its job hiding us, but shouts and the *pop-pop-pop* of gunfire reach us from the other side.

I grit my teeth, frustrated I can't use my powers here in the mortal world like Thorne and Emberly can. If I could call up my electricity right now, I'd be running toward the angel-born who attacked us, frying anyone who gets in my path.

"Don't phase," Thorne says, as if reading my mind. "They're as defenseless in the mortal world as you are."

"Defenseless? They have guns and they're shooting at us. They also just blew up half the cottage."

"Relatively, I mean."

Someone pops into existence in front of us and I'm so shocked to see Greyson that I don't react quickly enough to stop his fist from cracking against Thorne's cheek. Thorne doesn't return the blow but tackles Greyson to the ground before he gets a chance to throw another punch.

Ash and Sterling appear next, eyes wide with shock as they take in Thorne and Greyson wrestling in the sand at their feet.

"Everyone stop!" I yell. "Thorne's not the enemy. Emberly and Steel are over there taking a beating though."

Thorne shoves off Greyson, and although they look confused, my friends refocus their attention toward the smoldering cottage, no questions asked.

"The spirit world is crawling with special ops angel-born," Sterling says. "This is the closest we could get to the cottage without being seen."

"They're expecting Camiel to phase back into the spirit world," Thorne says.

"Camiel?" Ash says, blinking back at Thorne.

"We'll have to explain later," I say.

An angel-born in all black tactical gear rounds the top of the sand dune in front of us. "There's more over—" Thorne hits him in the chest with a ball of angel-fire, shutting him up. He falls and slides down the dune toward us. Sterling grabs the large gun slung over the guy's shoulder as Ash checks his pulse.

"He's still alive," she says.

"Pity," Thorne says, and she shoots him a glare.

Generally speaking, I'm against angel-born deaths. I'm with Thorne on this one though. That angel-born would have filled us full of bullets without a second thought if Thorne hadn't taken him down.

Another explosion makes the sand beneath us shake, and we all crawl up the dune and peek over the top. Camiel is flying over the burning remains of the cottage, shooting angel-fire at any Nephilim he spots. Steel and Emberly materialize from the spirit world running right at us with four rifle-toting angel-born on their tails. Emberly is transformed, her golden armor and wings out, but she looks to be trying to haul Steel along.

"I've got this," Thorne says, and then jumps into the air.

The angel-born chasing Emberly and Steel aren't expecting Thorne, so he's able to quickly pick off the first one. After the Neph goes down from a ball of angel-fire to the chest, the other three catch on and start shooting at him.

A bolt of fear zips through me as I watch Thorne twist and turn in the air, dodging sprays of bullets. Without my abilities, and carrying only a dagger that my parents gave me back on the *Dauntless,* there's nothing I can do against angel-born with guns but watch helplessly.

Thorne manages to pick another one off with a stream

of angel-fire, but two are still shooting as they chase Steel and Emberly.

Pop pop pop.

Gunfire detonates next to me, and I look over to see Sterling using the rifle he took from the downed angel-born, giving Steel and Emberly and Thorne as much covering fire as possible. He hits one of the angel-born in the thigh and he goes down. Emberly and Steel catch sight of us and sprint up the dune just as Sterling tags the last Neph following them in the shoulder.

"Someone want to explain to me why we're fighting against other angel-born?" Sterling asks as Steel and Emberly stumble over the crest and fall to the sand next to us.

"Long story," Steel answers with a grimace. Emberly starts fretting over him, and I notice that one of his legs and part of his back is badly burned.

With a beat of his wings, Thorne flies in the direction of Camiel and continues to fight the angel-born with him. I chew on my lip as they duck and turn through the air to avoid the gunfire as they blast angel-fire at their opponents.

"Never thought I'd see the day. Thorne and Camiel fighting side by side," says Ash, who's on her belly beside me, her eyes wide with disbelief.

Two days ago, I would have had the same reaction.

Greyson moves to the other side with Emberly and Steel, trying to clean Steel's wounds with a bottle of water, so Ash and Sterling are the only two still next to me at the top of the dune watching Thorne and Camiel finish off what's left of the angel-born.

Suddenly, Thorne jerks and plummets toward the ground. I'm on my feet and running toward him before anyone can stop me. Sterling and Ash shout to come back but I ignore them, my eyes glued to Thorne's body as he disappears on the other side of the cottage.

I pick up my speed.

The cottage is a raging inferno. The heat blisters my skin as I near it, making it feel like my eyelashes and brows are being burned off, but I don't stop sprinting around the corner. I spot Thorne just in time to see him throw a giant ball of angel-fire. The angel-born it rushes toward tries to dodge the attack but just isn't fast enough. The angel-fire consumes the Nephilim completely, showing me how much Thorne was holding back before.

Thorne's gaze is fixed on the burning body of the angel-born when I reach him, his hand pressed over his left bicep.

"Thorne," I shout as I eat up the last few feet between us. "Are you okay?" There's blood leaking from between his fingers. It makes me furious.

"I'm fine," he says, his eyes strangely vacant.

Jittery and anxious, I scan Thorne from head to toe, but besides a few scratches on his face from the initial explosion, and what must be a gunshot wound on his arm, he looks all right. Even so, I can't shake the pit of fear that's formed in my chest.

Camiel lands on the ground next to us, sweat dripping down his face. He stumbles a step before catching himself. I move to steady him, but Emberly appears suddenly, brushing past me to throw herself in Camiel's arms. She squeezes him tightly, not noticing the strained look on his face.

"Is Steel okay?" I ask.

"Steel's fine," says a deep voice. I check over my shoulder to see him and the rest of my friends congregated.

Emberly lets go of Camiel and returns to Steel's side.

"They're all down . . . for now," Camiel says.

"What about all the ones we saw in the spirit world?" Ash asks, keeping her gaze alert.

"Taken care of," Camiel answers.

Steel nods. "They all phased into the mortal world when they realized Camiel was here."

"We've got to get out of here," I say, hearing faint sirens in the distance. Most likely the human fire and rescue team on their way.

"We've got a ride down the street," Greyson says, nodding his chin in that direction.

"Let's go," Steel says, and we all take off, following Ash, Sterling, and Greyson to a large black SUV.

The vehicle is large but still won't fit all of us, which now includes an eight-foot angel with six wings. Thankfully, Sterling knows how to hotwire a car, and we steal an ancient maroon Cadillac with a back seat large enough to fit Camiel and his wings. Emberly climbs in next to her dad and Steel takes the passenger seat next to Sterling. Thorne dematerializes his wing, folds in the metal one, and we get into the back of the black Suburban with Greyson and Ash in the front. We don't get more than a half mile before two firetrucks and a police car zoom past us, headed toward the blaze.

"Where are we going?" Greyson asks, his eyebrows knitted as he sneaks a peek at Thorne in the rearview mirror. He seems uneasy, but I can't hold it against him. Last time they met, Thorne broke Greyson's leg.

"Just follow Sterling," I say.

Camiel is in the car ahead of us, and right now he's the

only one who knows where we need to go, so we need to stay close.

Thorne angles his body away when I try to check his wound.

"Let me take a look," I order, but Thorne just says, "It's fine," and pulls away again.

"It's not fine," I snap. "You're leaking blood all over the seat and floor."

Thorne's face, which had been sun-kissed from our time on the island, is now bleached of color.

"There goes the deposit," Greyson grumbles, but I don't waste time shooting him a withering glare.

"Here," Ash says, handing me some bandages. "I know our group. I came prepared."

"Thanks," I say, and then turn back to Thorne. "If you pull away from me again, I will knock you unconscious to take a look at that wound."

Thorne gives me a look I can't interpret, but finally turns his body so I can reach his left arm. Peeling back his fingers reveals a round bullet wound leaking a steady river of blood. I gently take his arm and inspect the back side, spotting the exit wound that's dripping as well.

Ash is twisted around in the front seat, trying to see what's going on. "Is it bad?"

I shake my head. "It's ugly and there's a lot of blood, but he'll live. And as a bonus we don't have to dig out the bullet."

Ash hands me a bottle of water and I do my best to clean both sides of his arm before wrapping it with gauze. Thorne watches me silently the entire time. My insides are a jumbled mess. I try to ignore unwanted feelings that threaten to punch through as I patch him up, but my hands shake as I work. I blame it on the aftereffects of adrenaline.

When I finish, the binding around his arm is tight, and thick enough to stop the flow of blood. But Thorne's shirt is covered in blood. He's a mess.

"Ash, reach into my bag and grab an extra shirt," Greyson says. "We can't have him looking like he just stepped out of a horror film."

Ash hands me the shirt while Thorne tries to unstrap the harness that keeps his prosthetic wing on. He has difficulty doing it with one arm. I reach forward to help him, and when our fingers brush a flood of warmth rushes over me.

My body is being a real jerk right now. We're running from angel-born assassins and power-crazed Elders, but I can't stop thinking about how yummy he tastes and how even though he's all sweaty and bloody I still want to wrap my arms around him and bury my face in his neck.

Clearing my throat, I get to work helping Thorne remove his harness and folded-up wing. His shirt has a couple of rips in it, so rather than putting extra stress on his injured arm by pulling it over his head, he just tears it down the front and shrugs out of it, which does nothing to calm my overactive libido. I practically sigh in relief when Greyson's spare shirt settles over his chest, blocking his abs from my view.

"So," Greyson starts, "seems like we have a bit of a drive in front of us, so which one of you wants to get us up to speed?"

For what feels like the millionth time I explain every-thing that's happened in the last few weeks to Greyson and Ash. They pepper me with questions, and when I get done they explain how Steel got them a message to get to Australia, and how Sable helped them get out of Seraph Academy unnoticed and onto a commercial flight. They'd been told very little besides the very bare-bones facts that I was alive and needed help, and then later the address of the cottage. Steel hadn't mentioned Thorne at all, which is why Greyson attacked him—at least part of the reason.

Greyson is going to have to get in the back of the line of people who have a bone to pick with Thorne.

Like every other time I've relayed the details of the last few weeks, Thorne remains silent the entire time, his gaze locked on the flat landscape that passes as we drove inland. After driving for about an hour, he lets me check his bandages, but doesn't even say much then.

"You've got to be kidding me," Ash says when Greyson steers the car into the parking lot of a McDonald's.

"Someone must have to go to the bathroom, or Sterling's just hungry," Greyson says as he pulls the SUV into a parking spot next to the Caddy.

Greyson rolls down Ash's window and calls across her to his brother. "What's up?"

"I gotta go . . . and I'm starved," Sterling says.

I snort a laugh as Greyson looks up at the ceiling and shakes his head.

Sterling jumps out of the car and jogs into the restaurant. Ash unstraps her seat belt, says she'll get enough food for everyone, and then is gone as well.

"I'm going to go see what our next steps are," Greyson says as he unbuckles and hops out of the SUV.

I start to get out and follow him when I notice Thorne doesn't move.

"You coming?" I ask.

He shakes his head. "I'll just chill here until my processed food arrives."

"Oh, okay."

I shut the door and round the front of the SUV. Greyson is standing on the other side of the car, talking to Steel through the open window, so I hop into the driver's seat Sterling vacated, twisting to look at Emberly and Camiel in the back.

"How you guys doing back there?" I ask.

"Vehicular travel is slow," Camiel grumbles.

Compared to flight, he's not wrong.

"So where are we headed?" I ask, which gets Steel's and Greyson's attention.

Steel and Emberly exchange a look, and no one answers me.

"What?"

"You really think leading Thorne to the origin of the Starfire Orb is a wise move?" Steel asks.

I glance at Greyson. He won't meet my eyes. Emberly just stares back at me with a crease between her eyebrows as she chews her bottom lip.

"What's this all about?" I ask.

"It's Thorne," Steel says. "If we take him with us, then he'll be able to go back in the future and retrieve the orb again."

I cross my arms over my chest. "I thought it was super hard to get the orb once it's returned to its origin."

"Hard, but not impossible."

"This is ridiculous. Thorne doesn't want the orb." *At least not anymore.*

Nobody looks convinced, least of all Steel.

I look over my shoulder at Thorne in the SUV beside us. He's resting against the headrest with his eyes closed. Despite the several layers of glass between us, all he has to do is stretch his hearing to catch everything we're saying.

"Just get over it, Steel. Thorne's coming with us. You can't deny he'll be an asset if we run into more angel-born, or one of the corrupt Elders." I shrug. "Or you can be a douche and Thorne and I can peace-out now before you've seen my awesome new powers in action. Honestly, a beach vacay in the Great Barrier Reef sounds pretty sweet right about now." I check my nails, which are disgusting, and pretend to be uninterested in his response.

Emberly sighs. "It does seem like he's changed," she says, looking at Steel. "He's put his life on the line not only for Nova, but also for us back at the beach. I'd rather have Thorne on our side than against us."

Steel sighs, clearly not happy, but nods. I look over to Camiel. He's fallen asleep again.

"Umm, is he okay?" He's been sleeping a lot.

"He's really weak," Emberly answers with a frown. "I think he's just recovering and needs the rest."

"He'll have time. It's going to take a day and a half to get where we need to go," Greyson says from outside Steel's window.

"And where is that?" I ask with an arched brow. If I have to ask another time, someone's getting a black eye.

"South Australia," Emberly answers. "To the opal mines outside Coober Pedy."

Thorne holds the burger in his hand like he's never seen one before. Ash delivered the first round just moments after I returned to the SUV, and then turned around to go grab the rest, leaving Thorne and me alone.

"You take a bite and chew," I say lightheartedly.

He shoots me a look that says he'd rather not, but then lifts the burger and takes a bite. I can instantly tell he hates it, but he dutifully chews and then swallows. "This is disgusting. How do humans consume these?"

I shrug as I munch on a fry. I think they're pretty tasty.

"I can leave," Thorne says quietly, his eyes fixed on the food in his hands and not on me.

My stomach drops. "You heard."

I have the sudden urge to punch Steel between the eyes, but I wouldn't want to incur Emberly's wrath. I'd never tell her, but when it comes to Steel's safety the chick can be downright scary.

"Your relationship with your friends is special. It's not something that just happens naturally. Devotion that would cause people to travel halfway around the world without an explanation as to why is unique and you shouldn't put it in jeopardy. Whether you're willing to admit it or not, losing your friends would cause you pain, and I can't bear the thought of your pain."

The things this guy says could make the coldest heart swoon. I know, because my heart was the iciest heart around and I can't seem to keep it from melting. Maybe the best thing would just be for Thorne and us to part ways now, but the thought of him just going off on his own makes my chest ache.

I shake my head. "No. You can't leave. We need you."

He looks up from his burger, his eyes searching. "You are traveling with the Angel of War and the most powerful Nephilim on the planet. You really don't."

I take a deep breath and blow it out, averting my gaze. "Fine. *I* need you. Is that good enough for you?"

Need him for what or why, I'm not yet sure or even

willing to find out, but that doesn't make the statement any less true. If he were to leave now—to just disappear out of my life as suddenly as he appeared—I wouldn't be okay.

Thorne places two fingers under my chin and gently turns my head. His eyes are a churning blue ocean and I'm suddenly scared I'm going to drown.

"That will *always* be good enough."

23

Camiel was right. Driving is so slow. We've been at it for twenty-eight hours straight with minimal stops and I want to pull my hair out. Most of us have switched cars at one point and taken a shift driving, but right now I'm stuck in the passenger seat next to Sterling as he belts out nineties boyband music at the top of his lungs.

I. Want. To. Stab. Him.

"If you don't stop singing, I'm going to rip out the sound system with my bare hands and beat you to death with it."

I twist in my seat, eyes wide as I stare at Ash in shock. I don't think I've ever heard anything so violent come out of the dark-skinned beauty's mouth before. She may be my new favorite.

"Yas, queen," I say, and hold out my fist for her to bump.

Ash bumps my fist with a smug smile. Sterling stops singing and says, "Ouch," but reaches over and switches the station to play something from this century.

Greyson rubs his ear. "Sweet relief. My ears were starting to bleed."

"Seriously, you guys?" Sterling says, casting a hurt look in the rearview mirror at Ash and then Greyson. He doesn't bother trying to guilt trip me; he knows that won't work. Ribbing Sterling is practically a sport for me, so he's used to it.

Greyson leans into the empty space between Sterling and me. He jerks his chin up, his gaze locked on the bumper of the maroon Cadillac in front of us. "Do you think it was a good idea to let them all ride together?"

No. It was a horrible idea. It's a miracle Steel and Thorne haven't ripped each other to shreds yet, but instead of saying that I feign nonchalance. "I'm sure it's fine. We've only seen them almost swerve off the road twice. They'll probably be besties by the time this trip is over. Inviting each other over for sleepovers and painting each other's nails."

Sterling snorts a laugh, knowing I'm full of it.

Yeah, that's never gonna happen. With each mile that passes I've gotten more and more anxious, but since it was my epically bad idea for them to ride together I'm not about to admit I made a mistake.

"Where are they going?" Greyson asks as the Caddy takes a hard turn into the parking lot of a seriously sketchy-looking motel.

"I'm not staying here if they don't have the voltage to handle my hair dryer," Sterling says.

Greyson shoots Sterling a look. "Seriously, bro?"

"We're not supposed to be staying anywhere," Ash speaks up from the back seat. "We were going to drive straight through."

"Maybe they just want to switch passengers again?" I offer, but my intuition says that's not it as I watch the

Caddy swerve, kicking up a plume of dust as it parks cock-eyed in a spot.

We're in middle-of-nowhere Australia and haven't even seen another car in the last fifteen minutes. If they just wanted to offload Thorne, they could have pulled over anywhere.

Steel jumps out of the car and jogs into the motel lobby. Thorne gets out of the car much slower and makes his way over to where we are parked just as Greyson hops out of the SUV to follow his brother.

I roll down my window as Thorne steps up.

Sterling leans over me and asks, "Does Steel have the trots?"

"Ew," Ash says, and I swat at Sterling until he sits back in his seat.

"What?" he says. "It's a legit possibility. Did you see the chili cheeseburger he ate at our last stop?"

Thorne casts Sterling a bland look, but I can tell he's trying not to smile. Maybe my friends are growing on him?

"Steel's digestive track seems to be running just fine," Thorne says with a straight face. "It's Camiel. There's something wrong."

"What's wrong?" I ask.

Thorne glances over his shoulder at the Cadillac. The sun's glare on the glass prevents me from seeing anything inside the other car.

"He passed out again and—"

"Has Steel been farting and smelling up the car?" Sterling cuts in. "That would make anyone go unconscious."

"Sterling," I snap, and then gesture for Thorne to continue.

"We can't wake him, and he seems to be burning up. The

idea was to get off the road, at least for a few hours, and see if his condition improves."

I don't like the idea of stopping. The orb hanging from my belt feels like it's burning a bigger hole in my pocket with every hour that passes. But if there's something seriously wrong with Camiel, stopping for a bit is probably wise.

Greyson and Steel return after a couple of minutes with room keys and we pile out of the SUV. It's no easy feat getting an unconscious eight-foot seraph angel out of the car and into a motel room. We lucked out that the doors to the rooms are all exterior and the place is so dead. We get him inside without being seen by any humans.

Once we have Camiel sprawled out on one of the two queen beds, Steel hands me a flat keycard. "This is for you and Ash. Em and I will stay here with Camiel. Grey and Sterling are on the other side of you."

"What about Thorne?"

He shrugs. "Thorne was snoring so loud for the last two hours I figured he could stay up and keep watch."

"Thorne doesn't snore," I say before I think better of it.

Steel's face darkens and I roll my eyes.

"Chill. We were alone together on an island for two weeks. I know the dude's sleeping habits."

Steel still looks unhappy, but like I care. Leaving Steel, I join Thorne on the other side of the room.

"I don't mind. Someone does need to keep watch," Thorne says before I get a chance to say anything.

"Eavesdropping again?" I ask with a tilt of my head.

I assume the glare Thorne shoots over my shoulder is directed at Steel. "It's not like he was trying to be quiet."

I sigh. *Those two.* A couple hours in a car together didn't do anything to improve their tolerance of each other. They're going to need to be separated sooner rather than later or it's going to come to blows again.

Thorne leans toward me like he's going to press a kiss to my forehead but stops himself. "Tell the others I'll take the first shift. When someone wants to relieve me, I can crash in the SUV."

I frown as Thorne leaves. He shouldn't have to sleep in the parking lot when the rest of us have beds. Granted, it's probably a lumpy bed-bug-filled mattress, but a bed none-theless.

Camiel releases a low groan.

"I think he's coming around," Emberly says.

The others rush over to crowd around him.

I use the distraction to slip out of the room and go search for Thorne. I find him around the back of the long two-story building, sitting on the top of a sun-bleached wooden picnic table looking westward, his feet propped up on the attached seat. He's strapped his prosthetic wing on, but it's folded up against his back.

That's good. Humans now know that the Nephilim exist, but it's still not a good idea to let anyone know what we are. The last thing we want is someone reporting that a group of angel-born are holed up in the motel. With the way the Council monitors transmissions, they'd probably be swarming this place within an hour.

"Hey," I say, as I sit down next to Thorne.

He doesn't say anything, but he tips his chin in way of acknowledgment.

We sit together in silence, looking over the countryside as the sun sets. It's not much to look at. Ever since we broke from the coast and started driving inland, the terrain has been mostly dusty, dirty, and flat. "Not the prettiest view, is it?"

Thorne leans back, putting his weight on his arms behind him. "I don't know. You might look out and see a dead landscape, but it's truly not. There are a number of different plant and animals who call this area home. The inhabitants of this land have had to adapt to survive here, making them strong. It might look desolate to most, but I find the lack of evidence of humans or angel-born and the wildness of the terrain soothing."

As I study Thorne while he watches the sunset, some hard truths come to me. Back on the *Soulless* he decimated his credibility with the Fallen and Forsaken, and no matter how much he's changed or what good he does, the world will probably always judge him harshly for the part he played in London.

When this is all over, where will he be able to go? What kind of life will he have left to build? He's not left with very many options. If he's looking for a fresh start, I'm not sure if he's going to be given that opportunity.

Maybe the only option for him is just to disappear somewhere in the spirit world far away from Fallen or Forsaken, or any being with angelic blood running through their veins.

Including me.

But even the thought of that is like a knife to the heart. When the time comes, will I be able to let go like I know I'm going to have to?

My gaze snags on the bandage I wrapped around his bicep. "Can I take a look?" I ask.

Thorne nods, and I gently peel back the cloth. The entrance and exit wounds are closed; the skin is puckered and pink. In a couple of days, or less, his skin will look flaw-less again.

I run my fingers over one of the new scars and Thorne's muscles tense. I look up at his face, thinking I've hurt him, but his eyes are closed, and his face is relaxed.

Crumpling the used bandages, I set them aside. Since the wound is closed he doesn't need them anymore.

"Who do you want to be?" Thorne asks, surprising me.

"What do you mean?"

"Where do you see your life going? Do you have hopes for the future?"

I release a shaky laugh. "Those are some deep questions."

Thorne stays silent, waiting for my real answer.

I release a breath. "I always assumed I'd take my place as an angel-born warrior and defender once I came into my powers, but with everything that's gone down with Malachi and the other Elders recently, I don't know that I see myself in that traditional role anymore. Things feel different now. I'm not sure what I'm going to do or where life will take me. Why do you want to know?"

Thorne brushes strands of hair behind my ear, his fingers grazing over my cheek and ear in the process. Even that light touch makes me shiver, and when I see his eyes darken, I know he's noticed. He takes a deep breath before answering. "I suppose I want to know so that when this is all over and we part ways, I'm able to imagine where you are and what you are doing."

Maybe I should be glad we're on the same page about what's going to happen, but hearing him lay it out there like it's an eventuality that's set in stone shreds me.

"What if . . . ?" I swallow, having a hard time finding the

courage to get the rest of what I want to say out. "What if when all this is over, I'm not ready to part ways?"

Thorne's eyes flare and he catches his breath, holding the air in his lungs. I can see the moment Thorne starts to hope. His face softens and warmth enters his gaze. I think he's going to say something, but instead he reaches up and cups my face, pulling me toward him.

This kiss is unhurried and leisurely, as if we have all the time in the world to explore each other's mouths. Just like every other time we've kissed, the world falls away, leaving just the two of us.

Scooting closer, I press my hand against Thorne's chest. Although he's exploring my mouth achingly slow, his heartbeat thumps rapidly.

He slides his hand into my hair, holding me in place as he pulls back just enough to say against my mouth, "You're killing me. I could kiss you for the next thousand years and it still wouldn't be long enough."

I don't have time to process his confession before he dives back in, his mouth gliding against mine, making me forget anything except him.

A bubble of emotion wells in my chest. The physical attraction between Thorne and me has been there from the beginning. From the very first moment I laid eyes on him a spark was ignited, but this kiss, more than any of the others we've shared is bigger. Weightier.

And devastating my soul, ruining me for any other man.

I savor each touch as if it were our first and last. My heart's fuller than it's ever been before, and there are words balancing on the tip of my tongue that I never thought I'd utter. Words that I can't hold back anymore.

"Thorne," I get out between kisses, "I—"

Suddenly, Thorne is gone.

I pitch forward, catching myself on the rough top of the picnic table and look up just as Steel slams his fist into Thorne's gut. Thorne doubles over, gasping for breath.

"Stop!" I scream, scrambling off the table and reaching for Steel's arm. I get a hold on his bicep, but he just shakes me.

"You think you can touch her?" he spits at Thorne, who's still trying to catch his breath. "You think you have a right to do that?"

Thorne coughs but then stretches to his full height, facing Steel head on. "No. I know I don't, and I know that I could live a lifetime and still not earn that right. But if stolen moments are all I'll ever get with her, I'm not noble enough to deny myself."

Steel steps toward Thorne, his fists clenched. "She's like a sister to me. I'll kill you if you touch her again."

Now wait a minute.

"Steel, you're out of line," I snap. "If I want to make out with an entire cohort of Fallen warriors, you don't get a say in it."

Someone gasps, and I glance over to see Ash, Greyson, and Sterling staring wide-eyed and slack-jawed at the scene unfolding before them.

Just how much did they catch? Did they show up before or after Steel yanked Thorne away from me? Did they see Thorne and me kiss? And if so, do I really care?

Steel growls and lunges for Thorne, leading with his fists.

Not again.

Steel gets another hit to Thorne's jaw, and I expect

Thorne to retaliate, but he doesn't. He barely defends himself as Steel wails on him.

"Steel, cut it out," I order, and try to reach the pair so I can stop this madness, but a golden arm, corded with muscle, wraps around my waist, holding me back.

Camiel? When did he get here?

"Give them a moment," the angel says. "They need to work some things out."

"With their fists?"

The seraph angel nods. "It's a long time coming. I think you know this isn't only about you."

I growl in frustration. Watching Steel wail on Thorne is a new type of torture. I flinch every time he lands a blow on Thorne. It's only Camiel's iron grip on me that keeps me from interfering.

Why won't Thorne fight back?

Finally, it gets to be too much. My skin starts to heat and the electric power that I'm only supposed to be able to call upon in the spirit world starts swirling inside of me. Sparks shoot up my arms and shock Camiel. He looks down at me with raised brows, releasing me immediately.

I'm going to zap Steel so hard the aftershocks will vibrate through him for a week.

But I don't get that chance. Camiel moving faster than I can track, shoots over to Steel, catching his fist midair.

"Enough," he says.

I run to Thorne, helping him to his feet. He keeps an arm around his ribs like they might be broken. One eye is starting to blacken, and his lip is split.

Forget zapping Steel. I'm going to kill him.

Jerking his hand free, Steel shoots Camiel an angry glare.

"You shouldn't get in the middle of this. This doesn't have anything to do with you."

"It doesn't have anything to do with you either," Camiel fires back. "If anyone should recognize what's going on here, it should be you." His gaze carries meaning that takes Steel a moment to catch on to, but when he does his eyes widen and then volley back and forth between Thorne and me.

"No," Steel says, shaking his head, his voice laced with a hint of shock-filled panic. "I won't believe it. He's not capable of that type of emotion. He was raised by a monster."

"He was," Camiel agrees. "But doesn't that make you wonder who he would have been if he hadn't?"

"What's going on here?" Emberly asks, the last one of the group to appear. She's utterly confused.

"What's going on here is that your fiancé's a giant douche," I say.

"Well, yeah, he definitely can be," Emberly agrees. "But that's not new."

"Hey!" Steel looks offended, but as she goes to his side she only has to lay a hand on his arm and he visibly calms.

"They're soul-bonded," Camiel announces.

My breath is knocked out of me and my muscles lock.

Soul-bonded? No way.

I look to Thorne, expecting him to refute what Camiel said, but he just stares at me like he's gauging my reaction.

Sure, we have a connection, but . . .

We can't . . .

We aren't . . .

Angels have a wonky relationship with time. The soul-bonded are angelic pairs whose love is so great, it bounces back through time, bonding their past selves. That means if Thorne and I are soul-bonded, we're destined to fall in love with each other at some point in the future.

Or maybe you already have, my mind whispers.

I find myself shaking my head in denial.

"Day-um. Shit just got real," Sterling says.

"Shut up, Sterling," Ash hisses.

I have to pull myself together. This isn't the time to fall apart.

Clearing my throat, I take a step away from Thorne. A flash of hurt skids across his features so quickly I immediately doubt if it was ever there.

An awkward silence falls over our group.

"Dad," Emberly finally says, and Camiel looks toward her. He seems surprised but pleased. I can only assume he's not used to being addressed that way. "We should get you back in the room. You're looking a little shaky again, and we don't want anyone to see you."

He nods.

"I'll stay out here and keep watch," Thorne says as he wipes at the blood on his bottom lip. He won't meet my gaze.

I'm handling this all wrong, but I'm in shock and utter overload, and hate that there's an audience right now. It feels like I'm having an out-of-body experience.

Thorne walks back toward the picnic table, slowly and with an arm still wrapped around his waist, and something snaps in me.

What am I doing? I'm Nova flippin' Kelly. I know what I want, and I take it. I don't care what anyone thinks.

The soul-bond thing threw me for a loop. I'm not ready

to have my feelings out there for everyone to see, but screw it.

"Let me get you something to clean yourself up," Ash says to Thorne, and then looks at me. "Come on. You can get settled in our room."

"No," I say forcefully, and Ash cocks her head.

In four long strides I'm in front of Thorne, taking his face between my hands and pressing my lips against his. He stiffens, and I remember his lip is busted and gentle my kiss. The kiss is really for show, but like the other times we've come together, everything falls away except him.

Thorne pulls back after only a few short seconds. Confusion swims in his gaze. "What are you doing?"

"Staking a claim," I answer and then straighten, looking each of my friends in the eyes, one by one. "This is happening. Get on board or get out of the way."

Ash gasps, Sterling's jaw drops, Greyson's eyes widen, and Steel grinds his teeth. Camiel stands off to the side, letting our group work this out on our own.

Emberly bites her lip to keep from smiling. "Let's get out of here, guys. We should get rest while we can. Tomorrow's going to be wild."

With a mix of looks, everyone turns and heads back around the motel. Emberly has to tug on Steel's arm to get him to move, but he leaves as well.

When it's just Thorne and me, he takes my hand, lacing his fingers in mine. The sun has set, but the sky is still a lovely shade of pink that reflects warm tones on Thorne's face as he stares at me.

I lick my bottom lip; his silence makes me nervous. "So yeah, that happened."

"It did indeed," he says, his voice deep and rolling over me like a physical touch.

He lifts my hand and flips it, placing a soft kiss on my wrist. I catch my breath, waiting to see what he does next.

"I didn't even know someone like you existed."

"Someone like me?" I ask.

Am I fishing for compliments? *Maybe.*

Thorne smiles, seeing through me.

Standing, he pulls me forward, looping my hands around his neck and wrapping his arms around my waist.

"I don't need to tell you you're beautiful, because you already know you are. And I don't need to tell you you're brave, or strong, or fierce, because you already know those things as well. I love that you know who you are and your worth. But what I meant by 'someone like you' is someone who sees me, because my entire life there's never been a human or angelic being who has."

I slide a hand from Thorne's neck to his cheek and brush my thumb over his cheekbone. He closes his eyes and tilts his face into my touch.

"I do see you," I say, knowing that the excuses I made for our connection were always just that, excuses. I might have been panicked or unsure when I considered Thorne and me before, but right now I'm oddly calm. "I see your flaws and your scars, but I also see the parts of you that you had to bury to keep your mother from cutting them out. Your compassion, your protective nature, even your soft heart. You're not perfect and neither am I, but it seems like we might be perfect for each other."

When Thorne leans down to kiss me, nothing has ever felt so right.

Thorne and I stay up until the stars are shining brightly. Eventually, I fall asleep sprawled across the tabletop with my head in his lap. When I open my eyes early the next morning, my back and hip ache, but it's totally worth it to wake up to him running his fingers through my hair. He runs the tip of one finger over the shell of my ear and I shiver. When he chuckles and does it again, I know he knows I'm awake.

I sit up, stretching and cracking my neck to work the kinks out.

"Did you get any sleep?" I ask, my voice husky.

"And miss a moment of having you nestled up on me? I would never."

Even though it would have been good for him to rest, I can't keep the smile off my face. He says the most perfect things.

"No one came to relieve us of lookout duty?"

"Greyson actually checked in after you fell asleep. I told him I had it."

Footsteps crunch on the gravel behind us, and when I look over my shoulder Ash is headed our way. "We're getting ready to head out," she calls.

Sliding off the picnic table, Thorne and I follow her back to the motel. I grasp his hand and he looks down in surprise before giving me a soft smile and squeezing my fingers.

The mood is somber when we enter the motel room. The drapes are closed, blocking out the early morning light. Camiel is awake but propped up against the headboard in one of the beds. His normally golden skin is ashen; sweat dampens his hair, making strands stick to his forehead.

"Camiel and I aren't going with you," Emberly says.

The non-reaction from the others tells me they've already talked this out. It's clear Camiel is struggling, so I don't need to ask why Emberly and Camiel are staying behind.

"I need to phase into the spirit world to heal," Camiel says, his voice weak.

Emberly frowns and hands her father a tissue when a coughing fit starts. "And I'm staying to watch over him."

"Emberly and I shouldn't be around the Starfire Orb anyway," Camiel says. "Our angel powers could set off the orb in unexpected ways."

That makes sense. Camiel was reluctant to go with us to return the orbs when we tried back in December. And when Emberly touched the other orb it switched its magical properties.

Steel's expression is unreadable. I can't imagine he's okay being separated from Emberly. The pair has been practically attached at the hip since the battle in London.

"You okay with this plan?" I ask, and he nods.

"My girl can take care of herself," he says with a lingering glance at the blonde angel-born.

Emberly gives Steel a soft but sad smile before turning to Thorne and me. "If he improves, we can fly to meet up with you, and if not the plan is for you guys to return here after and pick us up. Malachi's not going to stop, so while you're gone I'm going to get in touch with some people I trust and figure out how to get us all to safety once we offload the orb."

I shrug. "The plan's okay with me if it's okay with all of you."

After a round of somber goodbyes, everyone except

Emberly and Camiel pile into the SUV. I dutifully ignore the looks my friends cast me when they think I'm not looking. Besides Steel, who's clearly still pissed about Thorne and me, the others don't seem to know what to say or how to act around us.

Thorne and I squeeze into the cramped third row of seats, but I don't mind the close quarters. It gives me the excuse to cuddle up next to him. Even sporting some new bruises and slightly bloodied from his tussle with Steel the night before, he looks and smells amazing.

Turning in her seat, Ash gives Thorne a smile that's part grimace, but bless her heart for even trying. "So, Thorne, what was it like growing up with Fallen and Forsaken?"

Thorne shoots me a look that says, *Is she for real?* before refocusing on Ash. "Lonely and dangerous."

"Oh," Ash says, and her face falls.

I'm not sure what answer she was expecting. We're all well aware of how brutal Fallen and Forsaken are, but she was trying with him, and I appreciate that. I nudge Thorne in the ribs, encouraging him to give her more than a three-word answer.

Thorne runs his tongue over his bottom lip and tries again. "I was the only child in the fortress, so I never had a playmate. In truth, I don't think I ever really understood what play meant as a child. For as long as I remember, my days were filled with sparring, drills, training, and education, as my mother was dead set on honing me into the perfect weapon. I had little downtime and no access to anything that would be considered frivolous."

Ash's face falls even further and I squeeze Thorne's

hand. My heart is bleeding for him. Thorne isn't trying to manipulate us into feeling bad for him, he's just being honest about what his childhood was like simply because Ash asked, and I encouraged him to.

Thorne's lips twist in a ghost of a smile. "Although for a time I did enjoy my time training with the barghests."

"Barghests?" Ash asks, and Greyson turns his head to listen. In the front seats, Sterling and Steel are arguing over the radio. I remember Emberly mentioning barghests. She said they were mostly scales and spikes instead of fur and had more teeth than any creature should. I prefer Cleo: deadly *and* beautiful, just like me.

"Hellhounds," Thorne explains, "although it's a stretch to relate them to mortal world canines in any way. They're a hundred times more vicious, and nothing about them is soft or cuddly. But I did find a small measure of pleasure when I was working with them and felt particularly connected to one. She was a fierce creature and I felt there was something akin to a bond between the two of us. Sometimes she would obey a command before I issued it."

That's kind of sweet. Like a boy with his dog, if the boy was training the dog to be a vicious killer.

The smile drops off Thorne's face. "But I made the mistake of naming her. When my mother picked up on my affection for the beast, she made me kill her."

Ash gasps, and Greyson mutters a curse under his breath.

"Thorne, I'm . . . I'm so sorry," Ash says, looking like she's about to cry.

I have to pinch my eyes shut to keep from letting them well with tears myself. When I open them again the entire car has gone quiet, and I notice Steel sneaking a glance at Thorne in the rearview mirror. His gaze looks troubled.

Thorne shifts uncomfortably next to me. "Yes, well, I'm sure my upbringing was vastly different than what Neph younglings are used to."

Understatement.

I lay a hand on Thorne's knee and squeeze, offering him what comfort I can. He doesn't want my pity, but I can still give him my support. Leaning over, I place a kiss high on his cheek and he turns his head to look at me when I pull back.

"I survived," he says, reading the sadness in my gaze.

I don't know what to say to that. In a perfect world he wouldn't have had to just survive his childhood. He would have been loved and cared for and cherished like every kid should be.

But we don't live in a perfect world, so surviving was truly the best Thorne could have hoped for.

I don't even know a tear has escaped until Thorne reaches forward and gently wipes it away. "Don't do that, I'm not worth your tears," he says, and my heart splits right open.

My eyes well and there's no way I can keep the wetness from spilling over. I bury my face in Thorne's chest. I know it bothers him to see me like this, but I can't not be close to him right now. He wraps his arms around me and pulls me closer, rubbing a hand up and down my back as I soak his shirt with my tears.

Someone clears their throat and then Steel says, "We're about an hour out."

The car falls silent again and I do my best to muffle my

crying. Steel or Sterling flips the radio on and an eighties power ballad plays softly through the speakers.

I've always considered tears a weakness, but although I'm overwhelmed by the depth of my emotions right now, I'm not weak. My reaction is an acknowledgement that what Thorne endured wasn't right, and also a confirmation that I actually have a heart. For that reason, I don't mind Thorne seeing me like this, but I wish we weren't in such close contact with the others. I've known Steel, Greyson, and Sterling practically my whole life, but this might be the first time they've seen me cry. This emotion doesn't belong to them, it belongs to Thorne alone.

When I finally gain control of myself, I sit up and wipe my face, pulling Thorne's hand into my lap so I can still keep connected with him. No one seated in front of us is turned in our direction and I'm grateful, knowing that is the only form of privacy they can offer us in this tight space.

Thorne stares at me as he brushes his thumb back and forth over the top of my hand. I close my eyes and lean my head back against the rest, not minding in the least that he's watching me the whole time.

24

When Steel stops the car and tells us we're there, I'm not exactly sure he has the coordinates right. We're north of the small town of Coober Pedy, and despite Thorne's sentiments from the night before about there being life in what might look like a dead landscape, I'm almost positive he's wrong about this area. Nothing looks alive here. It's like a deserted alien planet or a dystopian wasteland. The landscape is dry and flat as far as the eye can see. The packed dry dirt under our feet is fifty shades of beige, and the only vegetation around are some small shrubs tossed about, but their brownness makes them blend into the rest of the scenery. I suppose there's an eerie sort of beauty to this place, but this much wilderness gives me the creeps.

"There's nothing here," Sterling says, being the first one of us to talk since we all exited the SUV.

"Did you expect there to be a city built up around the orb's origin?" Greyson asks his brother, and Sterling shrugs.

"I guess not. It just feels so . . ."

"Isolated," Thorne says when Sterling's words fail him.

"Being way out here, it almost feels as if the orb never wanted to be disturbed," Ash says, and her comment resonates with me. I don't know why the orbs exist in the first place, but I do know the world would have been better off if they'd never been unearthed.

"All right, where do we start?" I ask.

Ash pulls her curls into a high ponytail. It's not that the temperature is overly hot, but without a breeze or a cloud in the sky the sun is more intense than when we were closer to the ocean. "Camiel said the origin was in an underground tunnel. So, I guess—"

"Over here," Steel calls out. He wandered off from the group almost the moment we got here. He's about fifty feet away on the other side of a small mound, looking down at the ground.

When we trudge over to him, he's gazing down into a hole about twice as large as a manhole. The sun shines into the space, so the drop is visible. I'd say it's about fifteen feet, a piece of cake for an angel-born.

"So, ah . . . we just head on down?" Sterling asks.

Camiel said when we get underground we should expose the orb and it will lead us to its origin. Sounds simple enough, but no one seems to be in a rush to go down the hole.

"Should I grab a flashlight?" Ash asks. She already has a backpack on with some light supplies, but I guess she left a flashlight in the car.

Thorne shakes his head. "The orb will give off plenty of light. Then, after we return it, our auras will cast a glow so we can navigate out of there."

"All right, it's time to offload this thing," I say and then step into the empty space, dropping into the hole and landing on sandy ground in a perfect crouch.

I've only just stood to my full height when Thorne lands next to me, his gaze watchful as he scans the darkness outside the ring of light. I glance around, seeing several tunnels leading in opposite directions.

The others drop into the space one-by-one, Steel coming down last.

"Which way?" Sterling asks as he peers into the darkness.

I open the pouch on my belt and pull out the box with the orb inside. "Let's find out."

The moment I crack the lid, we're all forced into the spirit world and bathed in the orb's silver light.

"I'll never get used to that," Ash says with a shudder, and I agree. Phasing is something Neph children learn to do at a young age and is a voluntary action. Being dragged into another dimension against your will feels like a violation.

Plucking the orb from the box, I hold it in an open hand and walk in a circle. When I near one of the tunnels, the orb's light intensifies, and when I move in the opposite direction it dims.

I glance back at the group and Steel nods. "Lead the way."

Once we enter the tunnel, the sunlight quickly disappears, but the orb's light is more than sufficient. Without looking, I know Thorne is following right behind me. It seems like the closer we become, the more attuned I am to his physical presence. Right now it's like there's a warm breeze brushing against my back and I wonder if that is a side effect to being soul-bonded or just all in my mind. I make a note to have a sit down with Emberly once things settle. If anyone can give me a heads-up about what to expect with Thorne and this bond down the road, it would be her.

The underground tunnels twist and turn and it isn't long before I start to feel like a mouse in a maze. Every time we come to a branch I repeat the same ritual, taking a few steps down one path and then the other watching the orb's brightness to see which way we should go.

"I hope someone is keeping track of these turns," I say when we venture down a new tunnel.

"I am," Ash says. "I'm typing the turns we made into the notes on my phone and so to get out we just follow the directions in reverse."

"Good, because if you weren't doing that we could get lost in these tunnels for years." With the amount of time we've been walking, I'd estimate we're at least a mile from where we started.

"Does anyone else hear that?" Sterling asks.

I don't hear anything down here besides our footsteps and breathing.

"The air seems different," Thorne adds. "Cooler and humid."

"Wait, I hear it too," Greyson says.

"Is that water?" Ash asks.

It's not until we've walked another few minutes that I hear the faint bubbling noise as well. The orb is bright enough to cast light several paces in front and behind us, but it doesn't shine in a straight line like a flashlight would, so we can't actually see very far down the tunnel. The trickling of water becomes louder, and the air chills until puffs of mist swirl around my face on every exhale.

"I should have brought a parka down here," Sterling says

as he walks beside me. He rubs his hands up and down his arms as he shivers.

I'm tough, so I try to play it off like the cold isn't affecting me, but I have to keep my mouth clamped shut to stop my teeth from chattering. I'm pretty sure if I looked in the mirror my lips would be blue. A tank top was such a good idea when we were out in the Australian sun, but not so much anymore.

A piece of fabric falls over my shoulders and I glance back. Thorne has stripped off his shirt. The only thing covering his chest is the harness for his metal wing. The soft material covering my shoulders and upper back is deliciously warm from his residual body heat, but it's freezing and Thorne's now naked from the waist up.

When I reach to slide it off and hand it back to him, he comes up beside me and stays my hand.

"I have a high tolerance for cold," he says, and my gaze drops to his bare chest, which is smooth and free of any pebbled flesh.

I must be staring for too long, because Steel clears his throat. I grin at the annoyed angel-born, completely unashamed. Thorne's body is a thing of beauty. I even caught Ash checking him out.

Tearing my gaze from Thorne, I refocus on the task at hand. The tunnels take a hard turn to the right, then almost immediately we're dumped out into a giant underground chamber, and we all grind to a halt.

I've never seen anything like it before. The space is the size of a football stadium with a domed ceiling that I'd guess reaches a hundred feet at its highest point. Giant icicles of various sizes hang down like glowing, bluish stalactites. The ground is sand so white it looks like snow.

Water trickles through cracks in the stone wall to the left and then slides over jagged boulders and into a small stream that cuts through the middle of the space and then takes a sharp turn to feed a pond that takes up the back half of the cavern. Beyond the pond, a golden starburst emblem glows against the stone wall on the far end. I'd bet my life that's where the orb needs to be returned.

"This is trippy," Greyson says, and I nod.

The air is still frigid and the orb in my hand is blinding, so I tuck it back into the pouch. The glow from the icicles and the emblem on the far wall light the space enough to see.

"Why doesn't that water sparkle?" Ash asks.

She's right. In the spirit world, water always shines like crystals, but the liquid seeping through the cracks in the wall and trickling over boulders to the stream isn't giving off any light. From where we stand the pond appears clear and smooth. The icicles hanging down from the ceiling glow, but they aren't shining like they should be.

"Don't know, don't care," Sterling says and starts forward. "Let's just get that orb back to its home and get out of here. This place gives me the heebie-jeebies. Not to mention I'm freezing my bits off and worried I'm going to compromise my ability to procreate if we stay here much longer."

"It's probably best for everyone if you don't reproduce anyway," I say with a cheeky grin. "Sterling Junior." I fake a shudder. "I'm not sure the world could handle it."

"Harsh," Sterling says, but shoots me a wink despite the dig.

As sad as I am to see him cover himself, I hand Thorne his shirt back and as a group we head toward the pond, our breath fogging the air in front of us. We easily leap over the small stream that bisects the cavern.

Sterling reaches the edge of the pond first.

"Hmm," Thorne makes a humming sound as he inspects the water.

"What?" I ask.

He tips his head back to look at the icicles above and then back down at the pond. "The water should be frozen."

That's a good point.

Sterling crouches down to test the temperature, but the instant he dips his fingers in the pool he shouts a curse and yanks his hand back, cradling it against his chest.

"Dude, what was that?" Greyson asks.

"That is *not* water," Sterling says. He uncovers his hand and I gasp.

The tips of his middle and pointer finger are missing down to the nail bed and look bloody and painful. Ash immediately shrugs off her backpack and starts rifling through it, pulling out a roll of gauze.

"Do you think they are going to grow back? This is my dominant hand, and that would truly suck to have two stumpy fingers." He's trying to make light of it, but from the look on Sterling's face as Ash wraps his fingers, I can tell he's concerned.

Something moves in my peripheral, and when I look over Thorne is crouched close to the pond's edge. My heart jumps into my throat. Whatever that liquid is, it's highly corrosive and I don't want Thorne anywhere near it.

"What are you doing?" I ask.

"I think I've seen this before," he says. Then he backs away from the edge and I can breathe normally again. "It's basically acid, but more potent and corrosive than anything in the mortal world." He glances up at the icicles again. "I'm guessing those are made of the same substance as well."

"Okay," Sterling says. "So no touching any of the liquid in this cave because it's liable to burn our faces off. Roger that."

"Let's just get this orb to its origin and get out of here," Thorne says, and I couldn't agree with him more.

Glancing at the golden starburst on the wall across from us, we're close enough that I spot a round indent in the middle of the emblem.

Bingo.

"Since swimming is out of the picture," Ash says, "one of us needs to fly over to the far wall and shove the orb into the middle of that gold starburst."

"Flying without clipping one of those icicles is going to be challenging," Greyson adds, eyeing the icicles warily.

I study the glowing shafts, noting they're in tight clusters and hang low, some of them almost kissing the surface of the pond. Greyson's right, flying through them will be tricky. And only Thorne, Steel, and I have the ability to fly since the others haven't gone through metamorphosis yet.

Steel has been uncharacteristically quiet since we dropped into the tunnels. Usually he's all about taking charge and issuing commands. Maybe Emberly has chilled him out a little. Or maybe it's something else, but he finally speaks up. "I could do it. My eagle form is more agile than angel wings."

"No, I'll do it," Thorne says. "I've seen your clumsy flying."

"I don't think so," Steel scoffs. "You don't even have two wings."

Thorne bristles and steps into Steel's space. "I can fly

straighter with one feathered wing than you can with two."

Steel takes a step forward and the pair are almost bumping chests. "There's no world where that is actually true."

I roll my eyes. They're pretty but stupid sometimes.

I don't feel like listening to Steel and Thorne squabble like an old married couple. I happen to have a pair of wings myself, and I'm the one holding the orb.

Pulling the orb out of the pouch, I release my wings.

"Nova, no!" Thorne shouts, but it's too late, I'm already airborne. And the first thing I do is almost fly right into one of the giant icicles.

Whoops.

Ignoring Thorne and my friends, I concentrate on getting to that emblem. The flying is tricky. If I fly too low I might accidently skim the surface of the acid pond but flying higher means I have to navigate around the icicles. After a handful of seconds, I start to gain confidence that I have a rhythm going.

I'm over halfway there when a loud voice echoes throughout the chamber. "Don't let her return the orb!"

I try to steal a glance over my shoulder, but the distraction causes me to wobble, and I clip one of the icicles with the tip of a wing; the feathers that brush up against it singe. I loop in a circle to steady myself and spot the group of angel-born pouring into the cavern.

My stomach bottoms out.

"Take her down," Malachi shouts.

My friends on the ground rush the group, waving their arms and shouting at Malachi, but his men don't listen and take aim with their weapons.

Thorne's in the air, flying low to the pond to reach me

quickly.

This is really bad.

A volley of projectiles, everything from arrows, to bolts, and even a couple of spears, shoot toward me. As if he has eyes in the back of his head, Thorne shoots upward, swerving to block their shots with his metal wing, but an arrow makes it past him, and I have to dodge to avoid it.

I slam into an icicle that's thicker than I am. Pain lances my shoulder and left wing and I instinctually fold my wings, causing me to drop toward the pond of acid below. I force myself to stretch my wings, but my left one won't cooperate, and I start to spiral.

I'm not scared of death, but this isn't the way I want to go.

Arms wrap around my middle, and I'm hauled into a hard chest. I bite my lip to keep from screaming as my abused upper back and wing rub against Thorne.

"Dematerialize your wings," he shouts in my ear. "I've got you."

With a thought, my wings fold back into myself and the pain dulls a bit. Thorne and I skim over the top of the pond, low enough to make me nervous as he brings me back to the edge. He lands, releasing me right away, and a wave of agony shoots down my spine.

This sucks so bad.

Thorne turns me, checking my back.

"How bad is it?" I ask, glancing over my shoulder at him.

He meets my gaze. "It will heal," is all he says.

I don't have the luxury of falling apart right now, so I shove the pain down. I'll deal with it later. Right now we have to deal with a psycho Elder on a power trip. *Goodie.*

Ash, Steel, Sterling, and Greyson stand between us and a

small angel-born army led by Malachi.

"You guys okay?" Steel shouts back to Thorne and me without taking his gaze off the armed Nephilim across the cavern.

"We're good," I answer.

Malachi steps forward, looking past Steel and the others to me, or more precisely to the orb I have clenched in my hand.

"I don't know what you all think you're doing, but you've gotten yourselves into some serious trouble." The acoustics in the cavern make sound carry, so he doesn't need to shout for us to hear him. His gaze travels to Thorne. "Conspiring with this enemy is considered treasonous." His gaze tracks slowly over each one of us. "But you can also add theft and insurrection to the list."

"And what about your crime of holding a seraph angel prisoner and experimenting on him?" I spit back at him.

A muscle jumps in Malachi's jaw, and several angel-born give each other sidelong glances, looking unsure for the first time. Unfortunately, most of them appear totally unaffected by my accusation, telling me they either already knew about what Malachi was up to, or are so conditioned to following orders that the truth makes no difference to them.

"We're looking to be lenient on you for your crimes," Malachi says. I don't need to ask about Thorne to know that his offer doesn't extend to him. Thorne will either be imprisoned for life or killed if we turn him over to Malachi. "But you need to hand over the orb now."

"What do you want it for?" I have no intention of turning the orb over, but I'm curious to see if he'll answer. I don't expect him to tell me the truth, or at least all of it, but how he answers will give me an idea of what message he plans to put out to justify his actions.

"We've lived in fear of the angels too long. They've hoarded power that should be ours."

It's true that there was a time that angels persecuted the Nephilim, but it's been centuries since that actively happened. The vast majority of Neph have never even come in contact with an angel before.

"The angels aren't our enemies," Steel says.

Malachi scoffs. "You younglings don't remember what it was like before. When we were in hiding from not only the Fallen and Forsaken, but angels intent on wiping us out, believing we were a cursed race. The angels might be playing nice with us now, but there's no guarantee they won't turn on us."

"The orb needs to be returned to its origin," I retort. "It's too powerful for the angel-born to possess. We may not have as much power as the angels, but that doesn't mean it's right for us to take theirs. What you did to Camiel was wrong. Especially since he's been a champion and protector of angel-born."

"I didn't want to have to do this, but you've left me no choice." Malachi lifts his arm and gestures to someone in the back.

Angel-born toward the entrance of the tunnel shift out of the way so others can come through. A familiar roar echoes throughout the chamber and my blood freezes.

"No," I whisper, and Thorne steps up closer, putting a steadying hand on my back.

The crowd continues to part, rippling down the center, until a cage is rolled up next to Malachi. Cleo roars and bats at the metal bars, creating sparks. Several angel-born back away from the thrashing bastet, but Malachi only glances at her smugly.

"Cleo." I take a step forward and Thorne catches me around the waist. He isn't holding me back, but rather reminding me to stay strong.

Cleo suddenly stops slashing at the bars, her head swiveling until she spots me. She releases a mournful mew that pulls on my heartstrings until I'm sure they're going to snap.

How did they capture her? *If they have Cleo, where are my parents?*

"What is that?" Greyson asks, and Ash shrugs.

"Let her go," I order.

I squeeze my fists and electricity starts to crackle over my knuckles.

Sterling glances back at me, his eyes wide when he spots my powers emerging. "Wicked cool," he breathes.

"I'm happy to release your pet," Malachi says. "After you hand over the orb."

I suck in a deep breath, my nostrils flaring. Closing myself off, I give the Elders a one-word answer: "No."

Malachi doesn't look surprised. He nods to an angel-born, who pulls their sword from their sheath. Cleo's smart enough to recognize the threat and starts going berserk trying to get out of the cage, but even though she's throwing her body against the bars, she's no match for the thick steel holding her captive.

I can't pretend to stay calm anymore. I can't let anything happen to her.

Electric power shoots up my arms. I'm ready to take that angel-born with a sword out if they even flinch in Cleo's direction.

Malachi holds his hand up, staying the angel-born. "Maybe this will change your mind," he says.

There's more commotion amongst the angel-born, and suddenly my parents are hauled forward, bound and gagged and bloodied and bruised.

This isn't right. They were supposed to be all right. I didn't want to leave them behind but they said they'd be able to talk their way out of any suspicion that was cast on them after I fled with Thorne and Camiel. My parents have been trusted and loyal members of our community for years, but now some of the angel-born they've known their whole lives, have fought beside, are standing idly by while they're being abused by the same people they've given their lives to serve.

I look at Malachi, ready to plead for my parents' lives, but the look on the cherub Elder's face makes the words stick in my throat. Up until this point, Malachi has presented himself as the benevolent Elder, concerned about the well-being of the angel-born race, but the smirk that lifts the corners of his mouth when he looks at me is downright evil.

He thinks he's won and he's enjoying my pain.

Vomit tries to work its way up my throat as I drag my gaze away from Malachi and back over to my parents. Even injured, the fire in their eyes makes it clear they aren't giving up. It's almost as if I can hear them encouraging me not to give up.

Digging deep, I transform my horror and absolute fear into something usable. My power floods my body, ready to be unleashed. Malachi is going down. If I have to take out the other angel-born in this cavern to see that happen, so be it.

25

I shoot a stream of electricity right at Malachi's chest, but he twists out of the way and my power hits the ground behind where he was standing, scattering angel-born in the vicinity. I take off toward Cleo and my parents. We're outnumbered at least ten to one. Freeing them will help with those odds. I focus on Cleo first. She's a creature of chaos, and chaos is exactly what we need to get the orb returned to its origin and maybe, *maybe*, escape with our lives.

My friends spring into action when I do. Steel transforms into a golden lion and charges toward Malachi and his small army of angel-born.

I flip the orb to Ash for safe keeping, and Greyson and Sterling close ranks around her, offering added protection for the orb. None of them have wings, so they won't be able to get it to the emblem on the far wall, but I'm confident they'll keep it safe in the meantime.

Thorne is right beside me as I jump over the acid stream. Malachi gives some sort of signal to his troops and the angel-born with wings release them and shoot over our heads, making a beeline for Ash, Greyson, and Sterling. The others rush at Steel, Thorne, and me, and I mentally prepare for the showdown. Angel-born without wings are just as formidable as those with, sometimes more so. The Nephilim who don't have wings, in combat situations tend to have powers and abilities that have been shaped and honed for offensive use. So although Ash, Sterling, and Greyson are most likely going to have to face off against fierce power angel-born, Steel, Thorne, and I are probably about to get smacked by some super strong angelic magic.

Even so, we don't hesitate as we clash with our first opponents. The only weapon I have on me is a dagger, but I don't even bother pulling it. With my powers, I'm the weapon, and every punch and kick I land is laced with an electric shock strong enough to put angel-born down.

I cut through the first few angel-born quickly. Steel works to my left, tossing Nephilim and batting at them with his paws, but he's careful not to use his mighty jaws on his fellow angel-born.

Thorne, on my other side, is not exercising the same caution. He uses his wing and angel-fire to clear the way to Cleo and my parents.

Some angel-born make it past us as we steamroll our way toward my parents and Cleo, and I try to keep my head in the game rather than worrying about my friends battling behind us. I know the moment the angel-born who passed us make it to the stream because their agony-filled screams echo off the cavern's domed ceiling.

"The liquid burns!" someone shouts. "Don't let it get on you."

There goes one of our few advantages.

Steel, Thorne, and I move steadily forward, but not fast enough for me. Wind cyclones around Steel as he grapples with virtue Neph who are using their affinity with air against him. Thorne uses his metal wing to block projectiles from the both of us.

Up ahead, beyond the group of angel-born slowing our progress, Malachi stands between Cleo's cage and my parents with only three other angel-born warriors. Two of them keep my parents restrained. The third, a throne angel-born, has his hands lifted to project a transparent domed barrier over them all.

Enough is enough. We don't have time to mess with all these small battles.

"Thorne," I yell over to him. "Take us out of this mess."

I nod my chin toward Malachi. He knows exactly what I'm asking. He reaches me in a single stride, scooping me up, and we're airborne.

Thorne lands us just outside the barrier. I meet Malachi's gaze through the transparent veil. He's clenching his jaw and there's anger simmering in his gaze. He didn't expect us to get this far, and he's pissed about it.

"The barrier," I say to Thorne, smashing my fist against it uselessly.

"Stand back," Thorne says, "I can burn it with angel-fire."

My parents renew their struggles, and the gag they put over my mother's mouth slips. "Protect the orb," she cries, and I whirl to see my friends passing it back and forth between them as they fend off attacks. But they're at a disadvantage against the fully matured angel-born with wings and abilities. They're only going to be able to keep the orb for so long.

"Steel," I yell, and Steel turns his large lion head toward me.

I point toward Ash and his brothers. He nods, and then in a flash of light he transforms into a giant eagle and flies toward them, leaving Thorne and me to free Cleo and my parents, and face off against Malachi.

Thorne has a huge ball of angel-fire formed between his palms. It's so hot I have to take a step away from him. He chucks the ball, and it hits its mark. The flames explode against the barrier, spreading until it's covered completely with red and silver fire.

"Thorne," I say, alarmed. My loved ones are inside the fiery inferno.

"Don't worry," Thorne says, "it won't burn them. It will just eat away at the barrier."

I shoot him an uneasy look, not convinced, but it's only a few heartbeats before the flames start to recede, the barrier disappearing along with it.

Malachi screams at his man to put up another barrier, but without the aid of spring water to charge his abilities, it's clear he's not going to be able to do that.

"Get Cleo. I'll handle Malachi and the angel-born," Thorne says and then charges forward, throwing a ball of angel-fire at the throne Neph.

I sprint to Cleo, who's pacing in the small cage.

Reaching through the bars, I pat her head and she purrs. "Just a sec, girl. Let me figure out how to get you out of here."

Cleo releases a disgruntled growl, unhappy with having to wait. I scan the cage for a lock or a release and find a coded padlock on the side. I'm about to fry it with my powers when I hear my mom yell.

"Killian, look out!"

I snap my head to the left in time to see Malachi transform into a tan lion with a black mane and take a swipe at my father, whose hands are still bound behind him.

My heart jumps into my throat, but my dad ducks and rolls out of the way. Thorne appears behind him and quickly cuts his bindings so he's free. It looks like Thorne has already incapacitated the other angel-born guard and freed my mom as well, so now it's him and my parents against Malachi.

Cleo roars, slashing a paw against the bars of her cage, demanding my attention.

"Stand back," I warn, and she moves to the farthest point of the cage.

I release a stream of my electricity at the lock, which sparks and catches fire. The door pops open. Cleo bursts out of the cage, going up on two legs to greet me. She licks the side of my face. It's gross but endearing.

Malachi roars loud enough to send a tremor throughout the cavern, and some of the icicles drop from the ceiling. The cries of angel-born ring out as they rain down upon them, no doubt burning straight through their clothes. I can only hope my friends didn't get hit.

Cleo drops back down to all fours and turns toward Malachi, baring her fangs at him.

"Go get him!" I tell her, and she takes off, disappearing before she reaches Malachi, but when he releases an enraged roar and a stream of blood starts flowing from his shoulder, I know she's attacked.

With Malachi momentarily distracted, I run over to Thorne and my parents. My mother has armed herself with a sword from one of her fallen guards and my father is searching the other.

"We're fine," my mom says when I reach them, taking a moment to pull me in for a quick hug. When she lets me go, she points toward the other side of the cavern, where my friends are fending off what remains of Malachi's army.

It almost looks like they're playing hot potato with the orb. One moment it's shining in Greyson's hand, the next Sterling is running with it in the other direction, then Steel swoops overhead with it in his talons as angel-born take aim at him with their crossbows. Flying over Ash's head, he drops it into her waiting hands.

"Go help them," she orders.

"We'll help Cleo keep Malachi busy," my dad says as he straightens, having just pilfered two battle axes from the unconscious angel-born at his feet. "But you need to help your friends return the orb to its origin. He's not going to stop until the orb is out of his reach."

After exchanging a quick look, my parents take off toward Malachi. They've fought together for long enough that they can practically read each other's minds, which shows as they break off at the exact same time, flanking Malachi as he tussles with an invisible Cleo.

Part of me wants to join them. My hatred for Malachi has grown tenfold in the last half hour, and my heart is with my parents and Cleo, but I disassociate myself from my feelings. The priority is still to get the orb out of play.

"Let's go," I say to Thorne, and he doesn't waste a moment. He wraps his arms around me and boosts us into the air.

The icicles aren't as dense on this side of the cavern, but Thorne still flies us close to the ground, not far over the bodies of the angel-born we fought. The ones that Steel and I fought are mostly just unconscious or too injured to fight, but the ones that Thorne faced off against didn't make it. I focus ahead, not wanting to look into the lifeless eyes of angel-born I would have died fighting with, rather than against, only a few short weeks ago.

We've almost reached Ash, who still has the orb and is dodging attacks from two virtue angel-born as they use their powers to send rocks shooting at her like bullets. Two winged angel-born spot us and jump into the air to intercept us, but Thorne is able to outmaneuver them. When we touch down though, they are right on us.

"Protect Ash!" I shout to Thorne, and spin toward the winged warriors, not waiting to see if Thorne listens to me.

I'm ready to blast my opponents with power when recognition flashes and I lower my hands.

Drake? Vespa?

Standing before me are two power Nephs who used to be in my parents' squadron. My hesitation costs me, because even though they know who I am they don't have the same reluctance about attacking as I do and come swinging at me with a sword and a mace. I hit the ground and roll to avoid the business ends of their weapons.

When I pop up, my eyes connect with Thorne's over Vespa's shoulder. He's using his metal wing to shield Ash from the stones the virtue Nephs keep pelting at her, but I can tell he wants to abandon my friend to come to my aid.

I shake my head, telling him not to come. I've got this.

Drake swings his mace straight at my head—super rude —so I throw a bolt of power at him that nails him in the chest, sending him flying back. Vespa gapes at me.

"How did you—?"

I don't let her finish her sentence. I hit her with a second blast that sends her soaring through the air as well. I start toward them, planning to double-tap to make sure they're out, when Ash's scream stabs my eardrums.

Spinning, I spot Thorne has taken out the virtue Nephs, and Ash is standing with her head thrown back, back bowed and mouth open in a silent scream. Thorne stands in front of her with his wings flared, frantically trying to figure out what's wrong. When his gaze lands on the Starfire Orb in her hand, he reaches out and tries to pry it from her grip.

I'm racing toward them when energy explodes from Ash, sending a wave of some sort of power shooting outward and knocking every angel-born, including me, to the ground.

A crack rents the air and I stare in horror as several large icicles break from the ceiling above the clear pond and fall, splashing into the acid-like liquid and sending a wave toward the edge.

"Look out!" Steel yells to his brothers, and all three of them start running, just barely missing the sloshing fluid.

Some other angel-born aren't as fortunate. Their cries of pain echo in the chamber.

Jumping up, I sprint over to Thorne and Ash, my breath catching in my throat as I look over Ash, who stands with a look of shock on her face as she inspects the most beautiful set of downy pearlescent wings I've ever seen.

Ash just went through metamorphosis.

"How did this happen?" I ask.

"The orb," Thorne says, nodding down at the stone still clutched in Ash's hand. "It sped up your metamorphosis too."

"Yeah, but it took more than an hour of exposure to do that."

"Its effects must be stronger here."

Maybe that's true. There's a lot of weird things about this cavern, so it isn't hard to believe that it's amplifying the orb's magic.

The Durand brothers appear. They're covered in cuts and bruises, but none of their injuries appear life-threatening. Steel will heal faster though; he's gone through metamorphosis and his brothers haven't.

I scan the cavern, noting the remaining threats. We've miraculously worked our way through the majority of Malachi's forces but we're still outnumbered. My parents and Cleo are still keeping Malachi at bay, but their fight has inched closer to our side of the cavern, and now they're battling dangerously close to the acid-filled creek. We only have a moment's reprieve as what's left of Malachi's men regroup.

"Are you okay?" Greyson asks Ash, awe in his gaze, lingering on her new white wings.

"Yeah, I'm fine. It's just . . . wow, right?" Ash says.

He nods.

"We need to take out the rest of Malachi's army," I say. "I don't think we'll be able to fly the orb to that emblem until they're out of the picture."

"Agree," Thorne says, and the others nod. "But let's get everyone juiced up first."

I don't have time to ask what he means before Steel shouts, "Incoming," and spins to intercept the first wave of angel-born, Grey right on his heels.

Thorne asks Ash for the orb, and after she hands it off she rushes to help Steel and Greyson.

"Sterling," Thorne calls. He tosses the stone to him. "Time to level up."

Sterling looks down at the orb in his hand and then back at Thorne. "Like just holding this glowing rock is going to —" Sterling doesn't finish his sentence before he's on his knees, gritting his teeth and breathing shallowly as his metamorphosis starts.

We're backed up against one of the cavern walls, so Steel, Greyson, and Ash hold the line as Sterling writhes in pain.

"When it's over, give it to the other one," Thorne says, meaning Greyson, and then joins the others.

Sterling looks up at me, his face red with the effort to keep from shouting in pain. "Agony," he grunts out.

I drop to my knees next to him, remembering how excruciating the experience was for me.

"It won't last for much longer," I say.

I go to rub his back, but when my hand connects with him, he's so hot it burns, and I have to yank it back.

Not able to hold it in any longer, Sterling throws his head back and lets out a pain-filled bellow. A bright light completely covers his body, growing in intensity until I have to look away.

When it dissipates and I snap my gaze back toward Sterling, a giant winged lion stands in the place of my fun-loving friend.

Whoa. I've never heard of a cherub lion having wings.

"Are you kidding me? He has wings?" Greyson says, disgruntled as he catches sight of his twin over his shoulder. "He's going to be impossible to live with now."

I shake my head as I snatch the orb off the ground at Sterling's feet. Greyson's not wrong, Sterling is going to brag about that forever. *Sucks.* I always hoped he'd turn into a bull when he went through metamorphosis.

Sterling paws the ground and clumsily flaps his new wings. After a few misses, he's able to shakily fly over the others, giving Malachi's troops something new to attack.

"Grey, heads up," I shout, and when he looks over I toss the orb at him. He snatches it from the air and Steel moves to cover him.

One more friend to go, then we're putting an end to this battle.

Ash looks over her shoulder at Grey as he takes his brother's place, her brow pleated and concern shining from her eyes.

"Switch with me," I tell her as I throw a sparking ball of electricity at the angel-born she's fighting with. Those two are close. If anyone should be with him when he morphs for the first time it should be her, not me.

She nods and then rushes over to Greyson, the ends of her pearlescent wings brushing the ground as she passes me.

It's barely a minute before a rush of power slams up against my back. I sneak a peek over my shoulder and see Grey standing with a brand-new set of brown wings and a look of utter confusion on his face. I'm right there with him. Greyson's a cherub Nephilim and should have shifted into one of three animals—a lion, an eagle, or a bull—not sprouted wings. Maybe the orb messed with the powers he should have inherited? After all, Sterling's lion shouldn't have wings either.

Something cuts a hot path across my thigh, and I gasp, looking down to see the bloody line my opponent sliced into my leg.

Well . . . shit. That's what I get for losing my focus.

From ten feet away Thorne catches sight of the split in my pants and blood dripping down my leg. I can already tell it's not as bad as it looks, just a shallow cut that doesn't affect my fighting, but the sucker sure is bleeding a lot.

Thorne starts toward me, abandoning his own fight just as I hit the angel-born who cut me with enough power to put her down. I open my mouth to tell him I'm fine when his eyes go wide and the end of a sword punches through his chest. He looks down, his face washed in shock at the blood-coated blade protruding from him.

I'm frozen, my heart refusing to believe what I'm seeing. My other friends battle on, oblivious that my world has just cracked and is on the verge of splintering apart.

Whoever sank the blade into Thorne's back pulls it out and Thorne falls to his knees, a trickle of blood leaking from the corner of his mouth.

I drop to my knees as well, certain my heart has stopped beating. And then I do what supernovas do. I explode.

26

I throw my arms wide; veins of electric power shoot from me in all directions, like tentacles that reach out and connect to my enemies. I've never used my powers like this before, but I know exactly how to aim it and it obeys me, wrapping around Malachi and his troops and avoiding my friends and parents.

Blue and silver zigzags of electricity connect me to each of the angel-born in the cavern, and when one of them tries to break free I tighten my hold, coiling my powers around them like a snake.

I stoke my power, and with a scream shove it through the connections, and every angel-born linked to me drops at once, dead before they hit the ground.

My friends' shouts and gasps echo in the chamber, but I'm not listening as I shuffle-crawl over to Thorne, who is lying prone and still on the sandy ground. His chest is still rising and falling, but there's a rattle with each breath. Blood bubbles from the hole in his chest and soaks his shirt. The hole in his back creates a puddle beneath him.

From the moment the battle started, I hadn't noticed the freezing temperatures in the cavern, but now my fingers feel like shards of ice as I slap my hands over his chest wound, doing what I can to slow the flow of blood. My hands shake as I apply pressure.

He's losing too much blood. Way too much.

"Don't move, we'll stop the bleeding," I say, my voice more confident than I am. On the inside I'm shaking like a leaf.

Looking over my shoulder, I yell to Ash for some bandages. She still has her small backpack of supplies on, but struggles to reach it with her large wings, so Greyson has to help.

When I glance back at Thorne, his face is ghostly white, the effects of blood loss already showing. Something warm and sticky presses against my wrist and I look down to see Thorne's blood-coated fingers grabbing me.

"Nova," he says barely above a whisper. "No regrets."

I shake my head. His words sound too much like a goodbye.

There's a commotion behind me, and I think my parents and Cleo have joined us. Sterling prowls back and forth in his lion form and I hear Steel talking with my mom and dad, coming up with a plan for getting over the acid-pond to return the orb, but I'm not listening to what they say. I couldn't care less about that blasted glowing stone right now.

Ash drops down on the other side of Thorne. "Help me turn him a little so I can get the entry wound packed."

Grabbing his shoulders, we angle Thorne over just enough so that Ash can shove a wad of bandages against his wound. Thorne grunts when we move him, the sound stabbing my heart. Ash takes over for me, applying fresh gauze to the hole in his chest. "Keep talking to him. Try to keep him conscious."

I grab his bloody hand, holding it against my chest. "Do you know what I thought the first time I saw you?"

Thorne gives a small shake of his head, his gaze latched on to mine like I'm his life force.

"I thought I'd never seen something so beautiful and fierce before."

He rolls his eyes, probably not appreciating being called beautiful, but it's true. Thorne is undoubtedly masculine, but he's so good-looking it's almost hard to look at him sometimes.

Ash lets out a shaky chuckle, probably remembering my reaction when we saw Thorne standing before the burning remains of Buckingham Palace.

I give him a wobbly smile, trying to act like I'm not freaking out right now when in reality I don't know when I've ever been so scared. "I asked Ash if you were moving in slow motion and said that even though you may be evil it didn't mean you couldn't also be smokin' hot."

Thorne tries to laugh but coughs up blood instead.

Cleo comes up beside me as Thorne struggles to breathe. She drops down on her haunches, leaning into me as she watches Thorne with what might be concern in her large hazel eyes.

"Sounds like you," Thorne says when the coughing subsides, quieter than a whisper at this point.

"What can I say? I'd never let a small thing like moral ambiguity sway my assessment of physical attractiveness." The comment was supposed to be light, but I have to shove the words past the lump in my throat and they sound as forced as they are.

Steel crouches down on the other side of me. "Killian, Ciera, and I are going to fly over to the emblem to return the orb," he says to us. "Then we're going to get out of here."

I nod absently. "Whatever. Take care of the orb so we can get Thorne help."

I try not to think of how far underground we might be or how long it will take us to get Thorne out and then drive him somewhere we can get medical help. If Thorne were a human, there'd be no way he'd make it, but he's an angel-born. A strong and stubborn one who's faced too much in his life to go out this way. He's just going to have to hang on.

I'm not paying attention, so I have no idea which one of them has the orb as my parents release their wings and Steel transforms into an eagle and takes off, but I'm not so distracted that I miss the roar that echoes through the cavern.

I twist toward Sterling, thinking he's messing around, only to see Malachi in lion form bounding over the acid creek, heading straight for us. I have no idea how he's not dead like the others. Maybe he could withstand more of my power because he's so old and powerful?

Sterling tries to intercept him, but in a blink Malachi's transformed into an eagle and soars over our heads on a trajectory for my parents and Steel as they shoot toward the starburst emblem on the back wall. He's fast, and reaches my mom first, knocking straight into her and sending her tumbling.

I gasp, watching her fall toward the acid pond, but my

father dives and scoops her up. Her wing is bent at an angle, so he has to fly her back to solid ground.

In a flash, Malachi reaches Steel and they start battling, both in eagle form, turning and banking around the acid icicles as they take shots at each other. Steel clenches the orb in one of his talons as they fight.

"Nova! Blast him!" Greyson shouts, but I can't. They're too intertwined. There's no way I can hit Malachi without taking out Steel.

My mom and dad reach the edge of the pond, and after setting my mother down on solid ground my dad shoots back into the air, weapons ready to try to intercept Malachi so Steel can get to that emblem. But the cherub Elder is strong and has the most experience fighting, and ties both of them up. With the threat of the acid pond below and icicles hanging down all over the place, battling Malachi is a dangerous endeavor.

"Come back," Greyson shouts. "Get him on solid ground and we can all take him on."

Steel banks left and swoops low, racing back toward us and Malachi takes the bait. He wants that orb badly enough to take on the lot of us for it.

"Nova, you have to go help them," Ash says.

I shake my head. "I'm not leaving him."

Thorne squeezes my fingers. "Go," he says, "I'm fine."

"Liar." He is anything but fine.

He scowls at me and then starts moving like he's going to sit up.

"What are you doing?" I say, pushing him gently back down.

"If you won't fight, I will."

I close my eyes, taking a deep breath through my nose. "Fine, but you will not give up on me."

If he thinks he can up and die on me, he has another thing coming. He knows how stubborn I can be. I won't allow it.

A whisper of a smile turns the corners of Thorne's mouth. "Wouldn't dream of giving up on you."

I look at Ash. "Keep him alive," I say, and then jump up, Cleo by my side as I rush over to where the others are tussling with the cherub Elder.

When I reach the group, Malachi is back in his lion form and Steel has shifted back into a man. Sometime in the few minutes I took my eyes off their scuffle to argue with Thorne, Malachi's injured my father as well. One of his wings hangs limply at an unnatural angle. He dematerializes it so it's not in the way, but I can see the pain on his face as he does.

"Malachi, this is enough," I say as I step into the circle around him. "Your troops are defeated, and you're surrounded. Stand down." I let my electric power light up my hands to let him know I mean business.

Turning to face me, he lets out a low growl, not looking the least bit ready to give up. I think he's going to charge me, but suddenly he whips around and attacks Steel, hitting him with his giant paw, and Steel goes sailing into a cavern wall.

The orb slips from Steel's grip as he slides unconscious to the cave floor. Malachi is on it in an instant, shifting into an eagle, snatching the orb, and then darting toward the cavern exit.

We can't let him leave with the orb.

I shoot a stream of my power at him, and it hits its mark,

wrapping around Malachi's eagle form like a whip. I yank on the connection and Malachi tumbles through the air. It all happens so quickly I don't think about where he is, and Malachi falls straight into the stream.

He lets out a screech so high-pitched and loud I worry that my ears are bleeding. In a flash he's turned back into a man, trying to crawl from the acid. He only makes it halfway before his body stops obeying him.

The sight is gruesome. The acid has burnt away most of his skin and eaten through muscles and bone, but he's still alive, clawing at the ground.

Greyson and my mom rush forward and try to pull him out, but when they try to grasp his arms they have to touch skin-less flesh and he lets out a scream like I've never heard before. By this time, most of his lower body is already gone.

Malachi is awful, a true villain, but no one deserves to die in that much pain.

Snatching a sword, I sprint to where Greyson and my mom are still trying in vain to help him.

"Stand back," I order.

Malachi looks up at me, his gray eyes pleading. He nods when he sees the sword in my hand. I bring it down on his neck, cutting his head off in one clean swipe.

The cavern goes eerily silent.

The orb sits in the sand at my feet, shining brightly. Picking it up, I turn, ready to hand it over to someone, but there are no more experienced flyers left.

"I think I might be able to do it," Greyson says, giving his wings a practice flap. He can hardly get into the air let alone maneuver through the columns of acid icicles. Ash is going to have the same issue. And even if Sterling were a practiced flyer, his lion form is too large.

I release my wings, gritting my teeth against the pain from the acid burns.

My dad joins us. Cleo paces in a circle around me and my mom.

"You're injured," my mom says.

"I am, but I can still fly. Get Steel up and then figure out how to move Thorne out of the cave. We have to get him medical help. I'll return the orb and be right behind you guys."

Looking my parents in the eyes, I wait for them to agree, and then look at Greyson. "Promise me you'll get him out of here."

"I promise," Greyson says.

With a nod, I jump and flap my wings, biting my tongue to keep from yelling in pain. When I fly over Thorne, I see him watching me with a look of concern on his face, but I have to block him out and trust that my parents and friends will take care of him.

Once I'm over the pond, all my brainpower goes toward maneuvering around the low-hanging icicles, which become more densely clustered the closer I get to the starburst emblem.

Thorne roars in pain. I can't stop myself from glancing over my shoulder to see them trying to lift him. I wobble in the air and the very tip of one of my wings brushes up against an icicle, the feather burning instantly. I keep my eyes fixed on the obstacles in front of me, but whether imagined or real, the phantom pain of Thorne's wounds pulses in my chest with every heartbeat.

When I clear the last icicle, I feel like crying in relief. With only a handful of flaps of my wings before I reach the wall, I grip the orb tightly, half scared I'm going to trip some unseen booby trap that will prevent me from reaching its origin—but suddenly I'm there. I try to keep my wing beats steady like Thorne taught me to hover in the air, but I still bob up and down, my hand shaking as I reach forward with the orb, moving as close as possible to the emblem without smashing into the wall.

I've nearly got it. I'm a foot away. Six inches. One inch.

The orb slides into the round opening in the middle of the emblem with a click.

There's a moment when nothing happens, then the starburst emblem flares with golden light and a wave of power explodes outward, forcing me back into the mortal world and de-materializing my wings.

I fall toward the deadly liquid below, frantically trying to bring forth my wings, but I can't. I only have wings in the spirit world. Without wings, I can't fight gravity and there's only one way to go . . .

Down.

27

"N O!" Thorne's scream rips through the cavern and is the last thing I hear before I plunge into the pond.

I'm tucked into a ball, expecting the acid to start eating away at my flesh, leading to a gruesome and painful death, so it takes a solid two seconds before I realize that isn't happening. The clear fluid around me doesn't hurt.

Though it is . . . *chilly*.

I swim to the pond's surface, taking a big gulp of air when I break through and noting that the air is considerably warmer than it was before.

"He's going to kill himself."

"Someone knock him out."

"Don't do that. He may not have the strength to recover from a head wound."

"He won't recover from blood loss if he doesn't stop trying to reach her."

My friends' shouts echo in the chamber, reaching me easily.

"Let me go!" Thorne roars through the madness.

"I'm okay," I yell, fearful he'll die before I can reach them if he doesn't calm down.

"Nova?" Thorne shouts. It's just one word, but I can hear the weight of his relief in my name.

"It's just water now. Keep going. I'll swim out and catch up with you guys."

Something crashes into the water to my right, splashing me and sending ripples over the pond. I look up and there are still icicles overhead, but they're melting and detaching from the ceiling, raining down upon the pond and cavern floor.

You've got to be kidding me. I can't catch a break.

Moving as fast as I can, I swim in a straight line for the closest edge, just praying I don't get impaled by a falling chunk of ice. The water sloshes all around me as icicles fall, but I make it to the shallows and then run the rest of the way out of the pond. The crunch of crashing ice fills the cavern, but Thorne's shouts as he rages against my friends rise above the noise.

I sprint toward them, keeping an eye on the chamber ceiling. There aren't as many icicles on this side, but I still have to dodge and weave, which eats up precious seconds to get back to the group and an out-of-control Thorne.

"I'm here. I'm all right," I say as I skid to a halt in front of Thorne, taking his face in my hands.

He was fighting against Steel and Sterling to reach me, but now he sags in their arms and they're the only things keeping him from falling to the ground.

His shirt is soaked with blood; his face and skin are white as a sheet of paper. His lids start to close, but there's a small smile on his lips.

"Greyson, help me bandage him so we can carry him out of here," Ash calls, and then orders Steel and Sterling to set him down carefully.

I want to hold his hand while Grey and Ash work to pack more bandages against his wounds and wrap gauze around him, but they need me out of the way, so instead I hover above them, wringing my hands.

Something bumps my thigh and I look down to see Cleo.

"What? How?" I murmur even as I'm moving my hand to rub behind her ear.

Cleo is a creature of the spirit world; she doesn't phase back and forth like we can. She shouldn't be here.

"We don't know." I look up to see my mom standing a little ways away. "When you returned the orb, it forced all of us back in the mortal world, including Cleo."

I shake my head. It's a problem for later.

Ash and Greyson finish, then Grey shows us how to link our hands to make a makeshift stretcher for Thorne. It's slow moving, but Ash leads the way as we travel through the tunnels as quickly as possible. I try talking to Thorne to keep him conscious but he's barely holding on, having used whatever reserve of strength he had to try to reach me.

It's an eternity before we reach the hole we first dropped into. Night has fallen and moonlight pours through the round opening above.

There's no gentle way to get Thorne out, but he stays silent as he's hauled up from a rope tied under his arms. I'm waiting at the top when they pull him out and notice that he's soaked through his new set of bandages and lost consciousness.

He's lost too much blood. I know he has. Angel-born are tough and hard to kill, but even though we're free of the tunnels, we're still miles away from any human medical facilities, and even farther from angel-born help. His wounds are too severe—he's lost too much blood to recover.

"He's not going to make it," I whimper.

The remaining members of our group jump out of the hole, but my attention is solely on Thorne and what are likely our final moments together.

He's going to die. I'm going to lose him.

"We've got to get him in the car," I yell, panicked and frantic, not wanting to believe what my heart knows is true.

Everyone starts to move into position to lift Thorne, when Emberly and Camiel suddenly appear, both outfitted head-to-toe in their golden battle armor. Camiel is still gaunt, but the golden hue of his natural skin has returned, and he appears alert and battle ready.

The next instant, more angel-born phase into the mortal world. I recognize Nikias and Sorcha, other Council Elders. Sable and Deacon appear as well, along with a half-dozen other angel-born I don't recognize.

"What happened?" Emberly asks, taking in our bruised and battered group, as well as Thorne's bloody body.

Steel steps forward and pulls her into his arms and they both visibly relax, the tension leaving their shoulders now that they are reunited. "We found the origin, but we were attacked by Malachi and his troops before we could return it."

"And the orb?" Camiel asks.

"Returned," Ash answers him and then looks over at me. "Thanks to Nova."

Sorcha, the red-haired and freckled virtue Elder steps forward. "We've arrested Zara and Draven and are trying to figure out who else might have been in on their plans. There'll be a trial to determine their fate, but where are Malachi and his troops?"

Her question hangs in the air and my friends look everywhere but me. I'm the one who killed Malachi. I'm the one who finished off the rest of his troops, but no one wants to say it out loud.

"Dead. All of them," I announce.

Thorne lets out a low groan, his fingers brushing against my hand. I grab it and hold it to my chest, making sure he knows I'm here. "We don't have time for a reunion or catch-up. Thorne needs help. He's—" My voice fails; I can't get anything else out.

Camiel shoos everyone away and then crouches low over Thorne. I can hear the others talking amongst themselves, most likely filling each other in, but Thorne and the barely perceptible rise and fall of his chest is my priority.

Camiel is silent as he holds a hand over Thorne's chest wound.

"Can you help him?" I ask, a sliver of hope lodging itself in my heart. If anyone can help Thorne now it would be a full-blooded angel, right?

At first Camiel doesn't answer. but then he shakes his head. "I can't," he admits.

I grab Camiel's forearm, something I'd never do if I were in my right mind. Angels have killed Nephilim for less, but desperation edges out my good sense. "Is your telepathy working again? Call a Celestial. They have healing powers, right?"

Camiel frowns down at where I'm gripping his arm, and then gently, but firmly, removes my hand. "Not all Celestials are as gifted as the one I commissioned to watch over my daughter, and even if they were, it would be too late. He's run out of time. I'm sorry."

A sob escapes my mouth. I shake my head. Strands of my hair stick to my tear-stained cheeks. "It's too soon. We didn't have enough time. We hardly had a chance."

I'm not making much sense, but the look in Camiel's eyes says he understands. He lost his soul-bonded partner as well, and the heartache from his loss shines through on his usually impassive face.

Leaning down, I whisper into Thorne's ear. "Thorne, wake up. Please." My voice cracks and his fingers twitch on the hand I hold between both of mine. I pull back and his eyelids are cracked. He's moving his mouth but doesn't have the strength to give voice to his words.

"Thorne, please don't give up. Now that we've found each other, I don't want to do life without you. I need you. I . . . I love you."

Thorne's breath catches and his eyes flare. He swallows and then tries to take in a gulp of air, but wetness rattles in his chest when he does.

He's moving his lips again and I lean in to try to hear him, only barely catching what he says.

"Love you too," he murmurs as his eyelids slide shut. His mouth curves into a soft smile like he's content, even a breath away from death.

No . . . no . . . you're not supposed to have love ripped away from you at the exact moment you find it. This isn't fair.

My heart is breaking into a million pieces that I'll never be able to put back together. I can't walk through the rest of my life with parts of me so broken.

It's silent except for my sobs. Cleo rubs her head into my

back, but not even her presence can soften this moment. It's jagged and raw and it feels like my insides are wrapped in razor wire. Every sob brings on a fresh wave of pain. Every breath is too heavy to heave. Even the tears dripping down my face scald.

Camiel's voice breaks through my bubble of agony. "I can't help him, but you can."

"What? How?" I don't look away from Thorne, worried he'll draw his last breath and I'll miss it.

I don't understand Camiel. I have no medical training. How can I help Thorne when he has a hole through his body that leaks more blood every second?

"There's a way for soul-bonded pairs to share their life force," Camiel says. Someone gasps but I don't bother to figure out who. "I can perform a ritual so that you can share your strength with each other," Camiel continues, "but you'll be connected on levels you aren't right now, and the bond between you will be irrevocable."

I tear my gaze from Thorne to look up at Camiel. "According to you, we're already soul-bonded. How much more connected can we even be?"

Camiel's gaze flicks to his daughter, who looks just as confused as I am, before returning to me. "This is deeper than even that bond. It's deeper than a marriage, and it's not just for life. It's for beyond that as well. You'll be connected to him in every way possible, including death, but it may save him now."

I fixate on the only thing he said that really makes a difference right now. "So I can save him? Share my life force or whatever with him and he won't die?"

Camiel nods. "Yes. It's possible for one member of a soul-bonded pair to save the life of the other, but once it's done you'll never be able to undo this connection. You'll be linked to Thorne for this life and the rest of eternity. His fate will become your fate, and your fate his. One of your deaths will mean the death of the other."

"Yes, yes. Whatever. Just do it," I say, watching the times between Thorne's breaths get further and further apart.

"Nova," my mother says, stepping forward. "Is this really what you want?"

I look up at my parents. Their faces are drawn; there's a deep pleat between my mom's eyebrows, and my dad's mouth is pinched. It's clear both of them would rather see Thorne die than me bonded to him, but this isn't their decision.

"I won't let him die." My words are hard. Final.

Pressing her lips together, she nods, understanding this is my choice and letting me make it.

Camiel makes everyone move away.

"This will be painful," he says, and I nod to let him know I understand.

I'd be lying if I said I wasn't nervous, but even though I've only known him a short time, a world without Thorne is unimaginable. If the price of keeping him alive is sharing my life with him, I'll pay it, gladly.

"Are you ready?"

I look up at Camiel and his face devoid of warmth. "Do it," I say, and he starts to speak in a lyrical language I don't understand.

I squeeze Thorne's hand, willing him to keep breathing and his heart to keep beating. If he dies before Camiel finishes, I'm not sure if this will work.

What starts as a pinprick of pain in my chest starts to expand, slicing straight through me and growing in size until I look down, fully expecting to see a blood-coated blade protruding from my body.

Camiel said it would be painful and he wasn't lying. I grit my teeth, determined to bear the pain if it means I'll be saving Thorne's life.

Eventually, the pain gets so intense it's all I feel, hear, or see. I lose everything besides the agony, and Thorne's hand still gripped between both of mine.

When the world starts to dim, I don't fight it. Oblivion would be a nice reprieve from the burning agony in my chest, so when the darkness starts to swallow me I welcome it with open arms and sink into its embrace.

28

wake in a soft bed with crisp sheets, a fresh set of clothes, and an awareness that tells me I'm not alone. When I crack my lids Thorne is there, sitting in a chair next to the bed staring back at me. The sun filters through the window, lighting one side of his face while the other half remains shadowed. He looks whole and well—and most importantly, alive.

I stretch and then flip over, scooting into a seated position and tucking my legs under me.

"Hi," I say, feeling uncharacteristically shy.

Thorne's face is expressionless as his gaze sweeps over me. "How are you feeling?"

I rub my chest. There's not even a whisper of pain anymore, but something seems different. Not exactly off but different. I feel changed. In what way I'm not yet sure.

I smile at Thorne, trying to give him the reassurance that I think he needs. "I'm great. Perfectly fine."

Thorne's features finally soften. "Good."

I swing my legs over the side of the bed and face him. He

presses back into his seat, putting some distance between us. I try not to overthink it.

"How long have I been asleep?"

"Three days," he says. "I just woke up a few hours ago."

"Where are we?" I ask, scanning the room.

I don't recognize the space, and there doesn't seem to be anything particularly special about it. There's a bed, the chair that Thorne's sitting in, and a dresser pushed up against one of the white walls. No personal belongings in sight.

"We're in a safe house outside of San Francisco. Steel and Emberly had to go back to Egypt to start dealing with the mess Malachi made, and Camiel has returned to his angels. Your parents are both here, and some of your friends. They needed some time to allow their bodies to recover from their metamorphoses."

Wow. We're finally back in America and I don't even remember the trip.

There's a long yawn from the ground on the other side of the bed and then Cleo's head pops up. Spotting me, she jumps on the bed, her weight making the frame groan, and flops down beside me, rolling on her back.

"And of course there's Cleo as well."

I run a hand over her soft fur, and she stretches lazily.

"Who changed us?" I ask, taking in the leggings and tank I'm wearing.

Thorne's mouth pinches. "I don't know, and I don't want to know."

I smile, thinking of how uncomfortable he'd be if he found out Steel had been the one to do it, but we have bigger things to discuss.

"So," I say, not knowing how to start this conversation.

Does Thorne even know what happened when he was seconds away from death? There wasn't time to consider the possible repercussions. My focus had been solely on saving his life, but really I made a life-altering decision for him. I have no idea how he feels about being bound to me in this way.

"So," he echoes, and then a smirk curves his lips as he arches a brow. "I hear you married us while I was unconscious."

It's good to see a smile on his face.

"Worse than that," I say with a smirk of my own. "Marriage you can end. Camiel did some weird angel voodoo and linked our souls or something. I don't know all the details, but I hope you don't mind because there's no take-backsies."

I wink, expecting him to immediately give me some reassurance that I did the right thing, that he's not upset we're connected on a deeper level than we were before, but he stays silent. The soft smile he does give me isn't convincing enough to hide the troubled look in his gaze.

"Are you, you know, okay with this?" I ask, gesturing between us.

Thorne reaches out and takes my hand, running his thumb over the back in soothing circles.

"Nova, what you did for me . . ." He takes a deep breath before going on, a look of wonder in his gaze. "No one has ever cared for me enough to sacrifice themselves like you did."

"Sacrifice?"

Thorne nods. "Our lives are tied together now, and so are our deaths. If I die, I'll pull you into the grave with me."

"Pfft." I wave his concern off. "I'm not worried about

that. Angel-born are long-lived, and I don't think either one of us are planning on dying anytime soon."

Thorne frowns. "I live with a death sentence hanging over my head. I'll never be safe, and that means you won't either."

Letting go of my hand, he shoves to his feet, his movements jerky as he stands in front of the curtain-less window. Cleo stirs next to me, flipping back on her stomach, her gaze moving between Thorne and me as if trying to work out what the issue is.

I slide off the bed, taking tentative steps toward Thorne. I don't need the link between us to tell him his emotions are stormy. The tense set of his shoulders and his refusal to look at me broadcast that loud and clear.

"Thorne, do you know why I did what I did?"

It's a beat before he answers me. "Because I would have died if you hadn't."

"Yes, I couldn't fathom living in a world without you. But really it's because . . . I love you."

His shoulders go impossibly tense, and he clenches his fists.

Rejection lashes against me like a crack of a whip and I recoil.

Cleo jumps off the bed, directing a low growl at Thorne before brushing up against my legs as she circles me.

Through my pain, I sense something deep in my chest, pain that doesn't feel like it's my own, but this connection with Thorne is too new for me to be able to sift through what exactly may be coming from him.

Thorne turns and leans back against the window frame.

"Would you have rather I let you die?" I ask, bitterness rising to swallow my pain.

Thorne runs a hand over his face and shakes his head. "No. Yes. I don't know." His gaze locks with mine, his eyes begging me to accept something that I can't yet understand. "I'll never stop being thankful for what you did. I may not deserve to live—"

"Don't say that," I snap. Thorne did bad things, but he's not that man anymore.

"What I'm trying to say is that being connected like this is dangerous for you, and only makes what's going to happen next harder for the both of us. I'm thankful to be alive, but I wish there'd been another way."

My stomach drops, my gut telling me that Thorne is dragging us to a ledge that he plans to jump right off of. Part of me wants to stop him from talking altogether, but the other part of me needs to know what he's leading up to. "What do you mean? What happens next?"

"I won't ever be safe around humans or angel-born, or even the Fallen or Forsaken anymore. If I want to survive, if I want *you* to survive, I have to leave and go into hiding, probably in the spirit world."

There it is. He's planning to leave me.

"Fine. I'll go with you."

He's shaking his head, determination shining from his eyes.

"Why are you doing this?" I whisper.

Can't he see the ways that he's breaking me. If he plunged a dagger right through my heart, I'm not sure it would hurt as much as his words right now.

"I'm just being realistic. We exist in two different worlds. I'll never fit into yours. That's on me. I've done too many bad things, caused too much damage, and I refuse to drag you down with me."

As we stand facing one another, I can almost see Thorne shutting down parts of himself, cutting off whatever he can to mute the connection that exists between us. Whether he's doing it to protect himself or me, I don't know.

"But we're soul-bonded," I whisper, reminding him that even if he won't admit it now, there's something strong between us that will never go away.

"Not every soul-bonded pair lives happily ever after." He looks away, almost like he can't bring himself to look me in the eye anymore.

And then it hits me.

"You were never planning on sticking around. You were always going to leave eventually."

Thorne turns, his shoulders stiff.

I take a step forward, moving into his space and demanding he answer me. "When were you planning to duck out? After we returned the orb? Or did you try to do it sooner but couldn't make a clean getaway?"

Thorne takes a deep breath, his chest rising and falling before he turns back to me.

"Once the orb was out of play and Malachi and the other corrupt Council members were taken care of, I figured you wouldn't need me to protect you anymore. You could go back to your life as if I never stepped into it."

I scoff. He's a fool if he believed I could move on with my life as if he hadn't crashed into it and stolen my heart.

Thorne sees the truth of that in my gaze. "Nova, I always knew stolen moments were all I was ever going to get with you. It's enough for me to know you're safe."

"I didn't need you to protect me against any of that, and I don't need you to protect me now. I'm a big girl. I've always done just fine taking care of myself."

"You're not wrong. Even those were just excuses to stay close to you for a little while longer."

"And now what? You've run out of excuses?"

Thorne scowls, his temper finally rising to meet my own. "I'm trying not to be selfish. You have a life. A beautiful life with friends and family who love you unconditionally. You have a noble purpose and a place where you fit, and if I could stay next to you I would . . . but I can't. Being with me would take you away from every good thing you have. Even if I'm not locked up, even if I'm able to get some sort of pardon from the remaining Council members, I'll be hunted for years, decades, perhaps centuries.

"There aren't enough good deeds to wipe away what I've done, don't you understand that? A life with me means a life on the run, never knowing where or when or even if you'll see your loved ones again. I won't take away all you have when I have so little to offer in return."

"So, you'll give up without even trying? Without even fighting for what we have, for what we could be together?"

"I'll give up *everything* to make sure you're safe and have the life and love that I never had, that I can never fully give you," he roars.

Cleo lashes her tail and gives Thorne a warning growl. He flicks his gaze down to her and then back to me, not looking the least bit intimidated. I absently pat her head to calm her down. I don't think she'd ever attack Thorne, at least not full out, but this isn't her fight.

Thorne and I stare at each other. Everything we've said, and everything we haven't, filling up the space between us.

I get that he thinks he's doing the right thing, but all he's really doing is smashing this beautiful thing between us. Everything he said about what I would have to give up to be with him is probably right. To the world Thorne is still, and will always be, a monster that should be destroyed. But what he doesn't realize is that I understand all that I'd be sacrificing, but for him, to have a life with him . . . I would. I'd leave it all behind to forge a path for us to be together, but to hear him say he's not even willing to try for us is breaking me.

"If that's how you feel. If you don't think I'm worth fighting for, then you're right, you're not worthy to be with me."

He flinches and I know I've hit my mark.

I can't hold my tears back for much longer. I turn and walk stiltedly out of the room and then out of the house with Cleo on my heels, only making it into the wooded area in the back yard before I break down. Cleo curls her body around me as I sob.

When I return to the house much later, Thorne's already gone. And he never comes back.

29

*L*ife seems to go back to normal for everyone. I do a decent job pretending it has for me as well. I return to Seraph Academy with Ash, Greyson, and Sterling, and with special clearance from Sable, Cleo comes with us too. I do what I can to push Thorne from my mind, training long hours and studying hard to fill every moment so my thoughts don't wander to him, but the nights are hard. I often have dreams of him and wake up with his smell lingering on the pillow next to me, confused over whether my nighttime visions are the product of an overactive imagination or something tangible.

I learn to go through each day by putting on a fake smile and taking one step at a time, but I live with a constant throbbing in my chest. Heartache that I don't know is mine or Thorne's. Whatever Camiel did connected Thorne and me in such a deep way that I sometimes sense twinges of emotions that aren't my own.

Days pass in a blur of academy life. My grades have

never been better, and I'm unbeatable on a training mat, but faking that I'm all right is starting to wear on me.

I stare out the window of Sable's office. Steel and Emberly flew into Colorado the night before and are giving an update on Zara's and Draven's trials, and what they're doing to root out more of Malachi's co-conspirators. When they finish, they move on to discussing the Council's plan to move toward an elected form of Nephilim government. Just like everything else, I pretend to care—but I really don't.

The truth is, I don't care about much these days.

I notice Steel shooting me concerned looks but I don't care about that either. As soon as there's an opening, I excuse myself, leaving not only Sable's office but the academy building as well to walk in the forest.

I've never been much of a nature girl, but I've been self-teaching myself survival skills since returning to Seraph Academy. Not that I need survival skills to take a walk, but it's late June and the mountains are beautiful, and I can be alone, which is the only time I can let my guard down these days. Everyone's been staring at me since I returned, which old Nova would have loved but new Nova doesn't appreciate.

A branch snaps and I sigh.

"You can show yourself. I know you've been tailing me for the last fifteen minutes."

Steel walks out from behind the tree he was hiding behind. "You looked like you wanted to be alone."

"Then why did you follow me?"

Steel studies me as we continue walking. He doesn't say anything until I look back and give him a *What?* Face.

"Ash is worried about you," he says.

I roll my eyes. "Ash is worried about everyone. That's kinda her 'thing.' The mothering-vibe is strong with her."

Steel nods in agreement and we fall silent as we meander through pine trees and over a small creek. We reach the edge of an overlook, and I take a seat on a boulder. I know Steel followed me out here to say something, and I'd rather he just spit it out. I don't have to wait long. He starts in right after he plops down next to me.

"I won't pretend to fully understand you and Thorne. I hate the guy, most likely always will, but I do know that if you have something like Em and I do, you shouldn't deny it."

I can't quite cover my flinch when Steel says his name. Of course I suspected Steel wanted to talk about Thorne, but I'd forgotten how painful it was to hear his name out loud. The rest of my friends have been extra careful to avoid talking about anything Thorne-related—at least in front of me—so this is the first time I've heard his name uttered in weeks.

"Being with Thorne means I'd have to give up everything I've known, and I'd probably have to live in the spirit world." I recite the words almost like they are memorized. It's the reason Thorne left, and I don't know what else to say.

Steel looks at me from the corner of his eyes. "If Em told me she wanted to live on the moon, I'd shrug and ask when we were leaving."

I sigh. "He left me, remember?"

"Yeah, that was messed up, but I can see where he was coming from. If I thought being around Emberly would hurt her, I'd probably leave her as well."

"That's stupid."

Steel shrugs. "Dudes aren't as smart as girls. Pretty sure that's a scientific fact. Sometimes we're so focused on solving a problem we don't step back to take in the big picture." He throws an arm around my shoulders, giving me a side-hug. "But no one can tell you how to feel or how to live your life. Maybe you can give him up—honestly, I'd rather that you did—I'm just saying that if you find out you can't, I get it. There are some things in this world that we just can't live without. If he's one of those things for you, then you shouldn't give him up no matter what anyone says."

I lift an eyebrow. "Including you?"

Steel lets out a deep laugh. "Especially me."

I chuckle with him, a bit lighter, but then sadness returns.

"He didn't fight for me, Steel."

"He might have felt that leaving you *was* fighting for you. Fighting for you to have a better life than he believed he could give you." Steel heaves a sigh. "Thorne isn't like us. If I hadn't seen him with you I would say he doesn't even understand what love is. Maybe what he needs is to see someone fight for him, so he understands what it looks like."

I'm silent for a while, running Steel's advice over in my head. I don't know if he's right, but I do know I'm miserable without Thorne and I still want to be with him. Maybe that makes me pathetic, but I don't want to let my pride stand in the way of living my life with the man I love.

"I don't even know how to find him," I finally say.

"Don't you?" Steel arches his brow, calling me out.

I know what he's alluding too. I haven't tested it yet, but sometimes there feels like there's a cord connecting the two of us, and if I just follow my instincts it would lead me to him.

I pack a single backpack and leave a note for my parents on my bed before Cleo and I slip out of Seraph Academy. I didn't tell any of my friends because I'm not good with goodbyes. Besides, I'm sure Steel already knows I'm leaving and can fill in the blanks for everyone else.

I believe I'll see my parents and friends again. I have hope Thorne and I will be able to figure out a way to safely interact with people—supernatural and otherwise—someday. But since I don't know when that day will come, the note I left my parents explains that I left Seraph Academy of my own accord with the intentions of finding Thorne to be with him. That was the easy part. The hard part is going to be knocking sense into Thorne that he's stuck with me, whether he thinks I'm better off without him or not.

Cleo walks beside me as we head west, crunching over sticks and pine needles as we travel deeper into the Rockies. Even though it's mid-summer, the night air is crisp here in the mountains, but feels good as it swirls around me.

I don't know where Thorne is. The reality is that it might take me a couple of days or a couple of months to find him, but I'm confident I'm headed in the right direction. My instincts have been screaming at me to head in this direction from almost the moment I arrived back at Seraph Academy.

We haven't been traveling for very long when I notice that the sensation inside, that connection that I associate with Thorne, grows stronger with every step I take. My heartbeat picks up with something that feels a lot like anticipation, but I don't know why until Cleo and I clear a set of trees and I spot a figure standing up on a grouping of boulders.

I freeze, recognizing Thorne immediately.

He stands with his back to me, looking out over the valley. Even though it's the middle of the night, I'm sure he can see every detail. The moon and starlight are more than enough for angel-born sight.

Cleo silently slinks back into the trees, sensing she should leave us alone.

I must be at least fifty feet away from Thorne when he realizes he's not alone. His shoulders tense and one of his hands spasms, then he turns, slowly, his gaze locking with mine.

I suck in a breath, feeling like I just got punched in the stomach. I wasn't expecting to see him this soon. Mentally, I'm just not prepared, and my mind whirls as it struggles to catch up.

Thorne jumps down from the boulders, stalking toward me. He stops a body length away.

"Are you real?" he asks, his eyes flashing in the moonlight.

"Yes," I whisper.

I'm gearing up to launch into a long-winded speech, an explanation for why I'm here. He needs to know that even if he's willing to give up on me I won't give up on him, on *us*, but Thorne moves so fast he blurs and the next thing I know his arms are wrapped around me and his mouth is on mine.

I gasp. Thorne takes advantage of the movement to run his tongue over mine and I'm gone.

I return his kiss like my mouth is starved for him, like *I'm* starved for him. My hands are everywhere. In his hair, gripping his shoulders, wrapping around his waist to tug him as close as possible. And Thorne is just as frantic for me as I am for him.

He grabs me under the thighs and wraps my legs around his waist, walking me backward until I bump up against something rough and cold. I think it may be a rock, but I don't really care, I'm just glad it allows him to press even closer.

Delicious bits of energy weave under my skin; goose bumps break out on my arms as we kiss. We need to talk, but we also need this physical connection. It's only now that I truly understand how badly my body has ached to be close to his.

Thorne breaks the kiss, his breaths coming out in harsh pants. His lips are wet and plump, and his hair is messy from my fingers running through it.

"I can't do it," he says, struggling to speak between breaths.

"Huh?" I give my head a shake, trying to make sense of his words.

He can't kiss me?

Well, that's a lie. He's actually quite good at that and I'm a little peeved he stopped to argue with me about it.

"I can't stay away any longer," he explains, and some of the fuzz in my brain disappears. "I know you're better off without me, and I know I can't give you the life you deserve, and you should have so much better than me, but I can't stay away any longer. I love you too desperately to let you go, and if—"

I cut him off with a punishing kiss. He's saying exactly what I didn't dare hope he would, but now that the words are coming out of his mouth, I know I don't need to hear them. I know how he feels about me. He's shown me with everything that he's done up until this point, including trying to leave me alone, but more than that, I feel *him*. I sense the tornado of emotions deep inside, and it's just as powerful as what I feel for him.

Any remaining doubts I might have had about us, any lingering fears that this wouldn't work or that Thorne would reject me again, are swept away. Thorne and I were always inevitable, even if it took us a little while to figure it out.

I pour all that I am and all my love into our kiss.

It takes us a while to come up for air. Thorne tries to tell me how much he cares about me two other times, but I pull him back to me. It's only when Cleo returns and starts to make noises that I release him.

Thorne leads us to a small cabin less than a quarter mile from where I found him.

"You've been here the whole time?" I ask, looking around the space in surprise.

Thorne nods. "I tried to leave, to go far away, but I couldn't. I have a confession to make."

"Ah-oh," I say as I turn away from the neatly made bed to look at him.

He lifts a hand to rub the back of his neck, looking adorably embarrassed. "I've been sneaking into your dorm room at night to watch you sleep."

I cock an eyebrow. "That is seriously stalker behavior."

Thorne winces. "I know."

"Well, at least I wasn't going crazy when I thought I

smelled you some mornings." I shake my head. "I can't believe I didn't wake up."

"You're a very deep sleeper. The snoring covered any noise I made."

Snatching a pillow from the bed, I chuck it at him. "Shut up. I do not snore."

He winks playfully and then drifts toward me as I continue to inspect the small living space.

I smile. It's like we're magnets drawn toward each other. It's been this way for us since the beginning but we're finally not fighting it.

When he comes up behind me, I turn and wrap my arms around his neck. I can't seem to keep my hands off him, but he doesn't seem to mind. He slides his hands to my hips to hold me in place.

"So, where do we go from here?" I ask.

"Wherever you want. I was only staying in this cabin to be close to you, but now that we're together we can travel anywhere." He means anywhere there aren't humans, angelborn, Fallen or Forsaken, but I get what he's saying. "You're my tether. I promise I won't ever let you go again. I was a fool to think I could do it the first time, and if I have to spend a lifetime making it up to you and letting you know you are worth fighting for, I will."

I grin. "I'm on board with you spending a lifetime making it up to me. Any ideas how you plan to do that?"

Thorne's gaze heats, and he brushes a finger over the shell of my ear and then down my neck, making me shiver. "I have some very specific ideas of how I plan to earn your forgiveness."

Like it is every time he touches me, my mind is already a little muddled, but I don't care a bit.

"Is that so?" I ask, shuffling closer so that our bodies meet.

Rather than answering me outright, he wraps his free arm around me and dips his head, pressing his lips against mine once again.

I smile, wondering if I'll ever get tired of the way his mouth feels against mine, but content knowing I'll have a very long lifetime with him to find out.

ANGELIC CLASSIFICATION

IN ORDER OF SPHERE

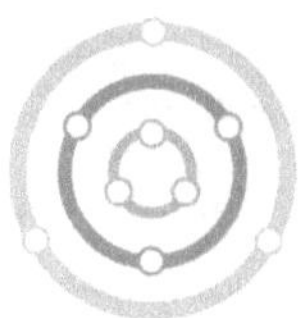

Angelic Spheres – The nine classes of angels are divided equally into one of three spheres. Each sphere has related roles and responsibilities and it's believed—but not proven —that the most powerful angels are from the first sphere with decreasing power down to the third.

Seraphim – Literally translated as, "burning ones," seraphim are the highest angelic class and considered the most powerful. Part of the first sphere of angels, these supernatural beings are said to have six wings and protect the throne of their Creator. There are no known Nephilim from the seraphim line, because not a single seraph angel rebelled and therefore there are no seraph Fallen.

Known Descendants – Emberly & Thorne

Cherubim – Part of the first sphere of angels, cherubim are the highest angelic class that rebelled. The Nephilim of this line can typically shift into one of three different forms in the spirit realm: a lion, an eagle, or a bovine. It's very rare for a Nephilim to be able to shift into two or all three of these forms.

Known Descendants – Steel, Greyson, Sterling, Aurora, Blaze, Eloise, Laurent, Silver, & Malachi (Cherub Elder)

Thrones – The thrones are part of the first sphere and are said to be natural protectors. Nephilim of this line can manipulate and build wards to protect the academies and compounds from supernatural enemies by pulling on energy contained in underground springs.

Known Descendants – Deacon & Draven (Throne Elder)

Dominions – Part of the second sphere of angels, Dominions regulate the duties of the lower angels as well as govern the laws of the universe. Dominions are considered to be divinely beautiful with feathered wings of various colors. The Nephilim of this line value friendship, family, and loyalty and tend to be the peacemakers of the angel-born world.

Known Descendants – Ash & Zara (Dominion Elder)

Virtues – These angels are known for their signs and miracles. Part of the second sphere, they ensure everything is acting the way it should, from gravity keeping the planets in orbit, to the grass growing. Nephilim of this line can control natural elements in the mortal world, but their abilities are more powerful in the spirit realm.

Known Descendant – Sorcha (Virtue Elder)

Powers – Part of the second sphere, these angels are considered the warriors of the angel hierarchy. As such, they are always on the frontlines of battle. They are known to be single-minded and focused on their cause. Nephilim of this line are skilled in combat and have a knack for military strategy. They are able to manifest wings in the spirit realm.

Known Descendants – Nova, Killian, Ciara, & Lyra (Power Elder)

Rulers – As part of the third sphere, these angels guide and protect territories and groups of people. They preside over the classes of angels and carry out orders given to them by the upper spheres. They are said to be inspirational to angels and humankind. Nephilim of this line tend to manage and govern different bodies of angel-born. Their natural talents veer toward shepherding and their powers manifest as defensive rather than offensive.

Known Descendants – Sable & Arien (Ruler Elder)

Archangels – These angels are common in mortal lore. Part of the third sphere, they appear more frequently in the mortal world than other classes of angels—with the exception of the angel class. Tasked with the protection of humanity, they sometimes appear as mortals in order to influence politics, military matters, and commerce in their assigned region. Nephilim of this line are skilled chameleons. They have the easiest time blending in with humans and many of them work as Keepers.

Known Descendant – Riven (Archangel Elder)

Angels – Perceived as the lowest order of celestial beings, angels—sometimes called "plain angels" or "guardian angels"—belong to the third sphere. Their primary duties are as messengers and personal guards. Nephilim of this line were believed to have been murdered over two millennia ago, yet it was recently discovered that they'd survived the massacre and were thriving in a hidden community, Eden. The powers of the angel-born of this line are still being discovered, but they greatly exceed what was previously recorded.

Known Descendants – Emberly, Shira, Aero, Stavros, Nikias (Angel Elder)

GLOSSARY

Angel – A winged supernatural being who protects both mortal and spirit realms from Fallen and Forsaken.

Angel-born – The common name for Nephilim. An elite race of supernatural warriors born of human females and male Fallen, and their descendants. They have varying powers and abilities based on their Fallen ancestor's angel class. They are stronger, faster, and their senses more enhanced than humans.

Barghest – A serpentine, dog-like creature most commonly known as a hellhound. Barghest have elongated muzzles and their bodies are covered in scales. Several rows of spikes protrude along their spines and a tuff of needle-like hair crowns their heads. They exist only in the spirit realm and are known to be highly aggressive, only trainable through the use of Enochian commands.

Bastet – A cat-like spirit world creature. Their bodies are slightly larger than a lion's and their distinguishing features are metallic gold striped black fur and large saber teeth. Bastets are apex predators who have a taste for Fallen flesh. When bonded with an angel they are fiercely loyal and have been known to fight in battle alongside their chosen angel companion. It's fabled that some bastets even have the ability to go invisible to stalk their prey.

Celestial – A fabled supernatural being that acts as a protector for angel-born. Nephilim tell their children fairy tales about these creatures, but their existence has never been confirmed.

Council of Elders – Comprised of the oldest Nephilim in each of the seven existing angelic lines: cherub, throne, dominion, virtue, power, ruler, and archangel. They are the closest thing to a ruling body the Nephilim have, yet—unless there is a global threat—their normal duties are to act as judges to help settle disputes between angel-born.

Dauntless – The Nephilim warship that operates in the spirit world.

Elder's Compound – A highly protected stronghold where the Elders of each Nephilim line are based, which consists of several buildings including lodging for over three hundred occupants, training centers, a vault for cherished Nephilim artifacts, and two pyramids. The compound is located in an area of Egypt called Farafra that's known for its hot springs.

Fallen – Angels who rebelled and were banished to Earth as punishment. They retained their strength, immortality, and wings, but lost their class specific angelic powers. They are unable to access the mortal world.

Forsaken – Fallen who have merged with a Nephilim—or willing human—and taken on the form of their host's body. They are able to travel between each realm unencumbered. Their appearance is hideous in the spirit realm, reflecting their true nature. Forsaken thirst for blood—although it's not their primary source of sustenance—and are unable to withstand the sunlight in either realm.

Keeper – Nephilim tasked with monitoring and collecting information about the human race.

Merge Zone – The twenty-mile radius around the epicenter of London where the mortal and spirit world collided when Fallen and Forsaken tried to break through the veil between realms. Within the Merge Zone, Fallen roam free and Forsaken can walk in the daylight. There is no human governing body in the Merge Zone and it is a dangerous place for both humans and Nephilim.

Mortal World/Realm – The dimension on Earth where humans reside.

Nephilim – The proper name for angel-born.

Phasing – When a Nephilim, Forsaken, or angel travels from the mortal world to the spirit realm or back again.

Seraph Academy – One of nine secret academies around the world devoted to the education and training of Nephilim children. Nephilim youth attend the academies from age eight until twenty, at which time they are considered fully trained. Seraph Academy is located in the Colorado Mountains near the town of Glenwood Springs.

Soulless – The Fallen and Forsaken run ship.

Spectrum World – What Emberly calls the spirit realm.

Spirit Gem – Small gems or stones of different colors that originate from the spirit realm and have various uses and properties. Some examples include concealing powers, amplifying natural abilities, creating shields, controlling objects or people, or forcing people into or out of the spirit realm. It is believed that there are yet undiscovered varieties of gems still hidden in the spirit realm. The orbs in the Council of Elders vault are both large spirit gems. Until recently, the Nephilim were not aware of their existence.

Spirit Realm – The plane of existence that can only be accessed by supernatural beings. The spectrum of colors differ in this realm and sound can be seen as ripples through the air. Angels spend the majority of their time in the spirit realm warring with Fallen for control of territories. Nephilim's angelic powers activate in this realm.

Starfire Orb - One of two spirit world magical objects that can force any human, Nephilim, or angel into the spirit world and keep them from phasing back into the mortal world. When the Starfire Orb and the other spirit world orb are combined it brings down the barrier that separates the two realms and creates a new one.

The Great Revolt – When the Nephilim rose up against the Forsaken and Fallen who had enslaved and used them as vessels for Fallen.

The White Kingdom – Also known as "Whitehold" this fortress is located in the Laurentian Mountains of Quebec, Canada. This stronghold was the primary training ground for Fallen and Forsaken and ruled by Thorne and the seraph angel, Seraphim. It remained a secret from the Nephilim for hundreds of years, but since its discovery it has been abandoned.

PLEASE WRITE A REVIEW

Reviews are the lifeblood of authors and your opinion will help others decide to read my books. If you want to see more from me, please leave a review.

Will you please write a review?
http://review.NovaAndThorne.com

Thank you for your help!

~ Julie

ACKNOWLEDGMENTS

My most sincere thanks goes to you, the reader. I'm so humbled by the amount of love the *Fallen Legacies* series has received. Thank you so much for embracing these books! I've lived with these characters and their stories for the last several years, and I feel so fortunate to get to bring them to life. And that's only been possible because you keep showing up, time and time again.

I thought the adventures would be complete with *Unleashing Fire*, but when I finished Emberly and Steel's tale, it just didn't feel like the end of the story . . . at least not completely. Nova kept nudging me to pen her adventure as well, and I'm so glad I listened! Nova is such a fun character to write. She says and does whatever she pleases. There's a freedom in working with a character like that. And Thorne . . . wow, he's complex and more layered than an onion. But I always knew there was more to him than what we saw through Emberly's eyes.

Supernova is truly my love letter to the readers who have cherished and championed this series. I hope you enjoyed the ride!

GET UPDATES FROM JULIE

JOIN MY NEWSLETTER

Please consider joining my exclusive email newsletter. You'll be notified as new books are available, get exclusive bonus scenes, previews, ridiculous videos, and you'll be eligible for special giveaways. Occasionally, you will see puppies. 🐶

Sign up for snarky funsies:

JulieHallAuthor.com/newsletter

JOIN THE FAN CLUB

ON FACEBOOK

If you love my books, get involved and get exclusive sneak peeks before anyone else. Sometimes I even give out free puppies (#jokingnotjoking).

You'll get to know other passionate readers like you, and you'll get to know me better too! It'll be fun!

Join the Fan Club on Facebook:
facebook.com/groups/juliehall

See you in there!
~ Julie

ABOUT THE AUTHOR

JULIE HALL

My name is Julie Hall and I'm a *USA Today* bestselling, multiple award-winning author. I read and write YA paranormal / fantasy novels, love doodle dogs and drink Red Bull, but not necessarily in that order.

My daughter says my super power is sleeping all day and writing all night . . . and well, she wouldn't be wrong.

I believe novels are best enjoyed in community. As such, I want to hear from you! Please connect with me as I regularly give out sneak peeks, deleted scenes, prizes, and other freebies to my friends and newsletter subscribers.

Visit my website:
JulieHallAuthor.com

Get my other books:
amazon.com/author/julieghall

Join the Fan Club:
facebook.com/groups/juliehall

Get exclusive updates by email:
JulieHallAuthor.com/newsletter

Connect with me on:

facebook.com/JulieHallAuthor

bookbub.com/authors/julie-hall-7c80af95-5dda-449a-8130-3e219d5b00ee

goodreads.com/JulieHallAuthor

instagram.com/Julie.Hall.Author

youtube.com/JulieHallAuthor

BOOKS BY JULIE HALL

Shadow Angel Series / ShadowAngelSeries.com

Fallen Legacies Series / FallenLegacies.com

Life After Series / LifeAfterSeries.com